PRAISE FOR BESTSELLING,
AWARD-WINNING AUTHOR
JOAN JOHNSTON
AND HER PREVIOUS NOVELS

THE TEXAN

"Awesome romance and mystery with a touch of
thriller thrown in. Lots of twists and turns that will
keep the reader hooked until the very end."
—*Huntress Book Reviews*

"A RIVETING BLEND OF ADVENTURE,
INTRIGUE AND ROMANCE . . . which builds to
a hair-raising, edge-of-the-seat climax. If you like
well-written tales of romance, adventure, and suspense,
THE TEXAN is a book you won't want to miss!
It's a story you'll remember long after the last page
is turned, with a truly unforgettable hero."
—*Romance Reviews Today*

THE COWBOY

"A WINNER . . . Joan Johnston [creates] unforgettable
subplots and characters who make every fine thread weave
into a touching tapestry." —*Affaire de Coeur*

"Joan Johnston has once again masterfully created very real
characters, a captivating story and interesting sub-plots."
—*Under the Covers*

JOAN JOHNSTON

COMANCHE WOMAN

A DELL BOOK

A Dell Book
Published by
Dell Publishing
Random House, Inc.
1540 Broadway
New York, New York 10036

This is a work of fiction. Names, characters, places, and
incidents either are the product of the author's imagination or are
used fictitiously. Any resemblance to actual persons, living or dead,
events, or locales is entirely coincidental.

Cover photo by Leo L. Larson/Panoramic Images

Dell® is a registered trademark of Random House, Inc., and the
colophon is a trademark of Random House, Inc.

ISBN: 0-440-23680-0

Printed in the United States of America

Published si   **3 0646 00122 5626**

December 2002

OPM 10 9 8 7 6 5 4 3 2 1

For my sister
Jeanne Elizabeth Owens

Still waters run deep.

COMANCHE
WOMAN

Prologue

IN HIS DREAMS, RIP STEWART ENVISIONED THREE SONS sweating shoulder to shoulder with him as his cotton plantation along the Brazos River blossomed in concert with the new Texas frontier. He had his sons' names already picked out before he ever married Amelia, chosen because she was the only daughter in a nearby Scots family of seven healthy children.

His eldest son would be named Sloan. Sloan would be strong and brave, a proud, capable heir to take Rip's place. Bayleigh would be Rip's surety. He would be the educated one, bred to be a loyal and steadfast help to his elder brother. Rip's youngest son would be named Creighton. Creighton would be the child of Rip's heart, the child he played with, and indulged, and lavished with his love. Creighton would be fiery-tempered and bold, demanding everything the Texas frontier had to offer a man, and getting it.

Unfortunately, Amelia gave Rip three daughters. That did not deter Rip Stewart. He named the eldest Sloan, the second Bayleigh, and the youngest Creighton, and set about to make his dreams come true.

Part I

SHADOW

Chapter 1

THE COMANCHE'S EYES NARROWED IN SPECULATION when he discovered the naked man and woman in the pond where he planned to water his pony. The white woman's belly was swollen with child and seemed to float on the sparkling surface of the pond. As he watched, the white man standing behind her splayed large, tanned hands across her overripe belly and pulled the woman back into his embrace.

The Comanche crouched the instant before the man turned his head abruptly in his direction. He remained absolutely still, and though he was in plain sight, the man's eyes flicked past him, unseeing, and finally returned to the woman. The Comanche smiled wolfishly. He could understand the man's distraction.

The man sought out the soft skin of the woman's neck with his mouth. The Comanche tensed as she leaned her head back into the man's shoulder so his tongue was free to taste her skin. The Comanche closed his eyes when the man reached up with his strong hands to cup the woman's breasts, already full and heavy for the coming child. He imagined holding his own woman, imagined the saltiness of her skin in the heat of the day, imagined the feel of her nipples peaking at his touch.

Disturbed by the sensual images he'd conjured, he blinked his eyes open. The white man reached for the single auburn braid down the woman's back and released the tie that bound her hair, spreading the silky mass with his fingers so it flowed like molten copper across his broad muscular chest and down his flat belly.

Such hair! What a glorious prize! The Comanche remained still, caught up in the beauty of the woman, the strength of the man. The couple was totally absorbed in one another, touching, tasting. The Comanche's jaw tightened in anger. *A man should not take such foolish chances with the woman who will bear his sons.* He could have killed them both and taken the woman's copper-colored hair to hang from his war shield. He pulled his knife from its sheath and edged closer to the pond. He would teach this *tabeboh*, this foolish White-eyes, a lesson.

The woman smiled teasingly and walked away from the man toward the opposite bank. She picked up his buckskin shirt and threw it to him as he stood in the water. Then she reached down and located a full, linsey-woolsey dress, which she pulled down to cover her nakedness.

When the Comanche was close enough to launch his attack, he shrieked his fierce war cry, a haunting, horrifying sound intended to freeze his victim.

Only this man did not freeze. He howled an equally fierce battle cry as he whirled to face his enemy. The Comanche found himself face to face with a Colt revolver.

The white man grinned, a feral smile, full of satisfaction.

The Comanche looked from the knife in his hand to the white man's gun—and smiled back.

"*Hihites*, Wolf," the Comanche said.

"*Hihites*, Long Quiet," the white man, also known as Jarrett Creed, replied.

"I'm glad to see you haven't forgotten everything you learned during the years you spent as a captive in my village," Long Quiet said in perfect English. He'd learned the white man's language from his *Comanchero* father, a white man who'd traded with the Comanches and taken a Comanche bride. "I thought you unaware of anything except your wife, and I believed you unarmed. Where did you hide the gun?"

"Cricket threw it to me with my shirt," Creed answered. He joined Long Quiet on the bank of the pond and pulled on his shirt and trousers.

"You wooden-headed ninnyhammer!" Cricket chided Long Quiet, softening her words with a welcoming smile. "It's a wonder you didn't scare me into having this baby a month early."

"My friendship won't always keep you safe from the threat of Comanche attack. You must always be vigilant."

"I'm always careful," Cricket shot back. "It's my husband who gets distracted."

Creed grinned. "You'll have to provide less of a distraction, then." He slipped one arm around his wife's shoulders and rested the other on her burgeoning belly.

"I hate always having to be on guard like this." Cricket wrinkled her nose to show her dissatisfaction. "Isn't there any chance the constant raiding by the Comanches will stop now that President Houston has talked the southern tribes into signing treaties?"

"I wouldn't count on it," Long Quiet replied. "The treaties only bind a few Comanches, and the peace will last only until they learn the white man can't be trusted."

"I don't think you're being fair," Cricket argued. "Most of us don't make a habit of lying, and we only want to live in peace."

Long Quiet's gray eyes turned flinty. "I've spent a lifetime traveling between *Comanchería* and the Republic of Texas. Thanks to Creed's father, I learned a great deal more about the white man's attitudes and ideas when he sent me to school with Creed in Boston. And I tell you, there can be no peace between the Comanches and the White-eyes."

"Does that mean we're never going to get my sister back from the Comanches?" Cricket asked, her voice a mere whisper. "You're still looking for Bay, aren't you?"

"Yes, I'm still looking."

"Have you heard anything? Has there been any word at all about where she might be?"

Long Quiet saw the pleading look in the eyes of his best friend's wife and wished he could give her some news about her older sister. For three interminable years he'd been hunting for the tall white woman with violet eyes and flame-red hair who'd been stolen from her father's cotton plantation by the Comanche called Tall Bear.

He'd searched for Bay among the villages of The People as Long Quiet, the fierce Comanche warrior. He'd searched for her among the wagons and shacks of the *Comancheros* as a half-breed, a gray-eyed Comanche in buckskins who wandered easily between the worlds of the Indian and the White-eyes. He'd even searched for her among the far-flung Texas settlements as Walker Coburn, well-respected friend of the Texas Ranger Jarrett Creed. All to no avail. Bayleigh Falkirk Stewart, second daughter of the richest gentleman planter in the Republic of Texas, seemed to have disappeared from the face of the earth.

"I haven't found her. But I will." Long Quiet turned away from the hopelessness in Cricket's eyes and confronted Creed. "I got your message to come. Why did you want to see me?"

"Let's go up to the house, and I'll tell you all about it," Creed said.

Long Quiet hesitated, frowning at the imposing white frame house in the distance that was at the heart of Creed's cotton plantation, Lion's Dare. Noticing Long Quiet's reaction, Creed turned from the direction of the house and headed instead for the shade of several nearby pin oaks. Long Quiet walked beside him, not apologizing for his disdain of the civilized comforts to be found in the house.

Creed helped Cricket sit down, then dropped to sit on the ground beside her, his back supported by a pin oak, one knee upraised, the other leg stretched out in front of him. Long Quiet sat down cross-legged across from the couple.

"I asked you to come because I need your help," Creed began. "You remember Luke Summers, don't you?"

"Sure. We worked together once. He's that young Texas Ranger, the one who made you so jealous with the attention he paid Cricket before you were married," Long Quiet replied.

Creed turned a sardonic eye on Cricket, who grinned back at him. "That's the one, all right. He also just happens to be one of my best Rangers. Unfortunately, for the past year Luke's been in prison with the rest of the Texans captured at the Battle of Mier."

"That's too bad," Long Quiet said. "I heard what the Mexicans did to the Texans who tried to escape. There's been evidence before of Santa Anna's heartlessness. What he did to the Texans who fought at Mier just proved it once and for all."

Jarrett Creed's bile rose at the thought of the senseless executions that had followed the Texans' escape attempt. The acid in his throat made his voice rough. "Recently the Mexicans moved the whole lot of them, over 150 men, to a place called Castle San Carlos in Perote, Mexico. From what I've heard, this new prison has walls thirty feet high and fourteen feet thick." Creed paused and added, "Luke's sent a message that he and the other fifteen men in his cell are planning to dig their way out."

For a moment Long Quiet didn't say anything. His voice expressed his disbelief when he asked, "They're going to dig their way out under fourteen feet of wall?"

"Never underestimate the determination of a Texan," Creed replied with a grin. "When they finally dig through, they'll need someone to meet them with horses, food, and guns and help them make their way back through the Mexican desert to the Rio Grande."

"Why do you need my help? Why not just take a few Rangers down to Perote and break them all out of there?"

"To put it bluntly, because the president of the Republic of Texas doesn't want to antagonize the president of Mexico. Sam Houston's hoping to talk General Santa Anna into recognizing Texas as a sovereign nation, so he's trying to avoid open hostilities between our two countries.

"Not only that, but Houston wants to keep the peace with Mexico while annexation negotiations are going on with the United States. That's why I need you. I can't get authorization to send any Rangers into Mexico. If they got caught, it could spell disaster for Houston's peace overtures and might start a war with Mexico that would put a damper on his hopes for annexation."

"How soon does Luke expect to be past the wall?" Long Quiet asked.

"He doesn't really know. He persuaded the Mexicans to put a wooden floor in his cell, complaining that the stone floor was too cold. He and his cellmates lift sections of the wooden floor to dig at night, then replace them in the morning. They're manacled at night, so the work is slow.

"Luke's guess was two months to dig their way out, but I'd like to have somebody down there in six weeks. We're getting our messages through a bribed Mexican guard, and I don't want to trust him any more than I have to. He's supposed to deliver another message when they've nearly finished digging."

"And if I don't go?" Long Quiet asked, wary of getting involved in what was clearly a white man's problem.

"Then I'll go myself," Creed said. "And damn the repercussions."

Cricket and Creed grasped hands. Long Quiet saw Cricket's other hand curl under her belly. He wouldn't wish to be gone at such a time from his own wife, if he'd had one, and he wouldn't ask such a thing of his friend. "There's no need for you to go. I'll do it."

"Thanks for helping, Walker," Cricket said, calling Long Quiet by the name his *Comanchero* father had given him.

"I've been worried sick about Luke. We hear terrible things about how the prisoners are treated, how they're starved and beaten."

"Sounds to me like Luke has done a pretty good job of taking care of himself," Long Quiet said. He turned to Cricket and said, "Now tell me, when is this child that's made your belly the size of a ripe watermelon going to be born?"

Cricket grinned and lovingly rubbed her rounded belly. "One more month. I can hardly wait."

"I will pray to the Great Spirit that he brings you a son," Long Quiet said.

"I'd be just as happy with a daughter," Creed replied.

Long Quiet knew from his friend's answer the distance that lay between them. A Comanche needed sons to carry on the war against the White-eyes.

"Will you stay for supper?" Cricket asked.

"I can't. I've been hunting with a small band of Comanches camped nearby, and we leave tomorrow for *Comanchería.*"

When Long Quiet rose to leave, Creed stood also and helped Cricket to her feet. "I'll meet you in Laredo a month from now with supplies for the prisoners."

The two friends clasped arms elbow to wrist in farewell. It was the first time they'd touched in a year, yet the joining was enough to express how much they were a part of one another. Unfortunately, the farther the whites invaded into *Comanchería*, the more difficult their friendship became. For although Long Quiet didn't kill without good reason, he knew the day was soon coming when killing would be necessary to stem the encroachment of the White-eyes upon the Comanche way of life.

"You'll keep looking for Bay, won't you?" Cricket asked, bringing Long Quiet from his bleak thoughts.

"Yes, I'll look. But she may not want to come—"

"I know she may not want to come back home now," Cricket interrupted.

Long Quiet saw the distress in Cricket's face. He knew she was imagining her sister's fate among the Comanches. He knew that fate firsthand, as did Creed. Most white women captives were repeatedly raped by the braves who took them, and they were often subjected to horrible cruelty from the women of the village. Bay might find herself awakened by a burning stick applied to her nose, might be beaten with thorny branches, might be tripped and kicked, bruised and cut.

"We don't know she was mistreated," Creed said in an attempt to ease Cricket's fear. "The brave who bought her from Tall Bear paid for her with a whole herd of stolen horses. That makes her value immense. Surely he wouldn't let anyone lessen the value of his property."

"Any man would treasure such a woman," Long Quiet said.

Creed noticed how Long Quiet's voice softened with his mention of Bay and wondered what it was about Bay that had captured his friend's imagination. Long Quiet had been more diligent about searching for Bay Stewart than Creed could credit to mere friendship. But he hadn't been able to get Long Quiet to admit to more than the desire to help his friend and his friend's wife.

"Farewell, *haints*," Long Quiet said.

"Farewell, friend," Creed replied. And then he asked, "You haven't changed your mind, have you?"

Long Quiet shook his head. "No." Then he mounted his pony and rode away.

Since Creed had never accepted his choice of the Comanche way of life as final, each time Long Quiet left, he was forced to confirm his choice again. If he hadn't valued Creed's friendship so much, he might have stopped seeing him altogether. For each time Long Quiet denied his white father's heritage, he did so with a little more regret.

As he rode to meet his Comanche friends, he thought of the choice he'd made so many years ago. Even if he were hav-

ing second thoughts, it was too late to change his mind.
The People needed him now more than ever. He'd learned
enough during his days of school in Boston to know that
the Comanches couldn't hope to survive the westward ex-
pansion rolling like a wave over Texas. Neither side understood the other, and from that lack of understanding hatred
grew. Long Quiet was a part of both worlds and wished
there were a way he could ease the enmity between them. No
solution had come to him, but he hadn't stopped searching
for one.

That evening, when Long Quiet reached the Comanche
camp he received an unwelcome reminder of the discord
between the Comanches and the White-eyes. A young buck
from a village far to the north in *Comanchería* had joined
their campfire. He was celebrating. He had just killed his
first white man.

The youthful warrior was dressed in the bright red shirt
and flat-brimmed hat of the white man he'd just scalped. He'd
drunk too much of the white man's firewater and began to
boast of his courage. He spoke of his strong *puha*, the spiri-
tual power garnered on his first vision quest. He held up the
medicine bag tied about his neck and swore it had protected
him from the white man's lead bullets.

"My medicine has proven very strong. I cannot be harmed
by any man. Nor can evil spirits hurt me. I am invincible. I will
speak of what I wish, even the longtime secret kept by my village."

Intrigued, Long Quiet asked, "What secret can a whole
village keep?"

The drunken young man peered owlishly at Long Quiet
and the other Comanches who surrounded the campfire in a
circle. He spoke in whispered tones of a white woman captive
kept hidden away in the village of a band of *Quohadi*
Comanches for the past three years.

"She is called Shadow. Her eyes smolder the deep, dark
purple of a stormy night and her hair burns like fire in the

sunlight. She is as tall as a man, but shaped very much like a woman. Her skin is the golden brown of honey—"

"If such a woman existed," Long Quiet interrupted, "I would have found her by now." His tone was harsh, for it was a well-known, even amusing, fact that he'd searched in vain for a woman with violet eyes and flame-red hair among the dark-eyed, raven-haired Comanches. His patience with the good-natured fun poked at his futile quest had worn thin over the years.

"But how could you know of her? None in the village may speak of her," the young man protested. "The one who owns her has threatened a curse upon the spirit of the man, woman, or child who tells of her existence."

"And you, foolish *tuibitsi*, do not fear such a terrible curse?" Long Quiet snapped.

"I am not afraid of Many Horses," the young man bragged, his hand gripping his medicine bag. "He is but a man and I . . ."

In the otherwise clear sky a cloud crossed the moon, blocking its light. The brave's face froze in a mask of fear as his glance skipped upward to observe the eerie phenomenon. His face contorted further and he lurched to his feet, clutching his medicine bag. His crazed eyes roamed the circle of Indians to whom he'd told his story.

"Do not heed my words," he pleaded. "I spoke only of a dream. There is no such woman. How could there be? You would have heard the tale long ago had she been real."

The young man staggered from the circle, mounted his pony, and thundered away into the night.

They found him the next day, facedown in a ravine. There was no mark upon him, but he was dead.

"He foresaw his death. That is why he ran away from us," Two Fingers announced, awestruck by their discovery.

"Many Horses must have powerful medicine," Forked River offered in a whisper.

"Perhaps we ought not to speak of what he told us lest our

lives also be in danger from this fearsome curse," Two Fingers warned.

Long Quiet suggested a more rational reason for the young man's death. "He was drunk. It is likely he fell from his horse and suffered a killing blow to his head."

"But there is no mark," Forked River argued.

Long Quiet grimaced. No, there was no mark.

"And even though he was drunk, his fear of the curse was very real," Forked River added.

Long Quiet knelt to examine the dead man again. As a result of his sojourn into the white world, he was no longer as superstitious as his Comanche friends. He would have argued the young man had made up the whole story, except the youth had mentioned the name of the Comanche—Many Horses—who supposedly owned the mysterious woman.

Long Quiet could ill afford to ignore this clue to Bay Stewart's whereabouts, coming as it did when he had all but given up hope of ever finding her. But the timing couldn't have been worse. He had a mere four weeks before he was supposed to meet Creed in Laredo.

Yet now that the Great Spirit had smiled upon him, he could not turn his face away. He would find the village of Many Horses and see the truth for himself. If the woman called Shadow was Bayleigh Falkirk Stewart, his quest was over at last.

Chapter 2

COMANCHERÍA
1843

AT FIRST LIGHT, LONG QUIET LEFT HIS HUNTING PARTY and headed north into *Comanchería*. For the next two days of his search for the *Quohadi* village of Many Horses, Long Quiet didn't see another human being, but the land teemed with wildlife, all adapted by nature to the rugged terrain. Deer, jackrabbits, prairie dogs, foxes, snakes, lizards, and birds of all kinds crossed his path. Thus, the flash of movement in the late afternoon sun was not unexpected.

But Long Quiet had learned caution so long ago it was second nature to him. He stopped and squinted his eyes against the sun, waiting until he was sure of what lay ahead on the trail. He smiled when he saw the mustangs strung out and walking steadily along the sun-baked plains. In the sweltering August heat, the wild horses rarely strayed far from water. He need only follow them to find a respite from the desert terrain. He tightened his knees slightly and the pinto beneath him responded by breaking into a steady jog.

He'd followed the mustangs for no more than a mile when they stopped abruptly. The stallion leading them whirled on his haunches and, teeth bared, nipped savagely at the mare directly behind him. She turned and fled, sending the rest of the herd in headlong flight in the direction from which they'd come.

Long Quiet paused, all his senses alert. Whatever had

frightened the mustangs was in all likelihood a danger to him as well. He was in no hurry to meet his death. He sought out an arroyo created over eons by the flooding waters of spring and settled down to wait unseen. He quivered involuntarily as beads of sweat dripped a ticklish path down the carved ridges and furrows of muscle on his chest and back. He ignored the flies that buzzed around him, while his slate-gray eyes searched the horizon.

His patience was soon rewarded. The quiet was broken by the bloodcurdling war whoops of one of the Comanches' deadliest enemies. That was followed by the sight of nine Tonkawa braves in full war regalia chasing a lone Comanche brave across the desert.

"Aieeeee! Haiiiii!"

The bruiting war cry of the lone Comanche echoed over the barren land. Suddenly, the Comanche, whose face was streaked in macabre designs with black war paint, wheeled his pony around to race headlong back into the midst of the Tonkawas. As Long Quiet watched, one of the Tonkawas fell, the Comanche's war club buried deep in his head. The Comanche screamed his defiance of the Tonkawas, who had momentarily retreated, and charged them again with only a knife to defend himself. Long Quiet admired the man's bravery in seeking a warrior's death.

Long Quiet headed up out of the arroyo to help the Comanche but jerked his mount to a halt when the warrior's horse stumbled in an unseen hole and fell, throwing its rider to the ground. The Comanche was quickly surrounded by the screeching Tonkawas, who raced in a circle around their victim, brandishing lances and tomahawks. One of the Tonkawas dodged in and pierced the Comanche with his lance before quickly retreating.

The Comanche did not rise.

Still hidden by the arroyo, Long Quiet held his mount steady. The courageous Comanche must be dead, Long Quiet thought, for if the brave had been alive, he would have continued fighting to his last breath. However, it was also possible the Comanche had only been knocked unconscious by his fall. In either case, Long Quiet's honor left him no choice except to retrieve the body of the Comanche brave.

He chafed at the additional delay this would mean to his journey north to find Bayleigh Stewart, but there was no help for it. He would not leave this brave Comanche in the hands of the Tonkawas, who ate the flesh of their enemies.

The remaining Tonkawas closed the circle around the Comanche, their vengeful bloodlust lending ferocity to their cries of victory. They retrieved the Comanche's pony, which had survived its fall without injury, and tied the Comanche's body on the animal's back.

When the Tonkawas started back in the direction the wild mustangs had originally been walking, Long Quiet assumed they were headed toward the water that gave life to the desert. He took a drink from the gourd he carried with him and noted he had enough of the precious liquid to last another day, or maybe two if he were careful. He squinted at the glaring sun, which had begun its descent. He would wait awhile and follow the Tonkawas. By the time they'd camped and settled down to roast their victim, he would have caught up to them.

Darkness claimed the land, leaving Long Quiet to make his way in the scant light of a half-moon and a scattering of silvery stars. He'd begun to fear he might lose the trail in the dark when he was aided by the contemptuous confidence of the Tonkawas. The flesh eaters had had the audacity to light a beacon fire, daring their enemies to challenge them. Yet the same bonfire that exposed the Tonkawas to their enemies also exposed their enemies to them.

Long Quiet waited in the darkness outside the glow of the campfire as the Tonkawas prepared the Comanche for their ritualistic feast. He was glad he'd come, especially when he discovered the Comanche wasn't dead. The brave, whose hands were tied behind him, was yanked to his feet by one of the Tonkawas. He stood swaying unsteadily in the ribboned shadows of the fire. The Tonkawa waved a sharp blade in the Comanche's face, but the brave stared stonily back at him.

A shiver ran down Long Quiet's spine as the Tonkawa slowly shaved a layer of skin off the Comanche's upper thigh. The Comanche never blinked an eye.

Long Quiet didn't think, he simply acted. He leaped onto the back of his pinto and urged the sturdy pony into a gallop. Often, as a boy, he'd practiced picking up various items from the ground at a full gallop. As a young man, he and his friends had practiced picking up a fellow Comanche between two riders, in preparation for the day when they would need to rescue a wounded friend from the battlefield. Only the strongest had been able to lift the full weight of a man by themselves. Long Quiet had been one of those, and his exploits had become legend. It was the legend who rode in fury toward the Tonkawas.

The flesh eaters were taken completely by surprise. It wasn't the thundering hoofbeats that frightened them so much as the inhuman howl that soared on the night air. They stood in numb indecision as the pinto stallion hurtled into their midst. Their eyes widened in terror as a near-naked giant yanked their prisoner up behind him and galloped away.

Long Quiet knew it was unlikely the Tonkawas would follow him in the dark. The Indians wouldn't take the chance of dying at night, leaving their spirits to wander in the darkness forever. Long Quiet also knew that with the first gray light of dawn, they would follow. He felt the man behind him attempting to free himself and pulled his mount to a halt. The wounded Indian slid off the pony's rump to the ground.

Long Quiet dismounted and cut the thong binding the Comanche's hands. "We must stop the bleeding of your wounds."

"It is nothing," the Comanche replied.

"Perhaps not. But I would not like to discover at first light that I brought you safely from the Tonkawa campfire, only to have you bleed to death later."

"As you wish, then."

Long Quiet reached into the *tunawaws* hanging from a thong at his waist, where he carried his mirror and war paints, searching through the tubular rawhide bag for something to tie around the Comanche's thigh where the skin had been cut away and his hip where the lance had stabbed him. He came up with a white man's shirt he wore occasionally. Neither man spoke as Long Quiet tore the rough linsey-woolsey into strips and bound the Comanche's wounds.

The Comanche was a head shorter than Long Quiet, but he was powerfully built. There was hard muscle under Long Quiet's hands where he wound the cotton strips. He marveled at the brave's silent stoicism in the face of what must be horrible pain, but he wasn't surprised by it. He'd already concluded this was an extraordinary man.

When Long Quiet was done, the Comanche said, "Two others who traveled with me died at the hands of the Tonkawas." For the first time, the Comanche seemed to wilt a little. He turned his head to gaze away into the distance. His voice was gravelly with grief when he continued. "They were both on their first raid. Their families have reason to be proud of them, for they died very bravely. They should be properly buried."

"Very well, then. Let us go and do it now, while the night hides us from our enemies." Long Quiet mounted his pony and reached down a hand to help the Comanche up behind him. Iron strength met his grasp as the Comanche threw his leg over the pony's rump. Long Quiet wondered how the man had managed to bend with the wounds in his thigh and hip, but the Indian sitting behind him gave no evidence of his recent travails.

When they located the two dead braves, Long Quiet saw what the Comanche hadn't been able to express in words. He hoped the young men had been dead when the flesh had been flayed from their arms and legs all the way to the bone. The two men worked quickly to reform the bodies into burial position, tying them into place with their knees bent up to their chests and their heads bent forward to the knees. It was hard work and would have been impossible if so much of the muscle hadn't been cut away. They moved the bodies to a deep arroyo and, after facing the two corpses toward the rising sun, covered them with rocks and dirt.

Long Quiet listened with respect to the chant sung by the Comanche on behalf of the dead warriors.

Mount your ponies and ride up to the sky
Brave warriors and strong of heart
Stay awhile in the Happy Hunting Ground
Then return to the bosom of the Earth Mother
And bring your power back to us.

Long Quiet reached over to support the Comanche, who seemed on the verge of fainting, only to have his hand brushed away.

"I must go home," the Comanche said. "You will come with me to my tipi and be my guest."

Long Quiet bristled at the Comanche's invitation, which had been no less than a command.

"I will give you a gift of many fine ponies. I would see my debt to you paid," the Comanche said.

Long Quiet's response was curt. He hadn't rescued the Comanche in order to be rewarded. "There is no debt."

"You saved my life. I would not have asked it of you, but neither did I refuse your deed. The debt is there."

"I have a journey of my own that must be finished," Long Quiet said, "but I will stay with you until the Tonkawas are no longer a danger."

"I do not need your help. But if you seek my protection, you may stay with me."

Long Quiet's eyes darkened as he fought to control his anger. "Do you question my courage?"

"Do you question mine?"

Muscles flexed and bulged and chests heaved as, like wild birds ruffling lavish plumage, the two men prepared to do combat. In another moment they would have attacked one another. The ridiculousness of the situation hit them both at the same time.

The hint of a smile curved the Comanche's lips. Long Quiet shook his head and let his mouth slant upward at one corner.

"I am too proud," the Comanche admitted.

"You have no horse or weapon. You are wounded. No insult was intended," Long Quiet replied. "I would be honored if you will join me on my journey."

"It is I who will be honored to journey with you. Will you give me your hand?"

Long Quiet reached out a hand in friendship to the wounded man. The Comanche took Long Quiet's hand and at the same time reached for the knife Long Quiet had tied at his waist. Long Quiet stopped the Comanche's outstretched arm where it was, suddenly aware what the warrior intended. He looked into the brave man's dark eyes, moved by the emotions he saw there.

"Such a rich reward is not necessary."

"Do you not wish it?"

"I did not say that."

The lone Comanche smiled as he grasped the knife and quickly cut Long Quiet's palm and then his own and pressed them together to allow the blood to mingle.

"Now we are brothers. What is mine is yours. You are welcome always in my tipi."

Long Quiet mounted his pony and reached his hand down to the Comanche. "Shall we go, *haints?*"

The Comanche stared for a moment at the man who with that simple word had named him both friend and brother, before he allowed himself to be helped onto the pinto.

They rode in silence through the night. Both men enjoyed the quiet solace of the vast plains. Both men felt as one with the Earth Mother. Although neither man spoke, somehow each knew how the other felt. Their unspoken communication firmed the unusual bond of respect that had been steadily growing between them.

The Comanche grunted once in pain when the pinto stumbled, but otherwise Long Quiet was able to ignore the wounded man's presence behind him. He let his imagination wander, his thoughts settling uneasily on the woman called Shadow. Was she the woman he sought? Three years ago he'd promised Cricket and Creed that he'd search for Bayleigh Stewart throughout *Comanchería*. He'd warned Cricket that after living among the Comanches, Bay might not want to return to the white world. Cricket had asked only that he continue his search. The decision about whether to bring Bay home could only be made if and when he finally found her.

He was less willing to contemplate the real reason why he'd searched so diligently for Bay Stewart all these years. No one who knew him would have believed it. He hardly believed it himself. For he was a man reputed to have only one use for women. Yet from the moment he'd first seen Bay Stewart in Boston, where she'd been sent to school by her father, she'd held a fascination for him. She'd stood along the wall at a cotillion, an ugly Texas duckling among the Boston swans. Tall. Gangly. Yet with a quiet dignity. He'd known she was different, as he was different.

He'd gone so far as to find out her name and where she hailed from, but he hadn't done more than that. For he'd always planned to return to *Comanchería*, and he didn't fool himself that she would willingly choose to share his world.

But then Tall Bear had stolen her from her father, and that had changed everything. If he could have found her in the first days and weeks of her captivity, he had no doubt she would now be his wife, the mother of his children. But though he'd searched like a man possessed, she'd eluded his grasp.

Now he was almost afraid to find her. What if she already

had a Comanche husband? What if she already had half-breed children? The worst of it was, he could imagine things no other way. He knew The People too well to hope she could have escaped that destiny.

Long Quiet unconsciously pulled the pinto to a halt. Could he take her away from her Comanche husband and children to return her to the white world? More to the point, could he tear her from a Comanche family to have her for himself? He sighed. He was ahead of himself, imagining problems when he wasn't even sure the woman called Shadow was actually Bayleigh Stewart.

The voice of the Comanche behind him interrupted Long Quiet's musing. "My people are to the north. If you must leave me to go another way, I will understand."

"I am also heading north," Long Quiet said. "I seek someone in the land of the *Quohadi*."

"I am *Quohadi*. Whom do you seek among us? Perhaps I know him."

Long Quiet hesitated before he replied, "An elusive Shadow."

The Comanche tensed. At that moment the sun cracked the edge of the horizon, sending a stream of sunlight into the shiny black curls that had escaped Long Quiet's long, thick braids.

Instantly, the wounded man slid off the pinto. He stepped forward far enough to see Long Quiet's gray eyes in the sunlight. His tone when next he spoke was no longer friendly. "Who are you? Who sent you here?"

Long Quiet hesitated before replying with forced calmness to the sharp demand. "No man guides my footsteps. I go where I will."

"No *tabeboh*, no hated white man, moves at will in *Comanchería*," he spat.

Long Quiet could see the Indian was furious at the discovery that he'd become blood brother to a man who didn't look much like a Comanche.

But I am Comanche!

It was a cry Long Quiet left unvoiced. He held back the sneer that formed in response to the Comanche's short-lived pledge of brotherhood. He should not have been so surprised or hurt . . . yet he was. With the last bit of courtesy he could muster, Long Quiet said, "I am no *tabeboh*. I am of The People."

"You will tell me more of the one you seek."

Long Quiet could hardly contain his wrath at the Comanche's haughty command. "When you ask in the words of a friend, I will gladly tell you what you wish to know."

The Comanche took a deep breath that made his massive chest appear even larger. His black eyes narrowed and his lips thinned in anger until they were nothing. Before he could snarl his response, a Tonkawa arrow landed in the dirt beside his moccasined foot.

Long Quiet extended his hand to the Comanche. "Mount quickly!"

For a moment Long Quiet thought the Comanche would refuse to join him on the pinto. But the whoops of the on-coming Tonkawas prodded him the way no simple words ever could have. His disdainful expression as he grasped Long Quiet's large, powerful hand made it clear he hadn't forgotten his animosity, only laid it aside.

Long Quiet leaned forward and spoke in the pinto's ear, and the pony responded by fleeing like the spring winds before a summer storm. But the gallant pony could only gallop so far with its heavy burden. Long Quiet sought a break in the landscape that would indicate a haven where they could stop and face their enemies.

"There!"

Long Quiet looked where the Comanche pointed. It wasn't much, a dip in the terrain, but Long Quiet headed toward it. To his amazement the ground fell away as they neared the dip, creating a gully. He urged his pony down into the wash, where both he and the Comanche dismounted.

"Here, take my knife. I have my bow and arrows," Long Quiet said.

In movements as smooth, swift, and silent as a rattler on desert sand, Long Quiet loosed four arrows from his bow, one after the other. Each one hit its target, and the odds were suddenly four to two. The startled Tonkawas retreated in the face of such a show of deadly force, screeching insults as they fled.

"They will return," the Comanche said, eyeing Long Quiet with new respect.

"I know."

Neither mentioned that they had only the single knife and a couple of arrows left to defend themselves. They simply looked at one another, acknowledging that each intended to fight to the death.

The Tonkawas taunted their enemies from a safe distance. "Cowardly Comanches! Why do you hide from us? It will serve no purpose. We shall wait here while your tongues dry up of thirst and the heat of the sun boils your blood. We shall wait here for you to crawl out on your bellies to us. There shall be no warriors' deaths for you skulking coyotes! Come out now and we promise to kill you quickly."

Long Quiet soothed his nervous pony before turning to the Comanche. "I have only enough water for a day, maybe two."

"Your horse cannot outrun them with both of us mounted on him. We will make our escape in the dark tonight," the Comanche responded.

"They will be waiting for us."

"I am not afraid to die. But before the sun marches farther in the sky, we have matters to settle between us." The Comanche clutched the knife Long Quiet had given him. His eyes glittered with malice as he turned his full attention to the other man.

"What do you know of Shadow?"

At that moment a Tonkawa brave leaped onto the Comanche's back, his knife poised to slit the Comanche's throat. Acting on reflex, Long Quiet put his arm in the way of the upraised knife and took the slicing jab himself.

The Comanche whirled and made short work of the Tonkawa with Long Quiet's knife. Then he stood for a moment with his head bowed as he thought of what he owed his blood brother. "You have given my life to me yet again."

Long Quiet turned his back on the frustrated Comanche, seeking some of the remaining linsey-woolsey in his *tuna-waws* with which to wrap his arm. As he worked the Comanche joined him, taking the material from Long Quiet's hands and binding the wound for him.

"I do not understand your willingness to risk your life to save mine, *haints*," the Comanche said gruffly. "I made you my brother and then did not act as a brother should. Now I find myself unable to think what I can give you that is a fitting reward."

"I have already said no reward is necessary, but you can tell me what you know of Shadow."

The Comanche's guttural voice shook with emotion when he spoke. "I do not know how you have learned of Shadow, but I will take you to her, if it is still your wish, when we have escaped these Tonkawa dogs."

"Then she exists?"

"Of course."

"What do you know of her?"

"I am Many Horses. Shadow belongs to me."

Chapter 3

THREE COMANCHE WOMEN SAT IN A SEMICIRCLE AT the edge of a colorfully decorated tipi preparing the ingredients for pemmican. Red Wing shelled pecans. Singing Woman beat dried plums into a pulp. She Touches First, sister to the *puhakut*, the village medicine man, pounded the main ingredient, dried buffalo meat, which she then dropped into a pot on the fire to be softened. As they worked, they talked.

A short distance away, far enough that her shadow would not fall upon any of the others, a fourth woman sat by herself. She combined tallow and marrow fat with the pecans, plums, and buffalo meat prepared by the other women and stuffed the resulting pemmican into large buffalo intestine casings. Later the casings would be sealed with melted tallow to make the container of pemmican airtight, so it could be eaten months, or even years, later. As she worked, she listened.

"Many Horses has been gone for two moons. He should have returned by now," She Touches First said.

Red Wing frowned. She had good reason to be concerned because her son, and the son of Singing Woman as well, had accompanied Many Horses on his raid. "Yes, two moons is a long time," Red Wing agreed. "I must admit I will not sleep well until my son, Eagle Feather, gives these old eyes a chance to see his face again. Do you think some ill has befallen them? Perhaps someone broke the tabu and spoke of Shadow's presence here."

"Surely not," Singing Woman chided. "None would dare to risk the *tabebekut*. No one could survive such a curse. And Many Horses has such powerful medicine since . . . since that one came to live among us." She paused in her work, and the lines of worry in her face deepened for a moment before she once again lifted her stone to pulp the plums. "They will surely be successful on their raid. I am eager to see what my son, He Follows the Trail, brings home for me."

She Touches First looked from Red Wing to Singing Woman. "Perhaps Shadow has decided to take away her medicine and leave Many Horses without his *puha*. If some ill has befallen them, then surely she is to blame."

Red Wing and Singing Woman shifted their glances toward the woman who sat a short distance away, but they did not look fully upon her. Such a thing was tabu. Had not the medicine man, He Decides It, told of the danger to anyone beyond Many Horses' family who dared to speak to her or cross her path? If they were also careful not to look upon her, was that not a way to be certain her medicine could not touch them?

"Why would Shadow deny her medicine to Many Horses?" Singing Woman asked. "He provides her shelter and food and keeps her safe from those who would take her away from her home here."

"Perhaps she does not wish to stay here," She Touches First suggested. "Perhaps she does not care who is harmed, so long as she is free to leave."

"I do not wish harm to anyone."

The sound of Shadow's voice brought a sly smile to the face of She Touches First and gaping horror to the faces of the two older women.

"It is tabu!" Red Wing gasped.

"Go! Go! Let us leave this place!" Singing Woman cried.

Red Wing and Singing Woman were gone in an instant, leaving the two younger women alone.

"It is you who should leave this place," She Touches First said, keeping her eyes carefully averted from Shadow. "Many Horses does not need your medicine. He was a great warrior before he ever brought you here and he will be a great warrior when you are gone."

"Why did you frighten them? Why do you call me a threat to anyone here? Why do you say I will take Many Horses' *puha* from him? It was your own brother, the *puhakut*, who said I had powerful medicine. I tell you, I possess no special powers. How could I harm anyone?"

"I did not say you could," She Touches First snapped. "But so long as you are in this village, Many Horses remains bound to you by the strong medicine he believes you possess. I want you gone!"

"So Many Horses will turn his eyes and his heart toward you?"

The woman called Shadow had often seen She Touches First watching Many Horses, and she had seen Many Horses watching the beautiful young sister of the *puhakut*. Yet they never acknowledged their interest in one another and rarely spoke unless necessary. The only explanation Shadow could find for the other woman's antagonism was jealousy. This was the first time she'd voiced that suspicion aloud. Before she could say anything more, She Touches First rose, and after casting a backward glance full of disdain, left Shadow alone.

The woman called Shadow drew her knees up to her chest and circled them with her arms. She closed her eyes and laid her cheek upon the soft buckskin skirt that draped her knees.

When she'd first been captured by the Comanches, Bayleigh Falkirk Stewart had prepared herself to face the horrors of rape and torture and slavery and endure whatever was necessary to survive. She was, after all, her father's daughter. Having been taught by her father how to make difficult decisions, she'd conceded, after considerable thought, that it would be better to live, even though battered and scarred, than to die.

The awful days after her capture when she'd been forced to flee with Tall Bear, and later when she'd ridden with Many Horses through the night, had been an agony of suffering. Thirst, hunger, humiliation, pain from an occasional blow; she'd suffered them all. But worst of all had been the overwhelming fear of what was to come. She tried not to think about it.

Rape.

She knew she was safe so long as the Comanches kept moving to escape anyone following them. It was when they finally stopped, when they made a campfire and settled down to relax, that she knew the time had come when she must endure or die. There would be no rescue.

Rape.

They'd untied her cramped legs from beneath her horse's belly but left the too-tight bindings on her wrists. They'd dragged her over to a cypress tree near a river and dumped her on the grass. She'd been too weak to stand, too weak even to moan, and had lain there in the evening dampness willing it all to be over. They'd left her there while they ate. She could remember their laughter, and remembered wondering what could possibly be so funny.

Rape.

It was dark, so dark, and she was cold. But how could that be? It was warm. July. She shivered. She reached out for something warm. She found it, something soft and warm, and curled her body around it. Then something equally warm curved around her arched back. She was safe. Warm and safe. She would never allow herself to be violated. She would die first. She could hear the excitement in their guttural voices.

Rape!

Oh no! Please God, no! She couldn't bear the shame, the horror of it all. Their voices were closer now, angry. And frightened? Of what? She forced herself upright, forced herself to open her eyes and confront her fears. The Comanches were pointing at her. She followed an accusing finger and stared with amazement at the wolf lying beside her. She turned and found another wolf stretched out on the other side and smiled at the sight of Ruffian and Rascal, two of Cricket's pet wolves. They'd been with her when she'd been captured by Tall Bear and must have followed her. She gave each wolf a hug of welcome.

When the Comanches tried to come near her, the wolves bared their fangs and lunged, backing up to stand beside her again as soon as it was clear the Comanches would keep their distance. She saw a Comanche raise his bow and arrow to kill the beasts, but he was stopped by the war chief, Many Horses. They argued among themselves, but Many Horses would not let them harm her or the wolves. At last Ruffian and Rascal, hungry for food, left her side.

She'd been approached warily by the Comanches, but when they'd found they weren't harmed by her touch, she'd been bound again and set on a pony. They hadn't stopped again until they'd reached their village. What had happened when she reached the village . . . she couldn't remember it without trembling. It had been awful.

But afterward she'd been left alone. All alone.

At first, being left alone had been a blessing. She'd feared the strange faces and strange customs, the strange foods and strange language. It had amazed her how quickly she'd adapted to all that strangeness. In fact, in a matter of weeks Bay was ready to make an overture of friendship to the Comanches who'd taken her from her home.

But no one would speak to her. No one would cross her path. And none of her efforts to change that situation made any difference. Many Horses' mother-in-law, Cries at Night, had spoken to her, but only in Comanche, and only to teach her the tasks a Comanche woman must know to do her share of the work.

In the beginning, she'd thought it was the language that created the huge barrier between her and the people around her. But after she'd learned a little Comanche, it became apparent something else kept the villagers away from her.

That was when she'd learned of the tabu.

Quite simply, because of the incident with the wolves on the trail and what had happened when she'd first been brought to the village, the *puhakut*, the village medicine man, had attributed some mystical power to her. He'd told the villagers she possessed medicine that could give strength to Many Horses—or cause him catastrophic harm. No one must interfere with her medicine, lest Many Horses be vulnerable in battle. The *puhakut* had declared it tabu for anyone in the village except Many Horses and his family to speak to her or even cross her path.

As if that hadn't been enough, Many Horses had added his fearsome curse, the *tabebekut*, as the penalty for anyone who brought the threat of harm to her, and that included speaking of her existence to those outside the village.

Bay's protestations, when she could finally speak the Comanche tongue, that the *puhakut* must be mistaken, had fallen on deaf ears. Her mystical power had remained unquestioned, and she'd remained alone. Many Horses obviously held her in some special esteem, but that role rarely included conversation that was more than one-sided. He would speak to her, but he didn't expect, or necessarily desire, a response. There had been no one to talk to, no one with whom to share the ache she felt at being so isolated in the midst of so many.

So Bay had begun to listen. She didn't eavesdrop by choice, nor had she ever gotten over the feeling it was wrong. And sometimes, like now, when she was faced with jealousy and resentment and fear, she wished she hadn't listened.

"Are you asleep, *Pia*, Mother?"

Bay opened her eyes to a pixielike face, with large black eyes, a button nose, and a sweetly curving mouth. A tiny palm cupped her cheek, and the small face angled so the two of them could easily see into one another's eyes.

"No. I was only resting." Bay sat up and made a lap for the little girl to crawl into.

Bay held the three-year-old child snugly to her. How she loved this child! Many Horses' wife, Buffalo Woman, had died in childbirth and Cries at Night had literally given the squalling infant, her grandchild, to Bay. From that moment on, in Bay's mind and heart the child had been hers. It was caring for Little Deer that had given Bay a reason for living during the lonely days when she'd begun to doubt the importance of simply surviving.

Little Deer took one of Bay's braids and held it up to the sunlight to see the red highlights sparkle in the sun. "Why is your hair not the color of the raven's wing?"

"The Great Spirit created each of us to be as we are. So my hair is . . ." Bay examined the braid that shone gold and red and tried to think what color she should use to describe it.

"Like the sunrise," Little Deer offered.

"Yes," Bay agreed, tapping Little Deer on the nose. "Perhaps you are right."

"Will my *ap'* be coming home soon?"

"Your father will be home when he has done what he went to do. I hope it will be soon."

"I miss him."

"I miss him, too."

Recently, Bay had begun to count the days, certain it couldn't be long before Many Horses returned from his raid in the south. "The day is nearly gone, Little Deer. Help me to put away this pemmican, and we will go and have our meal. Maybe if your *ap'* smells our good cooking he will find his way home to us."

But Many Horses did not come home, and as Bay drifted off to sleep, she wondered for the thousandth time if she was fated to spend the rest of her life among the Comanches. She knew her family must have searched for her, but she was hidden every time a stranger came to the village.

After three years of captivity, she harbored very little hope that anyone would ever find her. And she feared that the one person she wanted most to find her, Jonas Harper, wouldn't want her back if he could see her now. Because the woman she'd become was nothing like the woman who'd exchanged vows of love with Jonas in Boston so many years ago.

It wasn't just that her skin had tanned and freckled from exposure to the sun or that her fingers were callused from hard work or that her feet had lost their delicate arch from running barefoot so much of the time. There had been fundamental changes inside Bay that she wasn't sure Jonas would like. Rip had taught her to rely on herself, but in comparison to her sisters, Sloan and Cricket, she'd been a sparrow among hawks.

In those long-ago days, Jonas had bolstered her meager self-confidence, had protected her from the fears of inadequacy she'd acquired growing up in a home with two outspoken sisters and an overpowering father. Jonas had been happy to find a woman who needed him, someone who depended upon him to sustain her sense of who and what she was. She'd clung to him as to a rooftop in a raging spring flood.

But she'd changed. Surviving, and then having responsibility for another human life, had given her a confidence in herself that hadn't been there before. She wondered if Jonas would like the more self-assured Bay she'd become. She wondered if he could love such a woman enough to make her his wife.

Of course, it was silly to worry about what Jonas wanted in a wife, Bay thought, yawning hugely. She was never going to see him again. She turned over and closed her eyes and sought out Jonas in a world of dreams, where he would want her even changed as she was.

What seemed like moments later, a strong tug on the rawhide string attached to her pallet startled Bay awake. Her dream of dancing in Jonas Harper's arms rapidly faded, leaving her disoriented. As her fingertips grazed the woolly buffalo robe beneath her, she realized she wasn't in her soft featherbed at Three Oaks. She waited for her eyes to adjust to the dark. The walls of the tipi slanted in on her. Her nose burned with the smell of rancid meat and woodsmoke.

Like the slow rising of the sun on a black night, the reality of her situation once again became plain. No longer was she Bayleigh Falkirk Stewart, daughter of Rip, sister to Sloan and Cricket. She was Shadow, white captive of the Comanche war chief Many Horses. And at long last her master had returned and summoned her to him.

Bay hurriedly put on her deerskin poncho, the long fringes tickling her naked thighs as she pulled it down. She quickly stood and added a fringed deerskin skirt. She tied the thong at her waist as she bent to check on Little Deer, who still slept soundly.

"Something is wrong," a voice announced from the opposite side of the tipi. "Had everything gone well on his raid, Many Horses would have waited with the others until morning and awakened the camp to celebrate their victorious return."

Bay crossed to kneel beside Cries at Night, not bothering to ask how the old woman knew Many Horses was back and had summoned her. Bay helped the old woman, who suffered from arthritis in her joints, get more comfortable before she answered in a whisper, "Many Horses would have called you also, *Pia*, had anything been seriously amiss."

Cries at Night was the closest thing Bay had ever had to a mother, since her own mother had died when she was a child. The older woman had been adviser and teacher rather than confidante, and since that was very nearly the same relationship she'd had with her father, Bay had been more than willing to accord the respectful title of Mother to Cries at Night.

The hard nomadic Comanche life had wrinkled the old woman's skin and toasted it dark brown. Because of Cries at

Night's black hair and dark eyes, Bay hadn't realized at first she was Spanish rather than Comanche and had once been a captive herself. That wasn't surprising, because now even the old woman's thoughts were Comanche. Several years ago, Cries at Night's Comanche husband had died in battle and she'd become dependent upon her son-in-law, Many Horses, for her support. Thus, both women had an equally strong interest in Many Horses' well-being.

Cries at Night took Bay's arm and warned in a low, raspy voice, "That proud man would die before he'd admit to any pain. Look well to Many Horses and be sure he does not conceal any wound from you."

"I shall do as you ask, *Pia*. Now go back to sleep. You need your rest."

Bay turned and stepped outside the tipi, welcoming the August breeze that cooled the perspiration on her body. She took time to stroke the speckled fur of the dog that lay on its back near the threshold.

"Hello, Stewpot."

The dog stretched and groaned with pleasure as Bay scratched its flea-ridden stomach. The Comanches never ate dog meat if they could help it, but during the past February and March, the "time when the babies cry for food," she'd barely saved this ugly hound from the cooking pot, thus earning it its name.

"Go back to sleep, Stewpot."

It was but a few steps to reach Many Horses' tipi. His war shield, decoratively rimmed with the scalps of his enemies, stood on a tripod nearby. There were blond scalps, black, red, and even gray. Bay shuddered as she passed by the gruesome trophies and quickly lifted the flap of Many Horses' tipi and stepped inside.

It had been brighter in the light of the half-moon, and it took a moment for her eyes to readjust to the dim interior of the tipi. A small fire had been lit, weaving eerie designs within the buffalo-hide walls. Bay moved instinctively toward the heat of the man who'd first become her master on a sweltering night very much like this one three years ago.

"Welcome home, Many Horses. I thank *Our Sure Enough Father* for bringing you safely back to me."

"It is good to be home, Shadow." Many Horses' gaze warmed with appreciation as he said, "I thought often of you while I was away. I had only to close my eyes to see your face. I remembered your eyes, the deep violet of a stormy night; your hair, the red of a young fox's fur; your cheeks, pink as primroses blanketing the earth; your face—"

"—shining like the moon in the sky," Bay finished with a smile. His words, the tender poem of a lover, were beautiful in the Comanche tongue, and the first time she'd actually understood what he was saying to her, she'd been embarrassed by his effusive praise—until she'd heard him using words equally poetic and beautiful to describe his favorite war pony. It had been a shock to realize she was but a possession—one he considered exquisite and unusual, but a possession nonetheless. Bay didn't even believe the compliments, because she thought the features he honored were not nearly so beautiful as they were simply an oddity among the Comanches, who were uniformly black-eyed and raven-haired.

"I am glad you find me pleasing. It is sad to know my beauty must share your thoughts with burning homes and bloodied bodies," she replied.

Bay knew the frown was coming even before Many Horses pursed his lips. She knew he lived by raiding, plundering, and killing, and he knew she hated it. Many Horses was a Comanche warrior, and his valorous actions proved his courage and gave him his pride. Over the three years she'd been his captive, she'd come to understand why he did what he did. But she'd never learned to accept it.

At least he was back alive and—was he well? Why had he not waited with the two young men until morning and made a triumphal entry into camp? "Where are Eagle Feather and He Follows the Trail?"

"They did not return. They both died bravely fighting our enemies, the Tonkawas."

What does it matter whether they died bravely? They're still dead, aren't they? Bay bit her tongue against the words she longed to hurl, knowing they wouldn't be welcome. She knew the honored manner of their sons' deaths would be of utmost importance to Red Wing and Singing Woman. She fought against feeling so much hurt for the loss of the two young men she'd known only through the overheard conversations of their mothers.

She swallowed her grief, asking instead, "And you, Many Horses? Are you well?"

"Of course, except for . . . I am well."

Bay tried to keep her anxiety from her face, but she felt certain Many Horses was hiding something from her.

Apparently, she hadn't hidden her concern as well as she'd thought, because he held out his arms to her and said, "I have more to speak of and I can see you will not rest until your hands have confirmed what I have told you. Come. Look for yourself."

Bay knelt on the edge of the huge buffalo robe that covered nearly the entire floor of the tipi. Many Horses was naked except for a breechclout. She let her hands roam his thick, muscular body to reassure herself there was indeed no wound he'd hidden from her. His skin was hot and slick with sweat, and she inhaled his familiar musky scent as her fingertips skimmed his body. To her dismay, she found a bandage at his waist, and then one on his thigh, which had been hidden by his breechclout.

"What is this?"

He grunted as she touched the cloth bandage at his hip. "Only a small wound from a Tonkawa lance," he soothed. "Nothing to be troubled about. It has already begun to heal."

"Let me see."

Bay had already started unwrapping the covering when Many Horses caught both her hands firmly in his and said, "First you must greet our guest."

"What?"

"I have brought someone home with me who wishes to meet you."

Bay couldn't have been more surprised if Many Horses had announced he'd brought his war pony into the tipi to spend the night. She whirled on her knees to seek out the dark figure near the entry flap of the tipi.

"*Haints*, this woman is Shadow. Shadow, this man is my friend and brother Long Quiet, to whom I owe my life. I was surrounded by my enemies when he came charging amongst them and rescued me. Then he saved my throat from the slashing knife of a Tonkawa dog before we finally escaped from our enemies in the darkness of the night."

The man in the shadows rose and resettled himself cross-legged in front of Bay.

Long Quiet fought to keep his features impassive as he felt a flood of desire for the lovely woman who sat before him. His quest was over. At long last he'd found Bayleigh Falkirk Stewart—Shadow, the mystical white woman the young Comanche buck had spoken of, with eyes the dark purple of a stormy night and hair the color of fire. He no longer had to rely on his imagination to remember her. Before him sat a flesh-and-blood woman who set his pulse to pounding and his loins ablaze.

She belongs to another man, he reminded himself.

Yet he couldn't keep from eating the sight of her with his eyes. She'd matured since he'd seen her so many years ago. Her body, once gangly with youth, was lush, her breasts a bounteous promise beneath the deerskin she wore, her hips slim. Her lustrous auburn hair hung in braids, but the bound curls escaped in tendrils at her temples, enticing his fingers to entwine with them. He understood Many Horses' need to honor her beauty with his poetry. He felt the need to do the same himself and regretted he didn't have the other man's ease with words.

"You did not tell a tale. She is very beautiful," he said softly. "A man would do well to possess such a woman."

Bay felt her skin flush at the Comanche's compliment. It had been all she could do to sit still for his frank, thorough examination of her face and form. She waited impatiently for permission to speak and despaired when it did not come.

"I have been trying to convince Long Quiet he should accept some of the ponies in my herd. I would not have returned at all without his help, and I wish to thank him," Many Horses explained to Bay. "But he will take nothing."

"I also add my thanks to that of Many Horses. I will be always in your debt for having helped him come safely home," Bay said.

Many Horses watched with a queer mixture of pride and jealousy the look of admiration for Shadow that he found on his blood brother's face. He pressed the wound at his waist with his elbow and flinched when his elbow grazed the place where his flesh had been flayed away by the Tonkawas. He did not like owing Long Quiet, but nothing he had said had convinced the other man to accept a suitable reward that would free him of his obligation.

However, Long Quiet had unwittingly revealed there was something Many Horses possessed that he desired very much: Shadow. Of course the flicker of desire for Shadow in Long Quiet's eyes had been inappropriate, and quickly hidden. Nonetheless, Many Horses had seen it.

He had never shared Shadow with another man and was not quite sure how the idea had come into his head now. Yet there it was. He turned the thought in his mind as he would have turned a new arrow in his hands, smoothing the shaft, looking for flaws. It galled his pride to be in the debt of the other man. And Shadow was the only thing he possessed in which Long Quiet had expressed an interest. No man could turn down such a prize.

Yet could he share her? He considered the danger the *puhakut* had warned him of when he'd first brought Shadow to the village. Surely this man could mean him no harm. Long Quiet had already saved his life twice. Still, Many Horses felt a sinking sensation in his stomach. He was about to share a highly treasured possession, one he'd come to recognize as solely his own, and could not shake the feeling of foreboding that descended upon him. He felt his jaw tighten in determination, aware his pride was forcing him to do a thing his warrior's instincts told him could have terrible consequences.

He spoke before he could change his mind. "I am glad you approve of Shadow. She shall be yours to serve you in whatever manner you wish, for so long as you are among us."

Bay's head snapped up, and she looked at Many Horses with horror. "You cannot give me—"

Many Horses cut her off with a wave of his hand. If he could have done so without looking foolish, he would have withdrawn his offer in that instant. He briefly considered playing the fool, but his pride rescued him from that fate.

What was done was done. There was no turning back. When he spoke, his eyes were focused on Long Quiet, and his voice was brusque.

"You would not take a single pony from me, *haints*, nor any other gift I offered, even though you saved my life more than once. You were right to refuse such tokens. For only a gift as priceless as the one I offer now could repay the debt I owe you. I wish to share with my brother everything that is mine. Surely you will not refuse my offer and leave me without honor in this matter."

Long Quiet was stunned. He opened his mouth to agree, then snapped it shut. He'd only planned to be in the village long enough to find out if Shadow was indeed Bayleigh Stewart and, if so, to ask her whether she wished to return home to Three Oaks. Now he'd been given a gift he'd only imagined. He had to remind himself this was a white woman—his friend Creed's sister-in-law. He felt the swell of desire within him and knew it would be better if he did not accept Many Horses' gift.

Long Quiet held his tongue.

Bay was in shock. She turned her head slowly to confront the man to whom she'd been temporarily given. His lips were pressed in a tight line, and he looked uncomfortable, and perhaps even a little angry. If she'd learned nothing else among the Comanches, she'd learned a man's honor was everything. It was clear Long Quiet recognized his dilemma: He could not refuse Many Horses' gift without causing the warrior to lose face. Bay's stomach knotted in agitation. Many Horses could not intend that she be used for *any* purpose. Yet she feared he did.

Bay allowed herself to examine more closely the stranger who'd saved Many Horses' life. Where Many Horses had the high, wide cheekbones and straight, prominent nose of a Comanche, this man's angled cheekbones and aquiline nose were more refined. His skin was more bronze than copper, his muscular chest slick and smooth, with only a provocative line of dark hair arrowing from his navel downward. Instead of being barrel-chested like Many Horses, his broad shoulders tapered to a narrow waist and hips.

She looked closer and realized his sin-black hair escaped from his braids in tiny curls at his temples and at his nape, much as her own did. She almost jumped when their eyes met. Intense gray eyes stared back at her. No Comanche warrior she'd ever seen had curly black hair and slate-gray eyes. It dawned on her suddenly that this was no Indian, constrained to obey Indian customs.

"This man is white!"

Long Quiet's face became forbidding. He stared straight ahead but said nothing.

"Truly, some white blood runs in his veins. But he is of The People," Many Horses replied firmly.

Bay watched surprise flicker in the stranger's gray eyes,

which immediately became blank again. "I do not wish to belong to this man."

"It is done."

Bay didn't mistake either the finality of Many Horses' words or the tone in which they were delivered. She'd faced few calamities worse than this during her time among the Comanches, but from those experiences she'd learned not to give up. In order to survive, it was necessary to keep fighting, even when all hope seemed lost.

"May we speak of this alone?" she asked.

"There is nothing to discuss."

The spark of anger in Many Horses' eyes warned Bay that to question his will was to shame him before his friend. A lump rose in her throat. She belonged to Many Horses as surely as the Negro slaves who worked on her father's cotton plantation belonged to him. It was clear Many Horses had made up his mind, and there was no one in the village who would dare to contradict any command he gave her. But she wasn't done fighting yet.

"Have you told Long Quiet that for the past three years you have allowed no other man to touch me? Have you explained that I am the source of your strong medicine in battle? Does he know the *puhakut* warned you to guard my person against the day when one would come to take me away and thus destroy you?"

Bay could tell her words had shocked Long Quiet, but before the stranger could speak, Many Horses repeated more forcefully, "There is nothing to discuss."

Many Horses was clearly enraged by her defiance. She folded her arms about her to try to still her trembling. There was no one who could save her now—unless the stranger . . .

She turned to survey Long Quiet's features and found nothing to tell her what he thought of what she'd said, nothing to give her any encouragement that her words had made a difference. She'd learned that even among the Comanches there were kind men and cruel men, and she prayed he wasn't one who believed in hurting women. Her eyes beseeched the silent man for some solution to her dilemma.

Bay might have been bound by Many Horses' desires, but it was clear Long Quiet had a will of his own. "If you give me this gift, it is I who shall be in your debt," he said. "Can a brother not save a brother's life without the need for such a prize?"

"You speak from your heart, *haints*, which is generous," Many Horses replied. "Let me be generous as well."

Bay shifted uncomfortably as Long Quiet searched her face for her thoughts. He seemed dissatisfied with what he found, and she let herself hope again he would refuse Many Horses' offer.

Those hopes were dashed when he sighed resignedly and replied to Many Horses, "You have been as stealthy as a wolf among the buffalo. I find I cannot refuse your offer. You well know I would welcome a soft pallet beneath me and a woman to wait upon me while I am here."

A rush of air came from Many Horses' chest, and it was only then Bay realized he hadn't been at all sure Long Quiet would accept his offer. Bay wondered what kind of man would dare refuse such an incredible gift. She saw the unexpected spark of possessiveness in Many Horses' eyes, quickly masked, and knew how generous his gift had been.

The three of them sat for a moment in silence, as though none of them could quite believe they'd actually agreed to this arrangement. Then Many Horses rose, and Bay and Long Quiet had no choice except to stand also.

"Show Long Quiet where he is to sleep. I will expect you to care for him as though we were one in body, as we truly are in spirit."

Bay watched as Many Horses reached out a hand to the white man dressed as a Comanche, who clasped it elbow to wrist.

"I will not forget the giving of this gift," Long Quiet said.

"I am not at all sure that when I leave I will not be in your debt."

Bay turned to Long Quiet, all pleasure at having met the stranger now fled, replaced with trepidation. "Come with me." She stepped outside the tipi and held the tent flap open for him. When he stood outside the tipi, she became aware for the first time how tall he was. She stood out among the Comanche women because she was the same height as Many Horses. This man stretched almost a head taller than she did.

When they reached the tipi Many Horses kept ready for visitors, Long Quiet reached down to lift up the buffalo hide opening to hold it for her. She searched his face and was surprised when he spoke to her in English instead of the Comanche tongue.

"Go inside. We need to talk."

Bay stood frozen for a moment before she ducked inside. When he followed her, she moved away from him to the center of the tipi, intent on starting a fire. She grabbed the flint and a handful of the kindling kept ever ready in the tipi and squatted down in the center of the spacious area near a circle of stones.

To her consternation, he sat down directly across from her. He made no move to relieve her of her task, for which she was grateful. She worked with the flint until a spark hit the moss and a thin line of white smoke rose from the tinder. She'd just taken a deep breath to coax the fire to life when he spoke.

"I've come to take you home."

Chapter 4

"OH MY." IT WAS AN EXPRESSION BAY HAD OFTEN USED at Three Oaks when she was stunned or pleased or dismayed. Right now she was all three. Yet the words felt strange on her lips and tongue. She wanted to say more, but it had been a long time since she'd turned her thoughts into English words and she was surprised by how much effort it took.

When she remained frozen, Long Quiet leaned over and provided the puff of air needed by the fire for life. "I promised Cricket I'd keep looking for you and that once I found you, if you wanted to go home, I'd take you back," Long Quiet said.

Bay's eyes hung on the man who professed to be her rescuer, who was suggesting that after all these years she could simply leave and go home. Then she realized what else he'd said. "You know my sister?"

"Your sister's husband, Jarrett Creed, is my friend. Three years ago, several warriors of the Comanche band who burned your father's home passed through my village and spoke of a beautiful woman with violet eyes and hair of flame who'd been captured by Tall Bear. I went looking for you and found Cricket and Creed instead. When it became apparent you were being taken too far north into *Comanchería* for them to follow safely, I promised Cricket I'd keep searching for you until I found you.

"I was sure it would be easy to find such a distinctive woman." He smiled ruefully. "As you can see, I underestimated Many Horses." His eyes roamed her face, from the huge violet eyes to the full, slightly parted lips and back again. "It's hard to believe word of your beauty wasn't carried on the wind to the farthest reaches of *Comanchería*."

His words had been spoken in a low, husky voice that touched Bay almost like a hand. Then his hand did reach out, and his fingers tipped her chin up so their eyes met. Bay felt herself sinking into his gaze. He seemed to absorb her, engulf her. It was a frightful sensation, but tantalizing as well. Bay felt the heat at her throat that became a blush on her cheeks. It was a curse of her fair skin that her emotions were so easily revealed.

"I meant only to please you with my words," he said, discerning her discomfort. He took both her hands in his. "I ask again. Would you like to go home?"

Bay freed herself from the disturbing caress of his fingertips before she answered, "It doesn't matter what I want. Many Horses would never let me go."

"Every woman has a price. I will buy you from him."

"He won't sell me to any man for any price," she insisted.

Long Quiet's gray eyes darkened dangerously. "Then I will steal you from him." The voice that spoke was arrogant, fierce, and uncompromising, the voice of a Comanche warrior.

"You would steal from your brother?"

Bay could tell her words had stung when he asked in a voice hardened by the need to control his rage, "Do you want to leave or not, Bay?"

Bay started at the sound of her English name spoken aloud. Bay. Bayleigh Falkirk Stewart. He was offering her a chance to take up that other life again. And it was plain he would do whatever was necessary to take her home. All that mattered was whether or not she wanted to go.

"If you only knew how I dreamed of this moment," Bay

whispered. "How I hoped someday someone would come and take me home." Bay laughed aloud. "And now you've come!"

She longed for the touch of another human being to celebrate her good fortune. But she'd learned hard lessons from the Comanches and dared not tread where she wasn't clearly welcome. She hugged herself with her arms and rocked back and forth where she sat, a ridiculously happy grin on her face.

As if sensing her need and her indecision, Long Quiet held out his arms to her.

Bay launched herself into his embrace, crying and laughing at the same time. She had to swallow over the lump in her throat before she could speak. "Every night I prayed for this. I can't believe it's really happening."

She felt Long Quiet's muscles tense as though he sought to push her away, and she clenched her arms tighter around his waist. "Please. Don't let go."

"I will hold you as long as you like," Long Quiet replied. He wanted to be happy for her, but it was hard when he knew that if he got his way, she would not be going home to Three Oaks once they left this place. She would be coming home with him to his village. Now that he'd found her, he had no intention of giving her up again. But there would be time enough when they were safely gone from Many Horses' village to convince her that her place was with him. "Does this mean you want me to take you away from here?"

"Yes. Oh, yes."

"I will make plans for us to leave before the sun rises."

Bay's mind raced to contemplate what she would be leaving behind. She wouldn't miss the loneliness. Or the grueling work. Or the whispers. Or the Comanches who'd spurned her because of the *puhakut*'s decree. But she would miss Many Horses, because he'd been kind to her when she'd expected cruelty. And the taciturn old woman, Cries at Night, who'd been like a mother to her. And she would miss Little Deer.

As Bay thought of leaving Little Deer, the smile left her

face. Her chest tightened and her heart skipped a beat. She hadn't considered what it would mean to leave Little Deer, because she'd never really expected to have to make a choice. Now that the choice was hers to make, she realized there wasn't any choice at all. She had a Comanche daughter. How could she abandon her child?

"Wait. I . . . I can't leave this place. It's too late. You're too late," Bay cried, struggling to be free of Long Quiet's grasp. "Let me go!"

Long Quiet had expected Bay to have second thoughts. He just hadn't expected them to come quite so soon, before the first blush of pleasure had even left her face. He held her tenderly in his arms. "Shhh. Don't cry," he soothed. "It is never too late. If you want to leave, you can. But have you perhaps found this life better than the one you left behind?"

"No, it's not that . . . not exactly," she amended. As awful as she'd first found life among the Comanches, at least they hadn't asked more from her than she'd been able to give. Rip Stewart had expected his daughters to be equal to the tasks a son might be asked to perform. While Sloan and Cricket had found such accomplishments easy, Bay had found herself inept and inadequate at many of them. She felt certain that was why she was the least and the last among his daughters in Rip's eyes.

Here, at least, she felt needed. She would be missed more by the child she left now than by the sisters and father she'd left behind three years ago.

Bay had no idea how long she'd been silent, but when she looked up at Long Quiet, she said, "I can't leave this place."

"Because you love Many Horses?"

Bay was taken aback by the question. She didn't love Many Horses, but she did care for him, and there was the matter of the supposed powers she wielded on his behalf. While she didn't believe anything she did protected Many Horses from evil spirits in battle, he did. "I won't leave him."

"If it were not for Many Horses, would you stay and live among the Comanches?"

Bay didn't like the tone of Long Quiet's voice or the frown on his face. Both seemed to threaten. Surely he'd never consider harming Many Horses. After all, they were brothers. It was best he understood the reason why she wouldn't leave this village before he let his thoughts take the dangerous turn that appeared to be coming.

"I have a daughter, Little Deer," she said. "I could never leave her."

Bay thought she'd misunderstood the look in Long Quiet's eyes because for a moment he appeared bitterly disappointed. When he finally spoke, his voice was hard and flat as he confirmed, "You have a child."

"Yes. A beautiful daughter whom I love more than I thought it possible to love anyone."

"Many Horses' child?"

"Yes."

Bay knew he thought she'd borne the child, and it was on the tip of her tongue to correct him. But she thought he might be less willing to let her stay if she spoke the truth. So she kept silent.

Long Quiet hadn't thought it would hurt to discover that Bay had in fact met the fate he'd suspected at the hands of the Comanches. It was just that for a little while he'd allowed himself to imagine what it would be like to have this woman for his wife, to imagine children that blended her features and his, and to imagine growing old together. He'd wondered for the better part of three years whether he could take her from her child, to have her for himself. Now he had his answer. He could not do it. And he found that knowledge as bitter as winter wind on his flesh, and equally chilling to his soul.

"Of course you would not wish to leave your child," he said. "I promised your sister I would abide by your wishes. I will leave here tomorrow alone."

"No!"

Long Quiet's brow furrowed at her outburst.

"I mean . . . do you have to leave so soon?" Bay hadn't had nearly enough opportunity to speak with this stranger, and if he left tomorrow it could be months, years perhaps, before she was given another chance like this.

If Long Quiet hadn't been so frustrated at the turn of events, perhaps he wouldn't have spoken quiet so frankly. But he was frustrated, and thus brutally frank. "It would not please me to stay here and know I cannot touch you."

"But Many Horses said you could—"

"I have never taken an unwilling woman to my pallet."

What was she supposed to say? She couldn't guarantee she'd be a willing partner. She wasn't sure she could find pleasure lying with any man. She'd once hoped to save herself for Jonas Harper, but those dreams had been dashed when she'd been taken captive by the Comanches. But was what he asked so much to give if it would keep him here a little longer? Besides, the thought of being with him in the way of husbands and wives left her oddly breathless.

"And if it pleased me to have you stay . . . and touch me?" she asked at last.

His smile flashed quickly, white against his deeply tanned face. "Then of course I would be willing to do whatever pleased you."

Bay returned his smile with one equally brilliant. "Then stay. Talk to me for a little while."

"It shall be as you ask. What would you like to talk about?"

"Anything—as long as we can speak in English."

"Agreed," Long Quiet said.

Bay laughed, almost drunk on contemplation of the pleasure of an entire conversation in English. "When did you last see Cricket and Creed? How are they? And the rest of my family? Is everyone all right?"

Long Quiet smiled indulgently. "Which question shall I answer first?"

"Please don't tease me." Bay placed her hand on his arm, and felt the muscles bunch beneath her fingertips. "Sloan was expecting a child when I last saw her. Did she have a boy or a girl?"

Long Quiet covered her hand with his as he replied, "I wish I could tell you something, but I haven't heard anything about Sloan's baby."

"What about Cricket and Creed?"

"The last time I saw them, they both looked very happy. Cricket's belly is swollen with Creed's child."

"Cricket? A mother?" Bay laughed aloud at the thought of her hell-raising sister chasing after a rambunctious son or daughter. "When will the baby be born?"

"In the new moon."

"I hope she finds as much happiness in having a child to love as I have."

Long Quiet's hand tightened painfully on Bay's until she said, "You're hurting me."

He immediately released her.

Bay had grown up with a father whose terrible rages, though mostly bluff and bluster, had frightened her. Over the past few years, she'd learned to give the appearance of courage even when she was quaking inside. But she found the sight of this angry man, who had her life completely in his control, terrifying. She grabbed at the only excuse she could think of to leave him.

"I'll get you some food."

"I'm not hungry. Stay." His voice was sharp, commanding.

"Surely you must—"

"Stay. Right now I need sleep. Can you prepare a bed for us?"

Bay was shocked at his request. Somehow she hadn't expected him to take advantage of her offer so quickly. It was one thing to make the promise she'd made. It was an entirely different matter to keep it.

"I can't."

The words came out in a whisper, and she put her finger-tips to her lips after she'd spoken, her eyes rounding as she admitted to herself the utter futility of her resistance. There was no way she could physically resist the strength of this tall, broad-shouldered man if he chose to take her as Many Horses had given him permission to do—as she herself had given him permission to do.

"You can't make us a bed?"

She saw him look around the tipi, finding the buffalo robes rolled and stacked to one side and the nearby moss-stuffed rabbit fur pillows.

"No. Yes. I meant I can't . . ."

"Can't what?"

His voice seemed cold, unyielding, or maybe that was her imagination at work. Bay swallowed, but her throat was so tight it hurt. She looked at Long Quiet, her heart pounding in her chest. He was a white man. Surely he understood her po-sition, why she'd made her offer, what she was feeling now. She decided to take the chance of speaking as frankly with him as he'd spoken to her.

"I understand the Comanche custom that allows Many Horses to offer . . . to share me with you, and I know what I promised. But I . . . I really don't wish to . . . You must under-stand how unnatural, how wrong such an act would seem to a white woman . . . such as myself. After all, you're a white man, you—"

"I am Comanche, a True Human Being. Do not dare to call me White!"

Bay's face blanched at the sharpness of his reply. What-ever thought she'd had of appealing to his understanding died a swift death. She closed her eyes and held her breath, wait-ing for his wrath to descend upon her.

"I only wish to sleep now," he said, his voice less harsh. "Make a bed for us."

Bay sighed silently. He'd given her a brief reprieve. She

didn't want to guess why. It was the *now* at the end of his expressed desire for sleep that curled her toes. Perhaps once they lay down together, he'd change his mind and reach for her. His tone, however, had brooked no refusal. She had no recourse except to make a bed for them.

Her nervousness increased as Long Quiet watched her spread the buffalo robe on the hard-packed ground and settle the pillows at one end. It was an imperfectly cured robe, one of the first she'd prepared by herself, but her fingers found comfort in its flaws. She rubbed a spot that was still stiff, where she'd missed softening the hide with a mixture of basswood bark, buffalo brains, and grease. She had learned to do better. She had learned to survive.

"The bed is ready," she said at last.

Long Quiet rose and crossed to where she stood, reaching for the string that released his breechclout. She clenched her teeth to keep from asking him not to bare himself. She carefully kept her eyes on his face, not daring to look down. Completely comfortable with his nakedness, he lay down on his back with his hands cradling his head.

"Come, join me," he said.

When she started to lie down fully dressed, he stopped her. "You'll be too warm in that deerskin. Take it off."

Bay felt a spark of anger at his demand. "I don't want—"

"That we should be together now is by your choice. I merely wish to see you. That is less than you've agreed we should have between us. Do you deny me even this?"

Bay bit her lip until it bled, but she said nothing.

Long Quiet shrugged. He was relieved that she'd failed this first test. Now he wouldn't have the torture of remembering her body when he'd gone away. "I will leave with the rising of the sun."

"No. Wait." The words were torn from Bay. For a while she'd been able to forget that this gray-eyed, English-speaking man was Comanche, but it was becoming clear there was nothing remotely civilized about him. A combination of anger and desperation gave her the courage to do what she knew must be done. Bay had never wished so fervently for a petticoat. She was naked beneath the deerskin.

With her eyes on her feet, Bay untied the thong at her waist and let the skirt drop to her feet. As the fringes of her poncho undulated against her naked thighs, she heard Long Quiet's sharp intake of breath. Her face flushed scarlet as she realized she'd unwittingly provided more temptation to him than she'd intended. She stood with her head bowed, her hands at her sides, unwilling to completely bare herself to his gaze.

He rose with sure, catlike grace to stand before her. His hands grasped the poncho and pulled it gently up from the waist, bringing her arms above her head as he released her from the garment. Her hands automatically crossed over her breasts.

"I want to see you."

He'd said it so softly, so gently, that she looked up to see if his gaze matched his voice. It did. There was no frightening, fiery desire, no uncontrolled hunger. Neither did she find anger or any intent to inflict hurt or humiliation. She let her hands drop slowly to her sides.

She could see him try, and fail, to control another sharp intake of air. His eyes flashed briefly with raw need, then his gaze once again became remote. She flinched when he reached out to touch the long, jagged scar on her ribs, but stood still as his fingers traced the scar to its end. She knew when he realized there were more scars on her back. His jaw muscles tightened and his eyes narrowed as his arms reached around her, his fingertips tracing the myriad trails of pain.

"Did he do this to you?"

The rage in his voice kept her silent for so long that Long Quiet drew his own conclusions.

"I won't leave you here with Many Horses. When I go, you'll come with me."

"No."

"You would stay with one who—"

"He didn't do it."

"Who else would dare?"

The silence in the tipi was deafening. Bay drew a ragged breath before admitting, "The *puhakut*."

There was an astonished pause before Long Quiet said, "And Many Horses said nothing?"

Bay sneered at his disbelief. "Would he dare challenge one who wields the power of a medicine man? He was not so foolish! I learned later that He Decides It had told Many Horses I must be tested by the spirits, to see if I was worthy of him. I . . . I tried to fight back, but he tied me down and . . . I pleaded, but no one stopped him.

"The first night, when I was left alone, two wolves came to sit on either side of me. The wolves would not let anyone near me. It was three days before . . . before the wolves left as mysteriously as they'd come. The *puhakut* declared it was a sign from the Great Spirit. He made it tabu for anyone except Many Horses and his family to speak to me or cross my path. I was left all alone . . ."

Long Quiet pulled her trembling body into his arms, his hands soothing her agitation, knowing no words could remove the memory of her pain. "The wolves that stayed by you were the ones Creed told me about, the ones Cricket raised?"

Bay froze for a moment, then smiled. Most Comanches would have been awed by her tale, but Long Quiet had looked for and found a reasonable explanation for what had happened. Once again she was reminded that this stranger who held her was at least half white. "I helped raise those two wolves from pups. They followed me here all the way from Three Oaks. As for why they came to sit beside me and why they left—I can't explain that."

Bay found Long Quiet's embrace more comforting than she'd expected, and allowed herself to enjoy his solid strength. It was a welcome relief to lean on someone else and not to have to stand on her own. As the moments in his arms lengthened, however, totally different feelings began to course through her. A tingling sensation, a sense of fullness, rose in her breasts. His body was changing, too. The rising tension between them forced her from his embrace.

"It was a long time ago," she said. "I've never understood why the *puhakut* proclaimed the tabu or why he didn't just let me die when the wolves left. But I haven't forgotten or forgiven his cruelty."

Long Quiet took her hand in his and stepped back to the buffalo robe that would be their bed. "Lie down with me."

Bay avoided looking at Long Quiet as she settled down flat on her back, her arms at her sides. He quickly joined her, placing himself close, but not close enough for their bodies to touch. She turned her head so she could see his profile. His face was all angles and shadows—hard, harsh, and tense. He closed his eyes, and within moments she could tell from his steady breathing that he was asleep.

What did he want from her? Why hadn't he taken her body to use for his pleasure? Perhaps he planned to take his pleasure of her when he woke. Should she flee him now?

Bay lifted herself up on her elbow to examine the self-professed Comanche who slept beside her. He was an impressive man, without an ounce of wasted flesh on him. He was all knotted muscle from his thighs to his lean waist and broad shoulders to the . . .

Bay discovered the flesh she so admired was flawed. There was a swollen red gash on Long Quiet's forearm. Why hadn't he said something so she could relieve his pain? She shook her head. He was probably as stubbornly proud as Many Horses. There was nothing she could do now, but she determined that when he awoke, she would insist he allow her to make a healing balm for the wound.

With that thought Bay drifted off to sleep and soon found herself dancing in Jonas Harper's arms. As she dreamed, his square jaw became more angular and somehow Jonas's moustache disappeared to be replaced by Long Quiet's sensually bowed upper lip. Just as Bay began to suspect perhaps it wasn't Jonas who was causing such a ripple of excitement with his lips at her throat, her dream was interrupted.

She cried out in fear, throwing up her arms to protect herself as an unexplained weight came hurtling down on top of her.

Bay blinked her eyes at the sunlight filtering into the tipi and found that Long Quiet had grasped Little Deer by her arms and was holding her outstretched before him. The little girl's chin quivered and her lips were turned down in preparation for the wail that would accompany the tears hovering in her huge black eyes.

"Give her to me," Bay said. When Long Quiet hesitated, she added, "She's mine."

His eyes became distant again, his face impossible to read as he settled the little girl in her lap.

"Good morning, *Pia*," Little Deer said. "*Kaku*, Grandmother, said I must wait for you to wake, but I missed you."

Cries at Night could be heard outside the tipi. "Little Deer, are you in there?"

"She's here," Bay called out. "She can stay with me for a while."

Long Quiet studied the child with the same intensity he'd used to peruse Bay. "She doesn't take after you much."

"She looks like her father," Bay replied, knowing that was at least the truth, if not the whole truth.

Long Quiet looked at the child again. He could find nothing of Bay in the little girl and wasn't sure whether that pleased or upset him.

Cries at Night stepped inside the tipi. "I would not have disturbed you, Shadow, but now that I am here, Many Horses has asked that I help you serve his guest in whatever way I am needed."

"Will you take care of Little Deer while I prepare a meal for our guest?"

"I will do it gladly. Is there anything else?"

Bay tried to decide whether she should ask the older woman to run an errand for her, then decided it was not too much to ask. "Would you bring my *parfleche* of herbs to me?"

"Of course."

"I will keep Little Deer until you return."

Cries at Night examined Long Quiet for a moment before she cackled to Bay, "He is a lusty one, eh?"

"What?" Bay gasped.

The old woman was gone with a speed that belied her arthritic limbs.

Long Quiet laughed at the old woman's observation, but seeing Bay's flushed embarrassment, he tied on his breech-clout. His eyes caught a movement by Little Deer in Bay's lap and the grin on his face faded.

Bay followed Long Quiet's searing glance only to discover that Little Deer had reached out to play with one of her nipples. Somehow Long Quiet's easy manner had allowed her to forget about her nakedness. Now she was forcefully reminded of it.

She tried to remove the child's hand. "No, *ona*, baby."

Little Deer resisted. "Pretty."

"The child is right," Long Quiet said. "Very pretty."

Bay grabbed Little Deer's hand and brought it up to her mouth to kiss it at the same time she hugged the child to her. When she looked up, the frown had returned to Long Quiet's face.

Mercifully, Cries at Night arrived at that moment with the rawhide bag full of healing herbs. Bay kissed Little Deer's cheek and gave her another quick hug before handing her to Cries at Night.

"Go with your *kaku*. I will come play with you later."

"Do you promise?"

"I promise," Bay said with a quick kiss for the little girl.

With the child gone, Bay became conscious again of her

nakedness and hurried to pull on her simple clothing. She would never get used to the Indians' matter-of-fact attitude toward their bodies. Young boys wore nothing until the age of eight or nine, young girls only a breechclout until puberty, and she'd spent her first days in camp constantly flustered by the sight of them. That feeling was nothing compared to the way her pulse galloped at the sight of the muscles and sinews along the naked flanks of the man sitting across from her.

Once she was dressed, Bay worked quickly. She poured water into the buffalo paunch hanging on sticks to one side of the fire. She put heated stones from the fire in the paunch to boil the water and threw in some carefully selected herbs.

Long Quiet remained lying comfortably on the buffalo robe, watching her work. "What are you making? Something to eat?"

Bay laughed. "No, not unless you have a taste for cotton." She held up a piece of brightly colored cloth she knew had been stolen from some Texas settler's home before dropping it in the hot water. "I'm making a poultice for the wound on your arm."

Long Quiet's hand reached reflexively for the wound. "It isn't necessary."

"Perhaps not, but I noticed last night the cut is pink and swollen around the edges. This poultice will draw out any poisons."

His voice was husky as he asked, "You examined me while I slept?"

"I only . . ." Bay's mind raced for an excuse to cover the truth. "I thought you, like Many Horses, might have been hurt in the battle with the Tonkawas."

With the same catlike grace she'd seen before, he rose and seated himself beside her. She flinched when his hand reached up to brush a curl from her brow.

"I find I like being cared for by you."

Before he could do what his eyes told her he had in mind, she used a forked stick to draw the cloth from the water.

"Lie down on your side," she ordered firmly. "And hold your arm so I can reach your wound."

He smiled, then obeyed her.

Bay held the hot cloth out on the forked stick and levered it over to his arm, allowing it to settle on the wound. The hissing sound Long Quiet made told her how hot the cloth was.

"It has to be hot to work," she said.

"I didn't complain."

"I didn't want you to think I'd hurt you on purpose."

"But you don't like me."

She kept stubbornly silent. The fact was she did like him, but she didn't understand why. Until she did, it would be better not to admit such a thing.

Long Quiet suddenly sat up so the cloth fell from his arm. He thrust his hands in her hair where her braid had come loose overnight and held her head steady while his eyes searched her face. Before she could resist, his lips brushed hers once, twice.

If he'd tried to invade her mouth Bay would have fought him, but his touch was so soft, so tender, that she let him have his way. It was her undoing, because once he'd accustomed her to the feel of him, his tongue made a gentle foray along the edges of her lips, enticing, tempting. When she opened her mouth to object, his tongue slipped inside.

Her whole body tensed with the unfamiliar feelings that shot through her. His mouth felt good on hers. But it shouldn't. He was a stranger. She'd been given to him to use as he wished, like a slave woman to a plantation rake.

So why wasn't she resisting him?

Bay opened her eyes and saw his eyes were open, too. He kept his hold on her but edged back so they could look at one another easily. His gaze was frighteningly possessive in contrast to the gentleness of his touch.

"You aren't going to . . . you won't . . ." Her voice failed her.

"For now, until I leave, you belong to me."

Chapter 5

No!" THE PROTEST SPRANG INVOLUNTARILY FROM Bay's lips as she struggled to free herself from Long Quiet's arms. He held her gently but firmly.

"I will have you."

Long Quiet's simple words sent Bay into a frenzy, and though she knew it was futile, she arched her body away in an attempt at escape. He captured her easily and pulled her wildly writhing body back into his embrace.

"Let me go!" she cried.

"Do not dare to fight him! You belong to him!"

Bay froze at the sound of Many Horses' thundering voice. She hadn't noticed the sounds of someone entering the tipi, but perhaps Many Horses' entrance explained the tautness she'd felt in Long Quiet's body only moments before Many Horses had spoken. Bay could almost see the hackles rise on both men's necks as a frisson of barely controlled antagonism arced between them.

Because she knew him well, Bay was aware of the coiled tension in Many Horses' body. He should properly have ignored her presence, but she caught his quick glance as he looked to see how she'd fared after a night in another man's bed. Her face colored when she realized he no doubt believed Long Quiet had taken her to his blanket during the night. She was sure Cries at Night must have told him she'd been naked when Little Deer had awakened her.

Bay saw a flash of regret on the Comanche's face. Many Horses' jaw muscles tightened as though he were grinding his teeth. His guttural voice rasped in anger. "I had not thought you would shame me thus, woman. His right to you is as mine. You cannot refuse him."

Despite the words he'd spoken, Bay had the feeling Many Horses' anger was directed not at her but at Long Quiet. As she started to rise, Long Quiet's arms tightened around her.

"There is no shame to you, *haints*," Long Quiet said, "in her refusal of me. It is a tribute to the feeling she has for you."

"She must obey me!"

"No," Long Quiet countered. "She must obey me. She is mine now . . . until I leave."

Many Horses struggled to hold his tongue but lost the battle only to ask, "How long will you stay among us?"

"I have not decided."

Bay felt the rivalry blossom between the two men. Long Quiet had once again become the consummate Comanche warrior, slipping back into use of the Comanche tongue and observing Comanche customs. She shook her head in disbelief. Both men were too proud for their own good, and she refused to be fought over like some prize of war they both thought they deserved. If that meant she must submit willingly to Long Quiet, then she would. "I will—"

Long Quiet cut her off abruptly. "Be silent."

When she opened her mouth to continue, his fingertips came to her lips in a gesture that was as much a caress as a warning. Then his hand slipped down to capture her breast. She watched in awe as he calmly turned his attention to Many Horses. "Did you wish to talk to me about something?"

Many Horses was trembling visibly. His fists clenched and then unclenched before he allowed himself to speak in a voice that was barely audible. "I must speak to the families of those who did not return and to the *puhakut*. Will you join me, *haints?*"

Bay saw the effort it took for Many Horses to control his sarcasm when he called Long Quiet friend. She was amazed by the extent of his possessiveness, and especially the fact that he'd let it show. The Comanche brave prided himself on his ability to be generous with what he owned, especially what was most precious to him—his horses and his wives. It must be especially irritating for Many Horses to discover in himself this sense of ownership, so foreign to him and his kind.

Long Quiet was furious with himself. He'd known all along that Many Horses prized this woman—so why hadn't he released Bay when Many Horses entered the tipi? He backed away from his earlier provocation by sliding his hand from Bay's breast to her waist. But he couldn't help thinking he would never have offered this woman to another man—no matter how great the debt, or how great the honor to be found in such generous giving.

"I am honored that my friend has asked me to join him," Long Quiet said. "But it has been long since I have eaten, and I must see to the welfare of my pony. If you wish it so, I will join you later."

It was a dismissal, one Long Quiet was entitled to issue since he was the host in this tipi.

"Then I will see you later, *haints*." Many Horses whirled and left, his back stiff with pride.

It was quiet in the tipi when he'd gone. Bay waited for Long Quiet to speak, but he merely stared after Many Horses, his eyes blank.

At long last he murmured, "He believes I have known you as a husband knows his wife."

Bay swallowed hard but said nothing.

"Would you have me tell him otherwise?"

Bay raised carefully neutral eyes to the man who held her in his arms, but she couldn't keep the bitterness from her voice. "And let him think his generosity was refused? I do not pretend to understand this custom of sharing. Use me or do not. Say what you will. I have no choice in the matter."

Bay watched him ponder seriously before he replied, "Then I will say nothing until I leave. Then I will tell him the truth of what passed between us . . . or what did not."

"I won't refuse you again," she said.

Long Quiet fought the urge to take her then and there, and it made him angry with her and with himself, for his own lack of control. "What makes you so willing suddenly to sacrifice yourself?"

"I will not have you two fighting over me like rutting buffalo bulls!"

"You will do whatever I ask without question?" he demanded.

Bay shivered at the coldness in his eyes. "Yes," she breathed. "Anything."

Long Quiet knew the courage it took for Bay to remain steadfast when she so obviously feared his power over her. He didn't want her afraid of him. He wanted her warm and willing in his arms. He wanted to feel the upward thrust of her hips beneath him as he drove deep inside her, making them one. He tightened his hold on her as though expecting resistance and lowered his lips to hers. At first she welcomed him, her lips soft and wet. As his tongue probed her mouth she reluctantly opened to him, but even as he tasted her sweetness he could feel her body rejecting his touch.

He raised his head and saw she was flushed, but whether from desire or embarrassment, he had no way of knowing. He dropped his hands in frustration.

"Get some food for me. I'm hungry."

Bay scampered away like a scared rabbit, relieved to be saved, even momentarily, from examining her strange reactions to Long Quiet's kiss. She didn't understand the emotions she'd felt at the touch of his lips upon hers. This man was not her beloved Jonas. Or even Many Horses. He was nothing to her. She should have been afraid of him, but what she'd felt in his arms hadn't even remotely resembled fear.

There had been pleasure. Much pleasure. No man had ever made her feel like that. She'd withdrawn her body in an attempt to make the pleasure go away, but it hadn't. She'd fled the tipi in fear not of Long Quiet, but of her own traitorous emotions.

Long Quiet lay back down on the pallet and folded his arms under his head to think. He didn't like the truth he'd discovered: He was besotted with her. He'd thought his attraction for her might have waned with time. Instead, it had intensified so much that he'd nearly caused a confrontation with Many Horses over possession of the woman. He tried to think of the humor in the situation. Who would have thought Many Horses would offer him his heart's desire? Or that he would be having second thoughts about taking advantage of the offer!

Long Quiet tasted the bitter gall of defeat. He'd wondered what he would do if Bay Stewart had a Comanche family, and he'd found his answer. He could not take her from this place if she wasn't willing to go. She'd offered herself to him, but it hadn't been a willing offer, and he found himself reluctant to take what he wanted by force.

But could he leave here without tasting of the forbidden fruit that had been so temptingly set before him? Could he sleep next to her warmth another night without taking her in his arms?

It was sheer madness on his part that he hadn't taken her last night. He wanted to show her the ecstasy a man and woman could share. While it was hard for him to understand her white sensibilities, she obviously hadn't left them all behind in the few years she'd been among the Comanches. She needed time to know him, time to acknowledge the fact that their destinies lay together. But in three and a half weeks, he had to meet Creed in Laredo. He could feel the tightening in his gut at the thought that he was going to get this close to realizing his dream but no closer. He shut his eyes to think.

Would she like him better if he came to her as the white man, Walker Coburn? He rejected the idea even as it formed. He could never live among the White-eyes. He was Comanche. If she were to accept him, it must be as one of The People.

When she returned, Bay found Long Quiet lying on the pallet with his eyes closed. Thinking he was asleep again, she bent to set down the food she'd carefully arranged on a piece of bark. Before she could do so, he opened his eyes. When he saw her he sat up cross-legged, waiting patiently for his breakfast.

If Bay had had any doubt whether Long Quiet was Indian or white, it was settled as she watched him dip into the bowl of mashed boiled corn with his fingers. He alternated between corn mush and bites of the venison she'd seared over a fire outside the tipi.

"Aren't you hungry?" he asked.

"I'll eat later."

"Why not share this with me? You've brought more than enough for both of us."

"I don't think—"

"I insist."

Bay didn't think she could swallow, she was so nervous, but Long Quiet wasn't giving her any choice. She edged closer to him and dipped her fingers into the bowl of corn mush. Their fingers brushed and she fought against the reflex jerk that threatened to sling mush into both their laps.

"Do you miss the White-eyes' ways very much?"

He was speaking in Comanche again, and Bay had to concentrate to find the words with which to answer. She licked her fingers clean before she said, "Some of them, yes."

"Which ones?"

She searched for the Comanche words for *utensils for eating* and realized there was no way she was going to be able to easily carry on this conversation in another language. She answered in English, "Utensils for eating."

"We can speak in English if you wish."

Bay nodded gratefully.

He smiled and wiggled his fingers as he said, "These are simpler to take along on a journey than knives and forks."

Bay held out her own fingers, which still bore a residue of corn mush, and smiled back. "But messier."

"That's easy to remedy."

Before Bay realized what he intended, Long Quiet had taken her hand and slipped two of her fingers into his mouth. He used his tongue to clean them and then sucked gently. She felt a tingling in her belly that somehow seemed misplaced at breakfast. His tongue grudgingly released her fingers as his hand withdrew them from his mouth.

"There. Is that better?"

Bay stared at her clean, wet fingers as though they belonged to someone else, then looked up at Long Quiet to find laughter in his slate-gray eyes. She wished she understood what he expected of her. The tension of wondering when, or whether, he was going to demand his right to bed her was becoming unbearable. She forced a wan smile in return. "Much better. Thank you."

He picked up the conversation as though what he'd done was nothing out of the ordinary. "What else do you miss?"

Bay replied wistfully, "Sitting in a chair, lying in a bed, having a room to myself . . ."

"How many share your tipi?"

"There are three of us." He raised a questioning brow, and Bay continued, "I live with Little Deer and with Cries at Night, the mother of Many Horses' first wife, who died in childbirth."

"Many Horses has taken no other wife?"

"No."

"Why not?"

Bay's brow creased in thought. "How can I answer that?

It's not as though there are no young women willing to become his wife." Bay thought of She Touches First, whose eyes rarely left Many Horses when they were anywhere near one another. "He simply hasn't chosen to take another woman to his pallet."

"I would not desire another woman, either, if I had you."

Bay's head jerked up and her eyes flew to Long Quiet's. "You mustn't say such things."

"Why not, when it's the truth? I want you as I've never wanted another woman."

"Then take me and get it over with!" Bay was sorry as soon as she'd spoken the impulsive words and covered her mouth with the back of her hand.

"I can wait. If I—when I spill my seed within you, it will be because we both desire it."

His calm, certain reply sent a shiver of fearful anticipation through Bay. She was helpless to move as he reached out to caress her cheek. The hand at her mouth dropped to her chest in an attempt to slow the hammering of her heart. She was confused. She should have been afraid of him, for she knew the joining of their two bodies would not be a gentle thing, despite the fact he'd shown he could be gentle.

"I must see to my pony before I join Many Horses," Long Quiet said. Without another word, he was gone.

Bay stood up unsteadily. When she turned to leave the tipi, she ran directly into Cries at Night.

"I am sorry, *Pia*," Bay rasped. "I was not watching where I was going."

"Help me sit," Cries at Night said. "These old bones need a rest already." As she collapsed on the nearby buffalo robe, she said, "Tell me about this man with whom Many Horses has shared his most prized possession. Who is he?"

"His name is Long Quiet. He rescued Many Horses from the Tonkawas, and in return Many Horses has asked that I serve him until he leaves us," Bay explained.

Cries at Night pursed an already much-wrinkled mouth. "I do not understand this."

"What troubles you, *Pia?*"

"I cannot believe Many Horses will allow Long Quiet to depart this village with the knowledge of your presence."

"Why not? Long Quiet saved his life. They are brothers."

"Did Many Horses seek out the medicine of the *puhakut* before he gave you to Long Quiet?"

"I . . . I don't think so. I don't know."

Cries at Night drew in a hissing breath and muttered, "It is bad. It is very bad."

"What is wrong?"

"How could Many Horses ignore the tabu and give you to another man? He has put the source of his *puha* in another man's hands. Pah! There is no help for it now. We will have to wait and see what the *puhakut* will have to say about all this."

At that same moment, She Touches First was anxious to find out the same thing. She came flying into the *puhakut's* tipi without waiting for permission to enter, because the news she brought her brother was so exciting she was willing to face his wrath if he chose to chastise her recklessness.

"He gave her away to a stranger!"

He Decides It had dropped a whole handful of pecans when She Touches First had come bursting in. He looked up irritably and asked, "Who gave who away?" before beginning a search through the matted buffalo wool beneath him for his scattered breakfast.

"Many Horses is back and has given Shadow away."

Those words stopped his hand where it was and brought his head up to meet his sister's eyes, which glowed with undisguised satisfaction.

"Are you sure?"

"As certain as the gossip of the women can make me. I tell

you Shadow spent the night in Many Horses' guest tipi with another man."

"Many Horses must be crazy! It is tabu for Shadow to be with—"

"—with anyone from the village. But, brother, all-wise *puhakut*, your tabu did not say anything about another man."

"I did not think it necessary. Shadow is the source of Many Horses' *puha*. He would never allow another man near her. I cannot think what would make him do such a thing."

At that moment, He Decides It heard keening wails of lament from the direction of Eagle Feather's tipi. "So. They did not all come home."

"Only Many Horses. Both who traveled with him were killed by Tonkawas."

A second set of shrieks joined the cries from the other tipi as Many Horses gave his sad news to the family of He Follows the Trail.

"Many Horses will come here next," She Touches First said. "What will you tell him of his decision to give away the woman? Will it bode ill for him or well?"

"I cannot say. I will have to hear the reasons for what he has done. Then I can make medicine to see whether the spirits approve."

He Decides It blamed the continued irritation in his voice on his inability to locate the pecans he'd dropped. But it was moments like this that brought home to him how staggering a responsibility it was to be medicine man for the village and to have the power of life and death over those who came to him for advice. Now he must interpret the results of Many Horses' impulsive gesture in sending Shadow to stay with a stranger.

Perhaps this was the excuse he needed to send the white woman away. He knew that would please his sister. She believed that the only thing keeping Many Horses from making her his *paraibo*, his chief wife, was Shadow's presence in the village. She was wrong, but he could not confess to his sister the falsehoods he'd told that had led Many Horses to reject her.

What should he do?

He Decides It grunted in disgust and dug deeper in the buffalo robe. He could think better on a full stomach.

She Touches First knelt down to help her brother gather up the sweet nuts he'd dropped. "Do you think Many Horses will let Shadow leave the village?"

"How can I say what he will do?"

"You can tell him what he should do!"

"I cannot lead him where he will not go."

"You gave that woman the power she holds over the greatest warrior in this village. You can take it away."

"How can I do that?"

"Tell Many Horses he has broken his tabu by giving Shadow to another man and that he must give back her medicine and send her from this place as quickly as he can."

"I must think about what I will say to Many Horses," he said. "Leave me now."

She Touches First dropped a handful of pecans into her brother's hand as she rose. "This is the best chance you will ever have to rid our village of that woman. If you do not do it now, the day will come when you will regret it."

With that warning, she left.

He Decides It threw the whole handful of nuts into his mouth, ignoring the bits of sand and buffalo wool that had been added, and chewed on the gritty mess while he pondered the situation. As *puhakut*, he knew much about the individual weaknesses of those who lived in his village. They came to him when they needed powerful medicine to allay their fears of the Great Spirit, of Father Sun, Mother Moon, and the Earth Mother. They expected him to know how to combat the evils of disease and famine. They sought from him an explanation of the births and deaths, the good hunts and bad, the successes or failures in war, that made their lives a frightening yet wonderful mystery.

He knew Many Horses believed his extraordinary success in battle and in the hunt over the past three years was due to his possession of Shadow and to his observance of the personal tabu He Decides It had imposed on Many Horses, which would not allow the war chief of the *Quohadi* to take from his captive that which he had wanted most. Only He Decides It knew exactly how high the price had been for Many Horses' powerful medicine.

Well, the *puhakut* mused as he ran his tongue around his teeth to collect the last residue of pecans, he hadn't exactly said it would be tabu for any other man to touch Shadow as a woman. But Many Horses must surely be wondering whether his *puha* had been weakened now that he'd given her to another man. It was up to him to settle the matter.

"*Hu!* May I come in?"

He Decides It made sure he was seated imposingly across from the tipi opening before he signaled to Many Horses, "*Hihites!* You are welcome here."

The haggard look on Many Horses' face confirmed that he wasn't sure what disaster he might have caused by his actions. He Decides It gestured Many Horses to a seat of honor at his right side. The *puhakut* sat silently, waiting for Many Horses to speak of the matter that had brought him here. He would not be forced by impatience into revealing what he knew.

He heard an uncharacteristic sigh before the war chief of the *Quohadi* finally said, "I am getting old."

The prospect of living to useless old age was horrifying for any Comanche to contemplate, let alone admit out loud, and it appalled He Decides It to hear such a thing from the mouth of a man in the prime of his life. He waited again for Many Horses to speak, exercising the patience for which he was well known.

"I must be getting old to have done such a foolish thing," Many Horses continued at last.

If he expected that comment to goad He Decides It into speaking, he was mistaken.

Many Horses smiled wryly before he spoke into the silence. "You were ever able to wait out the most cautious prey. I see I must speak plainly or be left to listen to my own voice. I have given Shadow to another man, to serve him for the time he stays here in the village."

He Decides It caught his grimace before it could curl his lips. This news complicated matters. How could he tell Many Horses he couldn't have back a woman he had merely *loaned?*

"Who is this man you have so honored?"

"He is called Long Quiet."

"Why have you chosen to share Shadow's medicine with this man?" the *puhakut* asked.

"He saved me from the Tonkawa dogs. He gave my life back when it was forfeit—not once, but twice."

"Would not a herd of ponies have been a better reward?"

"Pah! He would not take them. Nor anything else I offered."

"He asked, then, for the woman?"

Many Horses hesitated before he replied, "No."

He Decides It frowned and shook his head. "Then I do not understand why you have acted as you have."

"I saw he desired her. I did not want such a great debt to remain unpaid, so I offered her. He did not refuse."

He Decides It grunted. Perhaps the savior of Many Horses had solved his problem for him as well. "For how many suns will Long Quiet stay among us?"

Many Horses flushed. "He has not said."

He Decides It rubbed at the wrinkles on the bridge of his nose. Perhaps now was the time to tell Many Horses that Shadow's medicine could no longer help him because she'd been possessed by another man. Perhaps now he should suggest that when Long Quiet left, it would be best if he took

Shadow along. But first, he must see what Many Horses believed to be the consequences of what he had done.

"Did you consider how giving the woman to another man will affect your *puha*?"

"I thought about it."

"And you did not think you should speak with the *puhakut* on this matter before you acted?"

Many Horses turned a stony countenance on the medicine man. "There was a debt to be paid. I paid it."

He Decides It felt the flush rising on his cheeks even as the choking fury of rage strangled his voice. Did the war chief of the *Quohadi* consider himself above needing the *puhakut*'s counsel? His rage increased when he considered the fact that Many Horses had not only flouted the *puhakut*'s power by not consulting him but had admitted his disdain of that power to the *puhakut*'s face. If He Decides It ignored this affront, it would be tantamount to admitting his medicine was not as strong as that of Many Horses.

Many Horses realized his mistake too late. He watched the *puhakut*'s darkening expression with a sinking heart.

"You would have been wise to think before you stepped upon another's feet," He Decides It said. "I will have to make medicine to see the results of your deed. For now, it would be wise if you walk carefully. There is no foretelling what effect the woman will have upon your *puha* now that she is in the possession of another man."

As a warrior, Many Horses couldn't help appreciating the awfulness of the purgatory in which the *puhakut* had left him. It was a fitting revenge for the insult he had unwittingly offered. As a Comanche brave whose whole life had been directed by powerful spirits that spoke only through the medicine man, Many Horses feared the consequences of the *puhakut*'s anger. As the proud war chief of the *Quohadi* and a once-close friend of He Decides It, he resented the *puhakut*'s veiled threats.

Many Horses' stomach churned, and he huffed out a

breath of air in the hope of relieving his discomfort. Had he been less frustrated by the events that had put him in Long Quiet's debt, and the subsequent sense of possessiveness that had taken him unawares, he would not have acted so impulsively. Now he would be forced to pay the price of his foolishness. He only hoped it would be a price the Great Spirit deemed he could pay with less than his life.

"We are to seek out the buffalo in a few days," Many Horses said. "Will it be safe for me to follow the hunt?"

"I cannot say until I have made medicine. Then we will see."

The two men stared at one another for a moment, each one measuring the other. Many Horses rose and headed for the tipi opening. Before he could stoop to leave, He Decides It spoke once more, in a voice more commanding for its quietness. "The woman may be lost to you."

Many Horses jerked upright as though he'd been stabbed in the back. He whirled to face the *puhakut*. "Seek your medicine with an open heart, *puhakut*. The woman means much to me. I will have her even at the cost of my life."

He Decides It controlled the shudder that threatened to shake him. He hadn't become as powerful as he was by showing fear when confronted with death. "I will do as you ask. But you must know," he said with a cunning smile, "I can only speak as the spirits direct me."

Many Horses snarled a "Pah!" before he made a quick escape from the tipi. He moved so fast he was almost running. He didn't realize where he was headed until he came to the tipi that housed Long Quiet and Shadow. He realized he'd left the *puhakut*'s tipi without waiting for Long Quiet to join him. He stood helplessly staring at the flap entrance. It was silent inside, which made him wonder what they were doing with their mouths that didn't leave them free to speak.

His unaccustomed jealousy ate at him like fire on dry moss. Unable to stop himself, he leaned over to lift up the flap. He peered inside, only to discover the dwelling was empty. His face burned with shame as he acknowledged the depths to which his possessiveness had sent him. He dropped the flap and looked around, gratefully finding the area deserted. He'd been spared the humiliation of making a fool of himself over a mere woman—a woman who wasn't even his wife.

He'd always prided himself on his generosity, had always been more than willing to share what he'd stolen on raids or brought back from the hunt. It was well known among the villagers that one had only to ask for something belonging to Many Horses to receive what had been sought. Many Horses hadn't realized how thoroughly *his* the woman had become in his mind. He turned on his heel and headed for his herd of horses. He would wait there for Long Quiet to join him. And seek within his heart a solution to the confusing feelings that assailed him.

Chapter 6

When Bay finished putting away the breakfast things, she went searching for Little Deer to fulfill her promise to play with the child. That was one of the things she liked best about the Comanches—they enjoyed playing when the work was done. When she stepped inside the tipi, where Cries at Night was sewing a knee-high fur-lined winter moccasin, the child was nowhere to be seen.

"Where is Little Deer?" Bay asked.

"She Touches First came to get her."

"Where did they go?"

"She took her to the shady spot by the creek where the other children are playing. If you are going there, will you bring back some water for me?"

"Of course, *Pia*." Bay picked up the water kettle and hurried off to find Little Deer, upset her place had been usurped, but knowing this was also the way of the Comanche. Children were to be enjoyed by everyone. It seemed to her, however, that She Touches First had taken an extraordinary interest in Little Deer from the first. *Not so odd*, Bay thought, *when you consider Little Deer is Many Horses' child.*

Bay couldn't have said why she was so upset to find Little Deer with She Touches First, except that it forced her to acknowledge that if she left the village with Long Quiet, Little Deer would scarcely want for love. She Touches First spent nearly as much time with Little Deer as Bay did. And of course Cries at Night and Many Horses loved the child. It was disconcerting to admit that she might need Little Deer more than Little Deer needed her.

Little Deer was laughing gaily, rolling a wooden ball to She Touches First.

Bay set down the kettle and called, "*Hu!* Little Deer."

"*Pia!*" The little girl came running and launched herself into Bay's open arms. Bay gave her a quick hug and set her down again. "Have you been a good girl this morning?"

"Yes, *Pia.*"

"Are you ready to play a game with me now?"

Little Deer turned and looked at She Touches First, who sat silently in the background. "I'm playing with She Touches First now."

It hurt to know Little Deer was just as happy with the other woman. But Bay was not so narrow-hearted as to deny the child the love of another. "If you want to play later, come and find me," she said, affectionately ruffling Little Deer's hair.

As Little Deer ran back to She Touches First, Bay retrieved the kettle. She walked the rest of the way to the creek lost in thought. When she got there, Bay dipped the heavy black kettle into the creek, filling it to the brim with water for Cries at Night. As her arm muscles tensed to bear the immense weight, the kettle was taken effortlessly from her hands.

Bay turned to find Long Quiet standing beside her. "I could have done that by myself."

"I never doubted it," Long Quiet replied with a smile. "But I wished to help."

It was the gesture of a white man. No Comanche male carried water for cooking. Bay searched Long Quiet's face for some explanation for his action, but she didn't find it.

"I thought you were to meet Many Horses in the *puhakut*'s tipi."

"I went there, but he'd already left." He avoided looking at her, gazing instead at their surroundings. The creek was at the bottom of a gully, so they were hidden from prying eyes. It would have been a good place to woo her, he thought. It was a vale for lovers, and she'd never looked lovelier, with the early-morning sun blushing her skin a rosy peach and turning her hair to molten fire.

"Did you want something?" she asked.

He wanted to know everything about her, to touch her, to make her his woman, to make her his wife. His heart ached with the futility of his wants. He said simply, "Will you walk with me?"

"I promised Cries at Night I'd fetch this water for her."

He set the kettle down on a flat stone. "We won't be long." He started to walk along the creek, not waiting to see if she followed.

But she did.

They walked for what seemed a long time to Bay, but still Long Quiet didn't speak. His brow had furrowed and his gaze was turned inward. At last, unable to bear the silence any longer, she said, "Has your pony recovered from the journey here?"

At her question, Long Quiet stopped and turned around, seeming almost surprised to find her there. "He's a fine animal. A little rest and some good grass, and he'll be ready to go again." He smiled before he added, "I didn't wish to walk with you to talk about my horse. I wished to speak with you about . . . about your life here. That is, if it wouldn't be too painful for you to speak of it."

Bay had shut out the memories of her first days and weeks as a captive, but at last she admitted, "I was lonely." When she felt Long Quiet's callused thumb on her cheek, she looked up into his gray eyes. She found the sympathy there disquieting. She took a step back from him. Her chin jutted as she added, "But I survived."

"You were beaten—"

"Why ask what you already know? You've felt the scars for yourself."

"—and you were raped."

It was then Bay realized she'd interrupted him before he'd finished speaking. How could she tell him of the fears she'd harbored when she was first captured? She'd been so certain rape would be her fate! How could she tell him that while she'd escaped that degradation herself, she'd witnessed the rape of other captives, that she'd seen them hurt and humiliated and been helpless to lift a hand to prevent it. Her heart had long borne the weight of guilt that she'd been spared what others had suffered.

Long Quiet watched Bay's eyes fill with tears. Her next words confirmed his fear that she'd been misused.

"I . . . I was . . . I've seen . . . I was afraid . . ."

Long Quiet saw her pain and knew that whatever had happened to her, he didn't want to hear it. "There's no need to speak of it." He reached out to touch her hair, but she flinched. He warned himself to be patient. He dropped his hand and continued to walk along the creek. "Tell me about your life before you came to live among The People. Were you happy?"

"Yes. At least as happy as I could be under the circumstances."

"What do you mean?"

"You'd have to know my father to understand. I could never seem to meet the expectations Rip had for me."

"What expectations could a father have that wouldn't be met by a daughter as beautiful as you?"

Bay's lips curled wryly at the compliment and she slanted a chagrined glance at Long Quiet. "I could have been a son." At Long Quiet's quizzical stare, Bay explained with a snort of laughter, "My father wanted sons. My mother bore him daughters."

"Ah." That was something a Comanche could well understand. Daughters had their uses, but sons were much revered and desired.

"I don't think you understand as much as you think you do," Bay said, the smile never leaving her face. "You see, my father raised us—his three daughters—to take over the roles he'd planned for his sons. My sister Sloan, who's a year older than I, is everything a man could wish for in a firstborn male—strong, brave, intelligent. My sister Cricket, who's a year younger than I, is my father's favorite—impetuous, headstrong, bold. And I . . ."

"And you?"

Bay shrugged. "I was my father's greatest disappointment. I couldn't ride well or shoot straight or stand the sight of blood. I'm afraid I had too weak a stomach for killing even to put food on the table. I couldn't—"

"Enough." Long Quiet hated the desolate look in Bay's eyes as she berated herself. "He's a foolish man if he expects such things of a woman. But didn't you tell me you cured a buffalo hide yourself? How could you do that if you can't bear the sight of blood?"

"I had no choice except to get over such delicate feelings," she admitted.

"And could you kill now?"

Bay's eyes clouded, becoming a deep dark purple. "I can do anything I have to do to survive."

"So your father was hasty in his judgment of you."

Bay raised her eyes to meet Long Quiet's. He was right. Her father wouldn't recognize her today as the same disappointing daughter he'd known.

This time, when Long Quiet's hand came up to brush a wispy tendril from Bay's temple, she didn't flinch away.

"I would speak now about us," he said.

"There is no *us*," she replied hesitantly. "I belong—"

"—to me."

Bay froze, bound by the touch of Long Quiet's knuckles feathering across her cheek. Slowly, giving her time to object, he reached his arms around her and drew her close. She didn't struggle. How could she struggle when he used no force? Nor did she defy him with her eyes or her voice. But she did nothing to encourage him, either. She simply submitted.

He was wary of her surrender, afraid to believe that she'd accepted him. "Are you willing? Is that why you do not fight me?"

"What purpose would fighting serve? You're stronger. You would win."

There was truth in her words, but Long Quiet felt compelled to chide, "There are ways a woman can make a man weak. Have you never learned to bow a man to your will?"

Confused, her eyes sought his. "What?"

"Like this."

She was unprepared for his gentle assault on her mouth or for the hands that roamed her body in supplication. His tongue sought the taste of her, his hands lightly skimmed the peaks and valleys beneath her deerskin poncho and were gone before she could mouth the words to protest.

In moments, his breathing was ragged and she could feel his heart pounding beneath the hand she had pressed against his solid chest. He tore his mouth away and leaned his forehead against hers, his eyes closed, his jaw taut.

She gulped a breath of air, trying to calm the pulse that leaped at her throat. The kiss had been a surprise. As was the barest touch of his hand upon her skin. She began to see what he'd meant. It was a heady thing to know she'd so completely conquered his senses.

She had relaxed, thinking he'd proved his point, when Long Quiet's hands grasped her waist, then dropped slowly to her buttocks as he lifted her up and into his body. She felt the hard evidence of his arousal, and froze. When she thought she would die with the waiting, he spoke.

"Can you feel me trembling? My blood races. My breath is stolen. And you say woman is weak? How can it be so when I'm robbed of my strength by your mere touch?"

No more so than I, Bay admitted to herself. She feared what she was feeling, because she didn't understand it. What was happening to her? She loved Jonas Harper. How could anything this white Comanche said to her affect her so strongly? Why was she feeling desire when she knew where that would lead?

Long Quiet tipped her chin up so he could see into her eyes. "You're trembling. Are you afraid of me?"

She shook her head but remained stubbornly silent.

"Then what troubles you, Shadow?"

"I know what men do with women who belong to them . . . as you say I belong to you. I know of the bruises, the bleeding—"

He tucked her head beneath his chin, seeking to comfort, to protect, to reassure. "I wouldn't hurt you."

"Why not? Am I not as other captives?"

He held her away from him so he could look into her eyes. He saw the fear and confusion there and said gruffly, "No. This is different."

"How? You've said yourself that I belong to you. What will stop you from using me as other white women are used by brave Comanche warriors like you?"

"I would not take you as an animal, without thought of your feelings," he argued, upset by the sarcasm in her voice.

"You're Comanche!" she spat.

"I'm . . ."

He would not deny what he was. But that didn't necessarily make him inhuman or cruel. A Comanche was no more cruel than the circumstances required, even though Long Quiet would have agreed that a lifetime of war demanded a heart hardened against the pain of others.

"Have I been unkind to you?" he challenged.

"No. But I'm still afraid."

"Of me?"

When she didn't answer, he dropped his hands abruptly and turned away. He could not undo the awful things he well knew must have been done to her. He knew he should leave her now, proving his good intentions, but desire clouded his thinking. He turned back to her.

"Come here," he entreated, his voice soft, as though he were beckoning to something untamed.

Bay came to him, but the moment his arms circled her she stiffened.

He stifled the muttered curse that sprang to his lips and said, as much to convince himself as her, "I can wait to have you until you've learned to trust me." He set her away from him and said, "I must go now and find Many Horses."

He walked away and left her standing there. He hadn't offered to carry the heavy kettle of water back to the tipi of Cries at Night. She snorted. Of course not. He was a Comanche. And that was a Comanche woman's work.

A cloud covered the sun, and Bay shivered as a breath of wind hit the perspiration on her body, cooling her. Joining her body to that of Long Quiet appeared to be inevitable. But how soon would it happen? Tonight? Tomorrow?

Over the past years, as hope of rescue faded, Bay had learned not to consider the future. She ignored what she was powerless to change. She turned and headed for the heavy kettle. She would live today and not worry about tonight . . . or tomorrow.

Long Quiet found Many Horses standing at the entrance to a brush enclosure that served as a corral. Within it roamed the most magnificent chestnut stallion Long Quiet had ever seen. Long Quiet edged up beside Many Horses and watched for a moment with the other man as the foam-flecked stallion lunged from one end of the brush enclosure to the other, seeking a way of escape.

"*Hihites*, Many Horses. Perhaps I should have looked at your herd before I rejected your offer," he said with a rueful smile. "What a magnificent animal!"

"Yes, but unfortunately he cannot be tamed."

"You cannot ride him?"

"I have tried everything I know, but he will not let me stay upon his back."

"Would you mind if I try?"

Many Horses arched a skeptical brow. "Of course not. But do you think you can ride a horse I cannot ride?"

"We will never know until I try, will we?" Long Quiet replied.

There it was again, the hint of challenge, of antagonism, that seemed always to be there between them. Both men sensed it, both regretted it, but neither was sure what, if anything, could be done to temper it. What Many Horses said next only heightened it.

"If you can ride him, he is yours."

Long Quiet watched the powerful animal fighting the constraints of the trap in which he found himself and couldn't help smiling. He felt a certain affinity for the stallion. In love with a woman he couldn't make his own, was he not also caught in a trap from which there seemed no escape?

"So be it," Long Quiet said.

Many Horses turned to look at his blood brother. "Will you try to ride him now?"

"No. I will deal with the stallion in my own time. There are other matters of which I must speak with you. I looked for you in the tipi of the *puhakut*, but he said you had left already."

"I was no longer welcome there. I offended the *puhakut* by giving Shadow into your keeping without first having him make medicine to determine whether it should be done."

"Is there anything a brother can do to help mend the harm?" Long Quiet asked.

Many Horses smiled. "I should have known you would offer. No. The *puhakut* and I have a rivalry of long standing between us. I did not even know it existed until I asked the *puhakut*'s sister to be my wife."

Long Quiet looked quickly at Many Horses. "Shadow told me you have no wife."

The bitter smile on Many Horses' face spoke for itself, but he added, "No woman has agreed to be my wife."

Long Quiet's astonishment kept him silent for a moment. "You are war chief of the *Quohadi*. What woman would not be proud to call you husband?"

"The *puhakut*'s sister," Many Horses said flatly.

"You desire her still?"

Many Horses nodded curtly.

"Has she taken another warrior as her husband?"

"Not yet."

"Then what keeps you from making her your wife?"

"Once She Touches First and I were lovers. We swore that we would spend our lives together. Then the day came when she refused to meet me along the banks of the creek anymore."

"Why?"

Many Horses was absorbed for a moment by the bit of wolf fur hanging from one of his thick braids, the symbol of Shadow's medicine. "Because I had brought Shadow to this village."

"Why should that make a difference to the woman who will be your wife?"

Many Horses' voice evidenced his confusion. "I do not understand it myself," he admitted. "But after I brought Shadow to the village, She Touches First would not speak with me. And when I brought ponies to her tipi, she would not accept them. I would have made her *paraibo*, but she refused me."

"Why have you not made Shadow your wife?"

"I cannot give Shadow the place my heart holds open for another," Many Horses replied.

"Have you thought of stealing She Touches First?"

"The *puhakut*'s sister? I am war chief of the *Quohadi*. I

need the *puhakut's* medicine to see me safely into battle. I would not dare to offend him."

"But now you *have* offended him by giving Shadow to me." Long Quiet took a deep breath before he said, "Shall I return her to you?"

"It would make no difference now. The damage is done. The *puhakut* has said he will make medicine and tell me what I must do. But I have been thinking. In anger, I told He Decides It that I would keep Shadow even at the cost of my life.

"Perhaps I am tempting the spirits to make such a boast," he admitted, his brow furrowing. "Perhaps the time has come that I should return the medicine Shadow brought to me. It can be easily done. I need only thank Shadow for the use of her medicine and then take this bit of wolf fur to the creek and let it be carried away. Then I will be free of both Shadow's medicine and the tabu."

Long Quiet asked what was uppermost in his mind. "If you give up Shadow's medicine, what will you do with her?"

Many Horses frowned. "I have not yet decided that. Perhaps I will trade her back to the White-eyes. She will bring a great price." He turned to Long Quiet. "Or perhaps you would like to keep her."

Long Quiet hardly believed what he was hearing. He forced himself to ask, "What about Little Deer?"

"The child is close to Shadow. But there are others who could care for her."

"What of Shadow's love for the child? She does not want to be separated from Little Deer," Long Quiet said.

"That may be so, but after all, she is only a woman. She will do as she is told."

Long Quiet wasn't sure what he was feeling at that moment. *Excitement.* There was the chance Bay would be his after all. *Sorrow.* When she became his, she would lose her child. *Anticipation.* He would fill her life with love and give

her other children so she would have no time for despair over
the one she'd lost.

"It is time to search for the buffalo. When we find them,
we can plan the hunt. Will you come with me, *haints?*"

Many Horses' words drew Long Quiet from his reverie.
"Yes, I will come," he said.

Long Quiet spent the rest of the day with Many Horses,
combing the surrounding territory for signs of buffalo. They
would need to find the herd before they could commence the
fall hunt. His eyes were on the ground, but what he saw were
visions of himself entwined with Shadow. He tried to imagine how she would accept the idea of living with him in his
Penateka Comanche village. Then he wondered how those in
his village would accept her. He tried not to think about how
his grandfather, who hated all White-eyes, would react, concentrating instead on a picture of Shadow round with child.
Then he pictured her with a papoose on her back and her
belly swollen with a second child.

He fought the smile he felt forming on his face. It would
not be wise to test the spirits by accepting this gift of happiness before it had been offered. He must be patient. He must
wait for events to unfold in their own natural time. He could
not rush headlong into the future. It would come to him when
the Great Spirit willed it so. His teeth clenched over a groan.
He prayed for Many Horses to make his decision soon. He
had only a few weeks before he was to meet Creed in Laredo.

Long Quiet contemplated sending a message to Creed that
he'd found Bay Stewart and couldn't come. But he thought of
Cricket, heavy with child, and knew he could not do it.

He would have to trust in the Great Spirit to make all
things come aright. He fixed his gaze once again on the
prairie around him and forced himself to see grass.

Chapter 7

IT WAS NEARLY SUNSET BEFORE LONG QUIET SAW BAY again. He found her sitting on a grassy knoll that overlooked the plain where Many Horses' large herd of ponies grazed. She held Little Deer snuggled deep in her lap and was talking and laughing with the child. A speckled buff and black hound lolled beside Bay, its nose resting on her knee. A breeze that smelled of horses ruffled Little Deer's cropped hair, and as Long Quiet watched, Bay tenderly brushed an errant raven strand away from the girl's eyes.

Bay's hands were constantly moving on the child, but Long Quiet felt sure she was unaware of how often she touched. A quick grasp of little fingers, the rub along a slender shoulder, a knuckle across a petal-smooth cheek . . . his loins tightened at the thought of having her touch him so freely.

She hadn't noticed him, so he stood silently, letting the mellow sound of her voice flow over him, caressing him where her hands did not.

Slowly, her words began to make sense to him. She was telling the story of how his friend Jarrett Creed had met Bay's sister, Cricket. He'd heard Creed's side of the tale. Now he cocked an ear, eager to hear what she said.

". . . he was a big man, but that did not scare Cricket. She liked to wrestle and she was sure she would win."

Little Deer giggled. "Oh, *Pia*, a woman cannot wrestle with a man."

Bay smiled, a curve of full lips, a flash of white teeth, and Long Quiet felt his body's avid response.

"Cricket could," she answered the little girl. "And she did. But this man was different from any Cricket had ever met, and not so easily beaten. When I came upon them at the pond, Cricket was lying atop Creed, bound to him by his strong arms. His hand covered her mouth to keep her from calling to her wolves, which were feasting nearby on a fallen stag."

The little girl's eyes widened. "Wolves?"

"Yes, wolves." Bay kissed the tip of Little Deer's nose. "They were Cricket's pets, and very friendly."

"Then what happened?"

"I waited and waited, hoping Cricket would win the wrestling contest. But they remained locked in one another's arms. So I took my bow and arrow—"

"Oh, *Pia!*" Little Deer interrupted, giggling. "You had a bow and arrow?"

"Can you not see me with a bow and arrow?"

Little Deer crowed with delight at the thought.

"I suppose it is funny to imagine it now," Bay said wryly, "but at the time I was not laughing. I approached them with an arrow nocked in my bow and demanded that the stranger take his hands off my sister."

"What did he say?"

"He warned me that if I shot at him, I might hit Cricket." Bay laughed ruefully. "Of course he could have no way of knowing he was right. I could not often hit the mark with my bow and arrow. But I knew that if I did not help Cricket, she might be hurt. So I stood my ground, and at last he released her. Then we marched him home to Three Oaks, to answer for the stolen horses he had in his possession."

"You were very brave, *Pia*."

"No, only very scared," Bay replied.

Long Quiet resisted the urge to correct Bay. Why did she

make so little of what she'd done? He knew from Creed's account of the incident that if it hadn't been for Bay's interference, Creed would never have been taken prisoner. His friend had described Bay as frightened but determined to force Creed's surrender. He was distracted from his thoughts by Little Deer's next question.

"Can I have a pet wolf?"

"What would poor old Stewpot think if you replaced him with a sleek gray wolf?"

At the sound of his name, the hound lifted his head from Bay's knee and thrust his wet nose into Little Deer's lap, begging to be petted. Both of them willingly complied, and two hands, one slender, one small, stroked the speckled fur until the hound's eyes drooped closed and he groaned in ecstasy.

Long Quiet grinned. He'd be groaning too, he thought, if he were the object of all that loving attention from two doting females.

"Hihites."

Two surprised faces turned to greet Long Quiet.

"Oh, I didn't know you were there," Bay said, feeling flustered. She had to fight to keep her gaze from straying from his face to his muscular chest and flat belly. Self-conscious beneath his warm gaze, she wondered whether she'd said anything in the past few moments she shouldn't have.

"You'll have to show me sometime how you handle a bow and arrow," Long Quiet said, flashing her a devilish grin.

Bay flushed. "It would be a waste of your time. I'm not—"

"—very good," he finished for her. "The important thing is that you were willing to try."

"The important thing," Bay contradicted, "is how good you become at what you try. My father always said good intentions don't put food on the table. Nor will they protect you from your enemies. My sisters and I understood that and accepted it. If you think about it, no Comanche would argue with it, either. I don't blame my father for demanding that I be skilled with weapons. I blame myself for not being able to fulfill his expectations."

"But you can't expect to equal a man's skill."

"My sisters did," she retorted. Bay lifted Little Deer out of her lap. She'd been sitting for a long time, and she unbent stiffly as she rose and took Little Deer's hand. "I must go prepare our meal now."

She headed for the village without looking back at Long Quiet. When Little Deer turned back and gave him a friendly wave good-bye, Bay gave the child a rather ungentle tug to get her started again.

He debated for a moment whether to call Bay back, but he feared they would only argue more if he did, and that was the last thing he wanted to do. He'd only meant to tease her, but it was obviously a sore subject for her, one that wouldn't bear pressing. What other unusual demands had her father made upon her, he wondered. And what other scars did she bear as a result?

He'd known a few men, most of them White-eyes, who used a brutal hand with their mounts, hardening the beasts' mouths so it took more and more pain to control them—and very little provocation for the beast to revolt. He wondered how thick a skin Bay had grown in order to avoid the pain of Rip Stewart's heavy handling. In his experience, it was rarely that a badly treated mount could ever learn to trust again. He wanted Bay to trust him. It was the first step toward the feelings he hoped she'd someday have for him.

He prayed it wasn't too late to undo the damage Rip had done.

When he arrived at the tipi that evening, Long Quiet saw that Bay had moved Little Deer's things in with them. He could tell she expected him to object to the sleeping arrangements, but he avoided the subject. Bedtime would be soon enough for the argument he feared was inevitable.

Bay wished she had more courage. She knew Long Quiet had seen the pallet laid out for Little Deer next to her own, yet he'd said nothing. He'd merely complimented her on the delicious meal she'd prepared and told her about his day. They could have been a Texas family sitting down to supper after a hard day working cotton. It felt so normal, and so nice. It made her wish things could always be this pleasant.

Bay had just gathered up the wooden bowls they'd used so she could take them down to the stream and rinse them out when Long Quiet reached over to wipe a bit of stew off the edge of Little Deer's mouth.

"I want to see all of your pretty face," he said with a smile.

Little Deer smiled back shyly and reached out to touch Long Quiet's chin. Bay held her breath, waiting to see what he'd do.

Long Quiet sat unmoving as Little Deer's tiny hand roamed the sharp angles of his cheeks and chin. At last her fingers twined around one of the black curls at his temple. She stretched it out straight, but when she let go it curled back up again. She laughed. "Do that to my hair."

Long Quiet twined a bit of her chin-length hair around his finger, then let it go and made a face of exaggerated disappointment when it immediately straightened again. "It does not stay curled like mine does."

"Do not be sad," Little Deer said, shaping Long Quiet's mouth back into a smile with her hands. "I still like you even though your hair is not straight like mine."

Bay's heart skipped a beat when Long Quiet reached up to cover Little Deer's hands with his own. He looked deeply into the girl's eyes and replied, "That shows a generous spirit. That is a very good thing for a Comanche woman to possess."

Bay wondered how he'd known the right thing to say to Little Deer, who puffed up with pride at being referred to as a woman. Bay knew she must look silly sitting there with three dirty bowls in her lap listening to the two of them talk, but she couldn't bear the thought of missing the dialogue between the man to whom she belonged and the child she felt belonged to her.

Little Deer angled her head sideways so she could look up at Long Quiet's face. He smiled down at her and said, "I was only a little older than you when I first came to live among The People. My *tawp*, my grandfather, used to tell me a story each night before I went to sleep. Would you like to hear my favorite one?"

"Oh, yes!"

Long Quiet settled the child more comfortably in his arms and began, "Once a Comanche was traveling across the desert and found a black colt that was all alone. The Comanche asked where the colt's mother and father had gone, but the colt answered that he did not know. The colt was very thirsty and the Comanche brave had water. The brave offered the colt some water, but the colt was stubborn and very independent and decided he would keep trying to find some water on his own.

"Two days passed while the colt got thirstier and thirstier, weaker and weaker. The brave offered the water again, and this time the colt said maybe he would take just a sip. While he sipped the water, the brave stroked the colt's nose and scratched that itchy spot behind its ears. The colt thought that felt very good, so when the brave asked if the colt would like to come home with him, the colt agreed.

"When they got to the Comanche's village, the brave told the colt to go and play with all the other ponies that lived there. That sounded like it would be fun, so the colt raced over to join them. But when he arrived, several of the ponies turned and lashed out at him with their heels. He shied away from them, only to be bitten on the neck and the rump by two other ponies. The colt raced back the way he had come and stood at the edge of the herd watching the ponies play with one another.

"The colt ran to ask the Comanche brave why the other ponies did not like him. The brave asked the colt to take a look at himself and then to look at the other ponies. Was he not different? The colt looked carefully at himself. He had four legs, a mane and a tail, a nose, two eyes, and two ears, just like all the other ponies. He did not see a single thing that was different and he told the brave so.

"That was when the brave pointed out that he was much larger in size than the other ponies. His coat was black, while all the other ponies were spotted or red or brown. While their manes and tails hung straight to the ground, his flowed in waves. The colt found it hard to believe that such little things would keep the other ponies from liking him.

"The Comanche brave assured him that those things made no difference to him, and that if the colt were just patient, the other ponies would soon discover the same thing for themselves and become his friends."

Long Quiet had been so involved in telling the story, he hadn't been aware of Little Deer's body relaxing in his arms. "She's fallen asleep."

"She was very tired, and your voice was soothing. It was a beautiful story. Did the other boys come to like you as your grandfather promised they would?" Bay ventured.

Long Quiet started at her perception. It wasn't until he was much older that he'd acknowledged how obviously the story mirrored his own situation. He'd only known it offered the hope of acceptance, and for a little boy who felt all alone, it had been the balm that had allowed him to survive his circumstances. "It was what I needed to hear at the time," he hedged.

"So they didn't accept you."

"Comanches are a very loving people. It didn't take long before the other boys forgot the color of my eyes and skin."

"But you were never really one of them," she prodded.

"I grew up knowing I was different," he admitted.

Bay took a deep breath and said, "Me too."

"What?"

"I was different, too. The neighbors weren't too accepting of the way Rip raised us, so we weren't always welcome when we showed up at some harvest social. I stopped going after a while. It hurt too much to be shut out. It might not have been so bad, I suppose, if I'd been more like Sloan or Cricket. At least they were always sure of Rip's approval."

"But you weren't."

"Not always." Then Bay corrected, "Not ever."

"So life is better among the Comanches."

"I didn't say that."

"You didn't have to. Would you go home, Bay, if you didn't have Little Deer to consider?"

"But I do."

"Answer the question."

Bay looked down at the bowls in her lap, filled with the greasy residue of their dinner. "I don't know." Home was not the place she would choose to be, but where else could she go?

Long Quiet struggled to hide his conflicting emotions. He was sorry she felt so unloved by Rip, but he was more than willing to make up for that himself. He would love her so much she wouldn't ever have to wonder again if she was wanted.

After what Many Horses had told him about his intentions, Long Quiet was glad to know that Bay had considered a future that precluded going home to Three Oaks. He wondered how well she would survive the loss of her child if it came to that. He would never have taken her from Little Deer by force, but the choice had been taken from him. He could not control Many Horses' decision.

He looked down at the girl sleeping peacefully in his arms. It was hard to begrudge the charming child the love he knew Bay felt for her. He was beginning to feel a few tugs at his own heart.

"I guess I should lay her down and let her sleep," he said.

Bay set down the bowls and went over to straighten the already straightened pallet. "You can lay her here."

Long Quiet did as she bid him. As soon as he'd laid her

down, Little Deer curled up into a ball. He sat for a moment watching her, imagining his own child lying there.

"You'll make a wonderful father."

Bay's words bore so closely on what he was thinking, he turned abruptly to her. "I have much love to give a child . . . and the child's mother."

Bay rose quickly to escape the intimate turn of the conversation. "I have to clean those bowls now."

"I don't mind if Little Deer stays here in the tipi with us," Long Quiet said, halting her in her tracks, "but you'll be sleeping with me."

"But she's always slept with me," Bay protested. She shifted nervously under Long Quiet's steady gaze.

"I won't let you put the child between us. It shall be as I say, or Little Deer will not stay here at all."

"All right," Bay replied sullenly. "You win."

Long Quiet stood up and grasped Bay's chin in his hand, turning her face up to his. "There is no winning or losing between us on this matter. I do not deny your need to love the child or the child's need for your love. But your duty at night is to me. Little Deer can have your pallet. You will share mine."

When Long Quiet released Bay's chin, she ran from the tipi with the bowls in hand. Long Quiet realized she was angry, but he didn't know what else he could have said. He turned to locate the pallet she'd put out for him and settled himself upon it to wait for her return.

Bay didn't stop running until she'd reached the creek. By then she was breathless, and her exhaustion had taken the bite from her anger. What was to happen would happen. She could not change it. But now she regretted having spoken so openly with him. She'd forgotten for a few moments why he'd come to the village in the first place. She'd revealed too much of the truth to Long Quiet about her past. But she'd thought it would help him understand why she wasn't sure she wanted to go home. Among the Comanches, she hadn't needed to try so hard to be something she wasn't.

Bay took her time getting back to the tipi, hoping Long Quiet would be asleep when she got there. It was a ridiculous expectation, and she knew it hadn't been fulfilled the instant she entered the dimly lit tipi. Long Quiet was wide awake. And he was waiting for her.

"Come to bed, Shadow."

"I'm not sleepy."

"Come to bed, Shadow."

"I have some sewing to do."

"Shadow . . ."

"All right!"

She wondered whether he expected her to undress again.

"It's too warm to wear what you have on. Take it off," he said.

She wondered whether he wanted her close to him.

"Come lie next to me."

She wondered whether he would touch her.

Bay shivered as Long Quiet's hand caressed the length of her body from shoulder to hip. "Your skin is softer than I imagined. More silky than my pony's nose."

Bay smiled despite her nervousness. "Your pony's nose?"

He chuckled. "It's very soft. I'll let you pet him tomorrow. You can feel for yourself."

"I'm not very good around horses."

"I'm not asking you to ride him, Shadow, only to pet his nose." His arm cinched her waist and he pulled her back against his body. The feel of her smooth back against his chest made him harden with desire, and he was sorry he'd pulled her so close, because there was no way she could mistake his reaction to her.

Bay could not help being aware of the warmth of Long Quiet's skin and his rigid shaft against her buttocks. She stiffened. It would happen tonight. He would not be able to wait any longer. A man like this . . . he would need a woman.

Long Quiet felt her tense, knew what she was expecting, and almost fulfilled that expectation. But reason came and held his hand and guided him away. "Not tonight, Shadow. When you are willing will be soon enough." With that, he placed a soft kiss on her shoulder and shifted away.

Bay lay trembling, afraid to admit how much of what she was feeling was relief and how much disappointment. The feel of his callused fingers on her hip, that had been good. The warm flesh of her back nestled against his chest, that had been good, too. The way her buttocks had spooned into his groin had been . . . natural. Why was she so afraid? She'd seen how gentle he could be. What did it matter whether he joined their bodies today or a week from today? She knew it was inevitable. Why couldn't she just submit and get it over with?

"*Pia?* Where are you?"

At Little Deer's frightened call, Bay rose on her elbow and replied, "I am here, *ona.*"

Little Deer sat up and rubbed her eyes, then crawled over to lie in Bay's arms. "I dreamed *Piamempits*, Big Cannibal Owl, was going to eat me up."

Bay turned to Long Quiet, daring him to make her send the child away.

"Put her on her own pallet, Shadow."

"She's just a baby," Bay whispered. "She's afraid to sleep by herself."

"Little Deer, you must sleep on your own pallet," Long Quiet told the girl.

"Why?"

Bay arched a brow as if to ask how he intended to answer that.

"Because I wish it so," he replied.

"Why?"

"Because a Comanche woman must learn to sleep on her own pallet until she is called to the pallet of her husband," he replied, staring at Bay until she blushed.

"Oh." Little Deer was clearly torn. She'd enjoyed Long Quiet's earlier approval a great deal. But clearly there were some things a woman must do that a little girl—who'd always slept with someone else—found a little frightening.

Long Quiet took the choice out of Little Deer's hands, scooping up the child and putting her back on the pallet across the tipi. "I will keep you safe from *Piamempits*. Go to sleep now, and in the morning I will let you ride my pony."

"You will?"

"Yes. If you sleep here tonight."

Bay was furious that he'd offered Little Deer a bribe and disgusted when Little Deer accepted it, blithely turning over to go to sleep.

"See," Long Quiet whispered. "She can sleep by herself after all."

Bay turned her back to Long Quiet and closed her eyes. She'd always loved sleeping with the child's body snuggled trustingly against her own. Tonight she felt cheated. And for the first time since she'd taken Little Deer into her care, she felt alone. Long Quiet was keeping his distance and he'd ensured that Little Deer would keep hers. As Bay drifted off to sleep, she was angry and frustrated and confused.

Bay awoke slowly, feeling the warmth of another body behind her. An elbow dug into the center of her back and jolted her awake. She became aware of the large hand splayed across her naked belly and realized there was no way it could be Long Quiet's elbow jabbing her in the back. Then she saw the small hand draped across her shoulder.

Bay began to laugh. She tried to do it quietly, but the guffaw in her chest escaped in unladylike whoops. She hugged herself with her arms and began to roll back and forth with mirth. Behind her she heard two grunts, one high-pitched and one low.

"What's going on?" Long Quiet bellowed, coming abruptly awake in a confused mass of arms and legs.

Squeezed between Long Quiet and Bay was Little Deer,

who now peered up with wide eyes at the ferocious expression of the rudely awakened man.

"I decided I would rather sleep here than ride your pony," Little Deer offered.

The guffaw Bay had been trying to control finally let go in a raucous "Hah!" Long Quiet's glare sent her into fits of hooting laughter. It was all she could do to get out, "Do I still get to pet your pony's no-ho-ho-ho-se?"

Chapter 8

BAY CARESSED THE SILKY SKIN WITH HER FINGERTIPS and then bent down to bestow a kiss. Who would have thought a pony's nose could be so soft? The pony whickered and backed up a step, shaking its head at this human nonsense. Bay smiled and reached over to scratch behind the pony's ears, noting that the pinto readily bent its head to her reach. How like its master, Bay thought. Seeking her touch but unwilling to be held. She wondered if this tame pinto knew it had been replaced by a fiery chestnut stallion.

She'd watched Long Quiet work with the stallion over the past two weeks as he slowly but surely tamed the animal with his touch. She'd watched them fight for dominance, the man and the beast. It had left her breathless when he finally sat upon the magnificent animal's back, the gentle master to a willing slave. She refused to find a parallel between herself and a horse. But it was there all the same.

She couldn't count the times over the past two weeks when she'd gone for water or wood or set out to gather wild fruit or roots or nuts and been met by Long Quiet. She wasn't sure how he knew where to find her, but he always did. He'd kept her company while she worked, and for that alone she would have been grateful. But he'd gone a step further and shared himself with her. No subject had been tabu. He'd told her she could ask him anything. So she had.

"Tell me about your family," she'd urged when he'd joined her as she gathered firewood.

"My father was a white man. He stole my mother, the daughter of a *Penateka* Comanche chief, and took her away with him. At least that's what my grandfather told me."

He'd laughed when she'd let the whole load of firewood fall in astonishment. As he helped her stack it up again, she asked, "Did you live in one of the Texas settlements?"

"No. My father was a *Comanchero*." At Bay's quizzical look, he explained, "A white man who traded with the Comanches. He belonged neither to the world of the White-eyes nor the world of the Comanches. A drifter, you would call him, but more often he was called less kind names.

"I remember he talked sometimes about his family back in New York. He'd argued with his father and gone west to make his own fortune." His lips twisted in what was not quite a smile. "We were never rich, but the land provided us with food to eat and clothes to cover us. My mother taught me the words of the Comanche; my father taught me the white man's tongue. I learned early to cross the borders between the white man's world and *Comanchería*. I was Long Quiet. And I was Walker Coburn."

"Walker. That's an unusual name. It sounds almost Indian," Bay said.

"It's a family name, handed down by generations of Coburns. Do you want me to help you carry some of that mesquite?"

Bay laughed. "Of course not. Do you want the women of the village to think you less than a man?"

Long Quiet shook his head. "If we were in Texas I'd have been thought less a man if I *didn't* offer to help you carry such a large load of firewood."

Noting the obvious differences in customs had made them awkward with each other, and she'd found an excuse to leave him.

A few days later she'd been sent to gather plums to be

dried for pemmican. She'd nearly filled her basket when he'd come along with a deer slung across his pony. He slipped off his mount and watched her work for a while. Before long, Bay found herself saying, "It must have been difficult for you, growing up like you did, to know where your loyalties lay."

"What do you mean?"

"Why, with a white father and a Comanche mother, and drifting back and forth like that between two peoples who hated each other, how could you know where you truly belonged? It must have been hard having parents who were so different and—"

Long Quiet cut her off with a wave of the purloined plum in his hand. "I belonged with my parents, and I don't think I ever much noticed the differences between my mother and father. They certainly never let their differences keep them from loving one another."

"It sounds almost like a fairy tale," Bay said, smiling dreamily as she picked plums and dropped them in the basket she'd brought along. "Where's your mother now?"

"She died of pneumonia when I was six."

"I'm sorry. And your father?"

Long Quiet spit out the pit and swallowed the last of the plum before he said, "My grandfather killed him."

"Oh, my." She'd just lifted the basket of plums into her arms and had to juggle not to drop it. His hands covered hers to steady her. They felt good, strong and sure. He didn't seem in any hurry to let her go, but she stepped back, and then, because she wanted to know, asked, "Why did your grandfather kill your father?"

"My grandfather, Stands Tall, hates all White-eyes. Because my mother had died the previous year, he had no way of knowing my father was his son-in-law. After he'd killed my father, Stands Tall took me captive. That was when he learned the truth—that he'd killed his daughter's husband."

"How sad! If only he'd known." Bay felt tears misting her

eyes, but since her hands were full, there was no way she could wipe them away. Long Quiet's thumb reached out and caught a salty drop. She felt a tingling deep inside when he raised his thumb to his mouth and licked it away.

Long Quiet took another plum from her basket and tossed it in his palm. His eyes were on her, but his thoughts were focused on the past. "I wonder if it would have made a difference if he'd known," he mused. At Bay's shocked expression, he continued, "Stands Tall was a far-seeing man. He realized years ago the danger of allowing the white man a foothold in *Comanchería*. He knew there would eventually be a battle for the land. He was right. It's already begun."

Bay had remained silent, unable to contradict the truth of what he'd said, unable to soothe his troubled look with a clever answer. But he hadn't let the subject rest, coming back to it in later days, worrying it like a lone wolf haunts an aging buffalo.

It wasn't until their conversation yesterday that she'd finally known what it was that bothered him. She'd been sent out to harvest pecans. It wasn't difficult work, but she had to do it on her knees or bent over, and after a while, her back ached. She'd just stopped for a rest and was stretching a knot out of her back muscles when he'd ridden up.

"Are you stiff?"

"A little."

"Let me help."

"I'll be all right. I—"

But by then his hands had slipped up under her poncho and his thumbs had found the clenched muscles just above her waist and were working their way up to the ache in her shoulders. It felt so good she forgot about objecting. Bay's eyes were closed and her chin had dropped to her chest. She was immensely enjoying the strong, certain touch of his hands on her skin.

She could hear the grin in his voice when he said, "I couldn't do this to a Texas woman."

"What?"

"You'd be all laced up in a corset and there'd be several layers of clothes between your skin and my hands."

Bay had flushed, but when she'd started to pull away he'd said, "Don't. I won't tease you anymore. I can feel how tense you are. Let me help."

It did feel good. And this wasn't Texas; it was *Comanchería*. "All right," she agreed with a sly glance over her shoulder, "but only if you tell me how you learned so much about white women's clothes."

"When I was seventeen, I left *Comanchería* and lived for a while among the White-eyes. I went to the white man's school and learned much about his ways."

"Standing Tall allowed it?"

From the corner of her eye Bay saw that Long Quiet's lips had compressed in a straight line. "It was not by my choice that I went, or his either."

"Oh." When he didn't offer any further explanation, she asked, "Where did you go to school?"

"In Boston."

She grinned in disbelief and turned to face him, breaking contact with his hands. "I went to school there, too!"

"I know."

"What?"

"I saw you once," he admitted.

"You did? When? Where?"

"At a cotillion. I even asked you to dance."

"No! I would have remembered." She searched his face, trying to imagine how he would have looked without the braids, with his bronzed chest covered by a stiff white linen shirt and silk vest, and with kerseymere trousers covering his long legs. His next words jerked her back to the present.

"You only had eyes for one man that evening."

"Oh. Jonas." She said the name sadly, as one would speak of the dead.

"I believe that was his name."

"Jonas wanted to marry me."

"And you?"

Bay dropped to her knees and began harvesting pecans again, collecting them on the piece of buckskin that lay nearby. In a moment Long Quiet dropped to his knees to join her. Knowing he was still waiting for an answer, she said, "Yes. I would have married Jonas in Boston, even without my father's permission, if he hadn't been called back home to Louisiana by his father's illness. But it hardly matters anymore, does it?"

When he frowned, she quickly changed the subject. "Tell me, did you try to find your father's family when you were back east?"

He hesitated, as though he wanted to pursue his own question further, but then answered hers. "Yes, I looked for them."

"And . . ." she prodded.

"I found them," he admitted. "My uncle, my father's younger brother, had inherited the family business."

"And what was that?"

He grinned. "A rather large New York bank."

"Oh, my." Bay looked down at the pecans she'd just spilled on the ground and blushed a bright red. Bay was frustrated by the fact that each time Long Quiet visited her, she became unusually clumsy. She had no explanation for the phenomenon except that whenever he was near, her mind wasn't completely on what she was doing. Fortunately, Long Quiet never seemed to notice anything amiss.

"What did your uncle say when he saw you?" she asked as they scooped up pecans.

"He offered me my father's inheritance . . . and a job."

Bay sat back and wiped the sweat from her brow. "You would have been rich! Why didn't you take his offer?"

"I didn't want his money. I always knew I would return to *Comanchería*."

"How did you know that?"

"It's the land of my grandfather, my home."

"What of your father's home?"

"My father had no home."

"It would be more accurate to say he had two homes." She forced him to meet her eyes before she said, "So do you."

He was silent for a moment, as though unwilling to admit the truth of what she'd said. He picked up two large pecans and, holding them both in one hand, closed his fist, crushing them against one another. When he opened his hand again, the shells had cracked, and he offered the sweet nuts to her.

"A man cannot have two homes. I am Comanche, a True Human Being."

She hadn't argued with him, but somehow they'd started comparing the Comanches, who were wanderers, with the whites, who stayed in one place. Long Quiet understood the need of the white man to possess the land, and he understood the need of the Comanche to roam free. But which one was right? Could they ever reconcile their differences?

Bay wasn't sure Long Quiet recognized the significance of the dilemma he presented. He talked around and around it, never seeming to come to the point. Until she'd realized that coming to the point would have meant making a final choice: Which side should he take?

And she was sure Long Quiet didn't want to have to make that choice.

Over the past two weeks she'd come to feel like she'd known Long Quiet all her life. She would have called the two of them friends, although she wasn't sure friends touched quite as much as they did. And he'd claimed her with his touch as surely as he'd claimed the stallion.

The fact they slept beside each other every night brought them even closer, so Bay felt the pain of his indecision as her own. Her heart went out to him, torn as he was between two peoples, bleeding for the wounded on both sides of the battle he foresaw in the future.

It didn't take much soul-searching to admit that she found in his plight a mirror of her own inner battle—between what

Rip wanted her to be and what she felt she could, or ought to, be.

The big difference was that a choice would eventually be forced upon Long Quiet by the inevitable conflict between two peoples; Bay could have gone on indefinitely walking the fine line between what her father desired of her and what she wished to be—if she hadn't been captured by the Comanches.

Her captivity had curtailed her father's plans for her life, but it hadn't really solved her problem, only changed it. She wasn't any closer now to knowing who Bay Stewart was than she had been three years ago.

Bay rubbed the pony's nose again, then ran her hand down his sleek neck. All she knew was that she dreaded the thought of a future without Long Quiet.

Long Quiet stood unobserved and watched Bay's easy familiarity with his pony. Two weeks ago it had been all he could do to get her to approach the animal. Things had changed since then. He'd wooed her in the only way he knew. He'd given as much of himself as she asked. He'd answered her questions. He'd touched her with gentleness. He'd dared to offer help in her woman's work when he knew his Comanche friends would have scorned him had they but known of it.

The labors of the day had borne their fruit in the darkness. She had sought him out to touch, a little at first, and then more and more, until he'd awoken this morning to find them so tangled it was hard to know where one began and the other ended. He took a deep breath and exhaled. He'd done all he could. The rest was up to her.

"*Hihites*, Shadow."

Bay jumped as Long Quiet stepped up beside her. He reached out to scratch the pinto's other ear. "I wish you wouldn't sneak up on me like that," she chided.

He grinned. "I didn't want to give you a chance to run away."

Bay turned and looked at him. "I wouldn't have run away." Her hand stilled on the pony's ear as their eyes caught and held. It was the pony's insistent nudge that broke the spell between them. Confused, Bay turned her attention back to the pinto. She scratched its ear once again, then, conscious of Long Quiet's hand so close to her own, dropped hers and moved away.

"I have something to tell you," he said.

She stopped and turned back to him.

"Let's go sit down where it's cool, so we can talk," he said, gesturing toward the late-afternoon shade of a nearby rocky butte.

Bay walked a little ahead of him. She settled herself with her back against stone that had barely lost the heat of the day and stretched her legs out in front of her. Long Quiet dropped down beside her, resting his forearms on his knees. His unfocused gaze instinctively searched the prairie for hidden danger in the clumps of spiny mesquite and catclaw shrubs. Fatigue bowed his shoulders and tightened the lines around his eyes and mouth. Bay thought maybe he hadn't been sleeping well. But then, she hadn't slept well the past two weeks, either.

While their days had been spent in pleasant conversation, their nights had been fraught with tension. Bay wasn't sure who was to blame for that. It was easier to name Long Quiet as the culprit. After all, he was the one who'd demanded she lie beside him. But he hadn't insisted that she seek out the heat of his body at night or that she burrow close. Bay blamed her actions on her loneliness. It had simply felt too good to be held in his arms not to take advantage of the opportunity.

This morning she'd awoken with her knee pressed intimately between his thighs, her breasts flattened against his chest, her nose and mouth nestled in the arch of his throat, her hands . . . Bay flushed as she remembered where her hands had been. One hand had been tangled in his hair, while the other had been curved snugly around Long Quiet's naked buttocks, holding him tight against her belly.

Bay closed her eyes and gritted her teeth as she remembered what had happened then. Long Quiet's callused fingertips had slowly traveled the length of her spine, from the dimples above her buttocks to the nape of her neck. She'd shivered and arched her body into his from thigh to breast.

There had been nothing to fear in their closeness, and she'd allowed herself to enjoy the pleasurable tensing within her body. She didn't for a moment suspect Long Quiet had more in mind than holding her exactly like this. After all, it had been two weeks and not once had he forced an unwanted touch. Nor was this touch unwanted, Bay had admitted to herself.

It was hard to say what would have happened if Little Deer hadn't chosen that moment to squirm in between them. In the light of day, Bay told herself she was grateful to the child. At least, she thought she was. But remembering the look on Long Quiet's face, she didn't think he'd been grateful at all. She looked at him now. Did he want to talk about what had happened this morning? Was that why he seemed so . . . distracted?

As though sensing Bay's eyes on him, Long Quiet turned to her. He straightened his back and leaned against the rocky butte, letting his hands hang off his bent knees. Then he shifted again, straightening his legs and letting his hands drop to his lap. But he couldn't seem to get comfortable. He rubbed at the frown wrinkling the bridge of his nose, then looked off into the distance. "I have to leave here soon."

Bay was stunned. "What?"

"I have to meet Creed in Laredo in about ten days." His voice grated with tension as he added, "Then I'll be going down into Mexico on some business, and I don't know when I'll be back."

"You never said—"

"It doesn't matter now what I said or didn't say," he interrupted irritably. "The fact is I have to leave. I can stay until the buffalo hunt is finished, but no longer. Once the hunt begins, we won't have much time together. That's why I wanted to talk with you now."

But he didn't say anything, just pursed his lips and stared out over the prairie.

When Bay couldn't stand the suspense another second, she blurted, "What did you want to talk about?"

"I want . . . I want to know if you've reconsidered your decision to stay here."

He sounded angry, and somehow Bay knew that what he'd said wasn't at all what he'd intended to say.

"I can't leave! You know that."

"Why not?"

Bay scrambled to her feet, away from the intensity of his stare. "We've been through all this before."

He came swiftly to his feet behind her, his strong hands clasping her shoulders to keep her from fleeing. "I'm asking again." He struggled for control, then said more quietly, "After this morning . . ."

Bay waited for him to finish his thought. When he dropped his hands, she turned to search his face. She took a deep breath and asked, "What about this morning?"

"If you won't come away with me, I want at least the memory of the two of us together. This morning I would have had that—you were willing, I think—had not Little Deer come between us."

She flushed, unable to admit what was nevertheless true. "What do you want me to say? That I am willing?"

"Are you?"

Bay bit her lower lip. She could tell Long Quiet was tense, anxious. But his eyes burned with desire. Anticipation sent the blood rushing in her veins. Fear knotted her stomach and choked her speech. This was so cold, so calculated. Why couldn't he have simply taken her and not made her responsible for the decision?

Sensing her fear, he spoke. "I will not force you, Shadow. Above all things, I want you willing."

Bay felt desire welling inside her. Yes! Why not say yes? Why shouldn't she know what it felt like to take this man inside her, to make him a part of her? When he left, she would be so alone! The memory of one night . . . and not a night with just any man, but this particular man.

She admired the patience that had allowed him to tame the stallion instead of breaking it. She appreciated the gentleness that had allowed him to hold a child in his arms and tell her a bedtime story. She respected the strength of character that had allowed him to do a woman's work undaunted by the possibility of another's scorn. And only this morning her body had heated to the touch of his hands.

Yet she was afraid to make such a monumental decision. No wonder she'd been such a disappointment to her father. Bay felt despair rising, and it brought a lump to her throat. She dropped her chin to her chest. Why couldn't she answer him the way she wished?

Long Quiet stepped back, and the chance was gone. With a fluid grace that never ceased to amaze her, he turned and strode away.

Long Quiet was in a killing mood when he left Bay, furious that he'd left the choice up to her, furious that she'd denied him. He tried to tell himself it was better this way.

But it wasn't. Now he would spend the rest of his life knowing he'd held her in his arms . . . but never made her his woman.

Chapter 9

BAY LOOKED OUT OVER THE HUGE HERD OF BUFFALO with an awe that hadn't diminished over the years. The hump-backed beasts drifted across the prairie like waves of water on sand, suddenly flooding the land and as suddenly gone again. Today, the Comanches would harvest what buffalo they needed for food and clothing to survive the winter. Both Long Quiet and Many Horses were among the hunters on horseback who circled the mammoth shaggy animals. The hunt was dangerous for all involved, and Bay shivered with the excitement she always felt during the hunt.

The past three days without Long Quiet had been miserable. One minute she hoped he'd come to her in the darkness. The next she was glad he'd made the break between them so complete. But until he left the village there was always the chance he would change his mind, and the thought of what would happen then had left her edgy and nervous. It was all she could do to wait quietly with the other women to butcher the buffalo once they were killed. After conversing so often with Long Quiet, it was harder to hold her tongue and merely listen when the women began to talk.

"Many Horses hunts without the protection of his *puha* because of Shadow," She Touches First said loud enough for Bay to easily overhear her.

"What has happened?" one of the women asked.

"He Decides It made medicine after Many Horses gave Shadow to Long Quiet. The *puhakut* told Many Horses he had broken his tabu by giving Shadow to another man and that it could be dangerous for him if she stayed in the village."

"Should that choice not be up to Many Horses?" another of the women pointed out.

"She has used her medicine to cloud Many Horses' eyes to the harm that may befall him," She Touches First said. "That is why he has refused to send her away. We should cast her out from among us and leave her to work her sorcery with the vultures and the wolves."

"If she is so powerful, could she not use her medicine against us as well?" Red Wing pointed out.

"The wolves will tear her flesh, and the vultures will pick her bones clean. Her spirit will wander the Otherworld crippled and blind. How can she then be a threat to any of us?" She Touches First replied.

Fear knotted Bay's stomach, but it was as much fear for Many Horses as for herself. Even though she'd denied having any special powers, Many Horses believed she did. How frightening it must be for him to know his *puha* had been destroyed by one impulsive act. How awful to know he no longer possessed any special protection from the perilous life he led.

Neither was she safe now. The accusation of sorcery was a serious one, for sorcery was one of the few crimes recognized by the Comanches. If She Touches First convinced the women of the village that Shadow was practicing magic, one of them would soon find a way to permanently end the menace she represented. She shuddered at the implications the *puhakut*'s decree held for her, and she was completely sobered by the risk Many Horses had taken by not following the *puhakut*'s advice.

"Ah! Look! The hunt has begun. May the Great Spirit guard Many Horses now."

Bay followed She Touches First's pointing finger and saw the buffalo shifting as the Comanches herded them in the direction of a deep ravine several miles away. There, the irrevocable push of the buffalo in back would send those in front over a precipice to their deaths.

Bay had only moments to stop Many Horses before he would be committed to the hunt. She didn't want to be the cause of his death. Without his *puha* to protect him he would not have the peace of mind, the certainty of success, that was necessary to keep him safe from the capricious buffalo. She had to convince him not to take part in the hunt.

Bay took off on foot toward Many Horses, so single-minded in her pursuit of him that she didn't see the buffalo bull that had been separated from the herd. Nor was she aware that the bull had caught her scent and was pawing the ground. She ran fleet-footed, skirting cholla cactus, jumping tumbleweeds and small hills like a deer in flight.

"Shadow! Look out!"

Bay heard Long Quiet's shouted warning and paused to look over her shoulder. She nearly stumbled in fright. An angry buffalo was bearing down on her at full speed, his eyes white at the rims and foamy saliva flecking his mouth. His trumpeting challenge was lost in the thunder of his hooves.

Long Quiet kneed his pony into the milling buffalo herd that separated him from Bay. "Run!" he shouted. "Run!"

His anguished cry set Bay in motion again, but it was a race she could not win.

Many Horses watched the unfolding drama as though it were happening in a distant time and space. He knew this was the awful moment He Decides It must have seen in his medicine vision. He'd warned Many Horses that if he kept Shadow, there would soon come a time when the Great Spirit would make him choose between her life and his own. Angry at the result of the *puhakut*'s vision, Many Horses had stubbornly refused to act upon it before the hunt. He saw now the folly of his decision.

Bay's breath rasped in gusts and a sharp pain pierced her side. Her legs ached and she pumped her arms harder to keep moving. She stumbled and almost fell, gasping when she managed to regain her footing. She could almost feel the fiery breath of the buffalo behind her, feel the earth trembling beneath her feet from his pounding weight.

Suddenly a pair of strong arms yanked her up off the ground. She clutched at the saving strength, barely aware of the low, murmuring voice soothing her fears even as callused fingers soothed her trembling body. Her face was pressed against a muscular chest and strong arms crushed her in their grasp. She inhaled the aroma of the man and realized it wasn't Many Horses who held her, but Long Quiet.

She jerked her head around to look for Many Horses, only to discover he'd driven his pony between her and the furious bull. She Touches First's warning rang in Bay's head and she struggled to be free.

Long Quiet tightened his hold on Bay and said in a voice harshened by his fear for her, "Be still. You're safe now."

"Yes," she gasped, "but Many Horses is not!"

His eyes searched out the other man and found the reason for her concern. "Stay here."

He dropped her off his pony onto shaky feet, and she stood there dazed as he raced away from her toward the rampaging buffalo.

Many Horses began to think the disaster had been averted and he need not die after all—at least not on this fine day. He'd distracted the buffalo from Shadow so it now chased him. In mere moments he would loose an arrow into the hump of the animal that would pierce through to its heart, and the threat would be vanquished. The bull was running unpredictably, but his pony was the best mount he'd ever had and well trained to anticipate and avoid the buffalo's path. From the corner of his eye he noticed Long Quiet had removed Shadow from danger and was now joining him.

"The kill is yours," Long Quiet shouted as he flanked the

buffalo on the other side to keep it from veering away from Many Horses' attack.

Many Horses drew his bow with such strength that the first arrow buried itself to the feathers. The second went all the way through the buffalo's hump. The giant animal collapsed in a heap, and the two men pulled their ponies to a halt shortly beyond it.

"I will make certain of the kill," Many Horses said, "if you will take Shadow back to join the other women."

"I would like to take Shadow across my knee!" Long Quiet said sharply.

Many Horses laughed. It was a sound of relief. Relief that Shadow, whose medicine had not yet been returned to her according to custom, was safe. Relief that his death had not been the price for her safety. "It is good she is so fleet-footed, is it not, *haints?* Perhaps I should warn her to run again," he said with a grin.

Long Quiet returned the grin. "She would not get far before I caught her. But I will go now, before she finds her way into more trouble."

When Many Horses turned back to the buffalo, he discovered She Touches First there ahead of him. He'd forgotten for a moment she was every bit as fleet of foot as Shadow. In fact, she'd acquired her name by having more than once been the first woman to touch a downed buffalo and claim it.

"You foolish man!"

Her accusation brought him off his pony in an instant and face to angry face with her.

"How dare you speak so to me, woman!"

"I dare because you *are* a foolish man. How could you not heed the *puhakut*'s warning? How could you risk your life for the white woman, Shadow?"

He grasped her by her shoulders. "What is my life to you?"

"You are war chief of the *Quohadi*. To lose you would be

to lose the strength of a leader. Should I not care whether this village is safe from our enemies?"

"Is that all I am to you?" he demanded.

"Once you would have been everything to me," she replied, her eyes fiery with disdain. "Your falseness put an end to that."

"I have dealt with you as you have dealt with me. The fault is not all mine."

She Touches First winced at the vehemence of his accusation. Her gaze ran freely over Many Horses' features until at last her eyes slipped to his mouth and fastened there.

Many Horses felt his body respond as She Touches First stroked his face with her eyes. He searched her face for some remnant of the love he thought they'd once shared, but her features were expressionless. He sighed with regret and said, "Give me a moment to take back my arrows, and the buffalo is yours."

She Touches First wasn't sure when she first realized the buffalo wasn't dead. In the ordinary course of things, Many Horses would have made sure of the kill before he retrieved his arrows. But they'd both been distracted by their argument and the unspoken feelings between them. Terror took the air from her lungs. She gasped, and gasped again, before she cried out, "Noooooo!"

Her shouted warning came too late.

The buffalo did no more than lift its head abruptly and Many Horses was impaled on a sharp, thick horn. The massive head tossed once, twice, and the Comanche warrior was thrown away from the buffalo like discarded pecan shells, a jagged gash in his belly that left bright red blood spilling onto the dry prairie grass.

A horrible scream rent the air and soared on the breeze, interrupting Long Quiet's tirade against Bay's carelessness. Their heads snapped around to discover its source. They could see a body on the ground not far from the buffalo that had chased Bay, but it wasn't apparent who lay there. Long

Quiet mounted, with Bay behind him, and galloped back toward the chaos that had erupted around the buffalo.

The effort to gore Many Horses had taken the lifeblood of the shaggy beast, but She Touches First hadn't paid the dying buffalo any mind, rushing instead to Many Horses' side. They'd been quickly surrounded by a host of women, all shouting and crying and angling for a better view of the wounded man.

The hovering women reminded Long Quiet of vultures. He threw himself off his pony and scattered the women as he would have scattered the black birds, with little concern for the injury he inflicted. Like the ugly scavengers, the women scurried to escape his avenging strength.

Bay had followed in Long Quiet's wake, so they both reached Many Horses' body at the same time. She Touches First sat with the warrior's head in her lap. Bay shoved past Long Quiet to kneel beside Many Horses, noticing for the first time the bloody entrails protruding from his wound. Many Horses' eyes were closed, and Bay feared for a moment that he was dead. Then she saw his chest rise and fall and she breathed a sigh of thankfulness. She wanted desperately to help but didn't know what to do. Bay's eyes met Long Quiet's, but she found no solace there. His eyes were as bleak as her own.

It was She Touches First who broke the ominous silence first. "The *puhakut* spoke truly. Many Horses' *puha* did not protect him. Shadow's magic must have helped the buffalo prevail against such a mighty hunter."

The excited chattering of the women stopped at the harsh accusation made by the *puhakut*'s sister, who continued, "Because of this woman, a brave man is hurt. Shadow cast a spell to make Many Horses keep her in this village when the *puhakut* warned him of the danger. Because of her—"

"Hold your tongue!"

The surprising strength of Many Horses' voice cut off She Touches First, but even his strong voice didn't give her any hope he would survive. With such a wound in his belly, if he didn't die quickly of blood loss, he'd surely die slowly and in agony of the poison sickness that usually resulted from such a wound. To see the man she had once loved with all her heart so mortally wounded kept her tongue wagging despite his command.

"She cast a spell on you!"

Bay noticed the cautious, fearful glances of the women and saw them edge farther away from her.

"I cast no spells," Bay said. She could see, even as she denied the charge, that their fear grew simply from the fact that she'd spoken directly to them. She realized too late it would have been better to have said nothing. Bay shouldn't have been surprised by the superstitious fears of the women, but she was. She was no sorceress!

"What happened here is no fault of Shadow's," Many Horses rasped.

"What of the words He Decides It spoke to you?" She Touches First challenged. "He warned that both you and the woman could not live in peace here."

This gossip titillated the growing crowd, which edged unconsciously closer in order to be able to hear.

"Keep your thoughts . . . to yourself," Many Horses warned in a low voice. "The decision was mine. Shadow had no say in the matter."

"Will you send her away now that you see how dangerous it is to keep her?" She Touches First countered in an equally soft voice.

Many Horses didn't answer her question. "Take me to my tipi," he whispered to Long Quiet.

Long Quiet called for one of the travois that had been intended to carry the butchered buffalo back to the village. With the help of several of the women, he gently lifted Many Horses onto the hide bed. His wound bled freely, leaving red ribbons along Many Horses' side.

Bay held Many Horses' hand as the travois slowly made its way to the village. "I do not wish you to die," she said.

His lips twisted into a weak smile. "It is too bad you are not a sorceress. I am afraid it will take some special kind of magic to keep me alive."

"I will find the *puhakut*," She Touches First said. "He will know if there is aught that can save you."

Many Horses closed his eyes against the pain that had begun when he'd been moved. Until then, he hadn't been aware how badly he was hurt. Once he'd seen his own purple and pink entrails poking through the skin, Many Horses had resigned himself to his death. His greatest regret was that he would not die in battle. He smiled grimly. At least he would not live to be a useless old man.

When He Decides It arrived, he was appalled to discover the grave nature of Many Horses' wound. He did not believe even his strongest medicine would be good enough to heal Many Horses. Strangely, he felt no sense of triumph. He had never hated Many Horses, only envied him. And there was no doubt the entire village would feel the loss of this great war chief. But he was *puhakut*, and his honor demanded that he do all in his power to save the war chief of the *Quohadi*. He Decides It took command and began issuing orders. His first was, "You cannot stay here, Shadow."

"But—"

"Do not speak. Go."

Bay felt an ache behind her eyes, but she could see it would do no good to argue. She squeezed Many Horses' hand one last time and, without looking back, left the tipi.

The *puhakut* turned to his sister and ordered, "Bring me seven pads from a prickly pear cactus."

At last he turned to Long Quiet. "Go and cut the tail from the buffalo that did this and bring it to me."

Once they were all gone, He Decides It found the gourd of water in the tipi and used some of it to rinse the blood from Many Horses' skin. Carefully, he pressed the gaping entrails back into the cavity where they belonged. Then he waited until the others returned.

"My buffalo medicine is very powerful," he said in an attempt to reassure Many Horses. But he couldn't resist adding, "Still, you should not have flouted the will of the Great Spirit. I do not know if my skill will be enough to counter such bad medicine."

Many Horses opened his eyes. "You are a good *puhakut*. I am sure if my life is to be spared, you will know how to accomplish it."

He Decides It felt a stab of anger. How could Many Horses taunt him about his power even now? Suddenly, He Decides It could not stand to think Many Horses would die without knowing how thoroughly his life had been manipulated by the *puhakut* . . . or why. He Decides It let his anger goad him into revealing his dark secret. "We should have been brothers-in-law," he said.

Many Horses paled. "It was my wish," he admitted. "But your sister did not want me for her husband."

"Oh yes. She did."

Many Horses frowned, thinking he'd misunderstood. "She refused me."

"Only after I confessed that you'd told me you found greater pleasure in the body of the white woman, Shadow, and that She Touches First would never be first in your eyes or your heart."

Many Horses' eyes lit with rage at the blatant lie told by the *puhakut* and his fists clenched at his sides. "You did not tell her of the tabu? That I could not touch Shadow . . . as a man touches a woman?"

"No."

Despite the fact Many Horses was gravely wounded, the *puhakut* feared he was going to attack him. Many Horses' attempt to rise was thwarted by his torn stomach muscles. He ground his teeth as he tried to keep from crying out with the pain. Finally, he recovered enough to demand, "Why?"

The *puhakut* shrugged. "I envied you."

"What did I possess that you should envy me?"

"You were much honored by the people of this village."

"No more than you!"

"It seemed so to me. You took what you wanted on raids and brought it back to the village to share with others. I had nothing."

"You never went hungry. You had ponies so it was never needful that you walk," Many Horses countered.

"Yes, but if you were not such a great war chief, I would have had little to show for my efforts as *puhakut*," he replied.

"I do not understand."

"What bounty you gave to the villagers, they brought to me," he explained, chagrined by the admission. "I did not plan to even things between us through She Touches First. But when the chance came to thwart your marriage, I took it. I had to lie cleverly to keep my sister from questioning you. And of course I lied to you as well."

"She loved me then . . . and now?" Many Horses asked.

"Yes."

Many Horses turned his head away so He Decides It could not see the tears that hovered in his eyes. It was hard to die knowing he had been cheated of happiness. It became harder to talk as his strength ebbed, but he could not stay silent. "I loved She Touches First . . . with all my heart. To watch her these past three years . . . and not to have her . . . has been hard for me. I wish you had not . . . told me the truth."

"I am glad he has revealed the truth," She Touches First said.

He Decides It whirled to confront his furious sister. "How long have you been standing there?"

"Long enough to hear the cruel trick you played on us. How could you lie to your friend? How could you lie to your own sister?"

"I am not proud of it," He Decides It retorted.

"But you waited too late—"

He Decides It cut off his sister's lament with a barking, "Pah! He is not dead yet. Did you bring the cactus?"

She Touches First opened a piece of rawhide to reveal the seven pads of cactus. At almost the same moment, Long Quiet returned to the tipi. "Here is the buffalo tail you requested."

"Good," He Decides It said. "Now leave me, both of you. I have work to do."

When He Decides It was alone with Many Horses, he put the buffalo tail in his mouth and blew on the wound to stop the bleeding. After burning the spines off the prickly pear cactus, he slit it and pressed the open surfaces of the cactus against the flesh all along the wound. Then he bound the whole of it snugly with rawhide.

"Now the healing is in the hands of the Great Spirit," he announced.

"I do not plan . . . to die," Many Horses gritted out. "And when I am whole . . . I will offer ponies for your sister."

The *puhakut* shrugged.

"Send Long Quiet to me," Many Horses said. "And tell She Touches First that . . . I want to speak . . . with her."

"As you wish." The *puhakut* rose to leave, but was stopped by Many Horses' pain-laced voice.

"And, *puhakut* . . ."

"Yes?"

"I do not forgive you . . . for this."

He Decides It met Many Horses' fierce glare. "I did not ask your forgiveness." He turned and left.

Long Quiet entered the tipi and knelt beside the wounded man. Sensing his presence, Many Horses smiled, although his eyes remained closed. "*Haints?*"

"I am here," Long Quiet said.

"Do you think Shadow . . . would make a good wife?"

Long Quiet's eyes narrowed as he speculated on why Many Horses had asked such a question. Tentatively, he responded, "She was not raised in the Comanche ways."

Many Horses chuckled. "I could not expect . . . very many ponies for such a woman . . . could I?"

Long Quiet's heart lodged in his throat and made it difficult for him to speak. "What?"

"So I will . . . give her to you."

"What!"

Many Horses took a shallow breath and huffed it out again. "Am I mistaken? You do not wish . . . to have her?"

"She will not have me. She does not wish to leave Little Deer," Long Quiet admitted.

"You would not take her . . . despite her wishes?"

"No."

Many Horses' brow furrowed in thought. "Then I will have to find another . . . to take her."

"You will not keep your most prized possession?"

Many Horses' voice was low but firm. "I should have obeyed . . . the *puhakut*'s decree. I will return Shadow's medicine . . . and take She Touches First as *paraibo*. Shadow cannot stay . . . in my tipi."

"I will take her," Long Quiet said.

"Good."

"For a few weeks I must go where she cannot follow. Will you keep her safe here for me?"

"Yes. But you must claim her . . . as your wife . . . before all in the village . . . and take her to your pallet."

"It shall be done. Now, as a brother, I have a favor to ask."

"Name it . . . and it is yours."

"I have no ponies of my own within this village to offer for Shadow."

"I have asked no bride price," Many Horses said.

"I would not shame Shadow by taking her without a proper gift. And I want all in the village to know the worth I place upon my wife. Thus will they fear my wrath should they seek to harm her."

Many Horses nodded in agreement. "That is wise."

"So I need your herd of ponies."

"All of them?"

Long Quiet smiled. "All of them. Except your favorite war pony, of course."

Many Horses returned the smile. "Of course. It shall be as you say."

"I will deliver them to her tipi this very afternoon."

Long Quiet had barely left the tipi when She Touches First entered. She hesitated near the opening. She had begged He Decides It to tell her whether Many Horses was going to die. Her brother had told her that all men must die sometime and, when she had looked stricken, he had given the only reassurance he could: Many Horses would live yet awhile, and if the poison sickness did not kill him, for many years to come.

She Touches First's nerves were strung as tightly as a fox skin on a willow hoop. Her whole future depended on what Many Horses chose to do with the truth he'd learned from He Decides It.

"Come. Sit beside me," Many Horses said.

She Touches First contained her emotions with difficulty. She could hear the pain in his voice and she shared his agony. Yet she had spent too long denying her love for Many Horses to feel comfortable expressing it now, even though she feared they would have only a short time left in which to share their closeness.

"Do you love me?" he asked.

"As the earth craves water." She hesitated, then asked, "Do you love me?"

"As the grass loves the sun." They still had not touched one another, nor did either make the attempt. Many Horses sighed. It was a sound of disgust, of disbelief, of frustration. "How could we . . . have believed his lies?"

"He was my brother. He was your friend. Why should we not have believed him?"

"Surely the love we felt . . ."

"Our love made us vulnerable to his lies. We cannot have back the years that were taken from us."

His voice was weak, and she could barely hear him as he said, "But can we share . . . the years to come. Will you share my tipi as *paraibo?* Will you let me love you . . . until the day the sun rises no more . . . on my face?"

She Touches First blinked at the tears that gathered in her eyes. He had offered her a future she had only dreamed could be hers at a time when she had no certain hope it would last more than a few hours. Surely the Great Spirit would not let him die now, not now, when he had yet to plant the seeds that would become a new generation of Comanche warriors.

"From now on," she said, "our lives will be as one. We will share the time the Great Spirit gives us . . . together."

She Touches First reached out a hand to touch Many Horses' face. He was unconscious. It was likely he had not even heard her answer. She forced herself to remain calm. Many Horses would not die. The strength of their love would give him the will to live. She did not doubt it. Her fingertips traced the line of his mouth before she lowered her lips to taste his.

"I will give you many sons to take into battle with you," she whispered. Then, because she was afraid to face the years ahead without him, she added, "Please, please do not die."

Chapter 10

BAY HEARD THE THUNDERING OF A THOUSAND HOOVES and searched for Little Deer to rescue her from the stampede until she realized the child was safe, playing near the stream with the other children. She raced from the tipi in time to see Long Quiet circling two hundred and fifty ponies around her tipi. She knew what such a thing would have meant to a young Comanche woman, but she hardly dared to imagine it could have that meaning to her, especially when she saw the grim look on Long Quiet's face.

She stood her ground as Long Quiet dismounted and walked toward her, aware of the gaping Indians who'd left their tipis and clustered around to find out what all the fuss was about.

"I have come to claim you as my *paraibo*," Long Quiet said loudly enough to be clearly heard by several of those close by.

Bay bristled at his arrogant tone of voice, which assumed her acceptance. "What if I refuse your offer?"

He stepped closer, so his next words could be heard only by her. "Of course you can always return my gift. But I do not advise it. You belong to me now."

"My place is with—"

"—your husband." A powerful hand grasped her arm,

pulling her along, until she suddenly found herself blinking at the dimness inside her tipi.

"Many Horses is taking She Touches First as his wife," Long Quiet said. "He would have given you to someone else unless I claimed you. Tonight we will share a blanket. And you cannot—will not—say no."

"But—"

"I will be waiting in my tipi when the sun leaves the sky, Shadow, my wife. You will come to me then."

He turned on his heel and left her standing alone. Bay sank to the dirt floor, holding her head in her hands. What was happening? Had Long Quiet really just claimed her for his bride? He hadn't sounded like a man terribly pleased by his good fortune. What would happen to her when he left the village? Did he plan to take her with him? The haven she'd created for herself in the Comanche village was crumbling around her ears.

She walked proudly from the tipi, her head held high, and began to drive the herd of ponies toward Many Horses' pasture—the sign that she'd accepted Long Quiet's extravagant proposal of marriage.

Despite her resolve, as the sun set, Bay searched for chores that would delay the time when she must submit to her new husband. It was nearly dark when she collected a kettle and detoured to the creek to draw water, thinking she would need it to bathe before the night was done. The darkness had never frightened her, yet tonight there were shadows moving around her which, although she peered at them intently, never materialized into anything. She'd almost reached the edge of the village when a raspy voice accosted her.

"Devil woman! Evil one! Go away from here. We do not want you among us!"

Bay whirled to search out the source of the hissing voice, but could find no one in the shadows. "Who's there?"

"Leave this place. Take your evil medicine and go!" a second voice spat.

Bay whirled back to search for the other figure, but again saw nothing but shadows. "I will not harm you," she cried. "Please, who are you?"

The taunts were terrifying. Bay stood still, waiting, but only silence greeted her. For a moment she debated whether to go on to the creek or flee to Long Quiet's tipi. She knew the fears of the villagers had increased when, so closely following Many Horses' injury and the accusation of sorcery by She Touches First, the hunt had been a failure.

The hunters had straggled back to the village in the late afternoon, surly, angry, because for some inexplicable reason the buffalo had turned at the last moment and escaped death at the precipice. Now the herd was miles from camp and still running. The villagers would have to follow the shaggy beasts and hope they could find them again soon. Otherwise they would spend the winter hungry.

Bay knew that tonight many a mouth watered at the thought of what had been missed as a result of the failed hunt. She could see it all in her mind's eye—the children crowded around begging for portions of raw liver covered with the contents of the gallbladder, the women feasting on a mixture of raw brains and the marrow from leg bones served in a dish made from the slaughtered buffalo's ribs, the men stuffing themselves with the roasted haunch.

It was no wonder she'd felt more eyes on her than usual. From overheard conversations, it was clear the entire village blamed her for the forfeited feast—as well as Many Horses' injury. Bay shivered when she heard another angry whisper. Unfortunately, she knew no way to counter their accusations. She could only ignore them. Bay picked up the kettle she'd dropped and continued on her journey to the creek.

Outwardly, she remained calm. Inwardly, her mind was turning every shadow into something horrifying. As she gradually became aware of a presence stalking her, her vivid imagination ran wild. It could be a roaming Tonkawa. It could be a hungry puma. Or it could be someone who wanted to make sure she could cause no more bad medicine for the village.

Whoever or whatever it was, she didn't plan to be a willing victim. She dipped the kettle into the creek, but only filled it halfway, so she'd be able to lift it easily. The enormous shadow moving closer sent her into action.

Bay recognized Long Quiet too late to stop the forward motion of the kettle, and the water drenched him from head to foot.

"I . . . I'm sorry! I thought you were . . ."

How ridiculous her fears seemed now! How could she admit them to the forbidding man who faced her? She dropped the kettle and fled, uncaring where she ran, simply needing to escape the humiliating situation and the wrath she felt sure would fall upon her for her rash act.

"Don't run from me!"

Long Quiet's shouted warning set Bay's heart to pounding in real fear. She looked back and saw him pursuing her. As it turned out, she was heading away from the village, so there was no hope someone would interfere and save her. Not that anyone would have dared to come between a warrior and his wife, she thought.

Bay scooted into a gully and followed along it looking for a place to hide. Just as she found a narrow crevice through which she might escape, Long Quiet's arms closed around her, dragging her back into his wet embrace, soaking her from shoulders to buttocks.

"I told you not to run," he snarled into her ear. "Stop struggling!"

Bay moaned once in defeat and then sagged in his arms, panting from exertion.

Long Quiet held the frightened woman as gently as he could, appalled at what had just happened. Did she fear and dislike him so much? He'd only meant to speak with her, to explain his feelings about the circumstances that had been thrust upon them. It was clear she wasn't yet ready to become his wife. And yet he had no choice except to demand she come to him.

His arms circled her waist, coming to rest beneath her breasts, and he could feel the rise and fall of her chest as she tried to catch her breath.

"I only wished to speak with you," he murmured in her ear. "Why did you attack me?"

"I didn't know it was you," she admitted. "Then, when I'd soaked you with water, I thought you'd be angry so I—"

"I am angry." Long Quiet felt her tense beneath his touch. "I'm angry that you don't trust me not to hurt you," he said.

Bay wished she could see his face. "I don't know what to expect from you," she whispered. "You said you would wait until I was willing. Now you drive ponies to my tipi and my feelings mean nothing. I've dreaded the sunset, not knowing what the night would bring." She paused and sighed wearily before adding, "I don't want to be your wife."

Long Quiet's grasp tightened, the only sign of his agitation. "Do you want to return to your white family?"

"Nothing has changed. I can't take Little Deer with me, and I won't leave her behind."

Long Quiet swallowed hard before he asked, "Is there another man you would have for your husband?"

Bay's eyes widened in surprise. She didn't know how to answer him. There was no man in the village she desired for a husband, but perhaps it would help him understand her feelings if she explained to him about Jonas. "There is a man I love, but—"

"Who is he? Is he willing to take you as his wife?"

Bay shook her head and let it fall forward. "The man I love is from the world I left behind. I have no idea whether Jonas would be willing to marry me after . . . after everything that's happened to me."

Long Quiet's jaw clenched at the name Bay had mentioned. He'd wondered if she still cared for Jonas Harper. Now he knew, and the knowledge upset him more than he cared to admit. Long Quiet grimaced, glad Bay couldn't see his face. He could hardly blame her for clinging to an unrequited love. Hadn't he done the same thing all these years? Yet despite the force of events that had pushed them together too soon, it was his intention to make her his wife. If he had to wait for love to come, then he would wait.

To be absolutely sure of what other obstacles he might be up against, he asked, "Are you certain there's no other man in the village you would rather have?"

"No. There's no one else."

He turned her in his arms and tipped her chin up so they could look into one another's eyes.

"Then I don't see that either one of us has much choice. I have taken you as wife. I am not sorry we are to be together, only sorry for the timing of it. But even that will come to some good. I know of no more sure way to stop the wagging tongues of those who would send you from this village than to make it clear that those who threaten my wife must answer to me."

"Their words are only that—words."

"Their whispered words will send you from this place to make your way alone, with no help from anyone! If you do not look for such a fate, you would do well to heed me."

"This is not the way I would have chosen to take a husband," she said wistfully.

"Nor I a wife," he replied. "We will simply have to make the best of the situation."

"I can never love you."

Long Quiet's face sobered. "You will bear my children. We will grow old together. Perhaps over the years your heart will find a place for me."

Bay was surprised at the earnestness in his voice and the somber expression on his face. She hadn't really thought about her relationship with Long Quiet in terms of years. Or children. She hadn't allowed herself to think at all. "You want children?"

"Of course. Do you not desire more children?"

Bay searched Long Quiet's face, wondering if her answer would make any difference to him. She decided to be honest, in case it did. "I don't wish to bear sons who will be murderers and thieves. I don't wish to bear sons who will torture and rape and enjoy it."

"I am Comanche. My sons will be Comanche."

Bay could feel his body trembling with fury. She swallowed her fear and said, "You asked how I felt. I've told you."

"White men also murder and steal. White men also torture and rape. They are not blameless in the conflicts that cause such hate between our two peoples."

"It's not like this everywhere," she argued. "In the East, there is no strife."

"There is no strife because the white man has pushed the Indian off his lands, with no regard to who was there first," Long Quiet snarled. "The white man treats all Indians as animals, not as human beings!"

"I can't change what's happened in the past," she said, "but I can do my best not to continue the enmity between our two peoples. I want to teach my children not to hate."

"To trust the White-eyes is to ask for death," Long Quiet said. "Their history is one of deceit, of lies and more lies. You would teach a son to listen to promises that will not be kept?"

"Someone has to take the first steps toward peace. Why not a son of ours?"

Long Quiet opened his mouth to argue, then realized what Bay had said. He'd lost the battle, but won the war. "A son of ours. That has a good sound. I like it."

Bay was shocked to realize their conversation had led her to think of *their* children as though they were a possibility, even a reality.

"Come," Long Quiet said. "Night is upon us."

Bay walked beside Long Quiet as though in a trance. Her life had turned onto a new path and she wondered what awaited her along the way. When they reached the creek again she stopped to pick up the kettle, but he took it from her hands. The gesture of a white man, she thought, from one who'd just defended the Indian ways. She smiled, but said nothing.

When they arrived at their tipi, Bay took a deep breath and asked, "May I have some time alone to . . . to prepare myself?"

"As you wish. I will see to the welfare of my pony and then return."

Bay watched Long Quiet as he walked away from her. He moved with grace, his muscular body lithe. She shivered at the thought of his hard, muscular flesh pressed against her own. But the fear she'd expected to rise within her didn't come. Sometime in the past few minutes, Long Quiet had replaced her apprehension with expectation.

Bay spread the buffalo robe across the dirt floor and plumped the rabbit fur pillows, thinking what it would mean to lay her head next to Long Quiet's for the long years ahead. Would she feel more of the tingling feelings she'd experienced when they kissed? Would he be gentle with her?

Her thoughts went around and around as she left the tipi to make arrangements for Little Deer's care. When she returned, she built a small fire and prepared a dinner for Long Quiet. Her nervousness increased as time passed and he didn't return. She jumped when the tipi flap finally lifted and Long Quiet stepped inside.

Bay's instincts told her to flee, and she began to struggle to her feet, held back by the fringes of her poncho, which had tangled beneath her knees.

"You need not rise," Long Quiet said, misunderstanding her attempt to stand. He crossed quickly and sat down beside her.

Bay froze.

Long Quiet's hand reached out to the small metal pot of food warming on the fire. He dipped a finger in and tasted. "It's good."

"It's ready whenever you're hungry," Bay managed to say.

"I'm hungry now. Shall we eat?"

"If you wish."

Bay served portions of the venison stew to both of them in carved bowls. She sat as far away from Long Quiet as possible and ate her food as slowly as she could, to postpone what she was certain would follow.

Despite her efforts to appear calm, Long Quiet was aware of Bay's nervousness. He sought a subject on which they could talk that would ease her time with him.

"Where is Little Deer?"

"I thought it better she stay with Cries at Night for tonight . . . I mean if we . . . that is . . . she wouldn't be . . ."

Long Quiet searched for another safe topic and said, "Cries at Night said she had enough rabbit skins with the two I caught today to make a pillow to replace the one she gave away."

"I didn't know you needed a pillow," she said.

"It's for both of us to share."

Bay flushed. "Oh."

Long Quiet recognized the futility of his efforts. There was no safe subject for them to speak of tonight. What was to come was too much on their minds.

"Come here to me, Shadow."

"My name is Bay."

"Bay was the name given to the daughter of Rip Stewart. Shadow is a good name for a Comanche wife. Come here to me, Shadow."

"Please . . ."

"Come."

Bay dared not disobey the command. She stood and walked the few steps that separated her from Long Quiet. She couldn't bring herself to sit down again.

Long Quiet reached out a hand and twined his fingers with hers, gently tugging on her hand until she was on her knees before him.

Bay was unprepared for the gentleness of his touch. She quivered as his callused thumb traced its way across her cheekbone and then down to her mouth.

"Look at me."

Bay couldn't.

He tipped her chin up and she found herself staring into his gray eyes.

"I wish only to share with you the pleasures of a man and woman becoming one."

He took the hand that had been entwined with his and brought it to his chest. "I am only flesh and blood, like you."

His muscles tensed beneath her touch.

"Your touch pleases me," he murmured. His other hand captured her nape and his mouth came down to meet with hers, their lips barely touching.

Bay tried to withdraw her hand from his chest, but he kept it there until her fingers began to move on their own across his smooth, sweat-slick skin.

Bay was frightened of the feelings that flickered to life inside her. She ached and didn't know why. She needed but didn't know what. She held back the sob that threatened to erupt, uncertain how long his patience with her would last and unwilling to test him so soon.

When she opened her mouth to protest, his tongue sought welcome there. The sensations were shocking, but she couldn't find the will to resist. He caressed the honeyed treasure of her mouth with lips and teeth and tongue.

Unconsciously, Bay's hands roamed his chest. He jerked when she skimmed a male nipple.

"Should I not touch you there?"

"You can touch me anywhere it pleases you to touch."

"But you—"

He grasped her jaw in his hand and turned her face up to his at the same time his hand skimmed across her nipple. She jerked, and he raised his brow.

She smiled as understanding rose. "Oh, my. And it feels the same for you?"

"Yes. The same."

Her thumb brushed his nipple again, and she watched as his nostrils flared and his eyes ate her with hungry glances. Simply touching his skin intensified the ache inside her. She was instantly aware when Long Quiet's hand caressed the bare skin of her midriff. Her hands stopped where they were, and she pulled away from him. She looked down at his hand, then back into his gray eyes, dark now with desire.

He continued his seduction, all the while searching her face with his eyes. "You are still wary of my touch?"

"A little," she admitted.

"But it pleases you."

Bay started to shake her head, but his hand reached up to cup her breast and she gasped.

"It is good we make each other tremble with need," he said, his voice husky and low.

She was startled by the warrior's admission that she could make him tremble, but she could feel from the hand caressing her breast that he spoke truthfully. That this fierce warrior allowed her to see him shaking with need made him infinitely less threatening.

"Don't let the other braves see you like this," she gently teased. "Think what they'd say."

"They would say I am but a man," he replied, "and richly deserving of such a fate."

His smile faded as he added, "I would have it no other way."

He released Bay long enough to pull her buckskin poncho off over her head. When his fingers sought out the tie on her skirt, her hands met him there.

"I will see all of you," he said. When she resisted his efforts, he added, "It is my right . . . and I have already seen you many times before."

This is different, Bay thought. But her hands fell away.

"Stand up," he instructed.

As she stood, he eased the skirt down the length of her body, baring it a little at a time, his senses inflamed by what he found. "You are very beautiful, Shadow."

Bay stared straight ahead, pleased by what he'd said but at the same time embarrassed by his lingering gaze. She expected him to lay her down and take what he wanted. Instead, he rose to stand before her. Before she realized what he intended, he'd released his breechclout.

Despite all they'd shared so far, despite the fact she knew rationally he wouldn't hurt her and that there was no rescue outside the tipi, Bay whirled to flee. She was caught before she'd taken two steps, crushed by strong arms that drew her into Long Quiet's embrace. She whimpered in fear, struggling against her inexorable fate.

"Shhh," he soothed. He turned her in his arms, bringing her breasts into the hard pillow of his chest, her belly into the cradle of his hips.

Bay moaned at the feel of his hardness against her softness. It felt good. It felt so good. There was no danger, nothing to fear here, only the welcome of home.

Long Quiet smoothed the hair back from Bay's forehead with his hand, then let his lips caress her temple, her eyelids, and finally her mouth. His tongue delved into that sweet cavern as his hands brought her belly hard against his need. His tongue mimed the dance of love he'd waited so many years to have with this woman. His mouth trailed down to the jumping pulse at her throat, then to the crest of her breast.

Bay's hips tilted into Long Quiet's in a purely instinctive reaction as her back arched to bring her breasts up to his searching mouth. Her hands clutched his back, her fingernails drawing crescents in the warm golden skin.

Long Quiet took the pebbled tip of her breast into his mouth, tongued it, suckled it, nipped it with his teeth.

The sensations shot from Bay's nipple straight to her belly, tightening like a wire between them, causing her to jerk her hips up toward Long Quiet's aroused manhood.

His head came up suddenly as he grasped her rounded buttocks with one hand and held her still.

Bay's head was thrown back over Long Quiet's arm, her mouth open, her eyes closed to concentrate all her attention on the delicious feelings racing through her. She tried to rub her belly against him, seeking the erotic sensations that had stopped when he'd stilled her against him.

Slowly, her eyes opened and Long Quiet's face came into focus. He was breathing heavily, and his facial muscles were taut. Her actions of the past few moments came flooding back to Bay in an instant, her face flushing with the horror of what she'd done.

She'd forgotten all about Jonas. How insidious was this emotion called desire! She couldn't desire Long Quiet. She hardly knew him. She certainly didn't love him. She loved Jonas.

"Don't," Long Quiet said. "Don't regret what's happening between us. It's good. It's—"

"Jooonaaas," she moaned.

Long Quiet's mouth came down brutally to cut off the hated name. She was his. Another man had no place in her head or her heart. In an instant he had her down upon the buffalo robe that served as his bed.

Gone was the gentle man who'd wooed her. Gone was the patience he'd shown earlier. Bay hardly recognized the man whose weight held her down. His thighs spread her legs apart while his large hand pinned her wrists above her head.

"Don't do this," she pleaded.

"I will put my seed in you and make a child that will be a part of both of us. Perhaps then you will realize that from this moment, forever, you are mine."

His hand came down between them, parting her nether lips. She tensed at this intrusion where no man had been before.

He slipped a finger inside her, finding her small and tight and slickly wet. His thumb searched, found what it sought, and applied pressure that caused Bay to buck her hips against him despite her desire to show him no response. "What are you . . . aaaah!"

Long Quiet lowered his head to her breasts, sucking and teasing, even as his hand continued to tease her woman's place.

Bay heard a groan and wondered who had made that wrenching sound. Her breasts arched up as her body begged Long Quiet to take more of her breast into his mouth. Her hips bucked, begging him to delve deeper with his hands. The groaning was constant now, cries and gasps and pleas that made no sense to her but were music to the ears of the man who was the cause of her distress.

Long Quiet felt Bay's body tensing, felt her desire cresting and, releasing her hands, grasped her buttocks and tilted her so she could more easily receive him. He placed himself at the entrance to her, dipping himself into the lover's dew that told him her delicate petals had flowered for him. Then he thrust inside her. He was past the obstruction before he realized it was there. Shock stopped him where he was.

Bay's dazed, pain-filled eyes opened, and she met Long Quiet's look of confusion.

"You were untouched," he said.

"Of course." Bay didn't understand his anger. What had she done? What was wrong?

"The child," he rasped. "Who does the child belong to?"

"She's mine."

Long Quiet's hand grasped her hair and yanked her head back. She arched up into his chest to avoid the pain. "The truth!" he demanded.

"She's mine," Bay persisted.

"Who carried the child? Who bore her?" He yanked her head back until she thought her neck might snap.

"Buffalo Woman, the first wife of Many Horses," she admitted as the pain became unbearable.

The tension eased on her scalp, but his full weight still rested on her chest. "I can't breathe," she said.

He released her hair, and she laid her head back down. He took his weight on his palms, which were placed on either side of her head, but he kept his hips hard against hers. It was then she realized he was still deep inside her, filling her full.

He began to move slowly in and out.

Bay gasped at the intense pleasure. Her eyes locked with Long Quiet's, her mouth open for a protest that didn't come.

His thrusts were powerful, reaching inside her, and the spiraling tension that had abated during his interrogation built again, more swiftly this time. Her eyelids sank closed as her body melted beneath the warmth of the man above her. Her back bowed, her hips thrust upward to meet him, quiver to arrow, sheath to knife, as her body demanded he end the war between them and bring them both peace.

His mouth covered hers to silence the frenzied groans that escaped, as the pleasure became so intense it bordered on pain. Then she was no longer conscious of him at all, only of the need to reach beyond herself for something that eluded her. She twisted her hips against his, ground her breasts against his chest, pulled his lips down to hers and sought out his tongue, sucking it into her mouth.

Suddenly her body shuddered. Her soul shattered. She clung to Long Quiet, only vaguely aware that he was shuddering too, as his body released his seed inside her.

It was long moments before Bay had a coherent thought, and when it came, it was painful. Her body had betrayed the man she'd loved all these years. It had responded to Long Quiet's loving with joyful abandon. And she had no doubt it would do so again . . . and again. Until she would have the child Long Quiet had promised her.

Her heart tucked her first love away in a safe place, where it would not be forgotten . . . or ripped out by the volcanic emotions Long Quiet had elicited from her with his hands and mouth and body. Her heart would always save a small corner for . . .

"Jonas," she whispered, unaware she'd spoken aloud.

Long Quiet was glad of the darkness, because he wouldn't have wanted Bay to see the desolation he felt at the sound of the other man's name. She had given him such great pleasure. Her own pleasure had been great as well. He'd known enough to be sure of that, and he was glad of it. She would forget the other man. Surely when she was heavy with his child, her heart would gentle toward its father.

His hand smoothed the hair from her brow where it curled, damp with sweat. "Go to sleep, Shadow."

A wolf howled in the distance, but the ululating cry spoke more of pain than of loneliness. Bay rose on her elbow and listened to the echoing wail. When she started to rise, Long Quiet pulled her back down into his embrace. "Where do you go?"

"The wolf is suffering. Perhaps he's caught in a trap."

"If so, he will be out of his misery soon enough."

Bay knew what that meant. A wolf made strong medicine. If found in a trap, it would be killed. She couldn't save herself, but perhaps tomorrow she could save the suffering animal. Bay worried whether she would be able to free the beast before it was discovered. As her eyes closed in sleep, it was she who was caught in the snare and Long Quiet who reached out to free her. She snarled at him, teeth bared and hackles raised. But he wasn't afraid. His voice calmed her, and his touch felt good upon her back. Bay arched beneath the taming touch and groaned her pleasure.

Long Quiet's hand caressed the sleeping woman. She was an enigma. He didn't have to understand her, though, to know he loved her. No man had touched her as he had tonight. No man ever would.

He would never give her back to Jonas Harper.

Chapter 11

BAY HAD AWAKENED NOT LONG AFTER LONG QUIET had fallen asleep, then shifted restlessly, unable to shut out the wolf's mournful howl, equally unable to ignore the warmth of her new husband's body beside her. She wasn't sure which of the two had kept her wider awake, but her red-rimmed eyes burned from peering into the darkness all night. She'd tried once to leave Long Quiet's side, but even in his sleep he'd clung to her, his arm draped heavily across her waist and his legs, ticklish with curly black hair, intertwined with hers.

Bay had tried to focus on the wolf's plight because she thought that when dawn came she might be able to do something to ease it. She was less optimistic about escape from the trap in which she found herself. She should have told Long Quiet sooner that she hadn't borne Little Deer. Well, she hadn't actually lied to him, had she? *But you didn't tell him the truth, either.* In light of his response of outraged betrayal, Bay was sorry for that. And worried.

Her heart ached at the thought of leaving the child she'd grown to love in order to follow her husband wherever he chose to take her. And where would that be? She had no idea where he made his home. She tried to imagine a log cabin somewhere in Texas, but couldn't picture it as well as a buffalo-hide tipi somewhere in *Comanchería*. Not that living in either place with Long Quiet would be such a horrible fate.

Last night had been a revelation. She hadn't expected the unbelievable ecstasy. Or the renewed craving for Long Quiet's touch that had surfaced during the night.

Bay groaned softly. What was wrong with her? How could she be thinking of the physical pleasure to be found with Long Quiet when this marriage meant she would lose her child? It was just that she'd pictured many times what it would be like to lie with Jonas Harper on her wedding night, and never had she even come close to describing the past night with Long Quiet. Nor had she known how seductive she would find the idea of making a child with Long Quiet—a child with his curly black hair and her violet eyes.

But as pleasant as she found the thought of Long Quiet's child growing in her belly, it did not allay the fear of losing the beautiful little girl she'd already held in her arms. No matter how far away Long Quiet took her, Bay would always wonder whether Little Deer was safe and happy.

When she remembered what Long Quiet had told her about his plans, it occurred to her that perhaps she could convince him to leave her here until he'd completed his trip into Mexico. She could spend that time giving Little Deer enough love to last her a lifetime.

Bay sighed when she realized there was finally enough light to make out shapes. Soon, dawn would arrive in all its splendor. She had little time left if she hoped to search out the wolf and free it before the rest of the camp awoke, so she tried once more to free herself from her lover's gentle bondage. She rolled a little sideways and his arm slipped away. She tugged her leg and his slid off. Amazingly, astoundingly, he turned over, and she was free.

Bay lay still for a moment, waiting to see if the change in position would wake him, but when his breathing remained steady, she slipped on her buckskin poncho and skirt and edged toward the tipi opening. It seemed to take forever, but at last she was outside.

In a few steps Bay found herself at the entrance to Many Horses' tipi, and for a moment she was tempted to step inside and see how he'd fared through the night. But even that short delay might mean that the hunters would reach the trapped wolf before she did. There was no logical reason for what she was doing, but Bay couldn't shake the feeling that she *must* free the wolf. She felt a kindred spirit with the animal whose mournful cry seemed so nearly to express her own pain at being trapped in a world of loneliness for the past three years.

Sometime in the early hours of the morning, the wolf's howls had ceased. Bay had only her recollection of the general direction of the sound to guide her. However, she also knew where the traps had most likely been set, and that was where she headed. She hurried anxiously through the gray predawn light, unable to escape the feeling of being followed. She glanced over her shoulder but saw nothing.

The stream she followed gurgled a bit, but otherwise, all about her the Earth Mother was silent. She soon found the first of the traps she sought. The metal jaws had clamped the life out of a large jackrabbit. She shuddered at the cruelty of such a death. The metal traps were evidence of how some Comanches had begun to adapt the white man's inventions to their benefit. One of the younger braves, Comes Running, had traded a number of good buffalo robes for three metal traps. He'd been laughed at by his friends for his foolishness, but their laughter had stopped when they'd seen how effectively the *tabeboh* traps worked.

Bay passed the rabbit by with no more than a glance, her walk almost a jog as the sun began to peer over the flat horizon like a lazy eyeball opening on a new day. She was moving so fast she almost stepped into the second trap, which hadn't yet been sprung. She gasped, then gulped back the bile in her throat. Her breath came harder with the pace she'd set for herself.

The feeling of being followed was even stronger now, and she stopped long enough to turn in a full circle. Nothing moved, but the birds had begun to chirp in the low bushes along the stream and a few bees had already begun their day's labors in the ironwood and blue sage blossoms coaxed open by the early morning light.

Knowing there were only three metal traps and that a willow snare wouldn't have held the wolf captive for long, Bay felt certain that if she could only find the third trap, she'd find the wolf.

She almost stepped on the gray mound before she realized what it was. Bay had come from downwind, giving the wolf no warning. The animal lay on its stomach, one bleeding paw caught in the trap's cruel metal jaws. She knew the instant its golden eyes caught sight of her, for the wolf rose up on three legs in a menacing crouch, ears flattened and vicious fangs bared. Its hackles, which stood in silver spikes, increased the already huge appearance of the animal. A low, pulsing rumble began in the wolf's chest.

"Easy there," Bay soothed as she moved closer. "Easy." She hadn't thought how she was going to free the animal, and she realized now there was little chance the wolf was going to allow her close enough to help it. As she closed in, the animal began to back away until it had reached the length of its clanking metal tether. She watched as the wolf jerked on the limb caught in the trap, further tearing the lacerated skin. Bay stopped, sure the wolf would yank its paw off before it let her get any closer. She stepped back a pace or two to give the wolf the distance it needed to be able to release the awful tension on the paw held by the trap.

With her attention focused on the wolf, Bay had forgotten the feeling that she was being watched. It returned now so strongly that she whirled, crouching, and brought up an arm to protect her head from whatever threatened. She huffed out the breath of air she'd been holding when she discerned it was only Comes Running, who owned the traps, and his two best friends.

Bay realized she could hardly confess she'd planned to release the prey from Comes Running's trap. She dropped her chin to her chest to think, but was drawn from her reverie when she heard the three braves arguing among themselves. Unfortunately, they were huddled together and speaking in whispers, so she could only make out snatches of their conversation.

"If it is true . . . let the wolf . . ."

". . . that would prove . . ."

". . . the *puhakut* . . . no time."

". . . let us do it now."

Bay wasn't sure exactly when it occurred to her the three men meant to harm her. They weren't even armed, except for a skinning knife Comes Running carried. But when they lined up three abreast and began to walk toward her, she backed away from the menace in their copper-hued, hawk-like faces.

Behind her the crouching wolf growled again, a rumbling deep in its chest.

Bay stopped in her tracks.

The Comanches kept coming.

Bay glanced over her shoulder at the wolf and saw that the margin of safety between her and its sharp fangs was slight. She tried stepping to the side to escape the wolf's path, but the Comanches spread the distance between them, cutting off her escape. She opened her mouth to warn that Many Horses would take them to task if they dared to harm a hair on her head, only to realize that he no longer stood between her and the superstitious villagers. Yet she still had a protector. Perhaps . . .

"My husband, Long Quiet, will be looking for me soon."

The three young men looked from one to another in some confusion. They whispered among themselves again, and this time, because they were closer, she could hear their conversation.

"Do you think Long Quiet will seek us out to answer for this?"

"How will he know whom to seek? We will act as surprised as the rest of the village when Shadow's fate is known. Besides, *we* will not do anything. The wolf will make an end to her."

"He will never think to look for us."

Bay realized they'd salved whatever fears they had of retribution from Long Quiet. She thought of screaming for help, but realized that even if she did, no one could come in time.

Comes Running stooped and picked up a fair-sized rock. The others followed suit.

"This is crazy," Bay muttered.

Comes Running threw his rock at Bay's foot, and she leaped backward to avoid it. Another rock came from the other direction and hit her on the ankle. When she jerked back from the pain, she was another step closer to the wolf.

Bay let a few of the stones hit her, but they were gradually being thrown harder and higher. It was only a matter of time before one was bound to hit her on the head and knock her unconscious. Inexorably, the pelting forced her backward. Bay's mind raced for a way to escape. The Comanches blocked her route in one direction, and the wolf in the other. Bay cried out as a particularly large stone hit her on the shoulder. Her body wrenched backward, and she turned sideways to provide less of a target.

"Have you forgotten the *puhakut*'s warning?" she demanded. "Have you forgotten Many Horses' curse? I am as I was, though Long Quiet's wife now. He will surely add his revenge to that of Many Horses and you will be doubly cursed for what you do here."

The thought that perhaps Many Horses' curse might yet have some significance held the three men momentarily motionless.

Bay gave a sigh of relief. As she stepped forward, she slipped on one of the stones that had been thrown at her. Bay waved her arms frantically, trying to catch her balance, trying to change the direction of her fall. She toppled like a wounded doe, her head landing inches from the wolf's snarling fangs.

Long Quiet had allowed Bay to escape his embrace because he wasn't sure what he wanted to say to her. After all his careful plans, after all his good intentions, he'd taken her in anger and by force. But she should have told him the truth about the child.

He felt the beginning of a smile. He knew it was absurd, but as shocked as he'd been to find her untouched, it had also pleased him to know no other man had possessed her, not even her beloved Jonas. And now that she was his, love would come. He was willing to be patient. As his grandfather had taught him, a bee that waits for the blossom to open can then sip its nectar.

The sun had fully risen by the time he'd dressed. He set out for Many Horses' tipi, expecting to find Shadow there. As he stepped inside, his nostrils caught the acrid smell of a burning feather. His eyes scanned the occupants of the tipi as he looked for his wife. Cries at Night sat next to the tipi entrance, needlework in hand, her arthritic fingers slowly setting beads on a buckskin shirt. Little Deer slept on a nearby pallet. She Touches First knelt beside an unconscious Many Horses, her hands clenched helplessly in her lap. The *puhakut* sat cross-legged beside the fire, where a kettle had been filled with water and was near to boiling. The *puhakut* threw a handful of herbs into the pot while he chanted a guttural incantation.

Long Quiet's eyes came to rest on She Touches First's face, which was taut with anguish, then shifted back to the *puhakut.* "*Hihites,*" he said in greeting. "How fares Many Horses?"

"He lives," the *puhakut* replied. "The wound is bad, but he is a strong man and my buffalo medicine is also strong. It would be best, though, if Shadow were to leave this village."

"She will be staying here for a while yet."

"It is not safe for her here," the *puhakut* said.

"What do you mean? Has someone threatened her? Where is she?" Long Quiet demanded.

"She has not come here this morning," the *puhakut* replied. "But it would be wise for you to watch Shadow closely lest some harm befall her."

"It would be even wiser for you to advise those who would harm Shadow that they will have to deal with me," Long Quiet retorted.

In an attempt to forestall a confrontation between the two men, Cries at Night said, "Perhaps she has gone to fetch some wood for your fire or water to wash with."

But she was too late.

"Do you threaten the *puhakut?*" He Decides It said.

"I do not threaten. And I will not offer another warning." Long Quiet pivoted and ducked outside.

Where was Shadow? He calmed his nerves by thinking that Cries at Night was probably right—Shadow had simply gone to fetch more water or wood. But Long Quiet couldn't rest until he knew for sure.

Bay opened her eyes to a sky that was a cloudless blue. It took her a moment to remember what had happened. She realized she must have been knocked unconscious by her fall. She could feel the wolf's panting breath in her hair.

"Shadow, don't move. Don't talk."

Bay heard Long Quiet's soft command and automatically started to rise.

"Don't move," he said quietly but urgently.

The three Comanches stood behind Long Quiet, who tried to take another step closer to her. The wolf bristled and bared its fangs.

Bay shivered and closed her eyes. What was the animal waiting for? Then she felt the wolf's cold nose against her skin.

"Oh, my." Bay lifted her head to look more closely at the wolf.

"Be still," Long Quiet warned tersely. "While I try—"

"The wolf won't harm me," Bay said.

While the four men watched in awe, Bay slowly sat up, put her arms around the wolf's neck, and hugged it. The animal merely whined as its rough tongue licked her face.

"It's Ruffian," Bay explained to Long Quiet. "That means Rascal is around here somewhere." Ruffian barked, and another wolf miraculously appeared.

The looks on the faces of Comes Running and his friends now bespoke terror as Bay was flanked by the two wolves. They quickly backed away from Long Quiet and were gone from the place within moments.

Long Quiet watched as Bay tried to release the heavy metal jaws of the trap holding Ruffian's paw. "You'll have to help me," she said at last.

"Will the wolves let me come near you?"

"I think so. I'll hold them while you try." Bay grasped a handful of fur on the neck of each wolf as Long Quiet moved toward her a slow step at a time.

"It's all right Rascal, Ruffian," she cooed. "He's a friend. He only wants to help."

The wolves growled, but their hackles stayed down, their ears slanted forward, and their fangs remained covered.

Long Quiet knelt beside the trap and released the wolf's paw, then stood and stepped back a pace or two, until the steady rumbling in the wolves' chests ceased.

"His paw is pretty torn up," Bay said, assessing the damage. "But I don't think he'd leave a bandage on it, and he'll be able to manage on three legs while it mends." Bay gave each of the wolves one more hug before she stood. "You'd better get out of here, fellows, before those Comanches come back." She tried to shoo the wolves away, but they refused to be moved.

"They don't seem to want to leave," Bay said.

"We should go back to the village," Long Quiet urged. "There will be trouble enough when the story of what happened here is told. It wouldn't be a good idea to let anyone else see you with the wolves right now."

"All right," Bay agreed. "Let's go."

They had not gotten very far before Long Quiet said, "I woke up and you were gone. What brought you here?"

Bay shrugged. "I heard the wolf howl in pain last night. I had to help it."

"You realize Comes Running and his friends intended that you should die."

Bay hesitated before replying, "Yes."

"And that this incident with the wolves will frighten the villagers even more, and convince them you have dangerous, powerful medicine."

"Can't I explain that I've known the wolves since they were pups?"

Long Quiet frowned thoughtfully. "I suppose you could try. But if that's the case, why did the wolf snarl at you first and then become tame?"

"I suppose Ruffian didn't recognize me at first. I certainly didn't recognize him."

A beehive of activity had erupted within the village as word of Bay's sorcery spread. The villagers scurried to get out of her way, and she walked unimpeded to Many Horses' tipi. When she and Long Quiet arrived, they slipped inside.

She Touches First looked from Many Horses to Bay and said, "I heard what happened with the wolves."

"And you aren't afraid to speak with me?"

"I care not what happens to me. I only ask that you use your medicine to save Many Horses."

Bay reached out a hand and laid it on the other woman's arm. She Touches First flinched, but didn't draw away. "If my wishes alone were enough, he would be well already. But I have no special powers," she said. "If I did, I would certainly help him."

"But you must—"

"I am sorry."

They heard another commotion in the camp. Long Quiet went to the tipi opening to see what was going on. "I think you better see this," he said to Bay.

"What is it?" she asked.

"Your wolves. They've come to keep you company."

Bay stepped outside and was thunderstruck by the sight of the two wolves sitting patiently outside the tipi.

Little Deer raced out of the tipi, her face a wreath of smiles as she shouted, "*Hu! Pia!* Is this my pet wolf?"

The wolves' hackles were high and they had crouched to spring.

"No, Little Deer. Stay back!" Bay shouted. As the whole village watched in amazement, she stepped between the child and the two ferocious animals. Long Quiet caught the child by the shoulders and held her back as Bay turned to face the beasts. Bay reached out a hand to the closest one, Ruffian, and he immediately rose and moved his head up under her hand to be patted. Rascal quickly did the same, both wolves wagging their tails in delight, clearly no more dangerous now than two tame puppies.

When Bay turned with a triumphant smile, Long Quiet's face was a thunderous cloud of agitation. He jerked his head to tell her to look behind her and she turned slowly to see what had upset him. What had merely been amazement on the faces of the gathered villagers had now become frightened awe. Whatever hope she'd had of convincing these

Comanches that she possessed no special powers was gone now forever.

Over the next few days, Shadow took the blame for sprung snares, sick babies, and tame ponies that bucked off their riders. It didn't seem to matter that such events were all normal occurrences in the day-to-day life of the village. Suddenly every such event had special significance.

To make things even worse, the two wolves had disappeared that evening, only to show up the next day. No one went unarmed to fetch water from the stream. Young boys no longer took old pieces of hide and hid under them to play *na-nip'ka*—"Guess over the hill"—because it took them too far from their grandmothers' watchful eyes. For the first time in memory, Bay was glad for the superstitious nature of the Comanches, because although there was talk of killing the wolves, no one dared.

Bay heard Long Quiet suggest to the men with whom he gambled away the early evening hours that the wolves had been sent to protect her from those who might wish to harm her. She was appalled at the tale but did not chide him, because although she could never catch anyone at it, Bay often felt as though she were being followed. She thought about confiding her suspicions to Long Quiet but decided against it. They would be leaving soon. At least, she thought they would.

There was another person equally concerned about when Shadow and Long Quiet would leave the village. The *puhakut* had been besieged by complaints from the villagers, demanding that he do something to rid the camp of the evil aura that surrounded it. And so, three days after the appearance of the wolves, the *puhakut* approached Long Quiet and asked, "Do you plan to stay among us long?"

"Is there some reason I am not welcome here?" Long Quiet challenged.

"None of which I am aware," the *puhakut* replied in a voice that, to his chagrin, trembled slightly. The *puhakut* shivered at the cold menace that had come to Long Quiet's eyes, the hardness in his voice, the tensing of steely muscles. Only the knowledge that the rest of the tribe watched their confrontation made him speak again. "But Shadow . . ."

Seeing the jerk of Long Quiet's muscles, the *puhakut* almost didn't finish his sentence. It was unnerving to think that this intruder could make him feel so uneasy. He chided himself for his fear. His medicine was very powerful. It had been enough to put Many Horses in his place. He would do the same with this pretentious warrior.

"But . . ." Long Quiet asked, his tone chilling.

"You must know there has been talk of Shadow."

"What talk?"

The *puhakut* took a deep breath. "That Shadow's medicine causes misfortune in the village."

"Who says such things?"

He Decides It hadn't expected to be confronted directly. He countered by asking, "Can you deny there have been a number of strange happenings in the village lately?"

Long Quiet snorted. "A burned finger? A lame horse? A sick child? How are these strange?"

The *puhakut* frowned. "Each by itself is not so unusual," he agreed, "but there have been too many such incidents to be easily explained."

"And you think Shadow's presence here is the reason for these . . . happenings?"

He Decides It had not gotten where he was without learning diplomacy. "I cannot say for sure," he hedged. "I do know the people fear what they do not understand. It would be better if Shadow left this place."

Long Quiet was frustrated and disappointed. He'd hoped to be able to leave Shadow in the village while he attended to his business for Creed, but it was beginning to look like that would be impossible. He tried once more to make his point with the *puhakut*. "Shadow is no sorceress."

The *puhakut* shrugged dismissively. "Perhaps not. But

look what happened to Many Horses. He has never been a careless man. How do you explain what happened to him? I cannot, except to say that he was warned to send Shadow from this place and did not heed that warning. Can you blame the villagers for their alarm when other unexplained accidents occur? Fear is a powerful enemy to reason. If Many Horses dies, I cannot say what will happen. There is great danger for Shadow so long as she stays among us."

Long Quiet was even more blunt than the *puhakut* had been. "I will kill any who threaten her."

In that moment, He Decides It knew real fear for the first time in his life. He had no doubt Long Quiet meant what he said. But that didn't change what would assuredly happen if the rumors continued and Shadow stayed in the village. His voice was soft as he explained what Long Quiet refused to acknowledge. "You must know she will not be threatened directly. One possessing such awesome power could do great harm if confronted face to face."

"What are you saying?"

"That none will think it wrong to end Shadow's life through stealth."

Long Quiet tasted copper in his mouth and tried to swallow it back down again. If he left Shadow in the village, sooner or later someone would come after her in the dark and she would be killed. He had no choice. He would have to take her away from here.

But where would be the safest place for his wife? Should he leave her in his *Penateka* Comanche village while he went to Mexico? What if rumors of Bay's sorcery made their way from the *Quohadis* to his *Penateka* village? Would his grandfather be able to protect her?

Or should he take Bayleigh Falkirk Stewart home to Three Oaks? And if he took her home to Three Oaks, would she willingly rejoin him in *Comanchería?*

The closer evening came, the more restless Long Quiet

became. He would have to make a choice soon. He had barely enough time to make the journey to meet Creed in Laredo.

He was on his way back from his second needless trip to check on the chestnut stallion when he was halted by a raspy voice from the shadows.

"Do not turn around. I came to warn you. Watch carefully tonight or Shadow will not live to see the morning."

Chapter 12

BAY NOTICED LONG QUIET WAS EVEN MORE RESTLESS this evening than usual. After she'd settled Little Deer on her pallet, she came to sit by the fire at the center of the tipi. She admired her new husband's grace as he paced the edges of the tipi. What was it about him that attracted her like a warm fire on a cold night? Bay picked up a pair of buckskin leggings she was making for Long Quiet and sewed steadily along the seam while she tried to think it out.

She was chagrined to admit that whenever she thought of him, her body responded as though he were actually touching her. And when he touched her, she had no willpower to resist him. Last night she'd melted in his arms the instant his flesh had touched hers. She'd lost all sense of caring whether what she was doing was right or wrong. She'd only wanted to feel his skin warm and slick against her own, to feel his tongue possessing her mouth and the corresponding thrust of his manroot deep inside her.

But it wasn't only the tumultuous lovemaking that had held her captive in his arms. It was the talk afterward. Not immediately afterward, of course. It had taken time for them to recover from the ecstasy of that moment when he planted his seed within her. For a while they'd merely lain quiescent, letting the shudders slowly ease the tension from their bodies, letting their minds descend from plateaus that could only be reached by two souls journeying together.

Eventually, he'd turned her in his arms and she'd nestled against him comfortably. Then they'd shared their thoughts as completely as they'd shared their bodies. At first they'd spoken of inconsequential things. Later they'd told stories of their childhoods. And finally they'd shared their hopes and dreams.

Long Quiet's words shook Bay from her dreamy remembrance of the past evening. "What did you say?"

"I said it's time for us to leave here."

"And go where?" she replied.

"To the village of my people."

Bay sighed. "Will they be any more accepting of me than the people of this village?"

"Of course they'll accept you. You're my wife."

"And none will resent my presence? Or despise me because I am a *tabeboh*, a hated White-eyes?" Bay could see her argument held some sway, because Long Quiet's brow furrowed. She knew he couldn't deny there would be some in his tribe, like Long Quiet's grandfather, who'd hate her simply because her skin was white. There had been too much enimity between their two peoples for the situation to be otherwise.

"At least none will wish to kill you," he said at last.

"Are you sure?"

Long Quiet wasn't sure, and it made him angry with her for making him confront the issue. He wondered whether there was any place in *Comanchería* where Shadow was really safe now that she'd been named a sorceress by the *Quohadi*. He knew it was his fear of losing her that kept him from suggesting she return to Three Oaks. But might he not also lose her if she stayed in *Comanchería*?

"We will leave soon to go to the village of my grandfather. Because you are my wife, he will not refuse to keep you safe." He paused and added, "Unless you would rather go home."

Bay's eyes were bleak when she raised them to his. She did not anticipate the warm welcome Long Quiet obviously expected her to receive in his village. Perhaps it would be better to go home after all. "Would you come with me if I went back to Three Oaks?"

"I have to go to Mexico."

"And after that? Would you come and live with me at Three Oaks as my husband?"

"I am Comanche. I will return to my village."

Bay's shoulders sagged. He seemed indifferent about which choice she made, even though one meant spending the rest of her life with him and the other meant leaving him forever. Did he care so little? "Do you want me to go to Three Oaks?"

Long Quiet wondered how she could ask such a question after what had passed between them the previous night. "No."

Bay carefully set her sewing aside. "Then why did you offer it as a choice?"

He met her gaze and held it. "Because I don't wish any harm to come to you."

"Because I belong to you?"

"Because you're my wife . . . and I love you."

Bay was overwhelmed by Long Quiet's admission. She hadn't even known she'd wanted him to say the words until he said them. But the simple phrase he'd spoken unlocked the chains around her heart. While she couldn't yet speak of what she felt inside for her Comanche husband, she reached out her arms to him.

Long Quiet dropped to his knees before her and his arms circled her, pulling her forward and crushing her to him. He kissed her feverishly, desperately, on her neck and throat and face, until he finally found her mouth and took it with the full force of his need.

There was nothing gentle about the way his tongue

claimed her mouth, nothing gentle about the way she returned his demanding caresses. His mouth left hers and
searched for the soft skin of her neck. He kissed. He sucked.
He bit her and sucked again.

Bay quivered at the alternation of arousing pain and exquisite pleasure. At her insensible, guttural groan he laid her
flat, his body mantling hers, his loins searching for her welcoming cradle and finding it. The hard length of his manhood
pulsed against her, and he pumped once before he stopped
and groaned. His hands grasped her hips and arched her upward. But it was not enough, not close enough, and in the
next moment her skirt was bunched above her waist and he
was inside her.

He stopped abruptly and looked at her. Bay saw the shock
in his eyes, as though he couldn't believe what he'd just done.
But she also saw the need and the desire, both of which
matched her own. Her hands clasped his firm, tight buttocks,
and she arched her hips upward, pulling him deeper inside,
holding him captive. His eyes closed and slowly opened
again. What had been banked coals was now raging fire.

She slid her hands up the length of his body, finding taut,
corded muscle, until she reached his shoulders. She urged
him down, down to her. His mouth sought hers, his tongue
searching out the soft skin behind her upper lip, then pressing
beyond her teeth and skimming her mouth, filling her, as his
manroot filled her body.

She sought to give as much as she received, but he held
her enthralled with his mouth and tongue. At last his mouth
sought the skin at her throat once more. She searched for
some part of him to kiss to show her love and found only his
chin. She nipped at it, kissed and sucked at it, and then
nipped it again.

Bay gasped as Long Quiet's mouth left her throat for the
pulse behind her ear, then dropped to her collarbone, then the
center of her throat, before setting off on a journey to realms
of delight. When buckskin barred his way, he yanked it off

her shoulders so that her breasts were free but her arms were bound. She moaned as he withdrew his body from her entirely. She throbbed with need. She ached.

"Why are you stopping?" she asked.

"I don't want it to end," he rasped. "I want to please you for more than just a moment. I want it to last forever."

When she would have said something, he closed her mouth with his, while his hand touched her nether lips, teasing, searching. She bucked against his restraint, but he used his strength to hold her still.

"What are you doing to me?"

"Giving you pleasure," he murmured. "As much as you can stand."

She groaned in answer as his thumb found what it sought. He dragged his tongue from the base of her throat to the tip of one breast and licked her there . . . like a cat tasting cream, and sucked . . . like a babe drinking mother's milk, and bit . . . like a hungry man.

She wanted to touch him. She wanted to share with him.

Suddenly his fingers slipped inside her, moving in a rhythm that had her thrusting against his hand in counterpoint. She fought the binding buckskin, panting, moaning, unable to speak but begging him with her body to give her release.

He murmured love words in her ear, urging her to take his gift, urging her to fly with him, and then his hand was gone and he was inside her again and they were one.

His moist breath rasped in her ear and his groans matched hers in aching need. She could feel him tensing even as her own body arched taut as a bowstring and began to spasm. Agonized sounds wrenched from her throat and she clasped him with her legs to hold him inside her, refusing to let him go.

He grunted and drove his loins against her, trying to get even closer, giving her the gift of pleasure he'd promised. He clamped his mouth on hers, muffling the cry that broke from both of them when he came.

It was a while before he eased himself away to lie beside her. He pulled her int his arms and, totally enervated, she allowed him to mold their bodies together.

"Sleep, Shadow," he whispered. "Tomorrow we begin our new life together."

Long Quiet smiled when he realized she was already asleep. He tried to stop his eyes from drifting closed, knowing there was some reason he had to stay awake. But nature's command was stronger than his will, and moments later he followed Bay into sleep.

The quiet ripping sound nudged at Long Quiet's consciousness. His eyes opened slowly, but he instantly became aware that something was wrong. He held himself still, waiting. The strange ripping sound began again. Long Quiet searched the edges of the tipi until he saw the sawing knife point glinting in the dim firelight. Whoever was cutting his way into the tipi had already created a sizable slit in the buffalo-hide wall.

Long Quiet eased himself from Bay's embrace and moved stealthily toward the tipi opening. Before he'd crawled more than a foot, his hand came down on another body. Instinctively, he clutched at what he'd found and woke the sleeping child who'd crawled close to sleep at the foot of their pallet. Little Deer let out a wail that woke Bay.

Long Quiet saw the knife point disappear, and he bounded for the tipi opening. "Take care of her," he snapped at a completely disoriented Bay as he headed outside.

Long Quiet ran quickly around the tipi but found nothing. Whoever had been there was gone now. He vented his frustration with a round of curses in English, none of which made him feel any better. He shouldn't have gone to sleep. What was he thinking to make love to Shadow. He pursed his lips ruefully. The plain fact was he didn't do much thinking around Shadow. She swamped his senses so he could only feel.

His heart pounded with the remnants of fear. He'd only

half believed the warning he'd received tonight, but here was proof that someone had deadly plans for Shadow. It was a good thing they were leaving in the morning. He wouldn't be caught unawares a second time.

When Long Quiet reentered the tipi, Bay had already quieted Little Deer and returned her to her own pallet.

"What happened?" she asked.

"Someone decided to come visiting." Long Quiet walked over to the slash in the tipi and slipped his hand through it.

"Oh, my."

"Why don't you go back to sleep now. I'll keep watch," he said.

Bay shivered involuntarily. "I don't think I could sleep now. Can I sit up with you?"

"You'll be too tired to travel tomorrow if you don't get some rest."

"I'm scared."

Long Quiet saw the plea in her eyes, saw how her body quivered with fear, and crossed to sit beside her. He pulled her between his thighs and wrapped his arms around her. His body was rigid with anger at whoever had been responsible for frightening her like this. "We'll both be exhausted tomorrow," he said.

Bay leaned back into his solid strength. "It's hard to believe someone wants to kill me."

"You're safe now. Tomorrow we'll be gone."

Bay shivered again but said nothing.

It was a long night for both of them. Bay managed to drowse but was immediately caught up in a terrifying dream. She was being chased by a hulking figure, and no matter how fast she ran, she couldn't escape. She could see Long Quiet in the distance, and somehow she knew if she could only reach him, she'd be safe. Just as she stretched out a hand to him, she tripped and fell. When something grabbed her ankle, she awoke with a scream, struggling violently against whatever held her prisoner.

Little Deer's yelp brought Bay fully awake, and she realized that what she'd felt on her ankle was Little Deer's waking hand and that it was Long Quiet who was trying to keep her hands from lashing out at the two of them.

"Shadow, stop. Wake up!"

Bay slumped in Long Quiet's arms. He released her and she turned and burrowed into his embrace as tears of frustration and fatigue gathered in her eyes. "I was having an awful dream—"

"You're safe now."

"—I was being chased and I knew if I could only get to you—"

"It's all right, Shadow."

Bay felt a small hand patting her back and then heard Little Deer say, "Don't worry, *Pia*. Long Quiet will keep you safe from *Piamempits*."

Bay choked on a laugh. If only it were the fierce mythological creature that she feared! She straightened in Long Quiet's arms, trying to come to grips with her fear. She wiped away the tears before Little Deer could see them, and then, when she realized this was her last morning with the little girl, her eyes blurred again.

"Come here, Little Deer," Bay said. She took the child in her lap, and Long Quiet's arms opened so he held both of them. "Today I will be going on a journey with Long Quiet."

"Can I come too?" Little Deer asked.

"You wouldn't want to leave your *kaku* all alone, would you? Cries at Night could not manage without your help. And your *ap'* would have no pretty daughter to make him laugh. No. You must stay here." Bay chucked Little Deer under the chin, and the girl made a dissatisfied face back at her.

"When will you be coming back?"

Bay's lips trembled, and she opened her mouth to answer, but no words came out.

At last, Long Quiet answered for her, "She is going to come live with me in my village."

Little Deer's face contorted in a frown of disbelief. "*Pia?*"

Bay's throat was swollen closed with the pain of leaving the little girl behind. "You will always be with me here," she said, thumping her fist against her heart, "as I will always be with you inside, here." She placed her open palm against Little Deer's heart.

Bay saw Little Deer was not impressed with her reasoning. The child threw her arms around Bay's neck, clutching her tight. "Do not go away, *Pia*. I promise to stay on my own pallet. I will be a good girl and not make you angry with me. I promise!"

Bay choked back the hysterical sob that threatened to erupt. "Oh, Little Deer, I'm not going away because I'm angry with you or because you didn't sleep on your pallet."

"Then why are you going away?"

"I have to go!"

"But why?"

How could she explain to Little Deer that the villagers believed she was a sorceress? The child would never understand. Bay turned frantic eyes to Long Quiet.

"Your *pia* is coming with me," Long Quiet said, "to be my *paraibo.*"

"Oh." Little Deer knew enough about a woman's role to understand that this was a very important position. "Someday I will be *paraibo* to a great warrior," she said.

"Yes," Long Quiet replied solemnly. "You will make a good first wife."

Once again the praise from Long Quiet mollified Little Deer, who now asked Bay, "Will you come to visit me sometime?"

Bay pulled the child into her arms again and hugged her tight. "Perhaps when you are older you can come visit me," she suggested.

That idea obviously appealed to Little Deer, who took Bay's face between her hands and said excitedly, "Could I, *Pia?*"

Long Quiet's suggestion that Bay prepare something for them to eat provided a further distraction to Little Deer, so the painful confrontation between mother and child came to an end. After they had a quick breakfast of plums and mush, Cries at Night came to get Little Deer. By the time Bay had finished straightening the tipi and stepped outside, Little Deer had joined her friends in a game of grizzly bear, in which the children tried to steal sugar (sand) from a grizzly and, if caught, were eaten (tickled) by the bear.

Bay memorized that picture of the laughing child, preserving the vision for the days to come.

Long Quiet had stepped outside the tipi after her and could see in her eyes her love for the child and her pain at leaving. He wondered if things would have been any different if he'd never come here. He shrugged his shoulders. He had come. Things had happened as they had happened. There was no help for what must be done. He offered the only solace he could. "She has a grandmother and a father who both care for her. She'll be fine."

"But will I?" Bay snapped in reply.

"Come," he said brusquely. "We must say our farewell to Many Horses. The sun is high."

Bay's mood had been so dark she hadn't noticed, but now that Long Quiet had pointed it out, she saw the cloudless blue sky from which the sun glared high and hot.

She followed Long Quiet to Many Horses' tipi, where they found not only She Touches First but He Decides It. Long Quiet greeted the *puhakut* and said, "My wife and I have come to say farewell to my brother, Many Horses."

He Decides It gestured to the unconscious man. "Perhaps if you speak the words, his heart will hear what you have to say."

"Will he live to hunt the buffalo again?" Long Quiet asked.

"He has lived longer than I thought he would. It may be

that Shadow will take with her the cloud that hides his spirit
and he will return to us."

Bay blanched at the *puhakut's* suggestion that she was responsible for Many Horses' failure to recover. She had never
loved Many Horses, but he'd been kind to her when she'd expected cruelty. He hadn't objected when Cries at Night had
offered her Little Deer to love. And for three long years he'd
kept her safe from harm, even risking his life to divert the
buffalo that had chased her during the hunt. For all those reasons and more, she was grateful to him.

"Please leave us for a while," Long Quiet said to the
puhakut.

He Decides It nodded to his sister, who rose from her
place beside Many Horses. When it seemed She Touches
First might speak, the *puhakut* shook his head. She lowered
her chin to her chest and stepped outside after him.

Bay followed Long Quiet the few steps to the pallet where
Many Horses lay. When Long Quiet sat cross-legged beside
his friend, she sat also. Long Quiet took the unconscious
man's hand in his and held it as he spoke. "I am leaving now
and taking Shadow with me. It is no longer safe for her here.
Yet I have much to thank you for, *haints.* For three years I
sought the woman you kept safe in this village. Now she is
my wife. I am sorry you cannot look into my eyes to share my
happiness."

Long Quiet felt the hand he held squeeze his fingers. His
eyes flashed from his lap to Many Horses' face in time to see
his friend's eyelashes flicker.

Bay gasped as Many Horses' eyes slowly opened and he
stared at Long Quiet.

"Come closer, *haints,*" Many Horses rasped in a voice
rough from disuse.

Long Quiet leaned closer.

Many Horses smiled. "So you have found a good wife, eh,
haints?"

Long Quiet smiled back. "Yes, a very good wife."

Bay blushed and bit her lower lip to keep silent.

"I think I shall take a wife also," Many Horses said.

"Oh?"

"Yes. But I will have to wait awhile, until I have stolen enough ponies to offer to her brother."

Long Quiet grinned and said, "That shouldn't take a clever thief like you very long at all."

"No," Many Horses agreed. "It shouldn't take long at all."

"And I will make a gift of a chestnut stallion to begin your herd," Long Quiet said.

Many Horses smiled. "I accept your generous gift. I wish you well, *haints*, and your wife also."

"You may wish her well yourself," Long Quiet said.

Bay lifted her eyes to Many Horses' face: They were bright with excitement and filled with admiration. "I shall never forget you," she said.

"Nor I you," he replied. "I will always remember your eyes, the deep violet of a stormy night; your hair, the red of a young fox's fur; your cheeks, pink as primroses blanketing the earth; your face—"

"—shining like the moon in the sky," Bay finished. Tears gathered in the corners of her eyes and fell unheeded down her cheeks.

Long Quiet returned the weakened grasp of Many Horses' hand and said, "We will meet again, *haints*. Do not doubt it."

"Until then," Many Horses said, "may you count many coups, may you steal many fine ponies, and may the Great Spirit fill your wife's belly with a son."

The sound of a much-loved voice had brought She Touches First to the tipi opening. When she saw that Many Horses was awake, she slipped inside and sat at the edge of the tipi, her eyes filled with the sight of him. Long Quiet walked past her and out of the tipi, but as Bay started to follow, She Touches First reached out a hand to stop her.

"Wait."

Bay stopped, startled.

"I am sorry for the way I treated you," She Touches First murmured. "And I thank you for giving back the life of Many Horses."

"I did not do anything."

"Do not deny your power. It is not necessary. I will not seek to do you harm because of it. But you must leave this place. I have already warned Long Quiet of the danger if you stay longer. Now, go. Go!"

Bay was bewildered by the words of the *puhakut*'s sister. She'd already warned Long Quiet? Warned him of what? Why hadn't he said anything to her? She left the tipi in a rush, anxious to question Long Quiet.

But Long Quiet was busy preparing the packs on their horses, and they'd left the village far behind before Bay had a chance to ask questions that by then hardly seemed important—since they'd left the supposed danger behind them.

"How does it feel?" Long Quiet asked when they could no longer see the vultures that circled the village searching for offal, or hear the sounds of the children at play.

"What?" Bay asked distractedly.

"To be leaving the place you've called home for the past three years," he explained. "How does it feel?"

"Frightening. Exhilarating. Sad. Wonderful."

"All that?"

"And more," she said.

"I'll try to make you happy," he said.

She didn't answer, simply turned to look back over her shoulder at what she'd left behind.

If she'd looked a little sooner, she might have seen a pair of dark eyes narrowed in spite, malevolent with hate, gleeful with satisfaction. After the thwarted attempt to take Shadow's life last night, Red Wing had decided upon another plan. She had been afraid She Touches First would warn Shadow, but apparently she had not. Red Wing smiled a nearly toothless grin at her cleverness. She had sent the source of Shadow's death with her on this journey, for there was an even greater evil packed within the evil one's *parfleche*. It would not be long now before the deaths of her son and the son of Singing Woman, both of which she was certain had been caused by Shadow's sorcery, were avenged.

Chapter 13

BAY AND LONG QUIET RODE UNTIL DUSK AND CAMPED not far from a small water hole. Bay was exhausted and sore. Her shoulders ached, her thighs were scraped raw, and her buttocks were tender. Her legs could hardly support her when she slid off her pony. She hid her weakness from Long Quiet, not wishing to prove herself a disappointment to him so soon after becoming a Comanche wife.

"I'll get some firewood," she offered.

Long Quiet saw her hobbling away and realized she'd be hard pressed to do the bending and stooping such a chore would require. "I'll do it while you unpack the ponies," he said.

Bay's eyes widened when he reversed their jobs. But he was gone before she could thank him. She loosened the packs on the ponies and put them on the ground. Long Quiet had shot and gutted two rabbits for dinner, but she had to skin them. She wrinkled her nose. She knew how to skin a rabbit, but that didn't mean she liked doing it.

She didn't bother to empty the contents of her *parfleche*, simply reached inside for her knife. The skinning went quickly, and Bay had time to dig a pit and arrange a circle of stones before Long Quiet returned with enough mesquite to last all evening. While the rabbit roasted on a stick over the fire, Bay arranged a pallet for them to sleep on. She eyed the *parfleche* she'd set near the fire, knowing it contained the winter leggings she was making for Long Quiet. She'd thought when she packed them that she'd sew on them in the evenings during the trip. She smiled ruefully. She was too tired to do anything more tonight than stretch out on the pallet and sleep.

When the rabbit was ready, they divided it between them. When they'd finished, they settled down on the pallet, close but not touching.

"How long before we get where we're going?" Bay asked.

"Tired of traveling so soon?"

Bay cautiously turned over, groaning when her muscles protested. "Just wondering," she gritted out.

Long Quiet reached out a hand to massage her shoulder. "I pushed a little harder today, knowing you'd be sore tomorrow. It's not much farther."

Bay had tensed at Long Quiet's first touch, but the strength of his fingers did too good a job soothing her aching muscles for her to think about objecting. She edged a little closer to Long Quiet to make his job easier, and when he nudged her with his palm, she readily flattened onto her stomach. He sat up beside her so he could use both hands to ease the soreness from her shoulders.

"You never told me why you're going to Mexico," Bay said.

Long Quiet's hands paused for a moment, then resumed as he explained, "Last year about this time, the Mexicans finally did what they've been threatening to do since Texas declared her independence seven years ago. They invaded Texas and captured San Antonio with an army of several thousand men."

Bay froze. "Why didn't you say something about this before?"

"Because General Woll and his army only stayed in San Antonio nine days. It was apparently just an expedition to see if Mexico could successfully invade Texas."

"And it succeeded!" The force of Long Quiet's hands on her back kept Bay from rising to confront him. "Texans all over the Republic must have been terrified."

"More angry than afraid, it seems. They put together an army of their own to retaliate against the Mexicans. The Texas army had orders from President Houston to invade Mexico and confront General Woll's army—if it looked like they could win.

"General Somervell led the Texas army south down the Laredo road, right through a post-oak bog. Between the animals sinking in quicksand up to their bellies and the men being drenched through with mud, they were in a pretty mean mood by the time they reached the Mexican border.

"Unfortunately, Woll's Mexican army was long gone and the Texans captured Laredo without getting a chance to fight off some of their aggravation."

Long Quiet's hands had moved down from Bay's shoulders to the middle of her back, and as he talked, his fingertips just skimmed the edges of her breasts. His touch seemed accidental, but Bay still felt a sense of languorous delight. "What happened then?" she murmured.

Long Quiet's hands tightened for a moment on Bay's back before he said, "That's when things started going wrong. Half the army decided they'd had enough revenge and headed home. The rest, led by a fellow named William Fisher, set out toward the Mexican town of Mier. Unfortunately for them, another Mexican army, this one led by General Ampudia, heard what was happening and surrounded the town.

"On Christmas Day, the Texans fought the Battle of Mier. Before they finally ran out of ammunition and surrendered, twelve Texans had been killed and twenty-three wounded. But they'd killed six hundred Mexicans and wounded two hundred more. As you can imagine, the Mexicans weren't feeling particularly benevolent toward their captives."

Bay felt tense but wasn't sure whether it was from the serious turn of Long Quiet's story or because his hands had moved down to massage her buttocks. Every once in a while his thumb would land in the crease between her thighs. She quivered with the thought of what would happen if she just turned over.

"You're shivering," Long Quiet said, his voice husky. "Are you cold?"

"No, I'm fine. I just—what happened to the Texans who were captured at Mier?" she said in an attempt to ignore the rapidly increasing sexual tension between them.

"Ah. They escaped, of course."

Bay smiled. "No, really. What happened?"

"They escaped," he said with a smile. His smile was short-lived as he continued. "But they'd been marched deep into Mexico before they fought free. The land around them was nothing but desert and barren mountains. They lacked food, water, and shelter. Almost all of them were recaptured. The Mexicans were furious, humiliated. General Santa Anna ordered that every tenth man who'd participated in the escape be executed."

"Oh, no!" Bay said.

"The Mexicans claimed they were being merciful." Long Quiet's hands, which had been moving steadily, stopped. "They used a lottery to decide who was to die. Seventeen black beans were put into a clay jar with 159 white beans. They forced each prisoner to draw out a bean. The seventeen doomed men were offered a meal and an opportunity to speak with a priest before they were lined up along an adobe wall and shot. Those who survived the lottery were taken deep into Mexico, where they've been ever since."

Bay sat up and faced Long Quiet. His somber expression gave little consolation for her fears. "So why are you going to Mexico?"

"Some of the Mier prisoners are attempting an escape. I'm going to meet them with horses and supplies and lead them back to Texas."

"Why do you have to go?" She hid her fear behind the sharp demand.

He shrugged. "Creed asked me to go. It looked like if I didn't go, he'd leave Cricket and go himself."

Bay could understand why Long Quiet had agreed to help Creed, but it still meant he would be putting himself in danger. Right now she didn't want to think about how much that mattered to her. No longer the least bit sleepy, she got up from the pallet and walked over to where she'd left her *parfleche*. She opened it and reached inside, yanking out the buckskin leggings she'd been making for Long Quiet and leaving the rest of the contents to spill out as they would. She marched back to the fire and sat cross-legged with the leggings in her lap, just staring at them.

"What are you doing?" Long Quiet asked.

"I'm going to finish these leggings."

"They can wait. You need to rest."

"I'm not tired."

"You can hardly move. Put your sewing away. Then come back and lie down beside me."

Bay stared for a moment at the buckskin in her hands before she said, "What if you don't come back?"

"What?"

"What if you don't come back from Mexico? I'll be alone in your village among strangers. What will happen to me?"

Long Quiet came and sat down beside her. He took the buckskin from her hands and pulled her into his embrace. "I think you have too little faith in your husband," he gently chided, but added to allay her fears, "My grandfather will make sure no harm comes to you."

"What if . . . what if someone accuses me again of being a sorceress? It could happen, couldn't it?"

She could hear the irritation in his voice when he answered curtly, "Anything is possible, but I don't think it likely."

"Let me go," she said. "I want to put your leggings away so the morning dew won't get to them."

Reluctantly, he released her. Bay gathered the buckskins and folded them carefully, aware that Long Quiet's eyes never left her. She was just about to stuff them back into her *parfleche* when he said, "Don't move. Don't breathe. Stay right where you are."

Bay looked down. Barely illuminated by the firelight, a small snake lay half inside and half outside her *parfleche*. The head was black, followed by a thin ring of yellow and a thicker ring of red. Then the pattern was repeated. She'd never seen a snake quite like it, but if Long Quiet's actions were any guide, it was dangerous.

She struggled to remain perfectly still as Long Quiet maneuvered closer. It was all over before she could blink. The snake's head had been severed from its body by Long Quiet's knife and she'd been yanked out of danger and enfolded in his arms.

"Shadow, Shadow," he whispered. He was trembling and his mouth found hers urgently, as though to reaffirm that she was alive. He clutched her to him as he tried to calm his shattered nerves.

"The snake was poisonous?" Bay asked breathlessly.

"Deadly," he huffed. "A coral snake."

"Where did it come from? I didn't see it crawling toward my bag, and it was tied closed until a moment ago."

"You didn't see it because it was already in your bag. Someone must have put it there before we left the village."

"But I'd already reached into that bag—twice! Once to get my knife and once for the leggings. Why didn't the snake strike then?"

"You were lucky." He looked down at the snake's severed head. Not even his grandfather could guard her against such surreptitious attacks. "We were both lucky. Maybe I shouldn't push that luck. Maybe it would be better if you went home to Three Oaks after all."

"For a visit, you mean? Until you return from Mexico?"

"No. To stay."

Long Quiet turned away so she wouldn't see the agonized look on his face. He'd searched for this woman for three years, had loved her for more years than that. He'd believed her lost to him forever because she had a Comanche family and then had discovered she wasn't bound to anyone after all. Then the Great Spirit had so turned the course of events that she had become his wife. How could he possibly consider sending her from his side? *How could he not?*

"I wanted to believe that the Comanches' fear of you was foolishness, but there's nothing foolish about this attack on you. It's not the first time someone's tried to kill you, Shadow. And despite my wishful thinking, it won't be the last."

"You don't know that it was someone from the village who put that snake in my bag."

"I can't prove it, no. But I won't take a chance with your life."

"It's my life. I can make that decision for myself," Bay said. "I'll go to your grandfather's village and wait for you."

"I won't take you there."

"Then I'll find it by myself," she challenged.

Long Quiet's nostrils flared in anger even as his eyes glowed in admiration for her courage. She'd already spoken of her fears, yet she'd willingly brave that danger to be with him. His heart swelled with love for her. "Don't you see you have no more choice than I do? To leave you in *Comanchería* is to condemn you to certain death. I can't let you stay here. I'll take you to your father's house."

Bay swallowed over the lump growing in her throat and managed to ask, "But you'll come back for me, won't you?"

You're my wife. Of course I'll come back for you.

But he only thought the words. What he said was, "There's no way we can be together, Shadow. You can't live in my world, and I can't live in yours."

"Can't? Or *won't*," she accused.

"It's the same thing."

"No, it's not. Why can't you live in Texas? What's stopping you?"

"Look at me, Bay. What do you see?"

"I see a man."

"In braids and a breechclout and—"

"You can cut off your braids and wear cotton breeches."

He looked at her as though she'd blasphemed. He ran a hand protectively over one thick black braid. A Comanche's braids were his one vanity. She might as well have been Delilah telling Samson to cut his hair.

"You said you loved me. How can you simply leave me on my father's doorstep and ride away?"

"Do you think this is going to be easy for me?"

"It's obviously easier than staying with me," she retorted. "You're just afraid to try living—"

"Enough! I tried living among the White-eyes," he hissed, "and do you know what I found?"

"What?"

"Hatred for the Comanche, fear of his cruelty, disdain for his intelligence, and pity for his simple gullibility. When I live with you in Texas, shall I ignore these insults to The People? Or shall I seek revenge for them?"

"Neither," she retorted. "Help those who hate to understand."

Long Quiet snorted in disbelief and said in Comanche, "*You do not tell a hungry wolf standing over a carcass that he should not have killed the calf.*" In English he continued, "The white man wants the Indian dead so he can take his land. I don't know if I can stand by quietly and watch that happen."

She frowned, sharing his concern, but asked, "What can you do to stop it?"

He bunched his hands into fists and held one out to her. "I can fight the white man as a Comanche."

"And what will that solve? You'll be dead, and the whites will still take the land." She covered his outstretched fist with her hand. "You can't stop the tides or hold back the horde. You can only live your own life in truth and honor. Can't you do that in Texas as well as in *Comanchería?* I want to be with you. I love you. I'm your wife."

"Not under the white man's laws," he countered. "Once I leave you at your father's door, you'll be free to find someone else . . ." He couldn't add "to love" because the thought of her loving another man was too painful.

She threw herself into his arms and clung to him. "Haven't you heard anything I've said? I love you and I want to be with you." She looked into his gray eyes and saw confusion and uncertainty. "You'll come back for me. I know it. And I'll be waiting when you do."

He pulled her arms from around his neck. "Don't wait for me," he said, furious with her for making him question beliefs he'd embraced for years. "I won't be coming back."

"If you tell me not to wait," she warned, equally furious, "I won't. I won't pine away for you, Long Quiet. I've spent too many years of my life pining away for a man who didn't come back for me when he promised he would. I won't make the same mistake with you that I made with Jonas. I'll carve out a life for myself that includes everything beautiful and good Texas has to offer, and I'll forget about you."

Long Quiet's features hardened at her reference to Jonas Harper. "So be it! Forget about me. As I will forget you." He retrieved his knife and kicked the dead snake away from her *parfleche*. He dumped out the remainder of the contents of the rawhide bag to make sure there were no more unpleasant surprises waiting to be discovered, then refilled it with her things. Bay stood beside him, holding the carefully folded leggings. When he was finished, she handed the leggings to him and he stuffed them inside the bag.

"Come to bed, Shadow. We have a longer journey tomorrow than I expected. You'll need your rest."

He reached out a hand to her, and when she took it, he led her to the pallet they would share. After she'd lain down, he lay beside her. Bay turned away from him, trying desperately to hide her grief. But one sob escaped, and then a second.

Long Quiet reached out a hand to comfort her, but Bay jerked away. "Don't touch me!"

But he remembered the times he'd refused comfort in anger when comfort was what he wanted most. So he ignored her struggles and turned her into his embrace. He held her tight, his fingers brushing through her silky auburn hair as she cried out her pain.

His hands eased the tension at the base of her back, then curved around her buttocks to hold her close. He was only conscious that she felt good nestled snugly against him. The sudden rigid arousal of his body caught him by surprise.

Bay wasn't sure when the need for comfort had become desire, but her arousal fully matched Long Quiet's. She arched her pelvis into Long Quiet's tumescence and heard the responsive groan deep in his throat.

"Love me tonight," she said in a low voice raspy from crying. "Give me a memory to keep me through the long days and nights without you."

Long Quiet kissed the corners of her mouth before his tongue traced the shape of her lips. He teased her, never fully satisfying her need, until Bay reached up and grasped his hair with her hands and brought his lips down to meet hers. They opened their mouths and tasted one another, searching for honeyed treasure. Long Quiet bit her lip and then soothed the hurt with the tip of his tongue. He sucked her lower lip into his mouth and nipped at it with his teeth. Then she did the same to him. They made love with their mouths while their hands roamed each other, touching greedily, with all the love they'd intended for a lifetime needing to be spent in a single night.

Their loving was intense, as moving as their first time together, as violent as their last. His hands sought the wet

warmth of her and she flowered for him. And then he replaced his fingers with his mouth.

Bay bucked in surprise and pleasure. "What . . . I
can't . . ." She gasped with sheer pleasure as he tasted all of
her with his tongue. When she crested on a wave of ecstasy,
he joined their bodies and made two into one. He filled her
full, thrusting deeply, surely, and when he felt her shudder
with fulfillment, he spent his seed inside her with a cry.

He rolled onto his side and pulled her tightly into his
embrace. "You will never forget me," he panted. Spent, exhausted, he could not stay awake to hear her reply.

But Bay said nothing. She lay awake far into the night and
watched her husband sleep. His face was not so harsh now,
although his cheekbones stood out in sharp relief. She
brushed aside a curl at his temple and traced his warm lips
with her fingertip. She laid her head against his heart and let
the steady beat soothe her to sleep. They had said their good-
byes. She had nothing left to hope for now.

Part II

BAYLEIGH

Chapter 14

LONG QUIET WAS GONE. HE'D BROUGHT BAY SAFELY to her father's doorstep, but no farther.

"You must go the rest of the way alone. The less your father knows of our relationship, the better. Do you understand, Shadow?"

"No," Bay cried. "I don't understand. I don't understand any of this!"

Long Quiet had clenched his jaw, biting back the retort Bay could see forming. He'd simply turned his pinto and ridden away.

Bay stood and stared at her father's house. Before her rose a two-story structure surrounded by a double gallery porch. It was painted a dazzling white that was almost blinding in the midday sun. The windows gleamed, reflecting the light like huge cat eyes. Rip had built almost a replica of the house that had burned down the day she'd been captured by Tall Bear three years before.

Bay noted only slight differences. The windows must be a little smaller, because the shutters were more narrow, and the round columns that held up the second-floor porch were more elaborate. The front door was made of sturdy oak and looked heavier than she remembered. But the three live oaks that graciously draped the house with moss-covered limbs and gave Three Oaks its name stood as majestically proud as ever.

She walked up the three steps and across the porch to the front door. She took a deep breath before reaching out and turning the shiny brass doorknob. The door opened and Bay was overwhelmed by the smell of the beeswax that had been used to polish the shiny oak floor in the central hallway. She wondered where everyone was. Then she heard voices from the dining room. Of course—they must be having dinner.

As she turned into the first doorway on the right side of the hall, her moccasin sank into the plush Oriental carpet that covered the parlor floor. She walked farther into the room, touching things as she went. Her hand smoothed over the brocade settee. Her callused fingertips tested the cool marble mantel above the brick fireplace.

She followed her nose to the dining room door. She stayed just out of sight beyond the doorway so she could observe without being seen. Rip sat at the head of a cherrywood table, where he'd always sat, with Sloan to his right and Cricket at the far end of the table. The fourth chair, the seat that had always been hers, was empty. Bay yearned to be sitting there now, yearned to turn back the clock, to make things the way they'd been three years ago.

Bay looked for changes in her family and found them. Her father, a huge bear of a man, sat as arrogantly straight and tall as ever, but deeper wrinkles etched his brow and somber lines framed his eyes and mouth. Gray now threaded through his rich auburn hair, which curled down over his collar. But Rip's eyes had lost none of their vitality.

In Sloan the changes were more subtle. She held her body more rigidly and her chin bore an even more determined thrust than it had three years ago. Her low, sensuous voice held a sharper edge than Bay remembered.

The changes in Cricket were most notable. She radiated happiness in her sparkling eyes and the burble of contained laughter in her voice. When she spoke, the contentiousness that had marked her character before her marriage to Jarrett Creed was missing.

They were eating clove-laced ham with honeyed sweet potatoes and buttered corn and peas. It was Cricket's favorite meal. Rip and Sloan were discussing the cotton crop that had just been harvested and sent down the Brazos River to market in Galveston. Sloan remarked how it had been a poor year but better than the last, and suggested perhaps they ought to put in a few more acres of sugarcane or corn next year. It was all so familiar. And all so very, very strange.

Bay rested her head against the doorjamb, unaware that she'd made herself visible to those in the room.

Cricket saw Bay first and came up out of her chair so fast it shot over backward, landing with a clatter. "Oh, glory!"

Cricket's precipitous action brought Sloan and Rip to their feet with equal speed. Rip grabbed for a gun as he rose, and Bay found herself facing a .44 Colt revolver.

Bay shrank from their intense stares and grasped the doorjamb with both hands to keep herself from running away. Her body trembled as she waited, watching her father's face to see how she would be greeted. She wanted to throw herself in his arms and have him hold her, reassuring her that he loved her and she was welcome home.

But Bay had never touched Rip so freely, and it was wishful thinking to hope he would greet her in such a manner now.

For a few seconds, Rip's face was blank. Bay swallowed hard as she realized Rip didn't believe what his eyes told him he was seeing. Had she changed so much? Wasn't he glad she was home? Hadn't he missed her? She tried to imagine herself as they must see her—in soot-darkened buckskins, her feet covered in moccasins, travel-weary, trail-stained, her hair braided and held in place with bear grease, her skin tanned and her face freckled, her violet eyes wide and dark with fear.

"My God," Sloan breathed. "Is that you, Bay?"

"Yes."

Both Sloan and Cricket remained frozen in place, jaws

agape, eyes wide. Their gazes settled on Rip, ceding to him the privilege of being first to greet his long-lost daughter.

Bay's eyes were on Rip, hadn't left him, in fact, since her discovery by Cricket. She searched his features, and it seemed the two of them carried on an entire conversation with their eyes.

I'm back, Father.

Where have you been? How have you been? What happened to you? How did you get here? Are you all right?

Did you miss me?

Is it really you, Bay? How I've missed you! You've grown. You're a woman now.

I've changed. Can you see I'm different than I was?

I can hardly believe you're alive, and here. Was your life hard? Did it change you much? Yes, I can see you're not the same. Where is my fragile Bay? Where did she go?

I'm here, Father. Please, can't you show me how much you missed me? Can't you hold me and comfort me as you did when I was very small?

I want to hold you as I did when you were a child. But it's been so long, Bay, since I have. I had to make you strong so you could carry on when I'm not here to help anymore. Did I keep myself too much from you? Is it too late to show you how very special you are?

Did you ever love me? Do you love me now?

I could never bear to be close to you; you reminded me so much of your mother. So gentle, so tender of heart that you couldn't bear to see any living thing suffer.

Please, please let me know I'm welcome here.

I know what you want from me, Bay. I'm just not sure I can give it to you.

I love you. I missed you.

It had taken only seconds for them to say with their eyes what was in their hearts. It took a moment longer before Rip said in a voice husky with emotion, "Welcome home, Bay."

He took the few steps necessary to put his hand on her shoulder, as he might do with a son. "Welcome home."

Rip's words released Cricket from the trance in which she'd been held, so just as Rip was reaching for Bay to draw her into his arms, Cricket's engulfing embrace cut them off from one another, and the opportunity to reach across the immense chasm that lay between them was lost.

Sloan had followed Cricket, quickly embracing Bay and then stepping back again, uncomfortable with this overt expression of love, uncommon as it was in this household.

"Goodness!" Cricket said with a laugh as she caught a whiff of Bay's hair. "We need to get you into a tub! But since we have dinner on the table, maybe you'd like to eat first."

Cricket grabbed Bay's hand and tugged her away from Rip and around to her chair at the table. "Sit here, Bay, and I'll fix you a plate of food. What would you like?"

"It all looks good." But Bay's eyes remained on Rip. She wondered if her father would have embraced her if Cricket hadn't interfered.

"Tell us everything," Cricket said as she set a plate piled high with ham and sweet potatoes in front of Bay. "How did you get here? Where did you come from? What was it like?"

Bay stared at the fork in her hand that felt so foreign, looked with confusion at the food she'd once loved, and tried to get comfortable in the straight-backed chair that forced her feet flat on the ground. "I . . . I hardly know where to begin. Why don't you talk while I eat? Why are you here, Cricket, instead of with Creed at Lion's Dare?"

"I'm here so my daughter, Jesse, can be christened at Three Oaks," Cricket announced.

"So you had a daughter," Bay said, smiling with pleasure. "Long Quiet said—"

"Long Quiet? Long Quiet found you? Is that how you got here? Did he bring you? Where is he?"

Cricket didn't leave time for Bay to get a word in edgewise, but Bay was grateful for the respite. Speaking English was a chore. She was glad she'd had the chance to practice with Long Quiet, for she still occasionally had to stop and say a word in her head before it would come out in English.

What should she say to them about her relationship with the half-breed Comanche? What could she say? She couldn't bear to tell them that she'd been married to Long Quiet and he'd abandoned her. It was hard enough for her to accept that he hadn't loved her enough to leave *Comanchería* and live in Texas. How could she hope to explain their relationship to her family?

"You don't have to tell us anything you don't want to," Sloan said.

Bay glanced quickly at Sloan, grateful for her understanding. But she had to say something, and it would be easier if she just got it over with now. So she explained, "Long Quiet found me among the *Quohadi* Comanches. I was owned by a war chief named Many Horses. Long Quiet convinced him to let me come home."

"Where is Long Quiet now?" Rip asked. "I want to thank him."

"He's gone to Laredo. He . . ." Bay couldn't speak over the lump in her throat. Was this going to happen every time she mentioned Long Quiet's name?

Cricket jumped in to fill the silence. "He's meeting Creed in Laredo. He promised to help out the Mier prisoners who are trying to escape from Castle San Carlos in Perote.

"Go on with your story," Cricket urged.

"I . . . I had a child named Little Deer. But I couldn't bring her with me. I . . ."

The stillness of the others brought Bay's speech to a halt. Of course, she realized, they thought the child was hers, and that would mean she'd lain with some Comanche buck. Well, that was the truth, even if they would never know the Comanche she'd lain with was Long Quiet. And she would not deny her relationship to Little Deer.

When she spoke again, she told them everything she

thought they would want to hear about her life among the Comanches and kept from them what she thought they wouldn't understand. She told them how Many Horses had been her protector and how she'd been accused of being a sorceress, which was why Long Quiet had been able to take her so easily from the village.

She didn't tell them she'd married Long Quiet. The pain and humiliation of being left by him was too great. Thus abbreviated, her story did little to satisfy the three curious minds at the table.

"So Long Quiet brought you home after all," Cricket said when Bay had finished. "He always said he'd find you. And he kept his word. I think we should have a party to celebrate your homecoming."

Bay turned pale. "You can't . . . I mean, I don't want anyone to know . . . people will think . . ."

"People will think it's about time you came home from gallivanting around England and the Continent," Rip said.

"What?"

"That's the story we told when you were captured," Sloan explained. "First that you'd gone back to Boston for more schooling, and later, when you still hadn't gotten back, we simply said you'd gone for an extended trip to the Continent with an acquaintance of Rip's who factors our cotton in England. Otherwise, we knew that when you did come home, it would be difficult for you to return. . . ."

Sloan stopped and bit her lip. All it would take to make Bay a social pariah was the knowledge that she'd been captured by Comanches. That fact alone would label her a fallen woman, unfit for the company of the local planters' wives and daughters. For it was a well-known fact that the Comanches raped their women captives. The question was there so clearly in Sloan's eyes that Bay actually answered it.

"I was never raped."

Sloan looked at Bay for the first time with her heart instead of her head. There was a sadness about Bay that made

Sloan wonder whether she hadn't suffered more than she'd admitted. How strange her sister looked. Not like her sister at all, but like . . . like some Comanche woman.

"I don't want to meet anyone," Bay said. "Especially not—"

"Damnation, Bay," Rip interrupted his daughter. "You have nothing to be ashamed of. We're having the christening for Jesse in a couple of weeks, and we'll just use that opportunity to let all the neighbors see you're back home safe and sound and none the worse for wear after spending a few years away . . . on the Continent," Rip finished.

"But I haven't been on the Continent."

"I know one particular young man," Rip said, too caught up in his hopes and plans to realize Bay had contradicted him, "who'll be delighted to know you're back. I've been putting him off for almost six months now, telling him you'd be home any day. He'll make a fine husband for—"

"I don't want a husband," Bay said, rising abruptly. "And I don't want to meet the neighbors or anyone else. I just want . . . I just want to be left alone!"

Three years ago, Bay would have turned and run. Now she just walked away and on up the stairs to the room that had been hers. She closed the door behind her in relief, then turned and realized that nothing in the room was familiar. All the things that had meant anything to her had burned with the house. Everything that tied her to the past was gone. She walked slowly to the window and looked out over the empty cotton fields. She didn't belong here.

She hugged herself with her arms, trying to get a grip on emotions that threatened to fly free. Long Quiet was lost to her. She would have to learn to survive without him. But if there was one thing she'd learned over the past three years, it was how to survive.

She whirled when she heard the knock at the door. Perhaps if she didn't answer, whoever it was would go away. The knock became more insistent. Bay sighed and crossed to the door. "Who's there?"

"It's me and Sloan," Cricket answered. "Let us in."

Bay knew she couldn't keep them out forever, and her sisters were both stubborn enough to stand at the door all afternoon if need be. She opened the door and stepped back. Cricket had come prepared. She carried a handful of clothes, brushes, a comb, and a pair of slippers. Sloan carried a large wooden tub.

"I figured you'd want to bathe off some of that trail dust," Cricket said.

Even as Cricket spoke, Stephen, the Negro servant who managed Rip's household, arrived with the first buckets of hot water. "It's a good thing you finally come home, young lady," Stephen said warmly. "I ain't tole nobody else where you really been gone to all this time, and I ain't gonna tell," he said as he emptied the buckets into the tub. "Wouldn't be right folks holdin' up their noses at you. Ain't your fault what happened. Shore 'nuf ain't."

"Thank you, Stephen," Bay replied. She stood aloof while Cricket made all the preparations for the bath. She was more than ready to exchange a warm tub for cold river water, and soap for the sand she'd used to wash herself during the past three years. Except she knew that when she stripped off her clothes, the scars she'd gotten among the Comanches would be visible, and she didn't feel like explaining anything else today.

If the roles had been reversed, Bay felt sure she would have been sensitive enough to offer Sloan or Cricket some privacy. But neither Sloan nor Cricket offered to leave, and they were trying so hard to do and say the right things that she would have felt callous asking them to leave the room.

When Cricket had finally shooed Stephen out the door for the last time, she turned to Bay and said, "Now, let's get you out of those filthy clothes. What is that smell in your hair, anyway?"

"Bear grease." Bay's voice was muffled because Cricket was busy pulling the poncho up over her head.

"Damn, Bay! Your back is a mess of scars," Sloan said.

"Oh, my God!" Cricket exclaimed. "You've been tortured!"

Bay grabbed the deerskin poncho that Cricket had removed and protectively covered her breasts with it. She backed up against the wall so her sisters wouldn't be able to see the horrible scars. "Surely you didn't think being a Comanche captive was all honey and roses," Bay replied bitterly. "What did you expect?"

Cricket said nothing. The tears in her eyes spoke for her. But Sloan admitted, "Frankly, I expected worse."

Bay snorted derisively. "I could always count on you to be honest."

"You don't seem to have been starved," Sloan continued, eyeing Bay's full figure, "and except for those scars you're hiding and a few more freckles and calluses, you don't seem to have changed much."

"The changes are inside," Bay snapped. "They can't all be seen."

"You're certainly more testy," Sloan observed with a wry smile. "But I guess that's to be expected. Things must seem pretty strange to you right now."

That bit of understatement made Bay burst out in hysterical laughter. Sloan and Cricket looked at each other in confusion, which quickly turned to worry as Bay's laughter became gasping sobs.

Bay quickly found herself surrounded by love, awkwardly offered by two people who hadn't had much practice at demonstrating their feelings. Cricket hugged her tight. Sloan put an arm around her shoulder. Both murmured soothing words of comfort, which were equally awkward for Bay to accept, because receiving comfort wasn't something with which she had much experience, either. For the moment, it was simply enough that she knew she was welcome here.

At last Cricket released Bay and said, "You don't have to take a bath if you don't want to. I only thought—"

"Oh, I do want a bath," Bay interrupted. "But I haven't had one in so long that—"

"We can give you privacy if you'd rather," Sloan offered. "We just didn't think you'd want—"

Cricket interrupted her to suggest, "I could wash your hair for you if you like, Bay, and—"

"I could scrub your back while you tell us all about Your Life Among the Indians," Sloan finished for her, as though she were reading the title to an exciting new novel.

Bay burst out laughing, but this time with happiness. "You two haven't changed a bit," she said. "Getting a word in edgewise when you're around isn't any easier now than it was before I left."

"Then you'll let us help?" Cricket asked.

"Yes, yes, I'll be glad if you stay," Bay said. In fact, it was wonderful to be able to talk and talk and talk. She was sure she wasn't going to get tired of their company anytime soon.

But Bay had overestimated her tolerance for the excitement of having two such inquisitive sisters, after such a long period of being so much alone. Long before the bath was over, Bay was wishing for the privacy she'd so readily abandoned at their pleading. She found that many of the things they wanted to know about were things she'd rather forget. She found herself avoiding direct answers to their questions and telling them about humorous incidents, distracting them from the more unhappy aspects of her life among the Comanches.

"I've got some muslin underdrawers for you," Cricket said as Sloan wrapped Bay in a large towel. "I can't believe you didn't wear anything under your buckskins."

"It really was fine," Bay insisted. Except the first time she'd had to bare herself to Long Quiet, she thought.

"If you say so," Cricket replied skeptically. "Now let me slip this gown over your head, and you'll be ready for bed."

Bay frowned. "Bed? It's the middle of the day."

"But you look exhausted," Sloan said. "Why not take a nap before supper?"

Cricket was already turning down the covers of a maple four-poster with two thick feather mattresses. Bay eyed the mattresses with longing. The bed looked tremendously inviting. "All right," she agreed. "I'll take a nap. But be sure to wake me up for supper."

Bay was already yawning by the time Sloan had adjusted the curtains in the room to shut out the bright sunlight. Bay climbed into the bed, thinking it felt heavenly. So soft. So utterly soft. Like Little Deer's skin. Or a pony's nose. Bay curled into a ball in the center of the bed and hugged herself, effectively shutting out the other two people in the room.

Enough. She'd told them enough. She'd shared enough. She needed to be alone now to give all those jumbled-up, confused feelings a chance to settle down.

"Get some sleep, Bay," Sloan said, resting a hand on her shoulder.

Cricket smoothed back the wispy tendrils of hair that had dried around Bay's face, then leaned over to drop a kiss on her sister's cheek. "Rest now. Don't worry about anything. Now that you're home, everything will be fine."

The sound of a man's angry voice startled Bay awake. Her dream of dancing in Jonas Harper's arms rapidly faded, leaving her confused and disoriented. As her fingertips grazed the soft feather mattress beneath her, she realized she wasn't in Many Horses' tipi. She waited for her eyes to adjust to the dark. No slanting tipi walls pressed down upon her. No smell of rancid meat and woodsmoke burned her nose. Bay pressed her fist against her mouth to stifle her cry. Where was she?

All too soon, the reality of her situation became plain. Shadow, Long Quiet's wife, was no more. She was Bayleigh Falkirk Stewart. And she was home at Three Oaks.

She couldn't face the thought of sitting at a table eating supper with her father and sisters, smiling and pretending everything was fine. Nothing was fine. The rough chambray gown grated on her skin. The muslin drawers were too constricting. The bed was too soft. And she grieved for those she'd left behind, especially Long Quiet.

Bay rose from the feather mattress and stripped off the clothes she wore. She wrapped her naked body in a cotton sheet and sought out the braided rug on the hard floor. She would lose herself in sleep. Perhaps in the morning everything would look brighter.

Only moments later the door was thrown open and a huge shadow spilled across her. Bay held her breath.

"Bay?"

That was the angry voice she'd heard, the one that had awakened her, the voice of her father. She kept her eyes closed, hoping he'd go away.

But he didn't.

He lifted her up into his arms, and she prepared herself to be put back into the too-soft bed. Instead, Rip sat down on the bed and settled her into his lap, one arm around her shoulders to support her. She heard his breath catch as his other hand roamed the scars on her back as though to erase them, to erase her pain. He huffed out the breath of air he'd been holding, then trailed his hand across her face, marveling at her cheekbones, tracing her eyebrows. His hand smoothed the hair from her forehead, and she could feel his breath fan her face, as he leaned down to press a fatherly kiss on her forehead.

She could not remember the last time he'd touched her with such tenderness. Why hadn't he reached out to her like this when she'd first arrived? Why wait until now, when he thought her asleep? She felt his thigh muscles tighten when the tear leaked from beneath her eyelash. She was sure he would speak then, was sure he would bluff and bluster as he usually did when caught off guard.

But he didn't.

He caught the tear with his thumb and wiped it away. Then he rose, lifting her tall woman's body as though she were but a child. He turned and placed her in the bed, covering her with the quilt and tucking it in around her chin.

Bay's throat was swollen so thick she thought she might choke. She wished for the courage to ask him if he'd missed her. She wished for the courage to tell him that she loved him.

"Stay in bed," he ordered, his voice brusque. "There's no reason to be sleeping on the floor. By the way, I've invited someone to come over for supper tomorrow, someone I know you'll want to see. I expect you'll be feeling better by then. Good night, Bay."

Then he was gone, without a word of explanation for what he'd done, without a word of love for his disappointing daughter.

Bay climbed out of bed and curled up on the braided rug. It was a small defiance, but defiance all the same. If he'd just look at her, he'd see the difference.

She wasn't his disappointing daughter anymore.

Chapter 15

 RISE AND SHINE!"

Bay came abruptly awake at Sloan's cheerful greeting, then realized she was sitting in the middle of her bedroom floor draped in nothing more than a sheet. "Hello. Good morning," she said, awkwardly pulling the sheet around her as she stood up. She mentally prepared a suitable explanation for Sloan as to why she'd slept on the floor and felt let down when Sloan didn't ask. Actually, Sloan seemed as uncomfortable as Bay felt, and busied herself spreading up the four-poster.

Despite being only a year apart in age, Sloan and Bay had never been good friends. Bay's interests had been too different from Sloan's, and Sloan's strong personality was a better match for Cricket's. So Bay wasn't sure what to think of Sloan's unexpected appearance this morning. When she heard a baby crying, she used it as an excuse to break the uncomfortable silence. "Is that Jesse?"

Sloan smiled and said, "Yes. She's quite a handful, even though all she does is eat and sleep."

"Where's your child?" Bay asked, returning Sloan's friendly smile. "Your son or daughter must be quite a handful, too."

Sloan's face paled and her lips flattened into a straight

line. She took a deep breath and said, "He doesn't live here. I gave him to the Guerrero family two years ago."

"What?"

"You heard me," Sloan said, yanking the bedcovers viciously. "I gave him away."

"Your son? You gave your own son away?"

Bay was dumbstruck. She'd known that the father of Sloan's child, the younger son of a wealthy Castilian Spanish *hacendado*, had been killed before he could marry her. But as of the day of Bay's capture by the Comanches, Sloan had intended to raise her child at Three Oaks. Having been forced to give up Little Deer, and knowing firsthand the agony of such a separation, Bay couldn't understand why Sloan would willingly have agreed to give up her child. But perhaps she hadn't been willing.

"Did Rip force you to give up your son?"

Sloan's bitter laugh didn't answer Bay's question as much as it raised others. "Rip didn't have anything to do with my decision. If he'd had his way, the child would be trailing around underfoot right now. Look, all this was settled years ago. I don't think about it anymore, and I certainly don't want to talk about it now."

"How could you do such a thing?"

"I said I don't want to talk about this," Sloan warned.

"Well I do!" Bay snapped. "What were you thinking? How could you give away your own flesh and blood?"

"My *bastard* son."

"Bastard?" Bay couldn't believe Sloan could apply such a word, and with such contempt, to her own flesh and blood.

"Yes, bastard," Sloan retorted. She turned angrily to confront Bay. "Antonio Guerrero never married me."

"I know that," Bay snapped, "but—"

"Did you know he never intended to marry me? Ah! I see that's news to you. Well, before you judge me, why don't you hear all the facts. Antonio duped me into carrying messages for him while he plotted to help the Mexican government invade Texas."

Bay gasped at the intense pain underlying the fury in Sloan's voice.

"He betrayed the Republic and he betrayed my trust in him. He was killed by one of his own men, who wanted to surrender to the Rangers when they were caught rather than fight to the death as Antonio intended to do. Do you wonder that I didn't want his son around reminding me every day how gullible, how stupidly trusting, I was? Yes, I gave the *bastard* to Antonio's family. The Guerreros were glad to have him."

"How could you give away an innocent baby?"

"Look who's accusing me of giving away my child! Didn't I hear you say yesterday that you had a child as well? Where's your child, Bay? Decided not to bring your Comanche bastard home with you?"

The flat of Bay's hand met Sloan's cheek with a loud *thwack*. Sloan's skin flamed red.

"Did I hit too close to the truth?" Sloan taunted.

Bay fought to hold on to her temper, appalled that she'd resorted to violence. "You couldn't be farther from it. I would *never* have left Little Deer if I'd been given the choice."

"You mean you'd have stayed with those brutal savages if you'd been given a choice?" Sloan asked, incredulous.

"They're not savages!"

"It's not savage to lasso a baby and drag it alive and screaming through cactus? It's not savage to rape a woman and leave her pinioned to the ground with a Comanche lance? It's not savage to kill and pillage and destroy for no good reason?"

"You don't understand!" Bay protested.

Sloan shook her head in disbelief. "Are you actually defending them?"

"It's not all one-sided, Sloan. They also love and—"

"Ahhhh, *love*," Sloan said with a cynical smile. "That explains everything."

This was not the Sloan that Bay remembered. This woman had been hurt and had hardened her heart against more pain. It was clear Sloan didn't think much of Bay's defense of the Comanches. To be honest, Bay thought, there was no defending the atrocities practiced by either whites or Comanches against each other. Yet each side seemed so sure it was right. For the first time Bay could see the extent of the problem faced by Long Quiet, who walked a narrow path between two worlds.

"What's going on in here?" Cricket said, stepping inside Bay's bedroom and closing the door behind her. "I could hear the two of you shouting all the way down the hall."

Cricket walked over to Sloan and touched the red mark that still stood out on her cheek.

"We were just talking," Sloan said, brushing Cricket's hand aside.

"So I see," Cricket said. Bay flushed when Cricket turned and looked inquiringly at her. "Would you mind telling me what brought you two clabberheads to blows?"

Sloan smirked. "Babies."

Cricket's brow arched in confusion. "Babies?"

"Bastard babies," Sloan clarified.

"Oh."

"Bay seemed to think I should have kept Antonio's baby."

"*Your* baby," Bay corrected.

"Not anymore it isn't."

"Hold it. Hold it!" Cricket said. "This isn't getting you stubborn, lard-headed mules anywhere."

"You're right," Sloan said. "I've got work to do and I don't have time to stand around arguing about the past. Rip asked me to come see if Bay felt up to doing some bookkeeping." She stared at Bay. "Well, do you?"

Bay swallowed the misery in her throat. "Yes, of course. I'll come down as soon as I'm dressed."

"Fine. I'll tell Rip." Sloan turned and left the room.

"How long has she been like this?" Bay asked, staring at the closed door.

"Like what?" Cricket asked.

"Bitter. Cynical. Angry. We were never close, but I don't think I ever felt so frustrated trying to talk to her."

Cricket crossed to sit on the bed. She pulled her long auburn braid around and chewed on the end of it before she spoke. "I can understand your feelings, Bay, believe me. But Sloan's decision to give her baby to the Guerrero family was made a long time ago. It's too late to do anything about it now. All that can result if you argue with her is to make things worse."

"How could you let her do it?"

"Nobody *let* her do it," Cricket retorted. "Rip was furious. But by the time he'd found out what she'd done, the Guerreros had Francisco and wouldn't give him up."

"Francisco?"

"That's what the Guerreros named the baby. They call him Cisco."

"Have you seen him?"

"Yes, once. I went to visit Cruz, Antonio's older brother, and he let me hold the baby. Oh, he's so beautiful, Bay. He has sable hair, just like Sloan's, and blue, blue eyes." Cricket pursed her lips thoughtfully. "Actually, I'd say he looks more like Cruz than Antonio. I don't know how Sloan could bear to give him up."

"Maybe if she saw the baby again she'd change her mind," Bay murmured.

"Are you thinking what I think you're thinking?"

"Could be," Bay said. "But speaking of beautiful babies, when am I going to see Jesse?"

"As soon as you're dressed. While you were sleeping I laid out a dress and muslin petticoat for you." Cricket gestured to the practical brown dress made of muslin delaine, a soft, lightweight wool. "It buttons up the front, so you should be able to get into it by yourself. I'll stay to lace you into your corset if you like."

"I don't think I'll wear the corset," Bay said. "I . . . it's just that wearing underclothes at all feels strange and I don't know if I could stand to be laced into a corset just yet. Maybe in a little while . . ."

"Nothing seems the same, is that it?"

"I guess."

Cricket's eyes narrowed appraisingly. "You seem changed, too."

"I do? How?"

"Well, for one thing," Cricket said with a chuckle, "I don't think that dress is going to fit as well as it might have three years ago."

Bay blushed as Cricket eyed her substantial cleavage.

"But that's not the biggest change," Cricket continued.

"It isn't?"

"Can you imagine the Bay who left here three years ago even daring to argue with Sloan, let alone raising her hand to anyone?"

Bay frowned, hurt by the slightly accusatory tone in Cricket's voice. "I suppose not. But . . ." Bay wasn't sure how to explain what had happened between her and Sloan. She wasn't really sure she could. Or that she owed it to Cricket to try. Stormy violet eyes challenged Cricket's inquiring gaze. When Cricket lowered her eyes, Bay admitted softly, "I guess that other Bay is gone."

Cricket met Bay's gaze again, her gray eyes sad. "I suppose so. I'll see you in Jesse's room when you're dressed. All right?"

"Sure," Bay said.

When Bay walked into the room down the hall, she found Cricket nursing the baby. She was appalled by the stab of envy that washed over her, even more so when she realized that what she imagined was Long Quiet's child at her breast. She would never have Long Quiet's child now.

She hurriedly stuffed her envy back into the hole it had crawled from and let herself be happy for her sister. "I never pictured you like this. I mean, all the time I was gone, I kept remembering you at the pond with Creed. But you look wonderful with a baby at your breast," Bay said.

Cricket blushed, but was obviously pleased by Bay's compliment. "Don't let Creed hear you say that. He already wants another one."

Jesse's mouth was playing with the nipple now rather than sucking. "She's finished," Cricket said. "Would you like to hold her while I put myself back together?"

Bay took the baby while Cricket buttoned herself back into her clothes. "Oh, Cricket, she's so perfect!"

"She is, isn't she," Cricket agreed with a grin.

"When is the christening?"

"As soon as Creed returns from Mexico."

"I thought he was just meeting Long Quiet in Laredo."

Cricket shook her head in wry acceptance. "He couldn't stand to miss out on the fun, and since Jesse and I would be safe here, he decided to go with Long Quiet. It won't really delay the christening that much, because we have to wait for Creed's brother, Tom, and his wife, Amy, to arrive from Tennessee anyway. They're going to be Jesse's godparents."

"When are you expecting them?"

"Sometime in the next couple of weeks, assuming the weather cooperates. If the rains start too soon, the roads will be mud pies."

"So Creed should be back in a couple of weeks?"

"I hope so," Cricket said with a laugh. "I don't know how I'm going to last even that long without him."

Bay's shoulders sagged at the thought of a lifetime without Long Quiet. She could never even share with her sisters the memories of their brief time as husband and wife. But as Bay handed the sleeping baby back to Cricket, she kept her bleak thoughts to herself. "I guess I'd better get downstairs and get to work."

Just as Bay reached the door, Cricket called out to stop her. "Bay?"

"Yes, Cricket?"

"It'll get easier."

"Thanks, Cricket, for understanding. I'll see you at supper."

The plantation office was on the main floor of the house, with one set of windows overlooking the front porch and a second set revealing vast cotton fields. Bay knew that a quarter-mile away, beyond sight and smell of the house, the cotton gin and baling screw were housed. The slave quarters for Rip's sixty field hands were a quarter-mile in the other direction. Out back of the house were the bachelors' quarters, which, Sloan had told her at dinner, hadn't been damaged by the fire.

The office itself was reminiscent of what it had been in the past—a room that smelled of leather and tobacco, with three rough rawhide chairs situated before a rock fireplace. Rip had re-created here the same bastion of power that had existed before the fire. Bay pulled down a heavy tome from the shelves that made up Rip's library and opened it to the current entries.

The first Tuesday of the month was the normal day of Wilkerson's advertised public sale of Negroes, horses, mules, and carriages in Houston. Bay discerned from the entries that Rip had attended the most recent sale and purchased one male African Negro and three mules. He'd also bought a score of hogs to be slaughtered by the hog boys. She also noted from the entries that the plough boys and hoe hands had been fitted with leather shoes for the coming winter.

"I see you found the books," Rip said, interrupting Bay's perusal.

"Yes. It looks like you've been busy."

"There's a lot more to do before the weather chills. Have to get a new gate built for the corral, along with some horse troughs, and there are some ploughs that need fixing. Oh yes, and the barn needs to be cleaned out. You know. The usual."

Bay felt a moment of sympathy for Sloan. In preparing his eldest daughter to one day take her rightful place as his heir, Rip had appointed Sloan as overseer for Three Oaks. It was Sloan's job to make sure Rip's will was done on the cotton plantation. Bay only had to keep track of everything that was accomplished and make sure supplies were ordered and available for all the work Rip dictated. Still, even that was a huge job for a plantation the size of Three Oaks. However, Bay was looking forward to the work to keep her mind off the past.

"From what you said at dinner yesterday about the poor crops, I expected to see the books in worse shape," Bay said.

"It's been bad enough," Rip replied. "Whole damn army of cutworms ate us out in the spring. Had no choice but to re-plant. Damned if we didn't get caught by army worms next. Stripped the fields sere! If that wasn't enough, we had so much rain late in the season the cotton bolls either mildewed or washed down to the ground, where they rotted out or got so stained as to be useless. Pickers should be out there right now snatching cotton, only what little there was has already been picked. It's been bad, all right. Second year in a row, too."

"Has it been this bad for everyone?"

"Peach Point and Evergreen have been even harder hit," Rip said grimly. "Longwood, Birchfield, and Pleasant Grove are about the same as us. Monte Verde seems to have escaped the worst of it, but we're all feeling the bite."

Bay smiled slightly at Rip's unintentional pun. It sounded as if most of the cotton plantations along the Brazos River had been victims of insects and bad weather.

"There'll be more homespun worn for a while, that's for sure," Rip finished. "Jesse's christening couldn't have come at a better time. People are ready to put their worries aside for a few hours and kick up their heels. Which brings me to the young man I've invited to join us for supper this evening."

"I'm not ready to meet anyone yet."

"You're as ready as you'll ever be," Rip said.

"I'm not ready to meet anyone who thinks I've been away touring the Continent," Bay protested, "when what I've actually been doing is tanning animal hides and sewing beaded moccasins. Don't you understand? Half the time I'm still thinking in Comanche."

"I'm disappointed—"

"Don't you dare!" Bay raged, jumping to her feet, her hands clenched in fists. "Don't you dare say you're disappointed in me. I survived. Against all the odds and when I didn't think I could, I survived!"

Rip's bushy red brows arched in amazement. "What brought all this on? I was merely going to say I'm disappointed that you don't feel more like meeting company."

Bay's face reflected her chagrin. "I'm . . ." Bay bit her lower lip. She would not apologize. She wasn't the least bit sorry for her outburst. "I can't forget what happened to me. I'm not the same as I was."

"I don't expect you are, but I have plans for you, Bayleigh Stewart, plans that were made long before some Comanche buck stole you from Three Oaks. I have no intention of letting you spend your life regretting and remembering your life as some goddamn Comanche's woman."

"It's my life. I'll choose how I want to spend it."

"The *hell* you will!"

"The hell I *will!*"

Bay gasped and clamped a hand over her mouth the instant she'd blurted the words that were Cricket's normal response to her father's challenge. In the past, about the time Cricket and Rip had gotten this far into an argument, Bay had been backed up against a wall somewhere well out of the way. Bay was appalled that she'd provoked her father, and if the ferocious look on Rip's face meant anything, he was ready to force her into a showdown right now. Despite the fact she had precipitated this confrontation, Bay had no urge to continue it. Yet neither did she run. She grasped the pen from the inkwell and held it poised over the ledger. "I have work to do. I'm sure you do, too. I'll see you at supper."

Rip's forehead wrinkled into a bemused frown before he sighed and left the room.

The tension gradually eased from Bay's shoulders, and she slumped at the desk. It wasn't going to be easy fitting back into this family. Her reactions were as confusing to her as they were to the others. She would just have to take one step at a time.

Bay finished her work with the books early and spent the rest of the day wandering around Three Oaks, checking out the new kitchen and barn, roaming through the orchards of plum and fig trees, and visiting the slave quarters to see Mammy Pleasant, who took care of the little ones while their parents worked in the fields. She wished there had been more to do in the office, because without the plantation business to keep her mind busy, she had too much time to think.

She recalled every step of her relationship with Long Quiet, from its inauspicious beginning to its conclusive end. She tried to figure out exactly when she'd started to love Long Quiet and decided it had happened when he'd pulled Little Deer into his lap to tell her his favorite bedtime story. She was amazed to realize he had all but replaced Jonas Harper in her heart and mind.

So it was quite a shock when Bay showed up for dinner, dressed in a watermelon-pink silk dress that tapered in a V from the shoulders to the tightly fitted waist, to find Jonas Harper waiting in the parlor.

"Hello, Bayleigh," he said.

Bay saw a handsome man with chestnut hair, a full moustache that covered his upper lip, sparkling tobacco eyes, and a flashing smile that charmed without half trying. When he opened his arms to her in the old familiar way, she hesitated only momentarily before stepping into his embrace. His arms closed around her so she felt safe and secure—even if she didn't experience the same nerve-jangling sensual attraction she'd felt with Long Quiet. She tried not to feel guilty that she was betraying Long Quiet, but the unease was there. And that made her angry, because *he'd* abandoned *her*, not the other way around.

She leaned her head back and searched Jonas's face for what he was feeling. "It's been a long time," she said.

His eyes dilated slightly with desire, and his lips curved in wry humor. "Four years. I've missed you."

"What are you doing here in Texas?" Bay asked. "I thought your father's business was in Louisiana."

"It was—is—I've branched out into Texas. I came calling six months ago looking for you, and your father told me you were traveling on the Continent."

Bay flushed, ashamed of the lie but unwilling to correct it. "Yes . . . well . . ."

Jonas took her hand in his and brought it to his lips. "I'm glad you're home."

Bay felt an unwelcome flutter in her stomach and thought perhaps it was simply relief that he hadn't seemed to notice the calluses on her fingers. She was somewhat alarmed at her reaction to Jonas's charm. After all, she was still in love with Long Quiet. "I waited for you in Boston, but you never came back for me like you promised," she accused.

"You'll never know how sorry I am for that," Jonas said, his tone too sincere to be doubted. "I couldn't come. There were unavoidable circumstances that kept me in Louisiana. But I'm here now, Bayleigh. And I don't intend to leave until I have your promise to become my wife."

Bay caught sight of Rip smiling and felt a vague sense of discomfort. She'd never told her father about her relationship with Jonas. Was it possible Rip intended to manipulate her into a relationship whether she wanted it or not? How could she hope to feel the same love for Jonas now that Long Quiet had come into my life? "A lot has happened to me since we last saw each other," she said to Jonas. "I'm not certain we would still suit one another."

Bay stood patiently while Jonas's eyes raked her body from the auburn curls atop her head, to her generous bosom, to the pink bow tied at her cinched-in waist, and down the length of her gathered skirt to the feet she'd squeezed into black pumps.

"We'll suit each other very well. But I agree we'll need time to get reacquainted. I want to marry you, but I'm willing to court you, Bayleigh. A woman should have that, don't you think?"

He knew all the right things to say, and Bay didn't know how to counter his smooth words. She wanted to tell him she already had a husband, that he would be her second, but that would cause more problems than she was ready to handle. She wasn't ready for another lover, but Jonas had also been a friend. And she needed a friend right now.

"Will you escort me in to dinner?" Bay said.

"Does this mean you're consenting to my courtship, fair lady?"

Bay looked out from lowered lashes at the man she'd once thought would be her one true love, and who had returned fully intending to take that role again. "Let's start with supper and see how things progress from there, shall we?"

"Of course, darling. Of course."

As Jonas escorted her from the parlor to the dining room, Bay shot a meaningful glance over her shoulder at Rip. She'd make her own decisions about who she'd marry.

It was a small defiance, but defiance all the same.

Chapter 16

IT WAS DARK, TOO DARK TO SEE FACES, TOO DARK EVEN to see shapes, but Long Quiet knew there was someone out there in the Mexican desert not far from him. He touched Creed's arm and knew his friend would understand the unspoken message: *Wait here. I'll find out who's there.*

Neither a stone turned nor bush crackled as Long Quiet made his way toward the rustling sound that had first drawn his attention. He could hear men whispering and tried to determine what language they spoke. Were they Mexican—the pursuers, or Texan—the pursued? But the sounds weren't distinct enough to make out. He'd have to get closer.

When he heard the hiss of inflating air, Long Quiet knew he'd be discovered momentarily. The coiling rattlesnake was as effective as a watchdog. Yet Long Quiet didn't dare move. Any movement on his part and the snake now coiling a foot from his nose would strike. The deadly buzz began, alerting those whispering in the darkness that something—or someone—had alarmed the prowling rattler.

"Shh! Shhh!"

Long Quiet could hear them warning one another to be still.

"You all right out there?" a voice whispered. "You find something?"

It was the confirmation Long Quiet had sought. He knew

now that he'd found the men who'd escaped from the Mexican prison called Castle San Carlos. He could say nothing without further alarming the rattler, but he knew if he remained still, the snake would soon move away. It seemed an endless time before the rattler's angry buzz settled to a steady *chik-chik, chik-chik,* and finally to a *chik, chik, chik,* and then silence. He waited a while longer to be sure the deadly night creature had gone on its way.

Long Quiet's attention had been so focused on the rattler that it took all his fighting instincts to counter the force of the wiry arm that suddenly circled his throat, cutting off his air. With a quick twisting movement, Long Quiet freed himself, bringing the other man's arm high up behind his back. He could tell from the thinness of the man's wrists and the leanness of his body that he was one of the prisoners. "I'm here to help," he said in English.

"Long Quiet?" an astonished voice asked.

"Yes, it's me. Is that you, Luke?"

"Yeah."

"Luke? You out there, Luke?" a voice called out.

"Dammit, Sammy," Luke hissed back. "Don't you know enough to keep quiet? You'll have the whole damn Mexican army down on us in a minute if you keep up that yammering."

"You find someone out there, Luke?" Sammy persisted.

"Yes, dammit. So will you just shut up, Sammy?"

"Hey, Luke, who you got?" a man called Chester called out.

"Goddamnedest bunch of farmers and storekeepers I ever met," Luke muttered. "Ready to fight in a minute, bullheaded and bighearted, but without a lick of sense. Come on. I'll show you where they are."

Long Quiet nodded and followed Luke down into a gully, where seven bedraggled men huddled around a tiny fire. Long Quiet knew from the looks on their faces as they scrambled to their feet that they didn't believe what they were seeing.

"Jesus!"

"Well, I'll be damned!"

"A goddamn Comanche!"

"How the hell didja catch a Injun, Luke? You was s'posed to be keepin' an eye out for Meskins."

Long Quiet cocked his head and listened for a second, then said in perfect English, "No need to look for them. They're on there way here right now."

Sammy's jaw dropped to the collar of his ragged shirt as he stammered, "Wh-what's g-goin' on here?"

Luke smiled when he could see Long Quiet in the firelight. "You're a sight for sore eyes. Is Creed out there somewhere?"

"Sure is. He's with the horses and supplies. You'd better get your farmers and storekeepers packed up and out of here in a hurry if you don't want to find yourselves right back in Castle San Carlos."

"Let's go, fellas," Luke said, kicking the fire out as he gathered his meager belongings.

"What's goin' on?" Chester demanded belligerently. "How do we know we can trust this dirty Injun?"

"This 'dirty Injun' is about to save your filthy hide, Chester," Luke growled. "If you want to argue with him about it, do it after we cross the Rio Grande. Understand?"

Chester grunted but kept his thoughts to himself.

"I thought there were supposed to be sixteen of you," Long Quiet said as they made their way toward where Creed waited with the horses.

"Not everybody was well enough to come. Half the men in our cell were either sick or dying with *vómito*. Hell, three of the men with me are still recuperating from the effects of the disease," Luke's voice rasped in anger. "The Mexicans don't need a firing squad to kill the Texans in Perote. Disease and neglect are accomplishing the same thing. Why the hell hasn't the Texas government done something to get us out of that hellhole?"

"You'll have to ask Creed that," Long Quiet replied. "But I think there's something else we need to take care of first."

The Mexican cavalry was almost upon them. They could easily hear the jingle of bits, the muffled plodding of unshod hooves, the clank of sabers, the grunts of men and animals as they made their weary way through the dark. Apparently, the Mexicans didn't know how close they were to their quarry.

The Mier prisoners silently ran for their lives, hell-bent on reaching the horses Creed and Long Quiet had brought. When one of the sick ones faltered, Long Quiet hefted him over his shoulder and kept moving. Luke did the same with another man, and Chester—huge, irascible Chester—did the same with a third.

Creed was waiting for them and assisted those who needed help in getting mounted. It seemed they would escape undetected when Sammy's bare foot slipped completely through the stirrup as he tried to mount. His startled horse bolted, dragging a yowling Sammy through the rocks and cactus after him.

Sammy's howls would have awakened the dead. They certainly roused the Mexican cavalry to action. While Long Quiet went after Sammy, Creed quickly distributed the Colt repeating revolvers he'd brought along, and the group of men the Mexican cavalry might moments before have broached like a stand of sagebrush, quickly became an impenetrable mass of spiny cactus.

"Bet that's Old Guts hisself out there," Chester shouted. "What say we get 'im, boys?"

Men who'd suffered cruelty and brutality for too long turned on their captors like avenging angels in the darkness.

"Here's for the Republic!" one shouted.

"Black beans, hah!" another cried.

"Texas! Texas!" a third chanted, firing several shots into the dark.

As several of the Mexicans shrieked and fell from their horses under the onslaught of the Texans' gunfire, their leader panicked. Somehow, the unarmed prisoners he'd been chasing had gotten hold of revolvers. He hadn't forgotten the lessons of Mier. Put a gun in the hand of one of these Texas devils and he quickly sent a host of Mexican souls to heaven.

"Los Diablos Tejanos!" he screamed. *"Retírense! Retírense!"* He urged them to retreat, yanking on the reins of his confused horse and spurring the animal away from the awesome firepower that had opened up on them. All around him men screamed in pain as the Texan guns spit bullets at them. *"Retírense!"* he cried again, using his saber to whip at the milling horses clustered in his path.

The Texans chased the Mexicans for nearly a mile, their bloodlust high, their need for revenge overwhelming. It was Luke Summers who finally called a halt to the carnage.

"Hold up there, Chester! Hey, Sammy, hold on. How about turning around and heading for home. Let's get out of this godforsaken land," he cried. "Let's go home to Texas!"

Soon his cry was picked up by laughing Texans with tears streaming from their eyes. In voices hoarse with emotion, they shouted, "Home to Texas! Home to Texas!"

Luke was giddy with freedom, wide awake, his blood pumping in the aftermath of battle, and totally exhausted at the same time by the effort he'd exerted with a body withered by so many months of near starvation. "Who knows the way home?" he asked, his teeth glistening white in the light of the rising moon.

"Follow me," Long Quiet said.

The tired prisoners were more than happy to give over control of their destiny to someone in authority. It was a long, grueling night, and Long Quiet listened with half an ear to Luke's nearly constant tirade against the Texas government, which had abandoned the prisoners of Mier to their fate.

When the sun rose on the ragtag men who'd escaped, Long Quiet saw why Luke was so angry. The eight men who'd tunneled under the walls of Castle San Carlos were emaciated, their bodies barely covered by the pitiful rags that had once been clothing. Some bore scars from beatings. All had bare feet. If the changes Long Quiet saw in Luke were indicative, these men had lived through a year of hell.

Luke Summers had aged. The brooding eyes that had so enticed the ladies of San Antonio now reflected a burning fury as well as a bleak bitterness. The well-developed back, the whip-lashed shoulders, and the muscular thighs all bore witness to the heavy work he'd done, but the flesh had dwindled to a shadow of what had been there before. His hair had grown to shoulder length and was tangled and dirty. There was little left of the charming young Ranger who'd drawn women to his bed like a Texas marsh drew mallards.

Luke was still asking Creed pointed questions days later, when they crossed the Rio Grande.

"Is Sam Houston planning to do something to free the rest of those men in Perote?" he demanded.

"I've already explained what's holding him back, Luke," Creed answered placatingly.

"About a half dozen times," Chester muttered under his breath.

Luke shot the man a quelling glance, and Creed continued, "Sam Houston doesn't want to take a chance of antagonizing the Mexican government. The last thing he needs is a war with Mexico while he's trying to negotiate annexation with the United States."

"Well, I don't like it," Luke retorted. "There ought to be some way to free the Mier prisoners without a full-scale war. What the hell happened to diplomacy?"

"I'm afraid there are too few Texas diplomats, and the ones we have are busy talking to United States congressmen and senators," Creed answered. He pulled his horse to a stop and turned to face the men who followed behind him. "This is it," he said. "You're on Texas soil now—at least what Texas claims is Texas soil," he amended with a grin. "The horses and guns are yours to keep, with my compliments. I wish you luck and hope you find your families well."

Creed soberly shook hands with the men he and Long Quiet had brought out of Mexico. They left in groups of two or three as they headed back to the stores, the small farms, and the lonely, hardworking wives they'd left behind nearly a year before.

"I'll be leaving you here, too," Luke said.

"Where are you planning to go?" Creed asked.

"Guess I'll head back to San Antonio and see what Captain Hays has in mind for a long-absent Ranger," Luke said. His brow furrowed in thought. "Maybe he's got some sway with the Texas government. I sure as hell want to find somebody who does and give them a piece of my mind."

"Why not talk with Hays and then come home with me?" Creed said. "I have a new daughter who's going to be christened Jesse Elizabeth Creed as soon as I get to Three Oaks. Cricket asked me to invite you to come to this shindig, and I'm extending my own invitation as well."

Long Quiet noticed that Luke's whole body tensed and his gaze became shuttered at the mention of Cricket. Creed had told Long Quiet that from the instant they'd met, there had been some kind of unspoken communication between Luke and Cricket and he knew they'd eventually become close friends. But what if Luke turned his charm on Bay? Would she be equally susceptible to whatever it was that made Luke so popular with the ladies?

Long Quiet's musing was interrupted when Luke smiled a heart-stopping grin and said "Sure, Creed. I'd love to come to your daughter's christening."

"Let's get moving, then," Creed said. "We've got some miles to cover yet."

"I'll ride with you for a while," Long Quiet said.

Creed frowned. "What do you mean, for a while? I thought you were coming to the christening too. Cricket's expecting you. Now that you've brought Bay home—"

"You found Bay?" Luke interrupted. "How is she? Is she all right? Where was she?"

"Whoa!" Creed said with a laugh. "Long Quiet found her in a *Quohadi* Comanche village and took her home. She's just fine."

Luke's interest in Bay sent chills down Long Quiet's spine. He eyed the other man suspiciously. "Why are you so interested in Bay?"

"Why, because she's Cricket's sister," Luke said. "Cricket's told me a lot about Bay. I feel as though I know her, even though I've never met her."

Long Quiet pulled his pony to a stop, barring Luke's path. "Leave her alone."

"What did you say?" Luke's eyes lit with challenge.

"I said leave her alone."

"What right do you have to be telling me how to act with Bay Stewart?" Luke demanded.

The truth was, now that he'd released his claim on Bay, Long Quiet had no rights at all. But the thought of Luke Summers—or any man—touching Bay Stewart tied his gut in knots. "I care a lot for Bay," Long Quiet said carefully. "I'd hate to see her get hurt."

"Don't worry," Luke replied. "The last person I'd want to hurt is one of Rip Stewart's daughters."

In the days when it had looked like he'd die in Mexico, Luke had wished he'd confided his secret to someone—the truth about his relationship to Sloan and Bay and Cricket. It was true he and Cricket had become good friends, but even she didn't know they had the same father. No one did, not even Rip himself. Luke would never do anything to hurt Bay. She was his half-sister. At the same time, Long Quiet's interest in Bay seemed to Luke to be more than merely the concern of the man who'd found Bay among the Comanches.

"You spent a long time looking for Bay," Luke said. "What was it like to finally find her?"

"Why does it matter to you, Luke?" Long Quiet asked, his eyes meeting those of the younger man.

"I wondered if maybe I should be protecting Bay from you."

Long Quiet felt the fury rising inside him and knew it came from the frustration of having to keep his relationship with Bay a secret. It could only hurt her for the truth to come out. But he could tell the other man enough to make his feelings for Bay plain, and to make it plain what he'd do if the other man hurt Bay.

So he said, "I would have been proud to make Bay Stewart my wife. I've wanted her since the first time I saw her, when she was in school in Boston. But in those days I planned to return to *Comanchería*. I knew Bay wouldn't be happy there, so I said nothing to her. Then she was stolen by Tall Bear. If I'd found her in those first days after her capture, I would have made her my wife and kept her with me in *Comanchería*. But it didn't happen.

"When I found her at last, I . . . I planned to marry her, to take her to the village of my grandfather and raise Comanche sons."

Creed pursed his lips thoughtfully. "Would Bay have agreed to that?"

Long Quiet smiled bitterly. "I wouldn't have given her a choice. But she would have been happy," he added. "None of that could happen, because she was accused by the Comanches of being a sorceress. I was damn lucky to get her out of *Comanchería* alive."

"So," Creed mused. "You love her. But she can't live in *Comanchería* . . . and you won't live in Texas."

Hearing the situation stated like that made it seem simpler than Long Quiet believed it was. "You know my feelings about living in Texas," he said in a voice that was steel gloved in velvet. "Am I supposed to reject everything I believe in for the sake of a woman?"

"I don't know," Creed said.

"Sounds to me like you just don't love Bay enough to want

to be with her," Luke said. "Otherwise, where the two of you live wouldn't make a damn bit of difference."

"Nobody asked you what you think," Long Quiet retorted.

Luke cocked his head and eyed Long Quiet. Maybe a little jealousy would nudge him into changing his mind. In his opinion, Long Quiet would make a fine brother-in-law. "If you don't want her, I'll take her."

"You lay one hand on her and I'll—" Long Quiet clamped his jaws tight over the rest of his threat, chagrined that he'd allowed the young man to goad him into speaking.

Luke grinned. "Guess you might have feelings for her after all. But all the feelings in the world aren't going to do you any good if you're in *Comancheria* and she's in Texas. If I know Rip Stewart, he'll find some wealthy planter and marry her off. Sounds to me like you're going to have to make a choice. You can live in *Comancheria* alone or you can live in Texas with Bay."

Creed joined the conversation, plainly on Luke's side. "You've been Walker Coburn before. Was it so terrible to be a white man?"

"You're suggesting I play a role for the rest of my life?" Long Quiet demanded.

"It isn't really a role, is it? It's part of who you are. You're half white—"

"And half Comanche! I'm not sure I can stand to live like a white man—staying in one place, living in a wooden house, raising the food I eat, bound by manners I have no use for, being friends with people who hate the people I love and have lived with my whole life. Do you realize what you're asking of me?"

"The choice is yours," Creed said. "Nobody can make you do anything. You can go back to *Comancheria*—"

"And lose Bay!" Long Quiet's agonized cry reflected the extent of the mental torture that afflicted him.

"You don't have to decide right now," Creed soothed. "Come to the christening. Try out being Walker Coburn for a couple of days and see how it feels. Bay will probably enjoy seeing you again, won't she?"

Long Quiet's features softened at the mention of Bay, then became strained as he remembered their last moments together. "I told her to forget about me."

"Have you forgotten her?"

"No."

"Do you think it's been any easier for her?"

Long Quiet sighed. "I suppose not."

"Come to Three Oaks for Jesse's christening," Creed urged. "Then if you still want to go back to *Comanchería . . .*" Creed shrugged.

Long Quiet felt sick. How could he live in Texas as Walker Coburn? Bay would need things that could only be bartered with goods or bought with money. What would he do to make a living for the two of them? He'd be bound to the land, stuck in one place. How would he survive within those constraints?

Long Quiet became conscious of Luke's presence beside him and looked up from his musing.

"If you love her," Luke said, "there really isn't any choice."

Long Quiet's eyes narrowed and his nostrils flared in anger. His fists clenched and unclenched as he sought to control his frustration. He wouldn't be pressured into making a decision by words like *love*. He gave Luke one last bonechilling glance before he kneed his pony and headed north for *Comanchería*.

"Do you think he'll show up for the christening?" Luke asked as he watched Long Quiet ride away.

"I don't know," Creed answered. "I've known Long Quiet for a long time. He understands what's happening to the Comanche way of life, how it's threatened by the arrival of the white man. How can he become part of a society that's threatening people he loves? It can't be an easy decision for him."

"It would be if he were really in love with Bay."

"A lot of things can blind a man to the fact he can't live without a certain woman," Creed said ruefully. "I ought to know. I was in love with Cricket long before I admitted it to myself. Long Quiet's spent a lot of years trying not to see what's right in front of his nose. He's going to have to want to see the truth about some other important issues before he'll be willing to admit to needing Bay. Because loving Bayleigh Stewart is going to turn his whole world upside down.

"I guess we'll just have to wait till the christening to find out what he decides."

Chapter 17

JONAS IS HERE TO SEE YOU, BAY."

Bay looked up from the ledger in which she was writing to find Rip waiting expectantly in the doorway. "Please tell Jonas I'll meet him in the parlor in a few minutes. I have a few things to finish up here."

"There's no reason to keep Jonas waiting. I can finish whatever you're doing," Rip countered.

"I'll finish it."

"You'll meet him now."

Bay set the pen down gently, too gently for it to have been other than a very calculated effort. She rose regally from the large rawhide chair behind Rip's desk, her violet eyes a stormy purple when they met Rip's. Her voice quavered slightly as she said, "Don't forget to subtract the butchered hogs from the last column of figures."

With great dignity, Bay walked across the room toward Rip, who blocked her exit at the last moment.

"What's the matter with you?" he demanded brusquely.

Bay jerked as though she'd been slapped. "What do you mean?"

"I mean," he said in an intense voice still low enough not to carry to the parlor across the hall, "you've been as ornery the past two weeks as a mule stuck belly-deep in mud. No matter what I say, you're bound to do the opposite. Ever since you got home you've been contrary. And I don't like it!"

"I can't help the way I am," Bay shot back in an equally suppressed voice. "If you don't like it . . ." Bay closed her eyes and touched her fingertips to the bridge of her nose to ease the tension. She had been irritable and out of sorts. But she couldn't explain to Rip that the more involved she became with Jonas, the more she felt she was somehow betraying Long Quiet—unless she also admitted the extent of her relationship with the half-breed Comanche.

Bay dropped her hand and opened her eyes. "I'll see Jonas now."

As she moved past Rip, he grasped her arm. "Wait. I know something's bothering you. Is there anything I can do to help?"

Rip's offer of help totally disarmed her. She almost reached out to him, almost blurted the truth. But at the last instant she held her tongue. There was nothing Rip could do to change Long Quiet's mind. His decision had been final. She would just have to learn to live with it. But it was high time she stopped making her family pay for misery she was suffering through no fault of theirs.

Bay forced a tentative smile to her lips. "There's nothing wrong with me that time and patience won't cure. And you've already helped," she said, "simply by caring." As she watched the flush rise in Rip's cheeks, she added, "I'll try not to be so ornery, all right?"

"Sure," he said gruffly. "I only want what's best for you, Bay. I know you cared for Jonas a long time ago."

"How did you know that?" Bay asked, astounded that Rip had known her carefully guarded secret.

He cleared his throat and admitted, "I have friends in Boston, Bay. I kept track of your comings and goings. It would have been hard not to know how you felt about Jonas."

Bay reached a hand up to Rip's flushed cheek. It was something she wouldn't have dared three years ago. "So when he came looking for me, you knew I'd already fallen in love with him once before."

"Well, there's that. And after all, he *is* very rich—"

Bay's tinkling laugh cut off Rip's blustering reply. "And therefore quite an acceptable husband," she finished.

Rip's flush deepened. "Get on, girl. He's waiting for you. I believe Jonas has it in mind to take you for a ride in his carriage. Be sure you wear a bonnet to protect your face from the sun." Rip reached out a hand as though to touch the small freckles scattered across Bay's nose but changed his mind and stuck his hand in his pocket.

Bay slipped quickly past Rip and crossed the wide hall to the parlor. Jonas was looking out the front window and didn't see her come into the room. She took advantage of the opportunity to observe him.

The years had been kind to him. His body was strong, virile in a way that would be attractive to most women, and his face was undeniably handsome. The fiery warmth she'd always felt inside at the thought of Jonas Harper still burned, but with a friendly glow rather than the heat of passion. The spark that had once caused her to pledge her heart to this man was no longer there.

Bay cleared her throat. "Hello, Jonas."

Jonas turned and walked slowly toward her with his hands outstretched. Bay reached out her hands in response, and he captured them, bringing first one and then the other up to his lips for a chaste kiss. Bay waited to see if she would feel some physical response to his touch, but it didn't come.

"You look lovely," he said. "And you'll look even lovelier when those freckles fade a little more," he said as his finger tapped her nose. "Would you like to go for a ride this afternoon?"

"That would be nice," Bay said. "Let me get a bonnet."

"I'll wait for you outside. You won't dawdle, will you?" he said with a grin. "I hate to be kept waiting by a beautiful woman."

"No," Bay replied with a wry smile. "I won't dawdle." Bay wondered if she'd ever dawdled in her entire life. If Jonas had known her as well as he thought he did, he'd have understood that dawdling wasn't something Rip would ever have allowed his daughters to do. As Bay tied her straw bonnet under her chin, she considered whether she could marry a man whom she now saw only as a good friend. She had no doubt Jonas truly cared for her. He'd even labeled his feelings love. But would it be fair to either one of them if she married him?

Jonas had a new team of high-steppers and the ride was fast enough that Bay was soon glad she'd come. The wind felt wonderful on her face, and the countryside went by in a green and gold blur. When the horses began to tire, Jonas slowed them to a walk.

"That was wonderful," Bay said. "Your team of chestnuts is magnificent." But not as beautiful as the chestnut stallion Long Quiet had tamed, she thought.

"Thank you. Coming from Rip's daughter, that's quite a compliment."

"What do you mean?"

Jonas laughed. "Only that Rip's a fine judge of horseflesh, and he promised me his daughters knew easily as much as he did."

"He was speaking of Sloan and Cricket," Bay corrected, "not about me."

Jonas laughed again. "Don't be upset. I'm glad you're not like Sloan and Cricket. I wouldn't like you nearly so much if you were."

"Oh, really?"

"You need a man to take care of you. They don't."

Bay felt a rush of indignation at the assumption she couldn't take care of herself, but she realized that until she'd been captured by the Comanches, she'd have agreed with Jonas's assessment of her character. "I think I might surprise you."

Jonas switched the reins over so he could free a hand,

which he then settled possessively on Bay's knee. "I want to take care of you, Bay. I'm a very wealthy man, in case you didn't know. I sold a portion of my father's business and invested the money in land on the Texas side of the Louisiana border. My holdings in Shelby County are so profitable I'm ready to buy property in the more settled areas of Texas along the Brazos River. I've already found a place where I'd like to build a house for us, a place where we can raise our children.

"For as long as I can remember, whenever I've thought of myself settled and with a family, you've been a part of that picture. If I can't have you for my wife, I don't think I'll ever marry."

"Jonas, I—"

"Don't say you haven't thought about becoming my wife, Bay, about having my children—little brown-eyed boys and redheaded girls."

"Jonas, I—"

"Marry me, Bay. I want you to come live with me and be the mother of my children. Ever since the first time I saw you in Boston, I've been smitten by you."

"No! Don't say any more, please. Jonas, I'm not sure I—" Bay stopped abruptly when she saw a cloud of dust in the distance. "Jonas . . . there's someone coming. Look. Over there."

Jonas turned to look where Bay was pointing and saw the red cloud that finally parted to reveal a man on horseback. In a frontier like Texas, it wasn't wise to take the chance that strangers would be friendly. Jonas had already gathered the reins to turn the buggy when Bay grabbed his wrist to stop him.

"It's Creed! And there's someone with him." Bay's heart was in her throat. She couldn't see the rider who followed Creed, but she wanted it to be Long Quiet. What would he think when he saw her with another man? He'd surely understand. At least he'd come back. He'd come back!

At Bay's insistence, Jonas waited for the two riders to join them. As they neared, however, Bay realized the man with Creed wasn't Long Quiet. It took all her willpower to keep her face free of the tremendous disappointment she felt.

However, once she looked into the face of the man with Creed, she found herself wondering who he was. She had the feeling she knew him, or that she ought to know him.

"Hello, Creed," she said when the two men had drawn their horses to a stop beside the carriage.

"Is that you, Bay? You're so grown-up! And so beautiful!"

Bay blushed with pleasure. "I . . . I want you to meet Jonas Harper," she said breathlessly.

"We've met. Hello, Jonas," Creed said, tipping his hat in greeting.

Bay's eyes strayed to the other man as she waited for him to introduce himself. His eyes were shuttered by some inexplicable emotion Bay finally identified as sadness. Tremendous empathy for the stranger's suffering washed over her, leaving her feeling his pain as her own. She looked away to break the spell that bound her to him.

"I'm Luke Summers," the young man said. He touched the flat brim of his hat with his finger and added, "Pleased to meet you, ma'am, Mr. Harper."

"Oh, please call me Bay."

Bay blushed again when Luke smiled at her and said, "Creed's right. You're a very beautiful woman."

Jonas hadn't missed the instant powerful attraction between Bay and the handsome young man who called himself Luke Summers. His voice was taut with jealousy when he announced, "I'm glad you admire my fiancée, Mr. Summers."

Luke turned to Jonas Harper and gave him a look that would have crushed stone. "Creed didn't mention his sister-in-law was engaged to you, Mr. Harper."

No one could have been more surprised by Jonas's announcement than Bay, whose mouth still hung slack from disbelief.

"That's because it hasn't been announced yet," Jonas replied as he slipped his arm around Bay's shoulders.

"I suppose congratulations are in order," Creed said. But he didn't offer any. He was too busy wondering whether Long Quiet knew about Bay's relationship with Jonas Harper.

Bay saw the confusion in Creed's eyes. Could Long Quiet possibly have told him about their relationship? Surely not, or Creed wouldn't sit silently by and watch Jonas staking his claim on her. She dropped her eyes to avoid Creed's piercing gaze. He could wonder all he wanted. She wasn't going to confirm anything for him. She shrugged her shoulders in an attempt to remove Jonas's arm. Grudgingly, he freed her from the possessive embrace and took up the reins again.

The ride back to Three Oaks seemed endless to Bay. None of the three men spoke to one another again, and Bay was too distressed to worry about soothing the antagonism between Jonas and the other two men.

When they arrived at the house, Bay turned to Jonas and said, "Thank you for the ride, Jonas." In a whisper, she added, "I want to talk to you about . . . about what you announced to Creed. I'm not your fiancée, Jonas." When he opened his mouth to protest, she reached out a hand to stop him. "Not now. We'll talk about this another time." She stepped down from the carriage without giving him a chance to help her and hurried into the house.

Jonas examined Creed and Luke with a jaundiced eye, but he was helpless to do anything except take his leave. He nodded his head to the other two men and departed with a curt, "I'll be seeing you."

"Not too soon, I hope," Creed muttered under his breath as Jonas drove away.

"What's going on between Bay and that Jonas Harper fellow?" Luke asked.

"I don't know," Creed replied, "but I sure as hell intend to find out."

Creed had no sooner swung down from his horse than Cricket flew into his arms. Creed took the time to properly greet his wife. Luke was grinning broadly by the time Creed's lips were finally free. "I guess you missed me," Creed murmured to his wife.

"Every day, all day," Cricket replied, breathless with excitement.

"I brought someone to see you. I cleaned him up a bit and bought him some clothes in San Antonio, but I couldn't do much about fattening him up. You'll have to take care of that with some of your famous biscuits."

"Hello there," Luke said. "Remember me?"

Cricket stepped out of Creed's arms and directly into Luke's. There were tears in her eyes when she said, "I'm so glad you're safe. I was so worried about you. And with good reason, it seems. Look at you. You're so skinny!" She ran her hands over him appraisingly as she hugged him again. "You must be hungry."

Luke laughed. "As a matter of fact, I am. What're you gonna do about it?"

"Why, feed you, of course. You are staying for the christening, aren't you, Luke?"

"I'd like to. I got an assignment from Captain Hays when I was in San Antonio—have to investigate some irregularities in the registration of land titles in Shelby County—but I can stay for a while. How soon do you expect it'll be?"

"We're still waiting for Creed's brother and his wife to show up," Cricket said.

Creed ran a hand through his black hair. "You mean Tom and Amy aren't here yet?"

"I suspect the weather's holding them up," Cricket said, tucking an arm around each man's waist and directing them toward the house. "We've had quite a bit of rain. The roads must be horrendous. But they shouldn't be much longer getting here."

"Guess you'll be our guest for a few days," Creed said to Luke. "You don't mind staying in the bachelors' quarters here at Three Oaks, do you? I've got some pretty fond memories of that place myself." Creed's eyes gleamed, and Cricket fought the blush that rose to her cheeks at the memory of the first night she'd spent with Creed in the soft featherbed at the bachelors' quarters.

"Just lead me to this pretty little baby of yours," Luke said.

"Oh, Luke," Cricket said. "You're going to love her. She's so beautiful." Cricket grinned. "She's got a few years to go yet before you can turn that charm of yours on her and have it work."

"What charm is that?" Luke asked innocently.

Cricket laughed and shoved the two men through the front door ahead of her.

Bay was waiting in the hall when the three of them came in. "Where's Long Quiet?"

Luke and Creed exchanged a glance before Creed answered, "He's gone back to *Comancheria*."

Bay suddenly felt dizzy. She would have fallen if Luke hadn't caught her.

"Sit her down over here." Cricket gestured for Luke to help Bay over to the rocker bench along one wall.

"I . . . I thought he'd come . . ." Bay closed her eyes in misery. She hadn't even admitted to herself that she'd hoped he would come to the christening. After all, he and Creed were best friends. She clenched her hands to hide their trembling. She was going to have to pick up the pieces of her life and keep on living. But, oh, how she missed Long Quiet!

Cricket sat down next to her sister. Her eyes questioned Creed. Why was Bay so concerned about Long Quiet? Cricket tightened her arm around Bay's shoulders. "I know you'd probably like another chance to thank Long Quiet, but I'm sure he understands how you feel."

Bay's head came up slowly. "Yes . . . yes . . . I'm sure he

does. It would have been nice to thank him again, but I suppose Creed can take my thanks and pass it along just as well." She looked up at Creed and could tell from the look in his eyes that he knew more than he was saying. "Will you do that, Creed? Next time you see Long Quiet, will you tell him I said thanks for everything?"

Creed's brow furrowed. "If that's what you want, sure. I'll tell him you're engaged to Harper, too."

Bay's eyes widened as she realized Creed had believed Jonas's announcement. "But I'm not!"

"Jonas said you were."

Bay shook off Cricket's supporting arm and stood up. "Jonas spoke out of turn. Yes, it's true he's asked me to be his wife, but I haven't accepted."

"Oh, Bay, that's wonderful!" Cricket said. "Are you going to accept?"

"I . . ." Bay stared at the three faces confronting her. Was she going to say yes? What was she waiting for? A man as proud as Long Quiet wasn't going to admit he'd made a mistake. He was never going to come back for her. And she could never go to him. She only wished she felt more for Jonas Harper than deep friendship. "I don't know," she said at last. "It's a big decision. I don't want to rush into it. I need some time to think."

With that she turned and crossed to Rip's office, closing the door behind her. She didn't want to think right now, and the best respite from thinking was to immerse herself in work. She pulled the ledger down from the shelf and opened it.

It wasn't long before Bay heard a knock on the door. She was only mildly surprised when Rip opened the door and entered. She'd known that word of Jonas's proposal would soon reach Rip's ears and that he'd want to hear from her why she hadn't immediately accepted.

"Cricket told me the good news. Of course you'll accept,"

he said. He smiled broadly. "I'll expect to have my next grandchild within the year."

If Rip hadn't said anything about children, perhaps Bay could have remained calm. But she'd only barely resigned herself to giving up Long Quiet. The added thought of never having his children was too much to bear. She rose and snapped, "I wouldn't count on it!"

"What?"

"You heard me. I haven't even accepted Jonas's offer yet and you already have me bearing his children. I won't have it!"

"What's wrong with bearing Jonas's children? You could do a lot worse than Jonas as a husband."

"I don't need another husband!"

It took the look of shock on Rip's face for Bay to realize what she'd said. *Another husband.* Bay closed her eyes, then opened them again. She'd let the milk spill, the cat out of the bag, the horse from the barn.

"You're already married?" Rip asked in a tight voice.

Bay laughed bitterly.

"Then you're a widow?"

"I'm not married. But I'm not a widow, either."

"Dammit, girl, it has to be one or the other," Rip insisted.

"He left me," Bay said. "He brought me home and then he rode away and left me."

Rip's eyes darkened as he realized the identity of Bay's husband. "You married that half-breed Comanche, Long Quiet?"

"Don't you dare speak in that tone of voice about my husband!"

"By your own word, he's not your husband. How can you defend a man who abandoned you? He couldn't have loved you very much if he left you standing on my doorstep."

"He loved me."

"How could he? He only found you a couple of weeks ago.

Or was that a lie? How long have you known that half-breed?" Rip snarled.

"Not very long. There were reasons why we . . . we had to get married."

The blood drained from Rip's face. "You're going to have his child?"

"No! No. There were other reasons that forced us to marry."

"But he didn't willingly make you his wife?"

Bay shuddered and admitted, "No."

"Then how do you know he loved you?" Rip demanded.

"He told me so."

Rip snorted. "Where is he now, this husband of yours?"

"He went back to *Comancheria*."

"Is he coming back for you?"

"I don't . . ." Bay took a deep breath and said, "No. No, he isn't."

Rip was silent for a moment, so Bay thought he might let the subject drop. But he didn't.

"So he just dumped you here and left."

Bay clenched her teeth in an attempt to stop the quivering of her chin. Rip always went for the jugular. It was part of what had made him so successful on the Texas frontier. She swallowed painfully over the lump in her throat, but though she opened her mouth to reply, no sound came out.

Rip's voice was surprisingly gentle when he said, "Don't waste your life mourning for him, Bay. You deserve some happiness. A Comanche marriage doesn't mean a thing here in Texas. Forget about it. Forget about him. Your Comanche could never have given you what Jonas Harper can—respectability, a comfortable home, and a rich legacy for your children."

What about love? Bay wanted to shout. But she said nothing. There was no winning an argument with Rip. "I don't know if I can marry Jonas without telling him the truth."

Rip reached out and held Bay with a hand on each shoulder,

forcing her to listen to him. "There's not a man in Texas, Jonas included, who would touch you with anything but contempt if he knew the truth. Think, Bay! You're destined for greater things than being some half-breed Comanche's woman. I've planned too long and worked too hard to have you end up pining away for some man who doesn't love you enough to keep you by his side."

"You don't understand."

"Don't defend him to me. He had his chance. Now it's Jonas's turn."

"But what if Long Quiet changes his mind?"

"If he ever changes his mind, it'll be too late. You'll already be Jonas Harper's wife."

Once upon a time Bay would have greeted Rip's dictum with resignation. But Bay had more to say, and so she said it. "The choice is mine. I'll make my own decision whether or not to become Jonas's wife."

Bay could hardly believe the look of approval in Rip's eyes, but there was no mistaking his smile when he replied, "All right, Bay. You know your own mind. I'll trust you to decide what's right for you. But think about it, won't you? Jonas will make a good husband, and you do care for him. I can't tell you what to say to Jonas about Long Quiet. But I will say it won't help for him to know. It can only hurt."

Rip turned on his heel and left. Bay stared after him for a moment, too numb to move. Rip had actually said she could make her own decision. She wasn't the only one who'd changed over the past three years. The Rip who could admit he cared, the Rip who could reach out a hand to help, the Rip who said she could decide for herself was not the same Rip who'd dictated to his daughters in the past. He'd mellowed with age, like a fine wine.

Bay visualized her father as he was, with threads of gray in his hair and wrinkles on his face. He wasn't a young man anymore. Were the changes in his personality simply the result of his getting older? Or, given a second chance, had he decided to treat her as more than a disappointing daughter? Whatever the reasons for his new behavior, Bay was more than willing to meet him halfway. She would try to be worthy of the trust he was showing in her judgment.

Unfortunately, all she wanted to do right now was lay her head down and cry. She barely made it to the chair in front of the desk before she collapsed with her head cradled in her arms on the desktop. She cried for the loss of her Comanche child. She cried for the father who was growing old. And she cried for the true love she'd lost and could never hope to find again.

Sloan had come to the plantation office to ask Bay to order more nails and had ended up hearing more than she wanted to of Rip's conversation with Bay. When she stepped into Rip's office, she found her sister with her head down on the desk, her tear-streaked face half hidden in her arms. Sloan hated seeing Bay suffer, especially over a man.

"Crying won't bring him back."

Bay jerked her head up at the sound of Sloan's voice. She quickly wiped the tears from her eyes with the sleeve of her dress.

"I ought to know," Sloan continued. "I cried enough tears when Antonio got himself killed."

"Long Quiet's not dead."

"He might as well be. Face it, Bay. He's never coming back. You're learning, the same as I did, that you can't trust a man not to hurt you. He'll take your heart and tear it in two and throw the pieces back in your face like so much useless paper."

"I love him," Bay protested.

Sloan laughed, and the harsh sound sent chills up Bay's spine.

"He used you. The way Antonio used me."

"No!"

"You're better off forgetting him," Sloan said, but her voice broke when she placed her hand on Bay's shoulder and added, "I'm sorry, Bay. Truly sorry."

When Sloan left, Bay wiped the tears from her eyes. Sloan was right about one thing. Crying wasn't going to solve anything. She couldn't believe Sloan was right about Long Quiet's using her, but the fact was he'd left her and he wasn't ever coming back. Admitting the truth was hard, and it left her hurt and angry. But it also left her free to make her decision.

Bay wasn't so distraught that she couldn't see what the future held for her. She could refuse Jonas's proposal, but what would that accomplish? She knew Rip too well to think he wouldn't find another man to present to her in Jonas's place. And maybe the next man wouldn't be someone she liked as much as she liked Jonas. . . . And at least Jonas loved her.

Her decision wasn't so difficult after all.

The next day Bay took special pains with her appearance. She donned a green cambric dress that left the tops of her shoulders bare, then followed the lines of her lush figure, cinching her waist tightly before it fell in gathered folds to the floor. The mint color emphasized her honey skin and complemented her auburn hair, which she parted down the middle and let fall in pert sausage curls that framed her face.

When Jonas arrived that afternoon, she didn't keep him waiting. "Hello, Jonas." This time she was first to extend her hands to him. She could see his delight at her appearance and his surprise that she'd made the overture to greet him for a change.

"You're lovely. Simply lovely," Jonas said, his approval making his voice husky. He brought her hands to his lips, but let them linger, taking his time and letting her feel his need in the pressure of his touch. He was smiling ruefully when he said, "Will you marry me, Bay?"

"Yes."

Jonas stood stunned while he tried to absorb Bay's agreement. "You will?"

"Yes, Jonas. I'll marry you." Bay felt almost ill, but the discomfort eased somewhat at the smile of pleasure that lit Jonas's face.

"We'll announce our engagement at the christening party," he said enthusiastically, "and get married at Christmas. How does that sound?"

"I . . . uh . . . fine . . . I guess."

Bay was cut off when Jonas's mouth came down to cover hers possessively. It was a practiced kiss and Bay wondered for a moment where Jonas had learned it. It amazed her that she could remain detached enough to make such an observation. Although Jonas's kiss was pleasant, she felt nothing of the fire she'd experienced in Long Quiet's arms. She tried to imagine baring herself to Jonas's gaze, allowing him to touch her freely. She shuddered unexpectedly but attributed it to the natural modesty she would have felt at having any man look upon her naked body.

"I can feel you trembling with pleasure, sweetheart," Jonas said, breaking the kiss. "Perhaps that kiss was a bit too forward, but I wanted you to have some idea of the delights in store for you when we're husband and wife. Shall we go find your father and tell him the good news?"

"You go," Bay said with a tremulous smile. She'd agreed to marry Jonas, but that didn't mean she was ready to endure Rip's sure-to-be-satisfied countenance.

"I'll see you later, darling," Jonas said.

Bay concentrated to keep from frowning at Jonas's endearment. She stood patiently as he dropped another quick kiss on her lips, before he headed in search of Rip.

Bay slid onto the settee as her knees buckled. What had she done? How was she ever gong to survive her wedding night with Jonas Harper? What was he going to say when he discovered that the woman he thought trembled at his amorous kiss wasn't even a virgin?

The next three weeks passed slowly for Bay. Jonas was delighted that she'd accepted his proposal. Rip stalked around the plantation wearing a perpetual grin. It was Luke who made Bay uneasy. His perceptive eyes watched her constantly, and it was clear he wasn't fooled by the smile she wore for everyone else's benefit.

At long last, Tom and Amy Creed arrived at Three Oaks with their five-year-old son Seth and one-year-old daughter Emily. The house was filled with the sound of children's laughter, reminding Bay all the more of what she'd left behind in *Comancheria*. With Tom and Amy's arrival, the christening—and thus, the announcement of Bay's engagement—was set for the third Sunday in October.

As the day drew near, Bay became more agitated. She had trouble concentrating on her work and began taking long walks down along the river after supper. She was taking such a walk when she became aware of a presence behind her. As though sensing he'd been discovered, Luke said, "Hello, Bay."

She turned to confront him. "I prefer to walk alone."

"I know."

"Then why are you here?"

"I wanted to ask you a question."

"All right, ask."

"Are you happy about becoming Jonas Harper's wife?" Luke searched Bay's violet eyes for the truth.

Bay forced herself to smile. "Of course I'm happy. I'm marrying a man who loves me, who's well liked by my family and rich enough to satisfy even my father. Why wouldn't I be happy?"

"You didn't say anything about loving Jonas."

"Didn't I? Of course I . . . love Jonas. He's a wonderful

man, a wonderful friend. I'm sure we'll be very happy together. There, does that answer your question?"

"Yes," Luke said. "It does." He turned and walked away, leaving Bay alone once more.

Bay sank onto a nearby log because her legs were trembling so badly they wouldn't hold her upright. Luke Summers hadn't believed a single word she'd said.

That wasn't surprising, because neither did she.

Chapter 18

I'M ENGAGED TO JONAS HARPER. BAY STARED DOWN AT the immense ruby set in gold that adorned her left hand. The ring, which visibly marked her as Jonas's future bride, felt heavy on her hand. She caught sight of Luke staring at her, a look of concern on his face, and smiled brightly at him. *I will be happy with Jonas*, she vowed fiercely to herself. *I will.*

The engagement announcement had been made immediately following the christening of Jesse Elizabeth Creed and had surprised and delighted the assembled planters, their wives, sons, and daughters. Nearly everyone present had made it a point to greet the prodigal daughter who'd returned to capture the heart and hand of one of the richest and most handsome bachelors in the Republic of Texas. Bay stood in a daze as she was approached by yet another of the multitude of well-wishers mingling in Rip's parlor.

"You're looking very well, Bayleigh."

"Thank you, Mrs. Kuykendall," Bay replied. Bay's smile looked genuine, but after two hours of politely greeting curious guests, she was having a hard time keeping it that way. She couldn't blame them for staring at her. After all, she had changed. It was just that what they saw as increased self-assurance garnered from attending fetes on the Continent actually resulted from three years of survival under the harshest conditions imaginable.

"I've come to take you away from all this," a husky voice rasped in her ear.

Bay turned to face Jonas but kept her strained smile in place. He, no less than anyone else, must be convinced of her happiness this afternoon.

"You're breathtaking," he whispered. "Come away with me and be my wife."

"I think I already promised to do that," she said with a strained laugh.

"Oh, there you are, Bay."

Bay turned sharply as she recognized the voice of Felicia Myers. Felicia wore a dress so stylish Bay was sure it must have been pictured in the most recent issue of *Godey's Lady's Book* from New York, but in a color that could most accurately be described as harlot red.

"Wherever did you get that dress?" Felicia asked, gesturing with her closed fan at Bay's simple lavender silk day dress.

"I made it," Bay replied.

"Goodness. I'd have thought with all the money Rip Stewart has he could afford to hire a seamstress."

"I think I see Amber Kuykendall," Bay said. "I haven't had a chance to speak with her yet. Will you excuse me, please?"

It was only after Bay escaped that she realized she'd left Jonas standing with Felicia. She turned and watched Jonas basking in Felicia's obvious admiration. A moment later she saw from the feline smile on Felicia's face that Jonas had returned the compliment. She watched Felicia's slim white fingers come out to stroke Jonas's sleeve . . . and felt nothing.

She should feel jealous. She should want to claw Felicia's eyes out. She should want to rescue Jonas from the clutches of that green-eyed lady tomcat in her harlot-red dress. What she felt was . . . faintly ill.

Oh, Bay. What have you done?

Surely she could learn to love Jonas as a wife should love her husband. Bay straightened her spine in determination.

She had no choice, for it was too late now to change her mind. Everyone who was anyone for miles around was here, and it would humiliate Jonas if she tried to back out of their engagement now.

But she needed a respite from the effort of appearing more happy than she was. Bay looked for someone she could be with and not have to keep up her smiling pretense.

She briefly considered Rip, but he was surrounded by planters, all talking about the poor cotton crop and how they'd manage if things were this bad again next year. Bay wasn't willing to broach the crowd of men to reach Rip. She'd endured enough looks at her slightly exposed cleavage when she'd shaken hands with each of them as they arrived. She had no intention of submitting herself for further ogling.

She sought out Cricket. She found her sister sitting in a large wing chair in the corner of the parlor with Jesse, still clothed in her lacy white christening gown, lying in her arms. Creed stood behind Cricket, obviously a proud father. They'd been joined by Tom and Amy Creed, Luke Summers, and Cruz Guerrero, Antonio's elder brother.

As Bay approached the group, she saw that Cruz's gaze kept wandering to the other side of the room. She followed his glance and discovered that the object of his attention was Sloan. She wondered why Cruz was staring so intently at his brother's lover. A second look at Sloan did much to explain Cruz's interest.

Sloan's normal attire around the plantation consisted of a red gingham shirt with a tan linsey waistcoat and dark brown fitted osnaburg trousers tucked into knee-high black Wellington boots—typical planter's garb. Tonight, she wore a pale blue silk dress, piped in two complementing shades of darker blue, that emphasized the womanly curve from her shoulders to the point where the V-shaped bodice ended at her tiny waist.

Because of Sloan's dominating presence, Bay sometimes forgot how much shorter Sloan was than herself or Cricket, who were both quite tall. In the powder-blue silk, Sloan appeared petite and delicate, characteristics Bay had never attributed to her sister. Sloan's huge chocolate-brown eyes seemed vulnerable, almost frightened. Her sable hair was caught at the base of her neck with a pale blue ribbon, giving her a childlike innocence Bay found disconcerting, especially since Sloan was a woman of twenty-two who'd borne a child.

As Bay watched, she realized Cruz was trying to catch Sloan's eye. Perhaps he wanted to talk to her about her son. Bay knew that even if Sloan wouldn't admit it, she must wonder sometimes how Cisco was faring with the Guerreros at Rancho Dolorosa. The longer Bay watched, the more convinced she became that Sloan was purposely avoiding Cruz. How awkward she must be feeling, Bay thought. As though to confirm Bay's conclusion, Sloan fled the parlor.

Bay forgot about seeking out Cricket's company and followed Sloan from the parlor, intent on finding her older sister and comforting her. Bay hunted through the four downstairs rooms without any luck and decided Sloan must have gone outside. She walked out the back door, fully expecting to find Sloan sitting on the bench at the base of one of the three oaks. Sure enough, she saw some movement within the moss-laden branches.

"Sloan? Is that you?" Bay called out.

"No. It's me," a masculine voice responded.

Stunned, Bay halted where she was.

The man who stepped out of the shadows bore little resemblance to the man who'd presented Bay with 250 ponies as a wedding price. His long black braids, a Comanche's pride, were gone, replaced by blue-black hair cut to the top of his collar. He drove his fingers through the wavy locks in agitation and succeeded in brushing them away from his face, except where a single black curl fell determinedly onto his forehead. He wore black boots, buff kerseymere trousers that fit him like a second skin, a black wool frock coat that ended just above his knees, an embroidered satin waistcoat, and a snowy-white tucked linen shirt with a stylish white silk cravat knotted at his tanned throat.

His voice when he spoke was low, husky with emotion. "I've been standing here trying to work up the courage to come inside and tell you how wrong I was ever to leave you, how nothing is more important to me than spending the rest of my life with you."

Long Quiet didn't give her a chance to speak, just swept her into his embrace, capturing her lips and searing her soul with the hot invasion of his tongue seeking the honeyed treasures he'd abandoned. One large hand threaded through her auburn curls and held her head still for his ravaging kiss while the other swept down her back and grasped her buttocks, pulling her tightly into the cradle of his thighs.

Bay was overwhelmed by sensation. Unable to resist Long Quiet's sensual onslaught, she joined it, grasping his silky hair in her hands and holding his mouth to hers as she returned his kiss with all the love and longing she'd held in abeyance. Her hands slipped down to his broad shoulders, then to his chest, where she already had three buttons of his waistcoat undone before she realized what she was doing. She jerked her head away from Long Quiet's kiss, her breathing so raspy it took a moment before she could say a word.

She used that moment to note Long Quiet's avid gaze, his nostrils that flared for the scent of her, his lips swollen with the force of his kisses, the sensual movement of his tongue as he moistened his lips.

"We can't . . . do this," she panted.

"No one can see us," he rasped in reply. "We're well hidden here. Let me love you, Bay. It's been so long."

"I—"

His mouth cut off her protest as he sought her lips with all the hunger and need he felt for her. Bay resisted for only a moment before her fingers tangled in his silky hair again and she gave herself wholeheartedly to the kiss. She blossomed under his loving, like a petal exposed to the golden rays of the sun.

Her body molded to his hard male form as his hands caressed her shoulders, then skimmed across her breasts beneath the lavender dress. His mouth found her exposed neck and shoulders, and Bay's head fell back to give him the access he demanded. Then his lips and tongue found the smooth swell of her breast above the lavender bodice and Bay felt the tips of her breasts tighten and swell with the fullness that heralded her need. If she didn't stop him now, she wouldn't have the will to stop him later.

"Long Quiet, stop," she protested weakly.

He nipped with his teeth at her breast through the dress.

Then, breathily, "Please stop."

His tongue laved her throat. His moist breath rasped in her ear.

"Oh, God, please," Bay begged. With her last bit of willpower, she stiffened against his caress.

Long Quiet responded instantly to Bay's rigidity. He lifted his head and searched her eyes. He saw pain and confusion in the violet depths. He stepped back and reached for her hands, taking them in his. "What's wrong, Bay?"

Then he detected the ring on her hand. He lowered his eyes and felt his stomach churn at the sight of the huge ruby. He raised his gaze again and saw in Bay's eyes the answer to his unspoken question.

He cleared his throat over the lump that had grown there and asked, "Who?"

"Jonas Harper."

He didn't bother to ask her if she loved Jonas. It had been Jonas's name she'd cried out the first time he'd made love to her. How could he have been such a fool as to let her go!

At the tortured look in Long Quiet's eyes, Bay felt a desperate need to explain. "We got engaged today. I . . . I thought I'd never see you again. I was sure you'd never come back for me."

Long Quiet released Bay's hands and dropped his arms to his sides. His hands balled into fists as his flinty eyes narrowed. "I nearly didn't come back, until I had a talk with Many Horses."

"Many Horses? Is he well? Has he recovered?"

"He's well enough to seek revenge from the Tonkawas. That's where I've been."

"Raiding the Tonkawas?"

"Come. Sit down with me," he said, "and I'll explain everything."

When Long Quiet reached out a hand to her, Bay stepped forward and took it. The frisson of sexual tension that arced between them from even this simple touch told Bay nothing had changed in the time they'd been separated. If only Long Quiet had come a few hours earlier!

Bay could feel the suppressed urgency in Long Quiet's grasp as he escorted her to the ornately carved wooden bench at the base of the live oak. Once they were seated, he asked, "How have things been for you since you came home?"

"Better than you'd expect," Bay replied. "Rip told everyone I've been touring the Continent."

Long Quiet shook his head in disbelief. "So none of the celebrants know that you're my wife."

Bay's tone was sharp with the hurt she'd endured during Long Quiet's absence as she said, "Am I your wife? We're not in *Comanchería* now, we're in Texas. A Comanche marriage means nothing here."

"You're my wife," Long Quiet said. "We don't need the white man's words to know what is in our hearts."

Anger and frustration that he'd come only a few hours too late to stop her engagement to Jonas spilled into Bay's voice. "You left me here and told me to forget about you. What was I supposed to think?"

Long Quiet's lips compressed. "I've admitted I was wrong to leave you. I believed it was the right decision at the time."

"And now?"

"Since I left you I've spent a lot of hours thinking about exactly why I'd chosen to stay and live among the Comanches. I didn't like the answer I kept getting. Then Many Horses painted a picture of my future without you in words so vivid they cried to be heard."

"What did he say?"

"That I'd end up a lonely old man with no woman to love or to love me, and no children to carry on my seed."

"I see."

"Do you, Bay?"

She avoided answering him, saying instead, "You've cut off your braids. Yet you told me you couldn't live in the white man's world. What will you do here in Texas?"

"I don't think I could work the land," Long Quiet admitted. "I'm not cut out for it."

"No, I suppose not. But that doesn't answer my question."

"I thought I'd raise horses. That's a respectable occupation even for a Comanche. I may even run a few cattle. I've been busy making plans. That's why I've been so long coming back to you. I went to my grandfather's village for my herd of horses, then drove them to Houston and sold them. I have enough money now to buy a piece of land where I can build a house for us."

"Take your hands off my fiancée!"

Bay's heart started beating double time as she realized what was about to happen. As she opened her mouth to explain things to Jonas, he grabbed her arm and pulled her to her feet. "You're too innocent for your own good, darling. Couldn't you see this gentleman was taking advantage of you?"

"Don't be ridiculous, Jonas."

"I'll take care of this, Bay. Why don't you go into the house?"

"I'd rather stay here."

Jonas looked annoyed, but Bay wasn't about to leave the two men alone.

Long Quiet had come to his feet in the same instant Jonas grabbed Bay, and it was only because Bay had quickly shaken her head that he hadn't already laid Jonas low. He stood tall and menacing, waiting for Bay to explain to Jonas that their engagement was off and that she'd be coming with him.

"Who are you?" Jonas demanded of the stranger. "I don't think I've seen you around here before."

"My name is Walker Coburn. Bay Stewart is my—"

"Friend," Bay interrupted, certain Long Quiet was about to identify her as his wife. He became tight-lipped with rage, but he held his tongue. "He's a very good friend," Bay said in an attempt to ease the tension between the two men. Bay could tell Jonas was making all the wrong assumptions about who and what Long Quiet was to her. But there was no way she could correct his mistaken assumptions without revealing the truth.

"I thought I knew all your male friends," Jonas said, never taking his eyes from Long Quiet. "Where did you meet Bay?" he demanded of Long Quiet.

"In Boston."

Jonas tightened his hold on Bay and asked, "What are you doing here at Three Oaks?"

"I came to make Bay my wife."

Jonas's whole body tensed. "I'm afraid it's too late for that. Bay is engaged to me."

"But she's going to marry me."

"The hell she is!" Jonas's fingers squeezed Bay's arm possessively until she cried out in pain.

Long Quiet clamped a hand onto Jonas's wrist and a moment later Bay was free and staggering away. Jonas grasped his injured wrist with his other hand and stared in shock at Long Quiet.

"Don't ever hurt her again," Long Quiet warned.

"How dare you threaten me. Do you know who I am?"

"You're a dead man if you ever hurt Bay again."

"We'll see who ends up dead," Jonas shouted, unnerved by

Long Quiet's calm voice. "You stay away from Bay. She belongs to me, and if you ever come near her again, I'll make sure it's the last thing you do."

Jonas was on the verge of attacking Long Quiet when Bay's voice halted him. "Stop this. Both of you, stop it!" She stepped between the two of them.

By now, sounds of the commotion in the backyard had brought several of the guests from the house. A small crowd had gathered to watch the altercation.

"Come with me, Bay," Jonas said. "We have to say good-bye to your father's guests."

"Stay with me, Bay," Long Quiet said.

Bay wanted to explain to Long Quiet why she had to go with Jonas, but there was no way she could say anything with so many eager ears listening. She could never humiliate Jonas in front of his friends. Even if she didn't love him the way she loved Long Quiet, he was entitled to save his pride.

"Let's go, Jonas," she said. Bay had never seen Long Quiet so coldly furious. Her eyes pleaded with him to understand. *I have no choice!* She turned and walked back to the house with Jonas.

Long Quiet was reeling from the painful blow he'd just been dealt. He told himself Bay had a right to be angry with him for abandoning her and that she had taken out her anger by choosing to go with the other man. But he knew she loved him. She couldn't have kissed him the way she had if she didn't still love him. And that meant she could still change her mind and be his wife. He would not make the same mistake twice.

This time he would woo her. And he would win her.

He was aware at once when Bay's father stepped within the haven created by the limbs of the concealing live oak. He'd expected opposition from Rip, and he got it.

"She's going to marry Jonas, and you're not going to stop her."

Long Quiet turned to face Rip Stewart. "She's already married. To me."

"Not in Texas," Rip countered. "Besides, what can you give her that can possibly compare with what Jonas Harper has to offer? He has wealth, property, respectability. What can you offer her?"

"I only need to find the right piece of land for my ranch, and I'll build a home for her."

"Were you planning to take my daughter to live in a dogtrot Texas house made of logs and chinked with mud? Bay deserves better. She's accustomed to better."

Long Quiet didn't bother to point out that Bay had survived with much less among the Comanches. He simply said, "She's my wife."

"Maybe she was once, but she's not anymore. She's engaged to Jonas Harper. She loves him. She's loved him for years. She doesn't need you, and she doesn't want you. Believe me, if she did, I'd be the last person to stand in her way. I'm only thinking of what's best for Bay. Leave her be."

Long Quiet remembered how Bay had called out Jonas Harper's name the first time he'd made love to her. And it was true Harper could give her the luxuries she'd enjoyed in the white world. What if Rip Stewart was right? What if Bay preferred the things Jonas Harper could give her? But surely his love meant more to her than having silk dresses or silver forks and spoons.

"Perhaps we should let Bay decide what she wants," Long Quiet said.

"You're wasting your time," Rip countered.

"It's my time."

"I don't want Bay hurt any more than she already has been."

"Neither do I."

Rip sighed and turned to leave, but stopped to shake his head and add, "You're a damned stubborn, single-minded man."

"So are you."

Once Rip was gone, Long Quiet slumped back against the huge gnarled trunk of the live oak. A snapping twig brought him upright, poised to fight.

"Whoa! It's just me," Creed said. "I heard what happened. Seems like you've got your work cut out for you."

Long Quiet leaned back against the oak again. "Seems that way."

"I'm glad to see you decided to fight for Bay."

"I love her," Long Quiet replied.

"Is there anything I can do to help?"

"Can you tell me where I might find a piece of land suitable for ranching?"

"As a matter of fact, I can. Cruz Guerrero told me this afternoon that Jonas Harper approached him a while back about buying some of Rancho Dolorosa. Cruz needs the money more than the land, and he's been seriously considering Jonas's offer. If you like, I can mention to Cruz before he leaves that you're also interested in the property."

"Do that. Tell him I'll make a trip out to Rancho Dolorosa tomorrow to talk with him about it."

"I'll see if I can catch Cruz now." Creed reached a palm out to his friend. "Good luck . . . Walker."

Long Quiet took Creed's hand and shook it firmly. "Thanks. I'll need it."

Chapter 19

BAY HAD PLEADED A HEADACHE AND PROMISED TO meet Jonas in the morning to talk, but she hadn't realized how hectic the next morning would be. Cricket and Creed were anxious to start for home and were taking Tom and Amy Creed with them for a visit at Lion's Dare. Luke was preparing to head for the Texas-Louisiana border, since he had Ranger business in Shelby County. The few neighbors who'd come from far enough away to stay overnight had left at daybreak, and Bay spent the few spare moments she had mentally preparing the speech she planned to give to Jonas.

Just before Cricket left, she pulled Bay aside. "Creed told me Walker's here in Texas to stay and that he says he loves you. I had no idea, Bay, that you and Walker . . . are you still going to marry Jonas?"

"No, I'm not. I care for Jonas, and I don't want to hurt him. I probably would have married him if Long Quiet hadn't come to get me. But now . . . of course I haven't had a chance to say anything to Long Quiet yet, and I won't until I've spoken to Jonas. I can't break our engagement right away, because it would cause too much talk. But I'm going to tell Jonas today that I can't marry him."

Cricket hugged Bay. "I'm so glad everything's turning out all right."

"So am I. Take care of Jesse. Maybe the next time I see you I'll be the one with the new baby."

"I hope so," Cricket said with a laugh. "I can't wait to see Walker playing the role of father."

Cricket and Creed had already driven away in their carriage, followed by Tom and Amy in theirs, when Luke sought Bay out. "I came to say good-bye and to tell you . . . ask you . . . how much do you really know about Jonas, Bay?"

"I've never had cause to doubt him, Luke. Is that what you're asking?"

"No. I mean how much do you know about his business dealings?"

"Not much. I know his father had business interests in Louisiana and that Jonas sold some of them and bought property in Shelby County. Why do you ask?"

"I'm headed to Shelby County to investigate charges of corruption in the land-title office. One of the men who's profited most by the alleged corruption is Jonas Harper."

"You must be mistaken, Luke. Jonas would never stoop to thievery."

Luke snorted in disgust. "That's what Rip said when I told him what I knew. For your sake, I hope you're both right. Just promise me you'll wait to marry Jonas until I've found out the truth."

Bay opened her mouth to tell Luke she had no intentions of marrying Jonas now that Long Quiet had returned, but since that might have suggested a lack of trust in Jonas that she didn't feel, she said nothing about her plans. "I'm sure you're going to find that Jonas is totally innocent, Luke, so you needn't worry about me."

"Damned stubborn, strong-willed Stewart women," Luke muttered.

Bay put a hand on Luke's arm to stop him as he turned to leave. "All right," she said, not totally sure why she felt the need to reassure him. "I'll wait."

The look of relief in Luke's hazel eyes was her reward. "Thanks, Bay. I'd better get moving."

"Take care of yourself, Luke."

"Sure, Bay. You too."

Bay had little time to contemplate Luke's accusations before Jonas arrived at Three Oaks. She greeted him in the parlor, dreading what she had to say because she knew it would hurt him.

"Good morning, darling," Jonas said, leaning forward to kiss Bay on the cheek. "Are you feeling better this morning?"

"Yes, Jonas, I'm fine. Won't you sit down?"

Jonas had seated himself comfortably in the wing chair before he realized Bay wasn't going to sit down. She was pacing nervously.

"What's wrong, Bay?"

"I don't know how to tell you," she said hesitantly.

Jonas rose and, taking Bay's hands in his, seated her on the brocade-covered settee before dropping down beside her. "Now, tell me what's wrong. I'm sure it's nothing I can't handle."

Bay took a deep breath and said, "I can't marry you, Jonas."

"But we just got engaged!"

"I know that, and I know we can't announce that we've broken our engagement until a decent time has passed. But then you can say you've changed your mind or that you discovered we weren't suited after all."

"But we're perfectly suited to one another."

"Oh, Jonas, it isn't that I don't care for you—I do."

"Then what is it, Bay?"

Bay fidgeted with the pink ribbon that streamed down the front of her light wool day dress.

"It's that other man, that Walker Coburn, isn't it?"

"I'm . . . I'm in love with him, Jonas."

"But you're engaged to me."

"Yes, I am," Bay agreed in an attempt to soothe Jonas's

growing agitation, "but that's what I'm trying to explain. We'll have to break our engagement. I can't marry you, because I'm in love with Walker."

"But you care for me."

"Of course I do."

"And you would have married me if this Walker fellow hadn't come here looking for you?"

Bay couldn't face Jonas as she admitted, "Yes."

"Then there's no reason for us to break our engagement, Bay. I love you, and you care for me. Walker Coburn doesn't figure into it."

"You'll find someone else, Jonas."

"No. There's no one else for me but you, Bay. I've had this picture in my mind from the day I met you—the two of us surrounded by our children. I'm not giving that up, Bay, especially not to some stranger who wanders in the day we get engaged and tries to steal you away from me."

Bay winced when Jonas gripped her wrist, because of the bruises he'd made the previous day. He didn't seem to notice he was hurting her again.

"Look at me, Bay," he said. Bay met Jonas's fierce gaze with reluctance. "You belong to me. I can understand how another man might find you attractive. After all, I find you exquisite. But he can't have what's mine."

"What about what I want, Jonas?"

"You want me."

"Not anymore," Bay said soberly.

"What if I told you that the fate of Three Oaks depends on your marrying me?"

Bay's heart began to beat a little faster as she asked, "What do you mean?"

"You know Rip's had a poor harvest the past two years."

"Yes. It's been the same for everybody up and down the Brazos."

"But everybody didn't have to rebuild and refurbish a house after it burned down. And everybody didn't have problems with a cotton gin that eventually had to be replaced. Rip had to borrow money. He mortgaged Three Oaks to do it."

"That's impossible. I've seen the books."

"Rip obviously didn't want you to worry your pretty little head about something you couldn't change. The truth is, I hold the note on Three Oaks, Bay, and because the latest cotton crop failed, Rip doesn't have the wherewithal to pay the amount due this year."

"Surely you're planning to extend the time he has to pay the note."

"Yes, of course I was . . . because he would have been my father-in-law. But without that relationship, I can't."

"Would you do it as a favor to me?"

"You know I would do anything for you, Bay. But you can understand that business is business. If I extended Rip's loan simply as a favor to you, without a family involvement, then all those for whom I hold similar notes would expect the same sort of consideration. In no time I'd be bankrupt myself. You can understand why I couldn't grant you such a favor if you weren't my wife, can't you?"

"No, quite frankly, I can't," Bay replied. "What you've said sounds suspiciously like a threat, Jonas. And I won't be threatened into marriage with you."

Jonas realized immediately that he'd made a tactical error, and quickly sought to mend his fences with Bay. "Of course there would probably be some way around the difficulty caused by our engagement being broken," he said hastily. "But to be equally honest, Bay, I simply couldn't afford to extend the note for more than another year in such a case, and then—"

"By then Rip could certainly pay what's due," Bay interrupted coolly.

"Perhaps," Jonas agreed. "Probably," he amended upon seeing Bay's gaze harden. "Well, what can I say?" he asked, exasperated at her unrelenting expression. "I have no control over the Texas weather or the worms that have wiped out the cotton two years in a row. Who can predict—"

Bay laid a hand on Jonas's arm to quiet him. "I understand what you're trying to say, Jonas. And I appreciate your concern. But I won't be coerced into marriage. Do you understand?"

This time it was Jonas's expression that hardened. He didn't like this side of Bay at all, but he supposed that it was what came of allowing a woman to spend so much time on her own traipsing around the Continent. Jonas had never been a graceful loser, but here the stakes were too high. He couldn't take the chance of offending his future bride by arguing with her. He had no choice except to capitulate. "All right, darling."

Bay patted his arm as a reward for his reasonableness. "I want a chance to talk with Rip about this," she said.

"By all means," Jonas encouraged, certain of Rip's support of his suit. He covered Bay's hand with his own as he added, "I'll abide by your decision. I love you, Bay. And I'd much rather have you for my wife than take possession of Three Oaks."

Bay held her breath as Jonas leaned over to press another chaste kiss on her cheek. "I'll see you to the door," she said.

"No need," Jonas replied with an understanding smile. "I know my way out."

Bay sat for a long time where she was, unable to believe the incredible claim Jonas had made about Rip's financial circumstances. Why hadn't Rip's books shown the severity of the debt Jonas had implied? It was hard to believe Rip had deliberately lied to her about such a thing, but apparently he had. And that could only mean the problem was every bit as critical as Jonas had suggested.

Bay felt a queasiness in her stomach that had nothing to do with the nervousness she'd felt earlier about confronting Jonas. What was she supposed to do now? Three Oaks was everything to her father. It was Sloan's heritage. What kind of daughter—indeed, what kind of sister—would she be if she had a chance to help and didn't take it?

She would simply have to confront Rip and determine the truth. Once she had all the facts she could decide whether it would be necessary to marry Jonas Harper after all.

Long Quiet heard the sharp crack of the rifle a second before the *thunk* of a bullet connected with flesh. His mount whinnied in terror, and a spurt of blood warmed Long Quiet's leg as the chestnut gelding buckled under him. Long Quiet reached out with his hands to cushion his fall, scraping his palms raw as they skidded along the rocks and dirt. The horse struggled against an inevitable death before it finally lay still. Long Quiet rolled himself into a tight ball in the cradle made by the horse's belly and legs and was soon lying in a pool of the animal's sticky blood.

Since the horse was down, the bushwhacker would know his one shot had found the animal and not the man. A quick look around convinced Long Quiet he couldn't make it to the nearest cover before whoever was shooting at him got another chance. He decided to wait it out. He could make his escape under cover of darkness.

Through the long day, the flies and insects were a trial, but it was the buzzards that became the greatest irritation. They seemed determined to make a meal of the horse and squawked in agitation when Long Quiet frightened them off. Even with those distractions, Long Quiet had too much time to think.

He only knew one person with a reason to want him dead. Of course he could be wrong. There was plenty of riffraff drifting around Texas. But it was more likely Jonas Harper had decided to eliminate his competition. There was no sense in confronting Jonas without proof. His time would be better spent preparing for the next attack.

He would be waiting when Jonas tried again.

The balance of Long Quiet's thoughts were spent on planning his future with Bay. It complicated matters considerably that she'd gotten engaged to Jonas, but he was convinced it was only a matter of time before she came to her senses and agreed to become his wife. He was certain he'd made the right decision in coming.

Yet it hadn't been easy deciding to live in Texas. He felt as though he'd shifted sides in the middle of a war. Of course there wasn't any war—at least not an overt one—but the feeling was there just the same. He only knew that without Bay his life was empty, as bleak to contemplate as an empty water gourd in the desert.

As darkness fell, Long Quiet had the rueful thought that he'd probably spent the day fighting off buzzards for nothing. Jonas Harper—or his hireling—was probably long gone. Long Quiet used the cover of nightfall to crawl a short distance from the horse's carcass. When he was clear of the animal, he rose and settled into a steady jog that brought him to the outskirts of Cruz's hacienda in little more than an hour. He searched for and found a place where he could rinse the worst of the blood off, but there was no way to remove entirely the effects of the day's events.

He hesitated at the fortresslike entrance to the hacienda. Comanches and Spaniards had been mortal enemies in Texas for hundreds of years. But he was no longer Comanche. The wizened old man who guarded the gate had expected Long Quiet earlier, so he escorted him to the house.

Long Quiet soon found himself in the cool, candle-lit interior of the adobe hacienda. The furnishings in the Guerrero home bore witness to Texas's possession by Spain and Mexico. Long Quiet sat in a heavy Mediterranean chair with a rawhide seat. He hesitated to set his glass of brandy on the delicate table beside the chair, for the elaborately inlaid Moorish table, with its spooled legs, looked more decorative than functional. Cruz stood at the other end of the large *sala*, the equivalent of a Texan parlor, his hand caressing a smooth blue Talavera jar.

Long Quiet had seen Cruz Guerrero in the past, when he'd competed at the *días de toros*, the roping and riding contests held at the end of the Spaniard's spring and fall roundup. He'd been impressed by what he'd found.

Cruz was tall, his body rapier-lean but laced with corded muscle. His gaze was hawklike, his mouth sensual above a cleft that rent his strong chin. Long Quiet looked for simple words to describe the aristocratic Spaniard and settled on *commanding* and *proud*. Despite those characteristics, Cruz had a reputation for gracious friendliness.

"I expected you earlier in the day," Cruz said as he handed a crystal glass to Long Quiet.

Long Quiet rolled the second glass of brandy between his palms as he'd learned to do in Boston. "I was detained by other matters."

Cruz raised a brow, eyeing the dried blood on Long Quiet's clothes, but didn't probe. "I understand you wish to start a ranch and need to purchase some land."

"That's right."

"If I sell to you, we will share a common border. I wish to know more of the man who would become my neighbor. Creed speaks very highly of you, of your integrity."

"Was it ever in doubt?" Long Quiet said, his eyes narrowing suspiciously.

"Excuse me, Señor Coburn. Perhaps I should explain my concern." Cruz walked over to one of the large rawhide-seated chairs and settled into it as though it were a throne from which he very comfortably ruled his kingdom. "Señor Harper approached me a few months ago about purchasing a great many hectares of Rancho Dolorosa land. Finances have been difficult for most Texans since we won our independence from Mexico seven years ago, and I must admit that since I paid my father's debts upon his death two years ago, the same is true for me. I found Señor Harper's offer attractive. I could put the money from such a sale to good use."

"So why didn't you sell to Harper?"

"At first I didn't sell to him because I wanted to find out more about him. After all, he would be my neighbor."

"And now?"

"Now I don't trust him."

Long Quiet leaned back in his chair and watched Cruz, waiting for an explanation.

"I am Castilian. My forebears were related to the royal family in Spain. Yet since we are not *anglo*, it has been a struggle to hold on to what is ours as more and more *anglos* move into Texas. The Guerrero family owns thousands of hectares of land, all of it deeded in grants from the Spanish crown more than a hundred years ago. So far the Texas government has held those deeds valid. If the Republic is annexed by the United States, there is always the possibility that Spanish land grants could be challenged. An *anglo* with a claim against a part of such a grant might very well be able to persuade those in power to cede to him what is not rightfully his."

"In other words, you think Harper is a thief."

"A very careful, very clever thief. But yes, a thief."

"What makes you suspect Jonas?"

"When I would not immediately sell him my land, certain unfortunate yet costly accidents began to occur. I do not like being threatened."

"And you think I'm more trustworthy than Jonas."

"Creed says you are. And I value his word. Creed also says you, and not Señor Harper, will marry Bayleigh Stewart."

"Yes, I will."

"*Bueno.* When you marry Señorita Stewart you will become part of my family."

Long Quiet sat forward in the rawhide chair. "What?"

"Sloan's child, Cisco, is my nephew. Bay is his aunt. I would much prefer having an honest man as my nephew's uncle. So you see I have very selfish reasons for preferring to sell to you rather than to Jonas Harper. I'll even loan you a few of my *vaqueros*, my cowboys, and some *mesteñeros*, some mustangers, to help you get started."

Long Quiet smiled sardonically. "I'd like to see the land before I agree to buy it."

"Certainly. I will show it to you tomorrow. There is a large adobe house on the property, where my grandparents lived before my father built this hacienda. I think you will find it comfortable. Will you stay here as my guest tonight?"

Long Quiet felt the thick adobe walls closing in on him. It would be hard to live in an adobe house after spending so many years in a tipi. But he'd better start getting used to it.

The thought came that it might be easier simply to steal Bay from her father's house and run with her. That was the Comanche way, to take by raiding. But where would he take her? Bay couldn't return to *Comanchería*. And he would have to kill her father and Jonas Harper both if he stayed in Texas and it was known she hadn't come to him willingly.

It seemed he was bound to the white world—however constraining its customs—if he wanted Bay Stewart for his wife.

"Yes," Long Quiet said at last. "I'd be pleased to accept your hospitality."

Bay had spent the rest of the day searching Rip's office for another set of books—the one that revealed his indebtedness—and thought her heart would break when she discovered it behind a collection of old reports on actions taken by the Texas Congress.

It was suppertime before Rip returned to the house. Bay confronted both her father and Sloan at the supper table with what she'd discovered.

"Why didn't either of you tell me you'd mortgaged Three Oaks?"

"You found the books," Rip said, his tone even.

"After Jonas told me about the debt," Bay admitted. "Why didn't you tell me?"

Sloan looked at Rip, who sighed and said, "It was my decision not to say anything. I didn't want you to worry. Besides, what could you have done?"

"Is it true you don't have enough money to pay what's due on the note this year?" Bay demanded.

"Yes."

"How could this have happened? I thought we had so much!"

"I made some bad investments, and of course the house burned and the cotton gin had to be replaced. We're not destitute, Bay. I've invested quite a bit in the cargo of several ships, but they're not due back to California from the Orient for another year at least, maybe two."

"But if you don't pay Jonas, he'll own Three Oaks!"

Rip laughed. "I've gotten myself into a bind, all right. But Jonas is a reasonable man. We'll work something out."

"I suppose it helps that I'll soon be his wife." Bay couldn't keep the aggravation out of her voice. Rip seemed so . . . so *cheerful*. Didn't he understand the gravity of the situation?

Rip's frown indicated he'd caught a hint of Bay's desperation. "Your being Jonas's wife has nothing whatsoever to do with our business dealings. Has Jonas suggested that it does?"

This was Bay's chance to detail her conversation with Jonas, but she hesitated to do so. After all, Jonas had withdrawn his initial threat, and it wasn't Jonas's fault Rip had invested unwisely, or that it would be—dear God—two years before his ships were back from the Orient. Rip seemed to think Jonas would have been reasonable enough to extend the loan another year if she hadn't gotten involved in what was essentially a business matter, and after their discussion she was convinced he probably still would.

But what if she married Long Quiet and Jonas ended up having to foreclose on Three Oaks two years from now? Then she'd be much worse in her father's eyes than simply a disappointing daughter. She'd be the reason he'd lost his life's blood—Three Oaks.

Bay shuddered. She couldn't handle the burden of that responsibility. She took a deep breath and made one last try at finding a way to save Three Oaks that didn't require her marriage to Jonas Harper.

"Is there anyone you could borrow the money from to pay Jonas?"

"I don't have anything left to use for collateral. The ships' cargoes could go down at sea, and everything else is already mortgaged." Rip pursed his lips ruefully. "I'm sorry, Bay. I wish you could have come home to find things in the same shape as when you left. We'll come out of this all right. I'll work something out with Jonas to tide us over until my ships sail back to California or the next bountiful cotton crop gets sold."

"And if the ships sink and the crop fails again?" Bay demanded, irked by Rip's optimism.

"Let's not predict a storm when the sun is shining," Rip cajoled. "Everything's going to be fine."

Bay dropped the subject. Arguing with Rip wasn't going to change the facts. If she didn't marry Jonas Harper, Rip was going to lose Three Oaks. Sloan would lose her inheritance.

And Bay would forever be his disappointing daughter.

In the quiet of her room that evening, Bay allowed herself the tears she'd been fighting all day. She wasn't a gambler by nature, and certainly not when the stakes were so very high as Three Oaks. Rip was sure everything would turn out fine. But then Rip had always gambled and won. Bay couldn't take that chance, and she was devastated by the non-gambler's choice she felt compelled to make. Wishing and dreaming and hoping didn't necessarily make things so. Otherwise she would never have spent three years among the Comanches.

Bay cried until her chest ached, until her throat was sore and raw, until her eyes were puffy and red. But her tears had changed nothing. She chewed on her lower lip until it bled, but could come up with no alternative. The only way she could be absolutely certain Three Oaks was safe was to marry Jonas Harper.

Once she'd made her decision, she realized she still had one more hurdle to cross. She must find Long Quiet before he made any more plans to stay in Texas. Because once she explained to him that she couldn't marry him, it was entirely possible he would return to *Comanchería*. That realization convulsed her body with wrenching sobs that she muffled in the soft feather pillows on her even softer featherbed.

It took Bay several days to locate Long Quiet. He was staying in an old adobe house near the Atascosito Road. She donned a pair of britches and a short gown and rode out early one morning to tell him what she'd decided.

She found the house without any trouble and was both relieved and disappointed when she realized it was empty. She almost turned around and went home, but the knowledge that she couldn't postpone this meeting pulled her off her horse. She led the animal into the musty-smelling shed that served as a stable before she turned back to the house.

As she stepped across the threshold, a yellow scorpion scuttled across the dirt floor. Bay could see tiny beams of sunlight streaming through the roof, which consisted of small branches of willow and cottonwood layered with grass and sod. She suspected it would leak like a sieve the first time it rained. Several small brown spiders had spun silver webs across the open windows.

Bay smiled wryly. Anyone living in this house would be even more exposed to the elements than if they lived in a tipi. She looked around for something to do to keep herself busy while she waited for Long Quiet and found a straw broom in the corner. It seemed silly to sweep a dirt floor, so Bay used the broom to send the spiders searching for new places to nest. She kept an eye out for the scorpion, which had apparently gone through a hole along the floor somewhere, since she couldn't find it.

The house consisted of only two rooms. She examined the contents of the front room as though it were going to become her home. It wasn't, of course; but she could imagine, couldn't she? The room contained a table and chairs for eating. A small empty pottery vase sat on the table. Bay imagined it full of Indian paintbrush or bluebonnets.

There was another table with a single chair that she could see was serving as a desk. A quick glance confirmed Long Quiet had already established a ledger with entries concerning mustangs and longhorns. She was surprised at the neat lettering, the precise-looking numbers. She shouldn't have been surprised, because he'd told her he'd been to school in Boston. But she was. Here was actual proof that he had one of the skills necessary to make a go of his ranch in Texas— that he was better qualified, in fact, than many white men, who could neither read nor write.

Finally, there were two heavy rawhide chairs cozily facing a fireplace, with a wool rug on the dirt floor in front of them. Bay imagined sitting with Long Quiet before a crackling fire, a mongrel dog lying at their feet and a cradle rocking between them.

She forced herself to leave that idyllic picture to examine the rest of the adobe house. In the back room, perched in an ornate Mediterranean wood frame, stood the largest bed Bay had ever seen. There was plenty of room for two people to make love there and never have to worry about feeling constrained. The table with six spooled legs beside the bed looked ridiculously fragile in comparison. At the foot of the bed was a trunk, which Bay supposed held Long Quiet's new clothes and other possessions. She resisted the urge to look inside.

The sheets were disheveled, as though Long Quiet had thrashed in his sleep. There was still a depression in the pillow where his head had lain. Bay set the broom down in the corner, removed her boots, and crawled up onto the bed. She carefully laid her head beside the depression made by Long Quiet's and reached down to pull the sheets up over her. She closed her eyes and breathed deeply. The sheets smelled of him. She turned on her side and curled into a ball.

How was she ever going to spend the rest of her life with another man?

Chapter 20

LONG QUIET SURVEYED THE OVAL-SHAPED BRUSH COR-
ral with satisfaction. Soon he'd be ready to go hunting for
mustangs.

"Is pretty good, no?"

Long Quiet turned to the short, spare Mexican who'd spoken. "It's more than good. Thanks for your help, Paco."

The middle-aged Mexican shrugged. "Señor Cruz, he say
work, I work. For you, for another—it does not matter. I am
like the mule, no? I obey when the master bids me lend my
back to his labor."

There was a trace of bitterness along with the resignation
in Paco's voice, but Long Quiet was too excited about the
progress he'd made on the corral over the past few days to
question the Mexican about it. "We'll start early again tomorrow, all right?"

"*Sí*, Señor Coburn. When the sun rises I will be here." The
Mexican slipped onto the back of his horse as easily as
though he were stepping over a low fence. "I send my sister,
Juanita, to come and cook breakfast for you, no?"

"No, but *gracias*." The Mexican had talked often of his
sister ever since he'd realized Long Quiet wasn't married.
While Long Quiet would have welcomed the help, he didn't
want the complications that accepting Paco's offer would un-
doubtedly raise. "I'll see you tomorrow."

"*Adiós*, Señor. *Vaya con Dios.*"

"*Adiós*, Paco."

It was a short ride from the brush corral to the house that had been built by Cruz's grandfather. Long Quiet eyed the adobe house that had become his home. It hadn't been as hard to live here as he'd feared. But that was because no one knew who he was.

To the planters he'd met at Rip's house he was Walker Coburn, the cocky firebrand who'd said he planned to marry Jonas Harper's fiancée. To the *vaqueros* and *mesteñeros* he was the *anglo* for whom Cruz Guerrero had said they must work, respected only for his grace on horseback. Neither Texans nor Mexicans would have accepted Long Quiet, the half-breed Comanche, in their midst.

But between the flat-crowned hat covering his short hair and the roweled spurs on his knee-high black boots, no trace of Long Quiet remained. The deception was easy. It was his knowledge of the deception and the necessity for it that he found hard to live with.

He stopped at the lean-to beside the house that served as a kitchen and started a fire beneath the kettle of black beans he'd left to soak all day. It would have been nice to come home to food that was already cooked, but he had nowhere to keep Juanita in the small adobe house, and that meant she'd have had to ride back and forth from the Mexican *pueblo* near the Guerrero's hacienda every day. Besides, he reasoned, it wouldn't be long before he'd be coming home to a meal cooked by his wife.

He walked to the well and drew a bucket of cool water. He scooped up a handful to dash on his face, rinsing it free of the day's sweat and dust. Then he pulled off his cotton shirt and, leaning over, sluiced the rest of the water from the bucket over his head. He threw his head back and shook like a dog, slinging drops of water across his broad shoulders and in a wide arc around him. He used the cotton shirt to dab at the remaining water that dripped from his nose and eyelashes.

He was tired, but glad the brush corral was finished. The four *vaqueros* Cruz had loaned him, known for their excellent horsemanship, hadn't bargained on having to work on foot. They'd done the work he asked, but they'd made their disgruntlement known. Long Quiet smiled. No one had worked harder or complained louder than Paco. He liked the wiry Mexican. Perhaps if he talked long enough, he could convince Paco to come to work for him permanently.

While he'd worked on the corral with the *vaqueros*, the *mesteñeros* were already scouting the watering hole used by a herd of mustangs. Most of the wild horses were chestnut or dark brown, but the herd also included a few of the highly prized *bayos*, cream palominos. Long Quiet planned to gentle one of the *bayos* and give it to Bay as a wedding gift.

He drew another bucket of water for his horse and when the animal had drunk its fill, Long Quiet led the gelding to the makeshift stable. The sight of a chestnut mare with a Three Oaks brand already munching hay in the single stall sent Long Quiet to the house on the run.

Bay felt something trail across her face. At first she smiled because the delicate touch tickled. Suddenly she remembered the yellow scorpion. Oh, God! It was on her face! She bolted upright with a screech, her hands batting at her face to get the creature off.

"Settle down! Stop that howling. What's the matter with you?"

At the sound of a human voice, Bay stopped screaming and opened her eyes. "Long Quiet? Long Quiet!" She threw her arms around him, strangling him with her grasp. "I thought there was something crawling on me."

"I was touching your face."

"Oh." Bay could feel Long Quiet's warm breath at her temple and was suddenly aware of her breasts flattened against his hard, smooth chest, of his arms wrapped around her, holding her snug against him, of his strong hands caressing her. She could feel the tension building in his body as his muscles flexed and tautened beneath her hands.

"Why are you here, Bay?"

"I had to talk to you." Bay knew she sounded desperate and tried to calm her voice. "You haven't bought the land from Cruz Guerrero yet, have you?"

"Yes, I have."

"Oh, no!" Bay hid her face against Long Quiet's chest.

He pried her arms from around his neck and pulled her away so he could see her face. Bay tried, but she couldn't bring herself to meet his eyes. He tipped her chin up, but she kept her gaze lowered.

"Look at me, Bay."

"I can't."

"What's wrong?"

Bay took a deep breath and blurted, "I've decided to marry Jonas Harper." She felt the muscles in Long Quiet's arms turn to rock beneath her fingertips. When he said nothing, she finally looked up at his face. His eyes were cold. His jaw jutted and his nostrils flared. He had never looked so much the noble savage.

"Why?" he said in a dangerously quiet voice.

"I . . . I . . ." Bay knew that if she was going to convince Long Quiet to let her go through with this, she'd have to convince him she loved Jonas Harper. But the words just wouldn't come.

"Do you love him?"

Bay breathed a sigh of relief that Long Quiet had made it easy for her. "Yes."

He didn't bother to contradict her. He simply lowered his mouth and captured hers, stunning her with his quick possession. She could feel his anger in the taunting kiss. His lips teased. His tongue coaxed. Bay felt herself melting like a wax candle in the Texas sun. His fingers thrust through her hair, tugging her backward until she was lying flat on the bed. His body covered hers, and while his mouth pillaged, his hands plundered. In moments Bay was writhing in pleasure beneath him.

His breath came in gasps as his mouth left hers and sojourned across her face and down her throat. His hands likewise journeyed from her breasts to her belly, stopping short of the place where she wanted them. Abruptly, he sat up, and while she watched he stood and unbuckled the *chaparejos*, similar to leather pants, that covered his trousers and let them fall in a heap on the floor. Heavy boots with large rowled Mexican spurs came off next, followed by buckskin trousers, until he was standing gloriously, starkly naked in front of her.

Bay hadn't taken her eyes off him. Shivering with desire, she reached out her arms, inviting him to join her. Instead of accepting her invitation, he pulled her upright to stand across from him. Slowly, he loosened the buttons on the short gown she wore, then drew it off her shoulders, leaving her in a lacy white chemise. Instead of taking off her trousers, he thrust his bent leg between her thighs and pulled her forward so she was riding it. With one hand he grabbed a handful of her auburn hair and pulled her head back to expose her throat to his mouth, while his other hand teased the peaked nipple that could be seen beneath the thin chemise.

"I love you, Bay," he murmured against her throat. "I think I've loved you forever."

Tears squeezed from Bay's eyes. "I . . . love you too."

"If you love me, you'll be my wife." It wasn't a question, it was a statement of possession.

"I . . . can't," Bay choked out.

Long Quiet raised his head so he could meet her gaze. "Jonas can never love you as much as I do."

"It's not that . . . it's . . ."

"It's the money, isn't it?" Long Quiet rasped, his voice flat. "And the respectability. Your father told me as much, but I wouldn't believe him."

He waited for her to deny it.

But she didn't.

"Can Jonas love you like this, Bay?" he demanded as his hands sent tremors of pleasure racing through her body.

Bay knew she was on the verge of admitting the real reason why she was marrying Jonas Harper. But there was nothing Long Quiet could do to help, and she couldn't afford to give him the chance to change her mind. She was already too aware of what she was giving up to save Three Oaks.

She laughed, a bitter, harsh sound, and said, "Why would I choose to live in a hovel like this, cooking and scrubbing like some Comanche squaw, when I can be waited on by servants, dining on china and drinking from crystal, if I marry Jonas?"

Long Quiet shoved her away from him as though she'd suddenly become a buzzing rattler, and she hit the adobe wall beside the bed hard enough to knock the breath from her. She couldn't speak for a moment, which was fortunate, because she might have taken everything back, so tortured was the expression on Long Quiet's face. By the time she could breathe again, he'd recovered his composure and his face revealed nothing of what her words had meant to him.

"Why did you come here today, Bay?"

"To say good-bye," she murmured. She gazed at him with all the love she felt, knowing that after what she'd just told him, he wouldn't want to touch her again. "And to tell you I'll never forget you."

As she watched, anger flared and then was banked, smoldering in Long Quiet's gray eyes. "Then I suppose I should give you something worth remembering," he said.

Bay flattened herself against the rough adobe wall and held her hands out in front of her as he started walking toward her. "Stop, Long Quiet, please . . ." When he kept coming, she gauged the distance between herself and the door. Just before he reached her she lunged, scrambling across the bed.

She was only halfway across the huge expanse when he

grabbed her chemise. It ripped down the back and fell away in two pieces, freeing her breasts but hampering her arms. She kept on crawling, but this time he caught her by an ankle. She whirled around, hands curled into claws, and reached out to scratch him. "Let me go!"

He used his hold on her ankle to get a better grip on her calf with the other hand. His weight held her legs down while he worked his way up her body. Bay grabbed a handful of his thick, curly hair and yanked. "Let go!" she shrieked.

He caught one of her wrists, but her other hand still clutched his hair. His head dropped suddenly and his mouth came down on hers. She bit at him. She bucked against him. She pulled his hair so hard she cried with the pain she knew she was causing him. But the more she tried to hurt him, the gentler he became.

"Yes, love. Be mine, love. Easy, love," he murmured.

The hand in his hair loosened, then drove through the wet curls again, only this time with urgent need, pulling his head down so his lips could meet hers. She thrust her tongue into his mouth in an erotic imitation of the way she wanted his body joined to hers. His hand released hers to find her breast while she sought out the flesh of his shoulder, then slid her fingers down his slick back to his hard, taut buttocks. Bay moaned.

"I'm yours, love. All of me. Whatever you want. Tell me what you want," he entreated.

She did. With her hands, with her mouth, with her heart. She wanted them together. Once again. Just one more time. She tugged at her trousers and drawers and he helped her pull them off along with her boots and then they were back together, flesh to seeking flesh. He made them one, confirming that they belonged together, promising that nothing could keep them apart.

Long Quiet could hardly catch his breath, but he wanted the words spoken now, while she was still in his thrall.

"Do money and respectability mean more to you than the love we share?"

Bay forced herself to meet his eyes and was agonized by the fierce need she saw there. Somehow she must make him give up the idea of having her for his wife. Somehow she must make him believe she would only marry Jonas Harper. "I love you, but there are other things besides love that have to be considered."

"Things like china and silver?" he snarled.

"Yes! You'll never be able to give me the things Jonas can. You're starting with nothing. Jonas has everything."

"I can get things too, if that's what you want."

"I can't wait—I won't wait to have the things Jonas can give me now."

He opened his mouth to speak and snapped it shut. He wouldn't bargain for her love. Their skin, bound by lovers' sweat, resisted parting as he tore himself off of her. His eyes were dark, burning hellholes. Proud. Angry. Empty.

How could she profess to love him yet say what she'd just said? She wasn't even choosing another man over him. She was choosing the things the other man had to offer her. He looked at her, her eyes wide and vulnerable, hinting of tears. She was obviously confused and didn't know what she wanted. It was all he could do not to pull her back into his arms and make it all very clear for her. He picked up her clothes and threw them into her lap.

"Get dressed and get out, before I do something I'll regret."

Bay dressed hurriedly, knowing Long Quiet watched her the whole time with condemnation in his eyes. How could she bear to hurt him? How could she bear to have him think her so heartless? If only she could explain. Would he still let her marry Jonas? She took one look at the proud, ferocious man standing across from her and thought it was more likely he'd skin Jonas alive. Without clothes to cover his naked strength, he looked much more like a savage Comanche than a civilized Texan.

"Long Quiet, I don't know what to say."

"Don't say anything. Just go. Get out!"

With a cry of anguish, she fled the room.

Bay rose from her seat at the desk and knew the moment she was upright that she'd moved too fast. Her body swayed, trying to find its equilibrium. Everything was out of kilter. The same thing had happened several times in the past week. She knew she hadn't been eating the way she should, but between making plans for her wedding and trying to find out whether Long Quiet was going back to *Comanchería*, she'd been too upset to eat. Besides, nothing seemed to sit well in her stomach. The dizziness got worse. She grabbed at the edge of the desk and missed, sending the crystal inkwell crashing to the floor. Aghast at the mess caused in Rip's office by the spilled India ink, Bay burst into tears.

Sloan heard the glass breaking in Rip's office and came to find out what had happened. She found Bay slumped in the chair at the desk, sobbing. Sloan knelt down beside her sister. "What happened? Are you all right?"

"No, I'm not all right! I'm exhausted and I feel like crying all the time. I can't seem to eat anything without getting sick. And lately, every time I stand up from the desk, I get so dizzy I think I'm going to faint. Oh, Sloan, I don't know what's the matter with me!"

Hearing the list of symptoms, Sloan stood up, shaking her head in distress. "I would have thought you'd have learned something from my experience and gotten married before you got yourself pregnant."

"Got myself . . . pregnant?" Bay quickly calculated and realized she hadn't had her monthly miseries since she'd first met Long Quiet. Her eyes flashed upward to meet Sloan's stark gaze. "Oh, my."

"At least you and Jonas can move up the wedding date so his child can have his name."

"It isn't Jonas's baby."

"Not Jonas's? Oh damn! Is Jonas going to be willing to keep a child that isn't his?"

"I'll never give up my child!" Bay was immediately sorry for her outburst. "I'm sorry, Sloan. I didn't mean that the way it sounded."

"I suppose I deserved it." Sloan turned away and brushed aside a tendril of hair from her face. When she turned back to Bay, the only emotion on her face was concern. "What is Jonas going to think, Bay, when you tell him about this?"

"He'll understand."

"Will he? I hope so, Bay." She put a hand on Bay's shoulder. "I do hope so." But somehow she doubted he would.

While Bay waited for Jonas in the parlor that afternoon, dressed in the most attractive day dress she owned, a pretty lilac-and-white-flower pattern piped with lilac, her thoughts were about how pleased and proud Long Quiet would be if he knew about their child. This was the child they'd vowed would bridge two worlds. All the plans they'd made. All the hopes they'd had. How could she even consider marrying Jonas now?

Because she had no choice. Because nothing, really, had changed. Three Oaks was still at risk. And now at least she would have a part of Long Quiet to love through the long years ahead with Jonas.

She'd spoken confidently to Sloan, but she really wasn't sure Jonas would still want to marry her. She shuddered to think what would happen to Three Oaks if he didn't. She'd always thought Jonas a generous man. She hoped she could convince him to show some of that giving spirit now. But how would he feel about becoming the father of another man's child? And what would she say when he asked who that other man was?

"Darling, you look beautiful," Jonas said, his hands outstretched as always. Only this time, when they touched, he drew her forward until he could kiss her lightly on the lips. "What could possibly be so troubling to a woman that she'd willingly wrinkle her lovely brow?"

Bay shoved back her irritation at Jonas's insinuation that a woman was unlikely to be troubled by momentous matters. "I do have a few things bothering me, Jonas," she said calmly. "I thought perhaps we could go for a ride this afternoon and I could discuss them with you."

"Of course, sweetheart. I'd be delighted to help. And it's a perfect day for a ride. The air's cool, crisp, as close to a fall day as I understand this part of Texas ever gets."

Jonas seemed to forget Bay's problem as he regaled her with a story of the good price he'd managed to get for some property he'd recently sold in Shelby County. Bay let him talk because, from past experience, she knew he didn't like to be interrupted. Jonas drove them to a shady spot along the Brazos River where they'd come in the past to picnic. When they arrived, he stepped down and secured the horses before coming around the carriage to help her down.

"Now, what's this problem that's been troubling you, sweetheart? Don't know what kind of flowers you'd like to have for the wedding? Can't decide on a menu for the midnight supper?"

"It isn't anything like that," Bay said.

"Oh? Then what is it?"

"Do you want to have children?" she blurted.

Jonas smiled. "Oh, darling." He walked the two steps that separated them and folded her in his arms. "Is that what's worrying you? Of course I want children. I told you that in the picture of us I've always carried in my mind, we're surrounded by our beautiful children. But you mustn't be frightened. I'll find a good doctor—the best."

Bay tore herself from Jonas's arms. "I'm not afraid. That's not the problem."

He frowned, perplexed and more than a little annoyed.

"Then what is it, Bay? I must admit I'm finding all this a little bit confusing. Why did you ask if I want to have children?"

Bay turned and faced him. "You've always been a friend to me, Jonas. In Boston I always knew I could count on you to cheer me up when I was sad or comfort me if I was feeling lonely. And if I had a problem, you were always ready to solve it for me. I think that's why I loved you so much."

Bay didn't realize she'd used the past tense, *loved*, until it was already out, but Jonas hadn't seemed to notice, so she took a deep breath and kept talking. "Now I need you to show all that understanding and thoughtfulness. Jonas, during the time we were separated, I was . . . I was . . . intimate with another man."

Jonas hissed in a breath of air. He took off his hat, then loosened his tie and collar and spat. His face ran the gamut of emotions from disbelief to fury and back again before he huffed out the breath of air and said through gritted teeth, "I've always believed a woman should save herself for her husband. But as you said, I am a forgiving man."

"There's more, Jonas."

"More?"

"I'm pregnant."

Jonas turned beet red. His mouth worked, but nothing came out except, "I thought . . . I had no idea . . ."

Bay stepped forward and put a hand on Jonas's arm. "Please, Jonas, listen to me. I'll be a good wife to you. You'll be the baby's father."

"No!"

"Does that mean you don't want to marry me anymore?"

Jonas grasped Bay's arms and pulled her close so they stood nose to nose. Bay looked down to avoid having to peer cross-eyed at Jonas.

"I'm not giving up my dream simply because of this . . . this obstacle," he said. "I love you, Bay, and I intend to marry you. We'll go away somewhere so you can have the child, and then we'll put it in a home for orphans—"

"Jonas, I—"

"—where it will be well cared for. But this will mean we'll have to be married right away."

"Jonas, I can't give up my baby."

"Nonsense. What can this child mean to you? The father can't have been . . . Who is the father, Bay?"

"It doesn't matter, does it?"

"Some Italian count? Some English lord? Some . . ." His face slowly flushed as he realized. "My God! Of course. It's that man from the party, that Walker Coburn! Isn't it?"

Jonas was shaking Bay, trying to get an answer from her, but he didn't need words. The stricken look on Bay's face was enough to tell him the truth.

"I'll kill him!"

"No, Jonas!"

"That son of a bitch isn't going to win. This isn't going to change things between us, Bay. You'll still be my wife. But you'll get rid of his brat!"

Bay gasped. "And if I won't?"

"I won't be father to another man's bastard."

"Then I won't marry you."

"You have no choice."

"That's ridiculous. Of course I do."

"Either you marry me, or your family will find themselves without a roof over their heads. Do I make myself clear?"

Bay had been willing to sacrifice herself on the altar of filial duty, but she could never agree to sacrifice her child. "I will never marry you. Never!"

"I don't make idle threats, Bay."

Jonas took a step toward her, and then another. Bay backed away from the dangerous intent in his eyes until she came up against a cypress tree. He kept coming until his body was pressed to hers from breast to thigh. Bay put her palms against his chest to keep him away, but he was too strong for her to have much success. One of his hands knocked off her bonnet and twisted in her hair while the other grabbed her chin and painfully jerked it up so she was staring into pitiless brown eyes.

"Oh you'll marry me, all right. You won't let your father lose Three Oaks. But there's no reason now for me to wait for our wedding night to take what I want from you."

He ground his mouth against her lips, drawing blood. The hand that had held her chin dropped to her breast, pinching, kneading painfully. He thrust his hips against her and, despite his fury, she discovered he was fully aroused.

Bay fought him, but the more she struggled, the more brutal he became. The hand tangled in her hair yanked her away from the tree trunk and pulled her head down. The pain forced her to her knees. He came down with her, knocking her onto her back, using his weight to hold her down as he pulled her skirt up around her waist.

"Don't do this. Please, Jonas!"

The ugly smile on Jonas's face frightened Bay. She didn't know this man at all. How could she have so misjudged him? They were too isolated for her to hope anyone would come to her rescue. If she didn't want to be raped, she was going to have to save herself. She let her hands fall to his chest.

"That's the way," he moaned. "Do for me like you did for your lover."

"All right, Jonas. What would you like me to do?" she asked. "A kiss. How about a kiss?" She raised her lips to his. When Jonas moaned she pushed lightly against his shoulder. "Turn on your side," she whispered in his ear. "I know a way . . ." she began in a voice promising pleasure.

The instant Jonas turned on his side, Bay slammed her knee into his engorged manhood with all her strength.

Jonas let out a howl that made the horses lunge and startled a family of sparrows out of the tree above them. He curled himself into a ball.

"You'll pay for this when you're my wife," he gasped.

"I'll never be your wife!"

"We'll see about that."

Bay climbed into the carriage and whipped Jonas's matched pair into a fast trot.

"Wait! Come back here. Bayleeeeiigh!"

Bay ignored Jonas, her thoughts already directed toward her confrontation with Rip. She couldn't marry Jonas, and if that meant her father would have to lose Three Oaks . . . She would have to face his disappointment and live with it. Bay shuddered as she laid the whip across the broad, sleek backs of Jonas's matched chestnuts.

Chapter 21

When Bay arrived back at Three Oaks, she immediately sought out her father. She found him in his office, paging through the debt ledger he'd kept hidden from her. When he saw her he quickly closed the book, swiveled his chair around to face her, and rose to his feet, all in one swift movement.

"What happened to you? Are you all right?"

For the first time, Bay became aware of her disheveled appearance. The sleeve of her lilac day dress was torn, and grass and dirt stained her flowered skirt. When she anxiously licked her lips, she discovered a cut at one corner of her mouth. A quick dab with her finger confirmed it was still bleeding. Her hair had a flyaway look that bore witness to the urgency of her escape from Jonas Harper.

"I was with Jonas," Bay said.

"Did he do this to you?" Rip demanded.

"I . . . we . . . had a disagreement," Bay said. "I told Jonas I can't marry him, and he got upset."

"He did this to you?"

Rip was almost out the door by the time Bay caught him. "Before you go anywhere, listen to what I have to say. I'm not excusing Jonas, but . . . just listen, please."

Rip crossed his arms over his chest. "Go ahead."

Bay paced the room nervously as she spoke. "When Long

Quiet came back for me, I knew he was the man I should be marrying. But when I tried to break my engagement to Jonas, he told me about the loans you'd made, about the mortgage on Three Oaks. He made it clear that the only way he would extend the note indefinitely was if I married him."

Rip covered his eyes with a work-roughened hand. "I should have known something was going on when you asked all those questions about how I was going to pay the note. But why would you ever agree to such a marriage?"

"Because if I hadn't, it would have been my fault if you eventually lost Three Oaks. And I didn't want you to hate me because I'd disappointed you again."

"Disappointed me? How could you think . . ." Rip groaned, but the sound never got beyond his broad chest. "So now you've broken the engagement, and Jonas isn't going to extend the note."

"Not unless I agree to marry him. I was going to do it, but . . . I just can't." Two hot tears slid down Bay's cheeks.

Rip moved toward her but was constrained by old habits from enfolding her in his arms to comfort her. He slid his hands into his pockets, letting his voice do the job for him. "Don't worry, Bay. I'll manage. But what changed your mind? I thought you loved Jonas."

"I did . . . but . . ." Bay knew she couldn't hide the truth forever. She might as well tell him now. But, oh God, how she hated disappointing him again. "I'm pregnant."

"Goddammit to hell! I'll take that son of a bitch Harper apart and feed him to the vultures."

"Wait!" Bay grabbed at Rip's arm with both hands. "It's not his baby."

Rip whirled on her. "Not his?"

"No."

She didn't have to tell him. She saw from the cold mask of fury settling on his face that he realized who must be the father of her child. "It belongs to that half-breed."

"He's my husband."

"Was. And will be again!" Rip said, grabbing her by the hand and hauling her after him. "I'm not having another bastard grandchild, and I'm sure as hell not going to take the chance of another daughter giving up her child to somebody else. Come with me."

"Where are we going?"

"To find a preacher. And then to find Walker Coburn. You're going to get married."

"But I told Long Quiet . . . he won't want—"

"I don't give a damn what he wants." Rip stopped to take a rifle from the rack above the mantel in the parlor. "He's going to have to face up to his responsibilities."

Bay knew that after all the lies she'd told Long Quiet, he wasn't going to want her back. The fact he was being forced to marry her was going to make things worse. The only thing that kept her from getting frantic was the knowledge that the closest preacher had to be two days away by horseback. By the time Rip got the preacher and returned, he'd be calm enough to realize there were other solutions to the problem.

"Thank goodness Elijah Hopkins bought Framington Farms last year. He's an ordained Methodist minister. Otherwise I'd have to ride clear to San Antonio and back for a preacher," Rip muttered. "We'll gather up Sloan on the way. I'm sure your sister won't want to miss your wedding."

Bay pursed her lips, chagrined that there wasn't going to be time for Rip's temper to cool. She didn't speak a word during the entire ride down the Atascosito Road. She was too busy thinking.

What if Long Quiet wouldn't agree to marry her? She took one look at Rip's grim face and the rifle he'd brought along. They were going to be married, all right. But how could she make Long Quiet believe she loved him no matter how rich or poor he was, after all the lies she'd told?

The more she thought about it, the worse she felt. Marrying Long Quiet was not going to end her problems with Jonas Harper. He'd threatened to kill Long Quiet, and then made it clear that he didn't make idle threats. Should she warn Long Quiet of the danger? And now Jonas would surely foreclose on Three Oaks.

Unless Rip was somehow able to do some fancy talking, she'd just caused her family to lose their home.

If Bay hadn't been too dazed to listen to the conversation going on around her, she'd have noticed that Rip appeared less concerned about his financial plight than she was. He and Sloan carried on a lively debate with Elijah Hopkins over what he ought to plant in his fallow field. Sloan said corn. Rip said sugarcane. Elijah wanted to leave it fallow for another year.

"Hello the house!" Rip called as they neared Long Quiet's adobe home.

Bay didn't expect Long Quiet to be there, but he stepped out onto the porch with a young Mexican woman by his side. Jealousy flared, and Bay felt the flush of humiliation on her cheeks when Long Quiet met her gaze.

"What can I do to help you?" Long Quiet asked.

Rip dismounted, slipping his rifle from its leather scabbard as he did. Bay noticed Long Quiet tense at the sight of the gun. His gaze slipped back to her, questioning, probing.

"I've come to see you live up to your responsibility to my daughter."

"I don't know what you're talking about. Bay made it clear the last time I talked to her that she didn't want a thing to do with me."

"Bay's carrying your child," Rip announced.

"Are you sure the child is mine?" he said, looking directly into Bay's eyes.

Bay gasped, devastated by the cruelty of his remark.

Rip started toward Long Quiet with a rasped, "Why, you—"

Long Quiet responded by crouching slightly in readiness to meet Rip hand to hand.

"Stop it! Both of you," Sloan said. "We came here to see

Bay married to Walker. It won't help for the two of you to kill each other."

"I already asked Bay to marry me. She turned me down," Long Quiet said. He glanced at the young Mexican woman, then back to Rip. "So I made other plans."

Bay died inside. He would never forgive her for the things she'd said. "This isn't going to work," she mumbled. "I should never have come here." She reined her horse around, but Sloan stopped her.

"This man is the father of your child. Your baby deserves a name," she said.

Bay understood what it had taken for Sloan to make such an argument. Sighing heavily, she turned her mount back around. "All right," she said. "Let's get this over with."

"I haven't agreed to this marriage," Long Quiet said.

"You can marry my daughter or you can die right now. Take your pick," Rip said.

"When you put it that way, I don't seem to have much of a choice, do I?" Long Quiet replied grimly. "Where do you want me to stand?"

Elijah Hopkins stepped down off his horse, thinking things were certainly done a little differently in Texas than they were back in Vermont. Although, as a father, he could certainly appreciate Rip's sentiment. A man should marry the mother of his children. "How about if the happy couple stands here at the threshold, and the rest of us will stand outside in the sunshine," he instructed.

"Where would you like Juanita to stand?" Long Quiet asked with a sardonic smile.

"Oh," Elijah said. "Well, how about on the other side of Rip over there?"

Long Quiet placed the young woman where he'd been told and then stood in the doorway to his adobe home, waiting for his future wife to join him.

Bay's head was pounding and her throat was swollen closed with bitterness, but she was determined not to give

Long Quiet the satisfaction of seeing how hurt she was. She kept her eyes lowered as she walked over to stand next to him.

"Let's see. I always like the couple to hold hands," Elijah said.

"Is that necessary, Reverend Hopkins?" Bay asked.

"Well, I always—"

Long Quiet took Bay's hand in his, eliminating the need for discussion. His hand was warm and firm, and oddly comforting.

"All right, now. Shall we begin?" Elijah asked, surveying those gathered.

"If we don't get started soon, the sun'll be down before we're done," Rip said.

"Well, all right then. We'll begin." Elijah thumbed to the wedding ceremony in his Bible and began to drone the traditional scripture of marriage in a voice that sounded like a nest of hornets.

When Elijah asked whether Walker Coburn took Bayleigh Falkirk Stewart to be his wedded wife, Long Quiet's hand tightened on Bay's before he said, "I do."

When Elijah turned to ask Bay the same question, she tried to answer but found she couldn't speak.

"Well, young lady, speak up," Elijah said. "Do you or don't you?"

"She does," Rip answered, grim-faced.

"She'll have to say so herself, Mr. Stewart," Elijah admonished. "I'm already overlooking the reluctance of the groom, and if the bride isn't willing either, I'm not sure I should go through with this."

"I do," Bay croaked.

"There, well, that wasn't so hard, was it?" Elijah said with a relieved smile. "Then, under the laws of God and the Republic of Texas—you are taking care of the legalities, aren't you, Mr. Stewart?—"

Rip nodded.

"—and the Republic of Texas," Elijah repeated, "I now pronounce you man and wife. You may kiss the bride."

There was a long pause before Long Quiet said, "I'd rather not."

Bay stood with eyes downcast, humiliated by Long Quiet's rejection.

There was an uncomfortable shuffling of feet before Elijah said, "Oh well, that's all right too. I guess."

"That's enough, Elijah," Rip said. "We've done our business here. Let's get you home before the sun's gone." Rip turned to Long Quiet and said, "Is there someplace I can take the señorita?"

Bay waited to hear Long Quiet announce that Juanita lived in the house with him, but was relieved when he said, "Her brother is one of my *vaqueros*. He'll be coming to pick her up soon."

Sloan drew Bay away from Long Quiet's side and put her arms around her sister. "You love him," she whispered in Bay's ear. "It shouldn't take you long to convince him that he loves you. It's a challenge worthy of a Stewart."

Moved by Sloan's show of support, Bay choked out, "I'll do my best."

"Take care of yourself, Bay," Sloan said. "And come visit us sometime soon."

Rip went so far as to take her hand in his. That small touch was enough to tell her how much the events of the day had affected him. "Take care, Bay," he said. "I'll expect you to stay in touch with us, and if we can be of help, let us know."

"I . . . I will. And if you need anything . . ."

Rip smiled. "I'll manage fine."

"About the loan—"

Rip cut her off gruffly. "Don't worry. I'll handle it. Let's go, Sloan, Elijah."

As Rip turned, his left leg seemed to crumple under him. Bay grabbed at his elbow to help him, but he recovered quickly and shrugged her away. "Leave be. I'm fine. Just caught my bootheel on something."

Bay stepped back. Rip had a harder time mounting up than he should have. If something was wrong, though, he hid it well. He smiled at Bay encouragingly and waved farewell before he turned his horse toward Three Oaks.

"Do you want to come inside now?" Long Quiet asked.

Bay looked from Long Quiet to the long-lashed Juanita and said, "I'd like to stay out here for a little while, if that's all right."

Bay watched her father ride away until he was no more than a speck on the horizon. She still couldn't believe she was married to Long Quiet. He'd seemed to understand her need to be alone. Maybe he needed to be alone too . . . although Juanita had gone back inside with him.

Before Bay had a chance to wonder exactly what Long Quiet was doing with the other woman, Juanita's brother Paco came to get her. And then Bay was alone with her husband.

"Come inside, Bay," Long Quiet said. "Dinner is ready for us on the table."

Bay watched while Long Quiet found another bowl and served her some of the chili and beans that were in the pot on the table.

"Sit down," he said.

"I didn't mean for this to happen," Bay said.

Long Quiet's head snapped around. "You don't have to explain anything to me. I want my son to bear my name, and now that we're married under Texas law, there'll be no question of that."

"Long Quiet, I—"

"In this house Long Quiet doesn't exist. He was a Comanche warrior. I'm a white man and my name is Walker Coburn. Use it."

Bay looked at the man standing across from her and realized that he was indeed a stranger, from the civilized trappings he wore to the uncivilized glint in his eye. She yearned for the gentleness of the savage she'd left behind in *Comanchería*. "Yes . . . well . . ." She forced herself to do as he asked and used the unfamiliar name. "Walker . . . I want to explain how all this happened."

"We both know why you chose to marry Jonas, and it's pretty clear why Jonas withdrew his proposal." Long Quiet stared at Bay's stomach. Then, as though he couldn't stop himself, he reached out his hand to touch her belly. Bay remained perfectly still, holding her breath.

He looked up at her and for an instant she saw a spark of the love they'd once shared. It was gone as he quickly removed his hand.

"Sit down and eat," he ordered. "You look tired."

From just that look, those few words, Bay took hope. For no matter what Long Quiet's—no, she corrected herself, Walker's—feelings at this instant—and she could tell he was both angry and hurt—she had nearly seven months to make him fall back in love with her before the baby was born.

Bay ate her chili, finding it spicy but delicious. She watched Long Quiet use a spoon with as much grace as a Boston aristocrat. It appeared he was following through on his decision to leave his Comanche heritage behind him.

"When I said I wouldn't marry you, why didn't you go back to *Comanchería?*" she asked.

"I would have eventually, but as long as I had a brush corral built, I figured I might as well take a herd of mustangs with me."

"Are you . . . are you sorry now that you aren't going back to *Comanchería?*"

"What makes you think I'm not?"

Bay's face blanched.

"Don't worry. I have no intentions of leaving here before my son is born."

"You couldn't . . . you wouldn't take my child away from me."

"You would have taken mine from me!"

"Not because I wanted to. Not because I had a choice," Bay shouted back. "I had to marry Jonas."

"Enough!" he said. "I don't want to hear your excuses. But let's get this straight now. I married you because I want my son. *And for no other reason.*"

Bay's eyes drifted to the bedroom. He followed her gaze and then met her violet eyes. Bay flushed.

"Oh yes, we'll share the bed—because it's big and it's the only place to sleep—but that's all we'll share. Do you understand?"

Bay stared at him. She hadn't realized how badly she'd wounded his pride, how completely she'd lost his trust, until she heard the conditions he'd laid down for their life together.

"Do you understand?" Long Quiet repeated.

"Yes. I understand."

They finished the rest of the meal in silence. Then Long Quiet sent Bay to the back room. Bay had no intention of making it easy for Long Quiet to reject her as his wife. She had her pride, too. If he weren't so stubborn, he'd have given her a chance to explain the extraordinary circumstances that had forced her to stay engaged to Jonas, and they'd be enjoying a real honeymoon tonight.

She stripped off the torn, grass-stained dress in which she'd been married, then took off her chemise and drawers as well. She left the candle on the bedside table burning. Lying flat on her back, she arranged the thin cotton sheet so it barely covered her nipples and outlined her entire body from breasts to stomach, hips to thighs.

"I'm in bed now."

A mass of confused emotions rose in Long Quiet as he heard Bay's soft voice calling out to him. It stung his pride to know Bay had only married him under duress, that she hadn't willingly foregone all the things Jonas could give her to come to him. It was awful to think he could only have her love by buying her the things she wanted.

Long Quiet wanted Bay to love him enough to take him

with nothing. And he didn't want the sparks between them when they joined their bodies in lovemaking to obscure her decision.

When he crossed the threshold into the bedroom, Long Quiet nearly abandoned his plan. His loins heated at the mere sight of her. He would have said she'd planned her alluring appearance, except it was clear from her reluctance to say "I do" that she hadn't desired this marriage.

He kept his eyes averted while he undressed, but it didn't do much good. He knew she was there. He blew out the candle and slipped into bed beside her. "Turn over and go to sleep," he said brusquely. If she turned over, perhaps he wouldn't keep imagining the sight of her lying there waiting for him to come to her.

When she turned over, it was worse. She had the sheet tucked under her arm and it slipped down in back so it came nearly to her waist, exposing the entire creamy expanse of her spine, from her shoulders to the dimpled rise of her buttocks.

He swore under his breath and turned on his side facing away from her. It didn't help that the bed was so soft, reminding him of the pillow her breasts and stomach had made for his head at the *Quohadi* village. He lay awake until he could hear the steady breathing that meant she was asleep, and then he let himself turn and look at her in the moonlight that seeped in through the bedroom window.

He'd never seen her hair unbound before. It lay in a copper nimbus around her head. He wanted to thrust his fingers into it, to bring her mouth under his and possess her. He craved the taste of her. He craved the touch of her. His hand hovered over her shoulder for a moment, as though he would turn her on her back, and then he withdrew it. There was a lot at stake here. Before he took her body, he must be sure of her love. He lay back down and within moments was sound asleep.

When Bay woke the next morning, she was alone. The bed sheets had been carefully pulled up to cover her shoulders and she wondered how Long Qui—Walker, she corrected herself—had felt when he'd done that husbandly chore. Bay knew she was going to have a problem calling Long Quiet by his white name. In her heart and mind he would always be Comanche.

Bay brought the covers to her nose to breathe in his masculine scent. She was determined to make him a good wife. He would never be sorry he'd married her. Bay heard a chair knock against the table in the other room and realized Long Quiet must not have left yet. What a lazy wife he must think her! Bay quickly put on her torn dress, which was all she had, and, keeping a lookout for scorpions and spiders, walked barefoot to the doorway between the two rooms.

When she lifted the blanket that separated the two rooms, what she saw almost made her take back the vows she'd just made.

"*Buenos días*, señora," Juanita said.

"What are you doing here?"

The pretty young woman smiled at Bay and said in broken English, "The señor, he asked me to come." Juanita was already clearing away the dishes Long Quiet had used for breakfast.

Bay felt nauseated and was afraid it had nothing to do with her pregnancy. What was this woman doing here? Why hadn't Long Quiet asked her to fix his breakfast? Some of their most pleasant times together in *Comanchería* had been when they'd sat down to eat together.

Bay was already uncertain of the role Long Quiet wanted her to play, and the appearance of this pretty woman in her home on the first day of her marriage wasn't helping her confidence. Had Juanita done more for Long Quiet than fix his breakfast? Had Long Quiet given his smiles, his tender looks to Juanita over the breakfast table?

"Are you hungry, señora?"

"I . . . uh . . ." Bay wished she could say no. She still hadn't decided in what role the other woman was cast, and she didn't want to owe her any favors. But she felt a familiar queasiness in her stomach and knew from experience that if she didn't eat a little something, it would only get worse. She admitted, "I could eat something, I suppose."

"*Bueno*. Is good for the *bebé*, no?"

The radiant smile on the woman's face startled Bay. Surely if Juanita had done more for Long Quiet than cook his food she wouldn't seem so happy about the baby. "Yes, it's good for the baby," Bay agreed.

Bay had expected the other woman to spend the day at the house, but shortly after she'd prepared breakfast and put some beans in water to soak in the lean-to, she announced she was leaving. "The señor, he says now you will do the cooking, no?"

"Oh yes," Bay said, smiling for the first time. Juanita was here to cook, had probably always been here to cook . . . at least she could salve her fears with that notion until she was proven wrong.

Paco had left a mule for Juanita to ride home, and when she rode away just before noon, Bay couldn't help hugging herself in delight. She would be waiting for Long Quiet with a wonderful meal ready to be served. He would not be sorry he'd counted on her. Bay spent the entire afternoon imagining how she would ask him about his day and how he would share his adventures with her. They were going to have a wonderful marriage. She'd make sure of it.

Not knowing when Long Quiet would return, Bay had supper ready a little before sundown, figuring he couldn't work in the dark. She hadn't found Indian paintbrush and bluebonnets—those only bloomed in spring—but she'd found some yellow sunflowers and filled the vase on the table to overflowing. She'd also placed two candles on the table for a glowing light she thought was nicer than the lantern. By the time it had been dark for two hours, she was worried. Two hours after that, she dumped Long Quiet's food in the fire in a fit of pique and went to bed.

But she lay awake, wide-eyed and frightened. Where was he? What if Jonas had followed through on his threats and Long Quiet was lying dead in a ravine somewhere? What if he'd gone to see Juanita? Or what if he'd simply decided to return to *Comanchería?*

There were no answers to her questions in the quiet night. All she could do was wait for morning. And pray.

Chapter 22

IT WAS NEARLY MIDNIGHT BEFORE BAY HEARD LONG Quiet's footsteps cross the threshold. He was moving quietly, as though he expected to find her asleep.

"I'm awake," she said, sitting up in bed, drawing her knees to her chest and wrapping her arms protectively around them.

"You should be asleep. You need your rest."

"I . . . I was worried about you."

She didn't ask him where he'd been, but the question hovered in the air between them.

He sidestepped it, saying, "I'm tired. It's been a long day."

Bay heard him taking off his clothes. His movements seemed slow—too slow, she realized suddenly. She scrambled across the bed to the small table where the candle stood and lit it. In the dim light she could see the bloodstains on his clothes and the dried blood on his face and neck.

"You're hurt!" She was at his side in an instant, helping him remove his tattered shirt. His skin beneath it was scraped raw, but there was no bullet wound, as she'd feared from the amount of blood on his shirt. She fetched the pitcher of water and poured some into a bowl. She tore off a corner of the ruined shirt and rinsed it in the water. He sat patiently on the bed while, hands trembling, she used the damp cloth to wash the blood, gravel, and dirt from the scrapes on his chest and arm and from the side of his face.

"What happened?"

"I had an accident."

Bay waited, but when he didn't say anything else she prodded, "What kind of accident?"

"A stupid one, really. After the *vaqueros* had all gone home, I decided to have one last try at breaking one of those mustangs I've got penned. I got thrown and hit my head and I guess it knocked me out for a while."

Bay's hands immediately reached for his hair, to search for the knot he must have on his head. Long Quiet grasped her wrists and pulled them down. "I'm all right. Leave me be and go back to bed."

Bay stared at him, her eyes wide, frightened by his unexpected brusqueness.

Suddenly his mouth covered hers, his tongue seeking hungrily, then gentling, soothing the hurt he'd done. Just as abruptly, he tore himself away. "Go to bed," he ordered, his voice harsher now than before. "You have to be up early tomorrow to make my breakfast."

Confused by the contradiction between his words and his actions, Bay backed away a step and then turned and climbed quickly into bed, dragging the sheet up over her shoulder as she turned her back to him. She wondered if he was hungry, but she didn't dare bring up the subject, because then she'd have to confess that she'd thrown out his supper. She'd only wanted to help him just now, but somehow she'd failed miserably. He didn't want her to touch him. And he couldn't even stand to kiss her.

Long Quiet blew out the candle and they were once more shrouded in darkness. He muttered a vicious curse and heard Bay whimper in response. He cursed again, more loudly, and stomped into the other room, throwing himself into one of the rawhide chairs that sat before the fireplace.

He couldn't let her touch his head or she'd have discovered there wasn't any knot. And there wasn't a knot because he hadn't been thrown from a horse. His horse had been shot out from under him. Again.

He knew now that whoever had shot at him before had done exactly what he'd intended to do when he shot Long Quiet's horse. This time, Long Quiet had been riding hard, knowing that Bay was at home waiting for him. His fall when the galloping horse had crumpled beneath him had caused the raw scrapes Bay had cleaned up. The blood on his shirt was the result of his impatience to get back to Bay. Knowing she'd be worried if he didn't show up, he'd tried to make a break for cover before it was completely dark. He'd felt his head explode in pain as a bullet creased his scalp and had felt the warm blood begin to run down his neck and onto his shoulder before he'd lost consciousness.

He'd woken in the dark, wondering why the bushwhacker hadn't finished him off. Maybe the arrogant villain thought he had. Maybe he hadn't been careful enough to make sure. Or maybe things were happening exactly the way Jonas Harper had planned them all along. Long Quiet leaned back in the chair, careful to keep the pressure off the spot where the bullet had grazed his head.

He'd had a lot of time to think on the walk home, and although the answer had been slow in coming, he believed he'd finally figured out what Jonas had in mind. Long Quiet had played games with a quarry before, similar to the game he believed Jonas was playing with him. Eventually, the object of the hunt became his own worst enemy, fearing his shadow, afraid and ineffectual, a shell of a man. It appeared Jonas wanted Bay to see Long Quiet craven and quaking before he finally shot him dead.

Unfortunately, divining what Jonas had planned didn't make it any less nerve-racking to endure. Because the truth of the matter was, for the first time in his memory, Long Quiet was afraid.

He wasn't afraid of dying. As a Comanche, he'd always considered dying inevitable. The only consideration was whether a warrior fought bravely to the end. And he would face death bravely however it came to him.

No, what he feared was leaving Bay alone and vulnerable to a smooth-talking thief—and bushwhacker—like Jonas Harper. But he didn't plan to die without ever having a chance to face the man who intended to kill him. Tonight he'd visit Jonas Harper and give a little of what he'd gotten.

But he'd take a moment to rest—and to be sure Bay was asleep—before he left again. His head throbbed. He reached up to check the crease, which had already scabbed over. The wound had probably left him more stunned than he'd realized. He could think of no other excuse for why he'd kissed Bay when he'd vowed to himself he wouldn't touch her until he was sure she no longer regretted giving up the things Jonas Harper had promised her. He shook his head in disbelief. Another moment and he'd have done a lot more than kiss her. Fortunately, his pride had reared its ugly head and saved him from himself.

Long Quiet's musing was interrupted by a cry from the other room. "What's the matter?" he called. All he heard was another low moan in response. He was up and into the bedroom in a matter of moments.

"What's wrong?"

"It's nothing," Bay said, teeth gritted against the cramp in her leg. She'd already clutched the muscles of her right calf with both hands trying to work out the cramp, but she couldn't help groaning as the muscles tightened even more despite her efforts. Since her pregnancy she'd been getting slight cramps in her legs when she stood too long during the day. But this one was much worse than any of the others.

Long Quiet lit the candle and pulled the sheet away. He hadn't paid much attention to what Bay was wearing while she'd ministered to him. Now he was quite aware that she was wearing only her chemise and knee-length drawers. He saw the flash of white skin in the shadows. He forced his gaze away from the darker nipples visible through the thin cotton chemise, focusing on the flesh she'd gripped in both hands. He knew at once what her problem was. He took her calf between his callused hands and worked his thumbs deep into the clenched muscles to relax them.

Bay was still curled over by the pain, unable to lie flat without worsening the problem, so their faces were close. She'd been too worried about Long Quiet before to notice how he smelled, but now every breath brought her the odor of a hard-working man. It wasn't an unpleasant smell—horses and honest male sweat. She wanted to reach out and touch him, but she didn't dare.

"How does it feel now?"

"Better," Bay said. "Thank you." Her calf muscles had begun to relax but still ached, and the arch of her foot began to tighten, threatening a cramp there. "Now my foot—"

"I'll get it." Long Quiet continued his massage down to her ankle and foot.

Bay groaned in relief. "That feels good."

Long Quiet massaged the muscles of her calf and foot, glad for the opportunity to touch her and know the touch was welcome.

When she was sure another cramp wasn't going to seize her, Bay lay down with her head on the pillow.

Long Quiet watched absently as she clasped her hands in her lap . . . actually, over the dark shadow at the apex of her legs. His hands never left her leg, but worked the muscle closer to her knee, his hands brushing the inside of her thigh. He felt her quiver before he slid his hands back down to her ankle. He took her foot in both hands and pressed the sole of her foot, ran his thumbs down the arch, eased each toe between his fingers.

It wasn't until Bay spoke that he noticed that she was quivering with tension.

"What do you expect from me in this marriage?" Bay asked softly. "I . . . I need to know."

Long Quiet's hands stilled. His eyes sought hers before he said, "Only that you be my wife."

Bay sat up so she could see his expression. "What does that mean, to be your wife? Is it only cooking and cleaning? Or does it include loving and sharing, too?"

He released a gust of air. "What would you like it to be?"

"I've always loved you."

"You told me once before that you loved me—and then made sure I knew that you loved the things Jonas Harper could buy you a helluva lot more. Don't speak to me about love. You don't know the meaning of the word."

"If you'll listen, I can explain everything."

He rose from the bed as though he were in danger of succumbing to some siren's lure if he stayed. "Just say what you want from me," he snarled. "Don't try to dress it up in a fancy wrapping with words of love."

"All right," Bay snapped, disgusted at having been cut off a second time while trying to tell him the truth about why she'd agreed to marry Jonas Harper. "What I want is you, inside me, pleasuring—"

Long Quiet's hand abruptly covered her mouth, cutting off the sensual request. "Do you know what you're asking for?"

Bay met his eyes with a determined gaze. Since she couldn't speak, she nodded.

"Then so be it," he rasped.

He dropped his hand from her mouth to her breast, cupping the new fullness the baby had caused. He lowered his head and kissed her breast through the cotton. He felt the nipple peak in his mouth and lifted his head to stare at the wet cotton.

"Please," Bay begged.

"What?"

"Don't stop. I . . . I need you."

He sought out the other nipple through the chemise and sucked it into his mouth. Bay groaned and arched beneath him, until she'd bucked up against his loins. He reached out his hands and grasped her waist to hold her close, then pressed her back down upon the bed and used his knees to spread her legs so he could settle himself between her thighs.

"Oh, Bay," he breathed. "You feel so good. It's been so long. I've missed you so much."

He tantalized her with his kisses, teased her with his tongue. She caught fire and he burned in the flame. In the Comanche camp he'd only wanted her desire. Now he discovered her desire wasn't enough; he wanted her love. He would find a way to have it, he vowed to himself. But he could no longer deny himself the warmth of her willing body.

He stripped himself and then her, anxious to make sweet, passionate love with his wife for the first time since he'd left her at her father's door. He was tender, even more so because of the child, his child, which she carried within her.

"Your stomach with the baby inside is so round," he marveled as his hands caressed her curved belly with all the gentleness he felt for the two of them, his wife and his child. "And it's not soft anymore, it's firm and taut, like a peach before it ripens. But you're still soft here . . ." He suckled her breasts as his child would suckle, and knew jealousy of his own babe's right to do the same.

Tears gathered in Bay's eyes at the wonder in Long Quiet's voice. He gave her ample proof that he cared for her as well as the child, through the warm wetness of his lips upon her naked breasts, with the love bites at her neck and shoulder, with the teasing, taunting foray of his fingers and mouth, preparing the way for his swollen shaft.

Bay held her breath at the slow, deep penetration, filling her, possessing her. She echoed his deep groan of satisfaction with an equally satisfied groan. And then she laughed because they'd both sounded so pleased with the feel of one another. She felt, as much as heard, his rumbling laugh in return.

She dug her fingers into his buttocks and wrapped her legs around him to keep him deep inside, but he wouldn't be bound. The slow, steady thrusts built in speed and strength, shoving her upward toward the head of the bed. She began to reach for the ecstasy with each thrust, feeling the tension build.

"More!" she panted. "Give . . . me . . . more!"

Then they were both out of control, their breathing ragged, their hearts pounding, their bodies slick with sweat, their voices spilling guttural sounds of pleasure.

"Please, now," Bay cried.

Long Quiet answered with a cry of exultation as he spilled his seed within her. He'd cherished Bay as he never had before, telling her of his love in the only way he knew. With his last bit of energy, he whispered, "Mine." Then he fell asleep, fulfilled, his head pillowed on his wife's breast.

Bay was still gasping for breath after Long Quiet had fallen asleep. It had been a tumultuous coupling, and as she brushed a curl from his brow, she claimed him as well.

"Mine."

A moment later she was also asleep.

Bay woke later feeling chilled. The covers had been pushed to the end of the bed by their lovemaking, and Long Quiet no longer lent her his warmth. In fact, he was lying as far away from her as he could get, on the opposite side of the bed. Slowly, she became aware he was also awake.

"The bed's too soft, isn't it?" she said, whispering because it was dark and the night seemed to require it.

He said nothing, and she thought he wasn't going to answer her. At last he replied, "Yes, it is too soft. I haven't slept much in a bed since I lived in Boston. It's going to take some getting used to."

"We could sleep on the floor," Bay offered.

Long Quiet chuckled. "There's not enough floor to sleep on. The bed takes up all the room. I guess we haven't much choice except to get used to it. Try to get some sleep. Morning comes early."

Sleep eluded them both. Finally, Bay said, "I can't sleep. I keep thinking about the mustang you were trying to tame—the one that threw you. Can you tell me more about what happened?"

"I'd rather tell you about the beautiful *bayo* mare I'm working with. I'm taking the time to gentle her rather than break her, as the *mesteñeros* are doing with the rest of the mustangs. I wish you could have seen her running with the herd, Bay," he said, his voice full of enthusiasm. "She's the most beautiful mare I've ever seen, sleek and graceful. I've only been working with her for two days and Lady's already starting to trust me."

"Lady?"

"I've named her Golden Lady," he admitted.

Bay wished she could see his features to know whether he was even a little red-faced at deciding upon such a beautiful, feminine name for a horse.

"I've been able to put a blanket on Lady's back and rest a little of my weight on her. She'll even let me rub her nose and—"

"You always were a great one for rubbing a pony's nose," Bay interrupted with a smile.

Long Quiet laughed. "You got to be pretty good at that yourself."

He was quiet then. Bay thought he must be thinking about the life he'd left behind. "Has it been hard for you to adjust to living here in Texas?"

"No." *Difficult, but not impossible.*

"Do you wish you were back in *Comancheria?*"

"No." *Because you can't be there with me.*

"Are you going to tell me any more about what you're thinking?"

"No." Only this time there was a smile in his voice. "It's all right, Bay. I'm not sorry I chose to live in Texas. It isn't as though I haven't ever lived as a white man. I have. Perhaps the finality of it hasn't struck me yet."

"But it doesn't have to be final, does it?" Bay asked. "You can go back to *Comanchería* to visit anytime you want."

"I suppose I can," he replied. "But listen to what you said. I'd only be *visiting*. It won't ever be my home again. I'll miss it."

"But you'll take our child to meet his Comanche relatives, won't you?"

"You still want me to take our child among the Comanches."

"How is our son going to be a bridge between two peoples if he doesn't know anything about one of them?"

"What would have happened if you'd married Jonas, Bay? How would *our* child have learned about his Comanche heritage then?"

Until he'd spoken, Long Quiet hadn't realized how angry he was with Bay for not telling him about the baby the instant she'd known. The thought of Jonas Harper raising his son put a foul taste in his mouth.

And if he didn't do something soon to put a stop to Jonas's games, the day might still come when his son would be calling Jonas Harper "Pa." That thought prodded Long Quiet completely out of bed.

"Where are you going?" Bay asked, startled to see Long Quiet dressing again.

"I have some business that needs taking care of."

"In the middle of the night?"

"It won't wait. Go to sleep, Bay."

"Long Quiet, I—"

"Go to sleep."

Long Quiet slipped through Jonas's bedroom window without making a sound. He wore nothing except a breechclout and he'd found his *tunawaws* and painted his face with fierce black stripes. Of course he had no braids, but he'd tied a fox-tail and several feathers into his hair, while a leather band at his brow held his raven-black hair from his face. He waited until nearly dawn, sitting cross-legged on the foot of Jonas's bed.

Jonas woke slowly, with a feeling that he wasn't alone. That made him think he must be in a hotel with a woman of the night, except the instant he opened his eyes, he knew he was home. His gaze flicked around the room, but found nothing. He frowned. He looked again and saw what appeared to be a war-painted Comanche standing at the foot of his bed with a knife in his hand.

He blinked and had opened his mouth to yell when a guttural voice commanded, "Don't cry out."

Panic-stricken, Jonas started to yell anyway.

A heavy hand shut off his voice by grasping his throat. "I said be quiet. I only want to talk to you."

Jonas had wet himself, and tears of humiliation and fright rose to his eyes as he struggled to breathe through the small air passage left to him by the Comanche's clutching fingers.

"Do you know who I am?"

Jonas's eyes went wide with recognition, and he clawed and struggled against the hand at his throat.

"Be still."

The hand closed tighter, cutting off Jonas's air, so he was forced to lie still or suffocate.

Long Quiet waited until Jonas opened his eyes again and stared at him before he said, "A Comanche's horse is his most prized possession, a source of wealth. I've lost two horses recently. Someone shot them out from under me."

Jonas was wildly shaking his head, but he stopped when it occurred to him that Long Quiet's knife was carving a tiny line along the pulse point below his ear each time he moved.

"But a Comanche is a generous man. I am willing to forgive

the loss of my horses, and I will take nothing from you in return."

Jonas slumped in relief and discovered that once he relaxed, breathing was easier.

"But I should warn you, if one of these accidents should happen again, if another horse of mine should die—for any reason—I'll come back to visit you again. And next time I'll flay you alive and cut out your heart when I'm done. Do you understand?"

Jonas nodded vigorously, adding a vertical line to the horizontal one on his throat, which created a jagged cross.

"Now, I know I've interrupted your sleep, so why don't you close your eyes and get some rest."

Reluctantly, fearfully, Jonas closed his eyes. He waited a moment before daring to open his eyes after the pressure left his throat. He glanced around the room, then leaned up on his elbows to search again.

The Comanche was gone.

Jonas opened his mouth to shout for help and noticed the acrid smell of urine. His face flushed as he rose from the bed and stripped himself of his soiled pajamas.

Who the hell did this Walker Coburn think he was, dressing up like a Comanche and scaring the hell out of him? Well, the time for games was over. He was going to kill Walker Coburn—or whoever the hell he was—and make Bay Stewart his wife. But he was in no hurry. He had a little business in Shelby County to settle first.

When Walker Coburn least expected him, he'd be back.

Chapter 23

BAY TRIED TO SLEEP BUT COULDN'T. WHEN DAWN came her eyes were red-rimmed with fatigue, and dark circles had formed in half-moons under her eyes. She rose to prepare Long Quiet's breakfast, knowing that in this, at least, she could please him. She already had corn cakes cooking on the fire in the lean-to when Paco arrived.

"The señor, he sent me to tell you he will not be coming here to eat his breakfast this morning."

Bay hid her disappointment as she said, "If you'll wait, I'll pack something for his dinner."

"My sister, Juanita, she has already done this."

"Oh." The stab of jealousy was quick and deadly. Bay swayed with dizziness that was not altogether due to fatigue.

Paco reached out a hand to steady her. "The señora, she should rest, no?"

Bay shook off his hand. "No, the señora has work to do. Tell the señor I'll see him at supper. That is, if he's coming home for supper."

Paco grinned. "*Sí*, Señora Coburn. I will tell him. *Adiós*."

Bay was determined to keep herself busy so she wouldn't have time to think about where Long Quiet had been all night long. She was digging a plot for a winter garden behind the house when she heard a wagon approaching. She ran around the side of the house in time to hear Sloan yell, "Hello the house! Is anybody home?"

Bay found Sloan unloading a huge trunk from the wagon. "What have you got there? Can I help?"

Sloan hefted the trunk over her shoulder. "Just tell me where you want this trunk."

"What's in it?"

"Your clothes."

"Oh, my. Bring it into the bedroom."

Bay hurried ahead of Sloan to the bedroom and shoved Long Quiet's trunk, which was centered at the foot of the bed, over to leave room for hers.

"Set it there," Bay said, indicating the empty space.

Sloan set down the trunk and immediately plopped herself down on top of it. "Whew! I forgot how heavy that was." She pulled a handkerchief from the pocket of her trousers and wiped the sweat from her brow. "So, how's married life?" she asked with a grin.

Bay was surprised by Sloan's friendliness. It occurred to her that Sloan might be as lonely as she herself was feeling at the moment. At any rate, Bay wasn't one to overlook a found penny, so she said, "It's not what I expected, if you want to know the honest truth." She sat down on Long Quiet's trunk beside Sloan and confided, "For one thing, there isn't much for me to do."

Sloan turned her head over her shoulder and looked for a long moment at the gigantic bed, then turned back to Bay and eyed the dark circles under her eyes. "Nothing to do, huh?"

Bay felt herself flush from the neck up. "Well . . . um . . . you know what I mean."

"What did you expect?" Sloan asked.

"I don't know that I ever really thought about it. At Three Oaks I always had bookkeeping responsibilities to keep me busy. When I was with the Comanches, I worked hard sewing and tanning and cooking. But I've always known what was expected of me. This is probably the first time in my life that

I've gotten up in the morning without somebody ready to tell me what to do."

"If you'd married Jonas, you wouldn't have had this problem. He'd have told you what to do."

"You're right about that," Bay agreed with a grin that said she wasn't sorry she'd missed that opportunity. "I feel a little like a bear that's woken up in spring and found everything still covered with snow. Things are kind of familiar, but the landmarks are harder to find."

"Don't worry," Sloan said. "It's bound to get easier. But you look tired. How have you been feeling? You aren't working too hard, are you?"

Bay smiled as she laced her hands across her belly. "All right, most of the time. But how long is this muzziness in the morning going to last? Was it like this for you, Sloan? I mean, when did you start feeling better?"

Bay looked up from her stomach to find that Sloan's face had paled to an unhealthy shade of white. She immediately reached out a hand to Sloan's shoulder. "I'm sorry. I didn't think."

"I've got to go now." Sloan rose, moving away from Bay's comforting hand.

"Please don't leave," Bay pleaded. "I promise we won't talk about the baby anymore if it makes you uncomfortable."

Sloan stopped in the doorway between the two rooms and turned back to her sister. "Look, Bay," she said, her voice taut with control. "I understand how happy you must be about your baby. It doesn't bother me to talk about it. Just because I . . ." Sloan swallowed hard and continued, "Just because I chose not to keep my child doesn't mean I don't want to share your happiness. But I really do have to go right now."

Bay thought Sloan was lying about not caring, and she wondered who Sloan was trying to fool most—Bay or herself. "I understand you have to go," Bay said, "but can I just ask one more question? If you're sure it won't bother you," she qualified.

Sloan's hands curled into fists, then relaxed as she said, "I told you it wouldn't bother me, and I do have time for one more question. Go ahead. What is it?"

"When the baby first moved, when you first felt life inside you, what was it like?"

Sloan turned her face away abruptly and stared out toward the front room. "I try not to think about it." Sloan turned back around, and Bay saw for the first time the anguish her sister had hidden so well from her family. "I try to pretend it never happened, that I never had a baby . . . But I haven't forgotten what it was like to have my child growing inside me."

There was the bitterness, the futility and sadness Bay would have expected to hear from a mother who'd given up her child. She ached for her sister and wondered whether Sloan had ever tried to see Cisco and whether, if she had a second chance, she would take her child back.

Sloan walked back into the bedroom and sat down on Bay's trunk. Bay grasped Sloan's hand in a show of support.

Sloan squeezed her sister's hand back and said, "I was in the barn the first time I felt the baby move, and it was like . . . like a small butterfly fluttering in your cupped hands, only it's happening here . . ." Sloan slid her free hand across her belly in a caress of her empty womb.

"It was the most glorious moment of my life. I had created a new life with the man I loved. Except Antonio didn't love me," she added quietly.

"I'm so sorry, Sloan," Bay said.

"Don't be." Sloan freed her hand from Bay's grasp and stood up. "I'm not sorry I gave up the child. It was for the best. I . . ."

When Sloan's voice cracked, she rose and walked quickly from the room and out the front door.

"Wait!" Bay called, racing after her. "Sloan, wait a minute."

By the time Bay got to the front door, Sloan was already seated on the wagon and had the reins in her hand.

"Good-bye, Bay," Sloan said. "I'll come visit again some-time."

"When?"

"Whenever you say," Sloan said, grinning as though what had happened in the back room had been left there along with all her painful memories.

"Then how about Sunday?" Bay asked. "Come for dinner on Sunday."

Sloan fiddled with the buttons on her vest for a moment. "All right. Sunday it is. See you then."

Bay could hardly wait for Long Quiet to come home so she could tell him about Sloan's visit. She was sure he wouldn't mind if Sloan came to dinner on Sunday. Just in case, she decided to provide him with an especially good sup-per before she told him about it. Thanks to the trunk of clothes, she would be wearing a pretty calico dress to greet him. She was in the lean-to when she heard the sound of a horse—no, two horses—nearing the adobe house.

Bay had lived on the frontier long enough to know that in the unexpected lay danger. She searched the lean-to for a weapon and found a long butcher knife. It would only be good at close range, but as bad as she was with firearms it was as good a weapon as any, and she would use it if she had to.

She inched her way along the wall of the lean-to toward a crack in the wall that gave her a view of the oncoming riders. The man riding in front was dressed in Spanish clothing, but Bay couldn't see his face because the brim of the flat-crowned black hat drooped in front. The other man, hidden behind him, rode a magnificent *bayo*.

Bay's heart raced, and she felt dizzy. She leaned back against the wall of mesquite posts and took a deep breath, trying to calm her jangled nerves. When she turned around again the face of the second man was visible. It was Long Quiet!

Bay threw the knife down onto the dirt floor and went

racing around the corner of the shed and directly into Long Quiet's path. The *bayo* pranced nervously as Long Quiet dismounted and tied the horse to the hitching rail in front of the house. He had barely turned around before Bay threw herself into his arms.

"I guess this means you're happy to see me," Long Quiet said with a chuckle as he embraced his wife.

"I was afraid it wasn't you. I didn't recognize the man riding with you." Bay turned her head to look and realized that the man was Cruz Guerrero. "Oh," she groaned. She turned to hide her face against Long Quiet's chest. "I feel so foolish."

"It is not foolish to be wary of strangers," Cruz said. "I apologize if I frightened you."

"No apology is necessary," Bay said. "You both look hungry. Come inside and sit down. Supper's ready and there's plenty. I hope you can stay and eat with us."

"I hadn't planned to stay long."

"Please. You'll be our first guest." Bay didn't know if she had feminine wiles, but she tried out a blazing smile on Cruz. She grinned even more broadly when it seemed to be working.

Cruz turned to Long Quiet, who added his encouragement. "It would give us some more time to discuss your suggestion. I think much better on a full stomach," Long Quiet hinted.

"But of course," Cruz said, relenting. "I will join you, Señora Coburn. I thank you for the invitation."

"Is this Golden Lady?" Bay asked, reaching out to stroke the palomino's nose. "She's beautiful!"

"Yes, she is. She's yours if you want her."

"Mine?" Bay moved from Long Quiet's embrace, using both hands to stroke the beautiful blond mane and the white blaze between the palomino's huge brown eyes.

Long Quiet grinned. "She needs to learn a few more manners, but I brought her home so you could see if you want her. What do you think?"

"I love her."

Bay looked up at Long Quiet to show her pleasure at the wonderful gift he'd given her, and he suddenly noticed the dark circles under her eyes. He felt responsible for her fatigue and realized he'd only made more work for her by bringing Cruz home. Now she would have to serve both of them before she could rest. "Then it's settled. She's yours. Let's go eat," he said.

Bay saw the displeasure shadow Long Quiet's gray eyes and wondered what had gone wrong. He was such a mystery to her. Perhaps he was only hungry and supper would put him in a better mood. "Everything's ready," she said. "I only have to find an extra plate for Cruz."

The meal that followed was a revelation to Long Quiet. It appeared Bay wasn't at all concerned that there weren't three plates of the same pattern in the house or that the pewter fork tines were bent or that they drank their coffee from pottery mugs rather than china cups and saucers. He couldn't understand how, if Bay had been marrying Jonas Harper for the silks and silver his money could buy her, she could be so obviously happy with the few simple things he provided in this adobe house.

But then, maybe he only wanted to believe she was happy because he couldn't bear to think her sparkling eyes and glowing smile were all an act.

"And now, *mi amigo*," Cruz said when the coffee had been poured. "Regarding that suggestion of mine . . . have you thought any more about it?"

Bay tried not to look as curious as she was. Of course Rip had always included her in his business discussions, but she knew that neither Texans nor Comanches were so open with their wives as Rip had been with his daughters. She waited to see what stand Long Quiet would take with respect to her involvement in his business.

Bay felt a small bud unfurl within her when Long Quiet said, "Let's see what my wife makes of this suggestion of yours." She leaned forward intently as he explained, "Jonas is pestering Cruz to sell him another tract of land. Cruz says he'd rather give me first crack at buying it."

"Can you use the land?" Bay asked.

"Yes, I've got a decent-size herd of stray cattle branded and I need a place to graze them."

"Then why don't you buy the land from Cruz," Bay said.

Long Quiet sat back and pursed his lips thoughtfully, then said, "I haven't the money to pay Cruz for the land outright or enough collateral to make a loan."

"Then why don't you take a long-term lease on the land," Bay suggested. "That way you'd have the use of the land without the need to make a large loan. You could pay some smaller amount each year. Jonas wouldn't be so interested in buying the land if he couldn't have the use of it for his lifetime, would he?"

The two men looked at each other, then stared in awe at Bay. "Why didn't I think of that?" Cruz said. "And the land would still be there for my grandchildren."

"Would it solve your problem with Jonas?" Long Quiet asked.

"*Sí*, I think it would. Jonas will not want the land if he must honor a lifetime lease. I think your wife has come up with a very good idea. I'll have my solicitor draw up the papers right away," Cruz said.

"This calls for a celebration," Bay said.

"Not right now. I've got an early day tomorrow," Long Quiet countered, thinking how much Bay needed to rest.

"And I have a long ride ahead of me," Cruz said. "Another time, perhaps."

Long Quiet saw Bay attempt to hide her disappointment and offered, "How about Sunday?"

Cruz shook his head. "I spend Sundays with my nephew, Cisco. I regret that I must say no."

"Why not bring Cisco with you?" Bay suggested eagerly. She held her breath, hardly able to believe the fortuitous turn of events that might bring her sister back together with the child she'd abandoned two years ago.

"I don't know."

"I'd love to see him. I'll bet he's adorable," Bay coaxed. "You know we're expecting a child of our own. If you come, it'll give Walker a chance to see what's in store for him. Please say you'll come and bring Cisco."

This time Cruz didn't even bother to check with Long Quiet before he agreed. "I cannot refuse the request of such a lovely lady."

Shortly, Cruz left. Long Quiet noticed that Bay seemed particularly nervous and wondered whether he'd made a mistake assuming she wanted to have Cruz come for dinner. "No second thoughts about having company for dinner on Sunday?" he questioned.

Bay took a deep breath. She couldn't decide whether or not to tell Long Quiet that she'd already invited Sloan.

"Bay?" Long Quiet closed the distance between them and turned Bay to face him.

"Uh . . . nothing." But the guilty look in Bay's eyes gave her away.

"What is it, Bay? Is there some reason why I shouldn't have invited Cruz to dinner on Sunday?" All kinds of jealous thoughts came to Long Quiet's mind, and his hands tightened on her shoulders.

Bay threaded her fingers anxiously behind her back. "I've invited Sloan to dinner Sunday, too. So there! Now you know my secret."

Long Quiet was startled into silence by her outburst. Then he broke out laughing. "Is that all?"

"You won't say anything to Cruz, will you?" She placed her palms against his chest. "This is a chance for Sloan to see Cisco, and I know if she sees him once, she'll want to see him again. But if Cruz finds out Sloan's going to be here, he might not bring Cisco and then—"

"Take it easy," Long Quiet soothed, reaching out his arms to enfold Bay. "I'll help with your little intrigue. But don't get your hopes too high, Bay. Sloan must have had good reasons for what she did, and they're not going to magically disappear when she sees her son again."

"Well, I didn't think they would," she said, rubbing her cheek against Long Quiet's shirt. "But Cisco's bound to be adorable, don't you think? All babies are. And Sloan will—"

Bay's mind was still occupied with scheming when Long Quiet's mouth covered hers. Startled, she jerked away from his touch. Eyes that had been a smoky gray turned almost black as his head lowered once more. This time she was ready, and his possession was no less fierce than hers. He lifted her into his arms and carried her toward the big bed in the other room.

"Come to bed," he murmured. "You need to rest."

"I'll rest," she promised. "Later."

Sunday morning dawned cloudy and gray. Bay only prayed it wouldn't rain. She wanted everything to be perfect, and sunshine was part of the beautiful day she had planned.

Long Quiet was aware of Bay's strange mood. She'd been nervous as a mare with a newborn foal all morning. Every time he came near her, she jumped. "It's going to be all right, Bay," he said. "Don't worry so much."

Bay looked at Long Quiet and wondered if he understood how important it was to her to reunite Sloan with her child. She couldn't have Little Deer back, but there was nothing to keep Sloan from being a mother again to Cisco—except Sloan's own obstinance. "Thanks for caring," she said.

They were interrupted by the sound of hoofbeats. Long Quiet stepped to the open front door and looked out. "Sloan is here."

"Hello, Walker," Sloan said. She stepped off her horse, and after releasing a package from the ties that held it to the saddle, carried it with her to the threshold.

Long Quiet and Sloan gauged each other, looking for any signs of hostility. When neither found any, it was Bay who released a sigh of relief. "Hello, Sloan," Bay said. "I'm glad you could come." She nudged Long Quiet aside so Sloan could come in the door.

"I've brought you a present," Sloan said, handing Bay the bulky package, which was wrapped in brown paper.

"What is it?"

"Open it and see," Sloan said with a smile.

Bay sat on a nearby chair and carefully opened the brown-paper package. "It's a quilt. Why, it's exquisite!" Bay opened the quilt up and let her fingertips roam the intricate multicolored design. "I didn't know you could sew."

Embarrassed to be found out, Sloan admitted, "I . . . I started while you were gone. With Cricket married and at Lion's Dare, it helped me pass the time alone at night."

Bay stood and hugged her sister. "Thank you." She grabbed Sloan's hand and tugged her along behind her. "Come on. Let's see how it looks on the bed."

Long Quiet followed after them and arrived in the bedroom doorway in time to see Bay open the folds and shake the colorful quilt out across the huge bed.

"How beautiful! And it fits," Bay said, running around the bed straightening wrinkles.

Sloan grinned. "I had to stay up late the past three nights adding more squares. I couldn't believe the size of this bed when I saw it."

"Yes, well, it is big all right," Bay agreed with a grin. She met Long Quiet's eyes and flushed at the amusement she saw in them. "I have a few things I need to finish up for supper. Want to help?"

"Sure."

Bay led Sloan out the front door, not giving her a chance

to focus on the table in the front room set for five, not three. They were in the lean-to when Cruz arrived in the carriage.

"Were you expecting more company?" Sloan asked.

"Actually, Walker invited Cruz for dinner, too," Bay said. "You don't mind, do you?"

"I . . . I suppose not. I owe a lot to Cruz Guerrero." Sloan self-consciously pushed a stray hair behind her ear. She'd tied her sable hair with a ribbon at her nape, as she usually did, but wisps were constantly flying free. It had become a habit to reach up and smooth her hair when she was nervous.

"I didn't realize you were indebted to Cruz," Bay said to make conversation. She wanted Cruz to have time to get inside with Cisco before they left the lean-to and joined the others in the house.

"Cruz was the one who arranged for me to see Antonio one last time before he was buried. And when I decided not to keep Antonio's child, it was Cruz . . ." Sloan's voice was shaking, but she managed to finish, ". . . Cruz who made the arrangements for his family to take the baby."

Bay used a pair of mitts to lift the heavy dutch oven off the fire. "I guess we can bring the plates out to serve this up whenever we're ready to eat."

Sloan followed Bay into the house but stopped square in the doorway at the sight that greeted her. Sitting in Cruz's lap was a small child, a little boy with dark brown hair and sky blue eyes who looked amazingly like the man who held him. The child looked up at her and grinned, a wide smile that, together with the sparkling blue eyes and the cleft in his chin, made him look even more like Cruz.

Of course, the two Guerrero brothers had looked alike, but there was nothing of Antonio's dark, betraying eyes in this innocent child.

"*Hola! Como esta usted?*" Cisco said.

"Speak in English," Cruz corrected.

Agreeably, Cisco repeated his greeting to Sloan in English.

"Hello," was all Sloan could manage in reply.

Seeing her sister's distress, Bay urged the men to take their places at the table while she and Sloan carried plates back and forth until everyone had a serving of the hearty stew she'd prepared. Sloan took the only seat left to her, which was directly across from Cisco, whose seat had been elevated with a small stool.

Bay noticed that Cruz hadn't taken his eyes off Sloan since she'd arrived. And if she wasn't mistaken, there was a great deal of admiration for her sister in his piercing blue eyes. But how was that possible? Sloan had been his brother's lover.

As the meal progressed, it became clear to Bay that not only was Cruz attracted to Sloan, but the feeling, whether Sloan knew it or not, was reciprocated. Bay found the relationship between Sloan and Cruz intriguing, since it had never occurred to her she'd be matchmaking, only that she'd be bringing Sloan together with the child she had given away. However, every attempt she made to involve Sloan and Cruz in a conversation seemed doomed to failure. At last she decided to take the bull by the horns.

"Sloan tells me you were the one who made the arrangements to provide a home for Cisco with your family," Bay said to Cruz.

"*Sí.* Sloan and I came to an agreement that made everyone happy."

Bay watched the blush rise on Sloan's cheeks and wondered what exactly had been involved in that agreement.

At that moment, Cisco begged to be let down. At first Cruz tried to keep him at the table, but it soon became obvious that the rambunctious boy had ideas of his own.

"You'll have to excuse me," Cruz said, finally standing to

leave the table. "I'm afraid Cisco doesn't ever sit still for very long."

Bay could see what was coming. Cruz would use Cisco's activity as an excuse to leave. She wasn't about to let that happen, especially when Sloan hadn't even touched the child yet. "Why don't you and Sloan take Cisco for a walk while Walker and I clean up here? Then we can all have some dessert," Bay said.

"You're asking for trouble," Long Quiet murmured in her ear.

"Maybe. Maybe not," she whispered back.

There was nothing Sloan or Cruz could do to avoid taking the walk together without admitting they didn't want to be alone with one another.

Sloan looked one last time at Bay but found no mercy in her sister's determined gaze. "All right," Sloan agreed reluctantly. "We'll be back shortly."

Sloan followed slightly behind Cruz, who trailed a foot or two behind Cisco, whose chubby legs were churning as he headed straight for the corral that held Golden Lady.

"*Caballo!*" Cisco yelled gleefully, dropping to his knees to wriggle under the bars of the corral.

Cruz grabbed Cisco by the waist and hauled the little boy up into his arms. "In English!" he chided.

"Why do you make him speak English?" Sloan asked when she saw the woeful look on Cisco's face as Cruz chastised him.

"Because his mother speaks English," Cruz replied.

Sloan met his steady gaze for a moment before she turned away, flushed because she was pleased and didn't want to be.

Cruz put Cisco down with a warning to stay outside the corral, and when the little boy had drifted out of hearing toward a patch of wildflowers, he turned back to say, "I want to be sure that when he is old enough to make the choice himself, he can speak to his mother if he wishes to do so."

"There's no need for that."

"I think there is."

"You have no right to make assumptions about what's important to me."

"I have *every* right," he retorted, "and you know it."

Sloan stood steadfast at his censure, unable to deny his words. They had an agreement. And if the terms were not exactly to her liking, she was still bound by it. "I spoke out of turn. He speaks English very well," she said by way of apology.

"Will you speak to your son, Sloan? Will you hold him in your arms as a mother should?"

She was trembling when she said, "You know I can't do that."

"Why not?"

"Because it would only lead to pain for me and the child."

"The child! The child! Can you not call him by his name? He is Francisco, or Cisco if you will."

"I . . . I thought he would look more like Antonio. But he doesn't. He looks like you."

Sloan met Cruz's blue eyes and saw the desire that never failed to frighten her. He wanted her. But they had an agreement, so she was safe.

Cisco interrupted the moment of awareness between them when he called, "Come see! *Bayo!*" The little boy had lost interest in the flowers and was headed back to the corral.

"Shall we join him?" Cruz said. He reached out to take Sloan's arm, but she flinched away. He started toward his nephew with Sloan at his side.

They walked up behind Cisco, who'd climbed up onto the lowest rail of the corral and stood stretched out with his fingers barely reaching the top rail. In his excitement at their arrival, he turned too quickly and would have fallen if Sloan hadn't been there to rescue him.

As he tumbled backward, she caught him at the shoulders

and knees so she was holding him like an infant. It was the first time she'd touched her son since the day she'd given him away, over two years before. He lay there for a moment staring into her eyes before he began struggling for a more upright, less babyish position.

Sloan accommodated him, and once she did, he seemed content to stay in her embrace. When Cruz would have taken Cisco from her, she held on. Sloan closed her eyes and enjoyed the feel of her child's arms and legs wrapped around her, the feel of his baby-soft cheek against hers, the fine curly black hair on his head tickling her chin.

She felt her throat closing in anguish and tried to squeeze back the tears forming in her eyes. She'd never forgotten or forgiven Antonio's betrayal. Would it have been any worse to have kept this living reminder of his perfidy? The child didn't even look like Antonio! Oh, dear God, it felt so good to hold her baby. Had she made the worst mistake of her life giving him up?

Cisco got impatient being held, and Sloan put him down to run again. This time when she met Cruz's eyes, she found a different emotion there.

"I don't need your pity," she cried.

"You deserve more than my pity, Cebellina, that is true."

"I don't want anything from you," Sloan said. But she did want to see Cisco again. And she wasn't sure how she could ask such a thing without giving Cruz any more encouragement to address her by intimate names like Cebellina, which he'd given her because of the sable color of her hair.

And there was the agreement. Always the agreement.

She turned to face Cruz, unaware that she'd squared her shoulders, which made her seem taller than her slight, five-foot-four-inch height. "I want to see Cisco again."

"Of course, Cebellina. I would never keep you from your son. Do you wish to come see him at Rancho Dolorosa?"

"No, no. I can't come to your hacienda." Memories of the awful confrontation there with Cruz's mother three years ago flooded her. The regal woman had stood beside Antonio's casket and casually offered to take Sloan's bastard child. Sloan could smell the incense burning in the dimly lit bedroom, could feel the stiffness of Antonio's dead flesh, could taste the bile rising in her throat at the humiliating offer.

Raising stark, pain-filled eyes, she asked, "Couldn't we meet somewhere else?"

Ready to do anything to ease her pain, Cruz offered, "Do you want me to bring him to Three Oaks?"

"No. Not at my home, either. What about here, at my sister's home?"

"You don't think Bay would mind?"

For the first time, a smile broke through Sloan's strained features. "She's the one who plotted all this in the first place. Somehow I don't think she'll be upset if we want to meet here."

They stood awkwardly, both aware of the momentousness of the occasion, but neither willing to be the first to comment on it. Finally, Sloan said, "I guess we should fetch Cisco and get back to the house."

Sloan made no move to touch Cisco when Cruz picked him up, and she was careful to keep her distance when they stepped inside the house. She shook her head ruefully at the clearly disappointed look on Bay's face. When they sat down for dessert, she said casually, "I have a favor to ask, Bay."

"Of course," Bay replied. "What can I do?"

"I'd like to come visit again next Sunday."

"You know you're welcome anytime, Sloan."

"Does that invitation extend to Cruz and Cisco as well?"

Bay's eyes narrowed as she looked from Sloan to Cruz and back again. "Of course, they're both welcome."

Sloan burst out laughing. "You'll be happy to know your devious little plan worked. I would like to see Cisco again, but we need a place to get together. How would you like having company for Sunday dinners for a while? I'll be glad to help out with the cooking."

Bay turned to Long Quiet and smiled serenely. "I'd love it."

Everything had turned out even better than she'd hoped. It wouldn't be long before Sloan had her child back in her arms for good.

Now, if she could only convince Long Quiet that she loved him. . . .

Chapter 24

AFTER THEIR COMPANY LEFT, LONG QUIET ENCIRCLED
Bay's waist with his arms from behind and rested his hands
on her belly. "That was a good thing you did for Sloan."

"I only wanted her to be happy."

He turned her around in his arms. "And are you happy?"

"I don't . . . I suppose I . . . are you?" she countered, unable to put her feelings into words.

"I have you." He leaned down to kiss her briefly, but she
noticed he hadn't answered the question.

She searched the face of the man who held her in his arms
and saw lines of worry at the corners of his eyes. Had they
been there before? She saw the tightness around his mouth.
Was that bitterness? Anger? She saw the faint creases on his
forehead. Had she contributed to those? Was there anything
in his countenance that spoke of happiness or contentment?
He'd said he had her. What if she wasn't enough? It was a
sobering, even frightening, thought.

"Are you really, truly happy here with me? Do you ever
wish you were back home in *Comanchería?*"

He smiled at her question, and all the lines of worry and
tension disappeared. "What brought that on?"

Her fingertips traced the feathery lines at the edges of his
eyes, then sought out the lips that curved now with amusement. She looked up expecting to find a sparkle in his eyes,

but there, in the gray depths, the sadness still remained. "I just wondered," she murmured.

Long Quiet knew what she was asking. How could he answer her? His fondest wish had been answered when her father had brought her to his doorstep and demanded that he take her as his wife. So, yes, he was happy with what he had—but he wanted more. He'd seen how her love overflowed on those she cared for, on Little Deer and now on Sloan and Cruz and Cisco. He would have given all he had to have it envelop him as well.

He felt the firm roundness of her abdomen pressed against him. There was happiness in knowing a part of them both grew inside of her. And there was happiness in knowing he could hold her and love her. His hands curved around her buttocks and he cradled her more firmly between his thighs. He felt her hands tighten around his waist in response. For now, it was enough.

"I don't know how to reassure you, but I think you want reassurance," Long Quiet said at last. "I can only say it doesn't matter to me whether I live in a tipi or an adobe house. My grandfather once told me, 'Happiness is a feeling inside that makes a gift of each day the Great Spirit gives you to walk upon the Earth Mother.' I never really understood that until now. Look at me, Bay."

He waited until she looked up at him and said, "To me, you are home and happiness."

Bay had never felt so needed, so fulfilled, as she did at that moment.

Long Quiet tried, but failed, to keep the bitterness from his voice as he added, "I'll try to give you the things you need to be happy, too."

"What if I said having things doesn't matter to me as much as being with you?" Bay replied.

He pulled her arms from about his waist and forced her to stay back so he could see her better. "You don't have to lie about a thing like that, Bay. You can't help the way you were raised. I can understand your appreciation for beautiful things, even if I don't share your need for them. And I don't intend that you should be deprived of those things forever simply because you're married to me. I promise to work hard for you, Bay, and someday we'll—"

Her fingertip silenced him. "Please don't say any more." If she loved him hard enough and long enough, maybe someday he'd believe that she didn't need to be surrounded by silver and crystal or dressed in silks and lace. He was everything she needed or wanted.

The loving between them began sweetly, as each sought acceptance and love from the other. It was a futile quest on which they were bound, for what they sought had already been given—they simply had not recognized the gift.

The days and nights that followed fell into a pattern of easy camaraderie during the day followed by stormy passion at night. Yet both Bay and Long Quiet remained frustrated by the misunderstanding that stood between them.

On Sunday, Bay looked forward to seeing Sloan again. Perhaps her sister would be able to shed some light on the problem. But Cruz and Cisco arrived first with a picnic lunch, and the moment Sloan got there they all set off in Cruz's carriage for a picnic spot Long Quiet had found while out hunting stray cattle.

They topped a rise and saw a huge old live oak that had grown up in the middle of a grassy field. It would have taken six grown men holding hands to circle the trunk of the tree. Its spreading branches created an expanse of shade the size of the manor house at Three Oaks. In the shade of the tree, delicate flowers that would have died in the hot Texas sun had flourished.

"This is wonderful," Bay said as Long Quiet helped her down from the wagon.

"Glory! This tree would make a great target for lightning in a thunderstorm," Sloan said.

"It is good we picked a day of sunshine to come here, is it not?" Cruz said, smiling as he took Cisco from Sloan's lap and set him on the ground.

"I can get down by myself," Sloan said when Cruz held up his hands for her.

"As you wish," he said, and stepped back.

Cruz brought the woven picnic basket over to the spot where Bay had laid out a quilt to use as a tablecloth.

"Go walk," Cisco demanded, grabbing Cruz's pant leg and tugging on it.

"Will you come with us, Sloan?" Cruz asked.

"I should help . . ." Sloan met Cruz's encouraging gaze and changed her mind. "All right. Yes, I'll come."

As Cruz, Sloan, and Cisco headed toward a slight rise at the edge of the shade, Bay busied herself setting out the food Cruz had brought—meat and bean tortillas, tamales wrapped in corn husks, shelled pecans, oranges, and *buñuelos*, crisp fried tortillas with a cinnamon-sugar topping, for dessert.

"What a feast! Everything looks so good." She broke off a piece of a *buñuelo* and popped it in her mouth. "Ummm, sweet."

"Let me taste," Long Quiet said, coming down on his knees across from Bay.

She held out another bite of the dessert, but Long Quiet chose to taste her instead. "Ummm, yes, that's sweet all right," he said as his tongue darted out for a bit of sugar on her lips, and then into her mouth for a taste of Bay. He toppled her over backward on the blanket and came down on top of her, keeping his weight on his arms.

Bay flushed. "Long Quiet, what are you doing?"

"Making love to my wife," he murmured, nibbling on her throat.

"Ah. What a good idea that is," Bay said with a smile as she arched her throat for his lips.

He teased her with light kisses, but his hips were flush with hers and every time he kissed her he pressed himself against her, until the kisses became more hungry and the thrusts more demanding.

Suddenly, Long Quiet rolled himself off her and threw his arm up to cover his eyes. He was breathing heavily, and Bay didn't have to look to know he was aroused.

She sat up and ran her fingers through the hair he'd mussed with his hands. "I guess that wasn't such a good idea," she said, breathing heavily.

"The idea was fine," Long Quiet countered with a rueful grin. He turned and propped himself up on his elbow. "It was the timing that was wrong." He scooted himself over so his head was in Bay's lap and relaxed with his arms stretched out above his head, his hands curved around her waist.

Bay's hands threaded through the curls on his forehead, brushing them away from his face. In a moment his eyes closed in relaxation. His hands slipped down to caress her buttocks and thighs.

"This is the way life was meant to be lived," he murmured. "A man doesn't need more than good food, fresh air and sunshine, and a woman to love . . ."

". . . who loves him back," Bay finished. When Long Quiet started to rise, she caught his shoulders and kept his head in her lap. "Please listen. I've been trying to explain for days now that—"

At that moment Cisco screamed shrilly. Both Bay and Long Quiet were on their feet in an instant, only to discover that it was a scream of delight. Cisco came running toward them, pursued by Sloan and Cruz. As they watched, Sloan scooped Cisco up in her arms and nuzzled his neck as he laughed hysterically.

"I'll get you for putting flowers in my hair," she taunted. "Take that!" Sloan kissed Cisco on the neck.

He laughed and twisted away, putting his hands up to protect his face.

"And that!" Sloan kissed him on the ear. "And that!" She kissed him on the chin.

Cruz came up behind her and held the brunt of Cisco's weight, cocooning Sloan between the two of them. Sloan stiffened as she realized what had happened. When another kiss didn't come, Cisco straightened up to see what had stopped the game.

"Kiss?"

Sloan leaned to kiss Cisco's nose, the sides of her breasts brushing against Cruz's arms as she did so. "That's enough kisses for now. Aren't you hungry?"

"*Sí!* Hungry," Cisco responded with all the enthusiasm of a two-year-old for food. "Down!" he demanded.

Cruz had to release his hold in order for Sloan to set the child down. She moved quickly from Cruz's arms and set Cisco on his feet. He headed on the run for the blanket covered with food.

Sloan turned to Cruz and, in a voice too low to be heard by the others, said, "Don't do that again."

Cruz didn't pretend to misunderstand. "You are too young to spend the rest of your life alone, Cebellina."

"Stay away from me," she hissed. "I want to see my son, but I won't if it means I have to contend with you touching me like . . . touching me." She shivered and crossed her arms as though to protect herself. It was the pleasure of his touch that frightened her.

"I will not touch you, if that is your wish." He gestured toward the picnic blanket. "Shall we go join the others and eat now?"

The rest of the afternoon passed pleasantly. While Cisco napped, Sloan and Bay took a walk together.

"How are things at Three Oaks?" Bay asked.

Sloan reached down to grab a stem of seed grass and chewed on the end, sucking out the sweetness at the tip. "As well as can be expected. Rip's still looking for a way to pay

Jonas. The note's not due until the first of the year, so he has some time to try to come up with the money."

"What will you do if he can't pay the note?"

Sloan threw away the stem of grass and grabbed another. "I don't know. I haven't thought that far ahead. My whole life's been planned with Three Oaks in mind. I can't imagine what I'd do if . . . if it wasn't there someday. I'm glad you didn't marry Jonas, though."

"You are?"

"Yeah. It's easy to see there's something special between you and Walker."

"He thinks I only married him because I'm pregnant with his child. He thinks I regret marrying him because he isn't wealthy."

Sloan snorted. "Why on earth would he think a foolish thing like that?"

"Because when I thought I was going to have to marry Jonas, I told Walker I needed the things Jonas could give me."

"Oh, for heaven's sake! Why don't you just tell him the truth?"

"I've tried. Every time I open my mouth, he interrupts me. Or we get sidetracked."

Sloan smiled slyly. "I bet."

Bay flushed but continued, "I've told him I love him, but he doesn't believe me. How am I going to convince him I'm telling the truth?"

Sloan dropped to the ground cross-legged, and Bay dropped down beside her.

"To start with, I think you have to tell him the real reason why you were going to marry Jonas, even if you have to tie him down to do it."

"And then?"

"Tell him the truth and see what happens. You might be pleasantly surprised."

Bay put a hand on Sloan's knee. "Thanks. I needed someone to talk to about this. I only hope you're right."

"Anytime," Sloan said. "Now I want to thank you."

"For what?"

"For returning my son to me. I don't know if it's because he looks so little like Antonio or because he's so adorable . . . or simply because I've dreamed so often what it would be like to hold my son in my arms—but it's easier to be with Cisco than I thought. I'm grateful to you for helping me find that out."

"Do you think you'll ever want to take him back?"

"Seeing Cisco on Sundays is enough for me right now. Let's not look too far ahead, all right?"

"Sure, Sloan."

"Guess we'd better be getting back. Cruz and Cisco have a long ride home."

The day was over too soon. When she was leaving, Sloan reminded Bay to be sure to talk with Walker, and Bay promised she would. But Bay hadn't counted on her pregnancy making her so tired. She lay down on the bed to rest after supper, and when she woke up it was Monday morning and Long Quiet had already gone to work with his *vaqueros*.

The week was nearly over before Bay found the right moment to talk with Long Quiet, and then their mood was so good that they ended up making love instead. Time slipped by, and the Sundays came and went.

If Long Quiet hadn't been so loving, if she hadn't felt so loving in return, perhaps Bay might have felt more urgently the need to clear up the misunderstanding that had marred their first days together.

But as the days became weeks and the weeks became months, it seemed to Bay that Long Quiet must have finally realized that she loved him for himself.

Every Sunday Sloan, Cruz, and Cisco came to dinner. Sometimes, if the weather was nice enough, Bay packed a basket of food and they ate under the old oak as they had the first day. The Sunday before Christmas was such a day. Bay had risen early, but even so, Sloan was already on her doorstep.

"What are you doing here already?" Bay asked.

"I thought maybe today we could have a—"

"—picnic," they finished together.

They laughed companionably. It had been quite an experience for Bay getting to know her older sister better. She liked what she'd found. It was still hard to assert herself with Sloan, but Sloan seemed to have developed a sensitivity to Bay's feelings. Bay wasn't sure which of the two of them had changed more. She only knew it was like finding a long-lost friend who'd been right there under her nose all the time.

"I'm way ahead of you," Bay said, threading her arm through Sloan's and walking her sister inside. "I've already got fried chicken, baked beans, some cheese, fruit, and an apple pie packed in a basket."

"Sounds wonderful. Cruz and Cisco should be here anytime now."

Almost as she spoke, Cruz rode up on his horse with Cisco planted in the saddle in front of him. That was something new, since Cruz usually brought the little boy in a carriage.

"Isn't Cisco a little young to be riding like that?" Sloan challenged.

"He's taken to riding like a bird to the air. All Spaniards are practically born on horseback," Cruz replied, not at all perturbed by Sloan's remark. Then, sensing Sloan's real concern, he comforted, "Besides, I have a tight hold on him. He's safe."

That seemed to be all the reassurance Sloan required, Bay noticed. Whether Sloan knew it or not, her trust in Cruz had doubled, and then doubled again over the past months. She wondered if Cruz was as trustworthy as all that. There was no doubt he cared about Sloan and about Cisco. But would he end up hurting Sloan? Would he be willing to give up Cisco when the day came that Sloan asked to have her child back, as Bay became more and more convinced she would?

Cisco squirmed in Cruz's arms trying to reach Sloan, until Cruz let go and the little boy launched himself into his mother's arms. Sloan hugged her son to her, rocking him back and forth as the two of them murmured to one another in a mixture of Spanish and English. Sloan was learning her son's language as he learned hers.

Seeing their happiness made Bay feel poignantly the loss of Little Deer, and she turned away from the pain. "I'll get Walker and we can go," she said.

They rode out to the gigantic oak and set their blanket in the sun, knowing they could move it to the shade as the mild winter day warmed even more. Sloan placed the basket of food in the shade and said, "Who's ready for a walk?"

"I think I'll lie here in the sun," Bay replied as she stretched out on the blanket.

Long Quiet lay down beside her and said, "A nap sounds good to me."

"Pick flowers," Cisco said, heading at a toddler's run for the blossoming winter sage on the hill.

Sloan grinned and turned to Cruz. "Guess we're going for a walk."

Cruz held out his palm to her, and after a moment Sloan put her hand in his and they headed for the spring.

"They look good together, don't they?" Bay said to Long Quiet as Cruz and Sloan strolled away together.

"Not matchmaking, are you?"

"Why not? I can remember when Sloan wouldn't let Cruz within two feet of her. Now they're holding hands. Anybody can see they're attracted to one another. Surely you've noticed it."

"Yes, but Cruz is dealing with a woman who doesn't know what she wants."

"That never stopped you," Bay said with a laugh.

A serious Long Quiet answered, "I guess you're right."

Beads of perspiration had formed above the bow of Bay's lip and Long Quiet entertained thoughts of what it would be like to kiss them away. In a moment his thoughts were transformed into action as he leaned over his wife and lowered his lips to hers. "You're a sorceress," he murmured. "You've cast your spell on me."

Sloan turned to call a request to Bay to join them and saw that she was otherwise engaged with her husband. Although it was doubtful Bay would have noticed her attention at that point, Sloan gave her sister the privacy she herself would have desired in the same situation.

However, Cruz didn't miss the blush that rose on Sloan's face at finding her sister making love to her husband in broad daylight. "It is the way of lovers," he said, "not to notice the rest of the world."

The memory of stolen moments with Cruz's brother, Antonio, swamped Sloan. Fleeting impressions of halcyon days, when she'd forgotten anything existed but the two of them, merged with memories of a darker time, when she'd learned that the man she loved had used her without her knowledge to carry messages in a sinister plot against the Republic of Texas.

Cruz damned himself for the agonized look on Sloan's face and sought a distraction that would keep her from remembering a time he wanted to forget as much as she did. "Why don't we take Cisco and go exploring?" he said.

"That sounds like fun," Sloan agreed readily.

Cruz scooped the little boy up in his arms, much against the child's wishes, and strode toward a hillock that would take them out of sight of the other couple. Once over the hill, he set Cisco down again and the little boy trudged away to explore on his own.

"Sloan, we have to talk," Cruz said, catching her hand before she could follow Cisco.

Sloan kept her eyes on her adventuresome son, letting none of the anxiety she was feeling show in her face. She couldn't, however, seem to stop the trembling that was giving her away.

Cruz led Sloan to a grassy mound, barely shaded by a scraggly mesquite, and pulled her down to sit beside him.

"What do you want, Cruz?" Sloan asked, hoping that by taking the initiative she could control the conversation.

"Only to tell you that you're a wonderful mother for Cisco."

Sloan clutched her hands together in her lap. "I don't know how you can say that. I abandoned my child at birth, then didn't see him for more than two—"

"That's enough, Sloan."

"—years, after which I—"

Cruz closed Sloan's mouth with his. His lips were soft on hers, gentle, seeking.

At first, she was too shocked to do anything. Then she found herself responding. Had she wanted this? His lips sought more, and his tongue came searching for the inner softness of her mouth. She shivered with wonder at the feelings bolting through her. It was so different from Anton—

Sloan panicked, jerking her head away and staring into Cruz's deep blue eyes as though he were a stranger. She wasn't supposed to feel anything ever again, and especially not for this man. He was the brother of her lover, the uncle of her child. And they had an agreement!

She scrambled to her feet. "How dare you. You promised," she hissed. "No touching. None!"

"Cebellina, I—"

"I don't want to hear your excuses," she spat. "I heard enough of them from your brother."

Cruz stiffened as the blood fled his face. Sloan was so enraged she never even noticed as she continued, "You Guerreros think all you have to do is snap your fingers and a woman will lay herself down for your pleasure. Well, not me. Damn you. *Not me!*"

Sloan turned and ran, heedless of her direction, which was

away from the site of the picnic, away from her son. Cruz raced after her, had almost caught up with her, when they were both halted by the sound of a child's shriek, followed by an awful silence.

"Cisco!" Sloan turned back in the direction they'd come, with Cruz at her side. Gasping for breath, the pain in her side making her limp with the effort to keep moving, Sloan finally reached the place they'd left Cisco.

Her eyes searched the terrain for her child and widened in horror when at last she spied him.

Long Quiet had found the taste of his wife so enticing he thought he could easily spend the rest of his life kissing her. His body was strung as taut as a bowstring with need, and Bay had teased him mercilessly by refusing to let him unbutton her dress to suckle her breasts. He'd retaliated by kissing her through the calico. He could feel the pebbled tips of her breasts with his teeth and tongue through the wet cloth. Bay was writhing with need beneath him, and he was certain she wouldn't be able to resist his entreaties much longer.

When Long Quiet first heard Cisco's shriek he ignored the sound, because the little boy had often shrieked with laughter, and he very much did not want to be disturbed. But his mind would not release the sound, and he realized all at once that this shriek had been different. It had been a shriek of terror.

He grabbed his gun from the blanket nearby and raced in the direction of the child's cry. He froze when he saw Cisco's body crumpled in the dry prairie grass, a Comanche brave kneeling beside the child with his bloody knife poised above Cisco's scalp. Long Quiet was astonished when the Indian's visage, distorted by his blood lust, lifted slightly at Long Quiet's appearance, and he recognized the face of his friend, Two Fingers, with whom he'd hunted often in the past.

"Two Fingers," he shouted. "Hold!"

Two Fingers, startled to hear his name called by a *tabeboh*, a hated White-eyes, paused long enough to try and identify the intruder. "Long Quiet?"

"Yes."

The Indian's lip curled over his upper teeth in a grotesque grin of pleasure. "You are just in time to share the moment of my revenge," he said, his guttural voice dripping with hatred.

"Revenge for what?"

"I take this boy's life to pay for the death of my son, Forked River, at the hands of the White-eyes."

"I am sorry your son is dead," Long Quiet said. "But I cannot allow you to take your revenge on this innocent child."

"Cannot allow?" Two Fingers raged. "It is already done. It needs only the scalping to satisfy my promise of revenge to the mother of Forked River."

"No."

Two Fingers looked from the gun in Long Quiet's hand to his friend's flinty gray eyes. "You will not kill me, *haints*. We have ridden too many trails together. You are Comanche, a True Human Being. A Comanche does not kill his brother."

Long Quiet watched the malicious grin widen on Two Fingers' face. What Two Fingers said was true. Must he choose, then? Was there no way he could avoid taking one side or the other? Would he have to kill his Comanche friend to save a white child's life?

"The boy is my nephew by marriage," Long Quiet said solemnly. "Will you kill one of my family?"

Two Fingers hesitated, clearly distressed by Long Quiet's pronouncement. "I am sorry this one fell beneath my knife. But I must have revenge for my son's death." Seeing no understanding in Long Quiet's eyes, Two Fingers demanded, "Have you become a White-eyes? Have you forsaken The People?"

"I have taken a *tabeboh* to wife, and I will live here among the White-eyes. As I am both Comanche and White, so will my son be of *both* peoples."

"At least you will have a son," Two Fingers snarled. "Mine has been killed by the White-eyes."

"I shall share my son with you, then, *haints*," Long Quiet said, his voice soft. "Will that not be a better balm to your wife's grief than the scalp of another's child?"

"What?"

As Two Fingers narrowed his eyes suspiciously Long Quiet continued, "When my son has passed six summers I will send him to stay awhile in your tipi."

Bay had come up behind Long Quiet and listened with fear and pride to Long Quiet's attempts to save Cisco's life without having to kill his friend. She bit her lip to keep from crying out as Long Quiet offered their own child in exchange for the life of her sister's son. She waited breathlessly to see whether Two Fingers would be swayed by Long Quiet's offer.

Two Fingers stood, releasing his hold on Cisco and sheathing his knife. "I will tell my wife that my brother has offered his son's laughter to fill the emptiness in her heart."

"So be it," Long Quiet said.

Two Fingers slipped onto his pony, and with a bloodcurdling war cry, disappeared over the hill.

Long Quiet turned to find Bay staring at him. He was afraid to meet her eyes, afraid to see whether she would fight him when he kept his promise to Two Fingers.

"Your heart is generous, my husband," she said in the Comanche tongue. "I am proud to be the wife of such a man."

Long Quiet opened his arms wide as Bay hurled herself into his embrace.

"You did the right thing," she said, hugging him fiercely.

"You are willing to share our child with another woman? A Comanche's woman?"

She smiled up at him. "I am also a Comanche's woman. I understand that it is the Comanche way to share the joy of children."

Long Quiet crushed his wife to him and fought the tears that threatened to unman him before his woman. "Come," he commanded. "We must see if there is anything we can do for the boy."

Sloan had reached her son only an instant after Two Fingers rode away. She extended a hand to touch him and it came away red with blood. "Oh, no! Please, no."

Cisco was lying on his face and the little boy's shoulder was bleeding badly. Sloan stared at the blood dripping from her fingers, afraid to touch Cisco again for fear of discovering he was dead.

Cruz checked Cisco's pulse. "He's still alive." He worked quickly, taking off his shirt and binding the knife wound tightly to staunch the flow of blood. He already had Cisco in his arms and was heading back toward the horses with Sloan when Bay and Long Quiet caught up to them.

"Rancho Dolorosa is closest," Cruz said tersely. "We can take him there."

"No! I want him at Three Oaks," Sloan cried.

"It's too far. You're welcome at Dolorosa," Cruz said. "Let's go."

Sloan stood in shock while Long Quiet took Cisco so Cruz could mount, then handed the boy up to him. Meanwhile, Bay gathered their belongings and tied them to her horse. "Come on, Sloan. Let's go," she urged her sister.

"I can't go there. I can't go to Antonio's home," she whispered.

"Yes, you can. I'll go with you," Bay said. "We'll all go."

Bay had never seen Rancho Dolorosa and was impressed by the huge whitewashed adobe house with its veranda overlooking the Brazos River. The house was surrounded by a high, fortresslike wall. Outside the fortress wall lay a village that included an old pockmarked Spanish church, a cantina, a frame mercantile store, and a dozen or more *jacals*, simple structures made of upright mesquite posts with thatched roofs in which Cruz's *vaqueros* lived.

An elderly Spanish servant opened the door to the house for them. As soon as Cruz was inside he sent the old man to

find the *curandera*, an ancient woman highly skilled in the
art of healing with plants and herbs.

"Have you sent for a doctor?" Sloan asked.

"The *curandera*, María, is the only doctor known to us
here at Dolorosa," Cruz replied.

"I want a real doctor," Sloan demanded frantically.

"There is no doctor close by who knows as much as
María," Cruz replied, his eyes quietly calming, even though
he did not touch her as he wished. He started toward the back
of the house, where Cisco's bedroom was located. He'd
barely laid Cisco down on his bed when a stately woman
dressed completely in black arrived in the doorway.

"What has happened to Francisco?" she demanded.

"Comanche attack," Cruz replied succinctly, busily un-
dressing the wounded child.

Bay saw that Sloan had frozen at the appearance of the
older woman. Cruz never paused in what he was doing but introduced the older woman by saying, "*Mamá*, you know
Sloan Stewart. My other guests are Sloan's sister Bayleigh
and Bay's husband, Walker Coburn. Bay, Walker, this is my
mother, Doña Lucia Esmeralda Sandoval de Guerrero."

The regal woman nodded her head at Bay and Long Quiet,
but Bay saw no friendliness in her beautiful blue eyes. Doña
Lucia turned to Sloan and said, "What are you doing here?"

"I came to be with my son."

"He is no longer your son. He is a Guerrero. You are not
welcome here."

Bay reached out to steady her sister as the blood drained
from Sloan's face. Before anyone could say anything more,
the *curandera* arrived at the door. Judging by the way she began issuing orders, the tiny old woman was used to being
obeyed. Bay couldn't help but feel confident when the old
woman stepped to Cisco's bedside and began to remove the
makeshift bandages.

Although María wore the oldest of rags for clothes, Bay
noticed they were immaculately clean. The old woman's dark

brown eyes were kind. The vigor with which she worked belied the age that showed in her wrinkled face and gnarled fingers. Bay saw that although Sloan was still afraid for Cisco,
the old woman's arrival had done much to ease her feelings of
helplessness.

However, the little boy's room, crowded as it was with his
toys, a chest, a massive Mediterranean-style bed, and a beautiful spool-legged table, was not meant to hold six anxious
adults.

"You will all have to leave," María said. "All except those
closest to the child."

Lucia Doña turned to those assembled in the room and
said, "I will stay with Cruz. Juan will see to your needs in the
sala."

"I'm not leaving," Sloan said.

"You gave up this child," Doña Lucia countered.

"He's my son!"

"I am the child's grandmother. It is I to whom your son has
turned in the dark night. It is I who have wiped the tears from
his eyes when he cried with a skinned knee. By what right do
you claim a place at his side? By what right do you claim a
place in the Guerrero home?"

"I . . . I . . ." Sloan faltered, and fell silent.

"Her right is equal to mine," Cruz said. All eyes riveted on
the imposing Spaniard.

Sloan waited with her heart in her throat to see if Cruz
would reveal the secret he'd kept all these years. She couldn't
breathe. Surely he would not disclose the terms of their
agreement. She pleaded with her eyes, *Don't tell them. Don't
tell them the truth.*

Cruz looked quickly at Sloan before he turned to his
mother and said, "She must stay. She is . . ." He ignored
Sloan's terrified gasp and finished simply, ". . . the boy's
mother."

Sloan closed her eyes with relief, struggling to hold back

the sob that threatened to reveal too much to those who watched her.

Not by the flicker of an eyelash did Cruz's mother disclose how she viewed her son's command. She simply turned on her heel and left the room. Bay felt Long Quiet's arm around her waist and then she was being escorted from the room as well. The last thing she saw as she left was Sloan's huge, liquid brown eyes riveted on Cruz's face.

Sloan swallowed over the lump that kept her from speaking in more than a whisper. "Thank you."

"I could not see you sent from your son's bedside by another woman. Even my own mother."

María interrupted to say, "I will need someone to help while I stitch this wound closed." She looked at Sloan, who nodded her acquiescence.

There was nothing said in the room while the *curandera* practiced her folk medicine on Sloan's son. When she'd finished she gave Sloan some salve to put on the wound and admonished her to change the bandages regularly. "I'll give you something to put in his drinks to keep him from being in pain," she said. "He is a strong boy. It is likely he will recover. Keep him still and let nature do its healing work." Then the wizened old woman left them alone.

Sloan slumped into the straight-backed chair beside the bed and stared at her child. She felt the pain in waves. She had begun to care too much. If Cisco had died she would have died along with him. It hurt too much to care. She'd learned that with Antonio. And again with Cisco. She refused to examine her feelings for Cruz. She simply would not—could not—put herself through agony such as this again.

She would remain at Dolorosa to nurse Cisco until she was sure he was out of danger. Then she would stay as far away from her son as she could get.

Cruz knelt at Sloan's feet and took her hands in his. "I hope you will stay until Cisco is well. I am sure my *mamá* will understand your need."

Sloan pulled her hands from his grasp. "You don't have to worry about your mother being distressed by my presence. I'll be gone from here as soon as I'm sure Cisco is out of danger."

"I do not want you gone."

Sloan met Cruz's intent blue eyes and found a wealth of wanting there. "I don't know what you expect from me. I've kept to the terms of our agreement, while you've crossed its boundaries more than once. I have plans for my life now that don't include you . . . or Cisco. I want you to stay away from me, and keep Cisco away, too."

"These past months you've been a wonderful mother."

Sloan sat up straighter in the chair. "These past few months I've been foolish. Don't you understand? I won't care for Cisco. And I don't care for you!"

"Saying you won't care—that you don't care—doesn't change the truth. And it won't make the pain any less if one of us gets hurt. I want—"

"No!" Sloan's brown eyes flashed with anger as she rose and brushed past him. She whirled back to rasp, "We have an agreement, Cruz. I intend to abide by it, and I'll expect you to abide by it as well—unless you'd like to release me altogether?"

A muscle worked in Cruz's jaw. He turned his face away so she couldn't see his reaction to her challenge, and then reached out and caressed Cisco's pale cheek. "As you say, we have an agreement. But no matter how far you go, no matter how long you stay away, Cisco will still be your son. And we will both love you."

Chapter 25

BAY DIDN'T SEE SLOAN AGAIN UNTIL THE DAY BEFORE Christmas.

"Hello the house!"

"Sloan? Is that you?" Bay came racing out of the adobe house and hugged Sloan as she stepped down from her horse. "What are you doing here? Is Cisco all right?"

"I'm on my way back to Three Oaks. Cisco's doing fine. He's going to be bed-bound for at least another week, but he's getting better every day. When he grows up, he'll have a fantastic scar to show his friends," Sloan said in a too-hearty voice.

"And you? How are you?" Bay questioned. "Goodness, come inside. I don't know where I left my manners."

"No thanks, Bay. I need to get home." Sloan walked with her horse to the well and drew a bucket of water, holding it so the animal could drink. "I came by to tell you . . . I'm not going to be seeing Cisco anymore."

"But Cisco loves you. How can you stop seeing him?"

"I don't want to argue about this, Bay. I only stopped by so you won't expect me next Sunday. I'm not going to see Cisco anymore, and that's final."

"But why not, Sloan?"

Sloan dropped the bucket on the ground beside the well and mounted her horse. "Will you and Walker be coming to Three Oaks for Christmas dinner?"

"No. We're going to celebrate here. But, Sloan, why—"

"Merry Christmas, Bay. I'll save your Christmas present till I see you in the New Year." Sloan put her heels to her mount and left Bay standing alone.

Bay was stunned by Sloan's decision, and confused because she couldn't see a good reason for it. She pulled her shawl closer around her against the chilly air and returned to the adobe house.

She shared Sloan's edict with Long Quiet when he came home that evening from working with his *vaqueros*.

"What I don't understand is why she won't see Cisco again," Bay said as she cleared the supper plates from the table.

Long Quiet leaned back in his chair until it was balanced on two legs. "Maybe she's afraid."

"Sloan's not afraid of anything."

"Maybe she's afraid the situation is getting out of hand."

"What do you mean?"

"Sloan's used to managing her own life and doing pretty much what she wants. She has no way of knowing whether something else will happen that might take Cisco away from her just when she's let herself start caring for him. Stepping back from Cisco is one of the few things she can control."

Bay forced Long Quiet's chair forward until all four legs were on the dirt floor. She wrapped her arms around his shoulders and laid her cheek against his. "Have you always been so wise?"

"I knew enough to marry you."

The slight tension in his body led Bay to say, "You do believe now that I married you because I love you and for no other reason, don't you?"

He didn't answer right away, but took Bay's hand from his shoulder and used it to draw her around to face him. "It's Christmas Eve, and I have a present for my wife. Shall I give it to her now?"

So his present was the answer to her question, Bay thought. "Yes, she wants it now."

Long Quiet left her to go outside to the shed and returned a few moments later with a large slatted packing crate.

"What is it?" Bay asked, as excited as a child.

"Open it and see."

The crate had already been opened once, so all Bay needed to do was lift the lid again. She shoved aside the straw that had been used for packing and pulled out a delicate china plate with a silver rim.

"Why, it's—"

"A set of china dishes. Now you won't have to be embarrassed when we have company," Long Quiet said with a grin. "And there's silverware to go with it, but it hasn't arrived yet. I ordered it too late to get it here for Christmas. Do you like it?"

"This is . . . I don't know what to say."

"I promised you'd have beautiful things to surround you," he said, his face becoming serious. "I hope these are all right."

"They're . . . they're beautiful," Bay said with a brilliant smile. She loved him too much to tell him the gift was all wrong, that it proved he still thought she needed *things* in order to be happy living with him.

And then he gave her another gift.

"I know that having these things isn't important to you," he said. "I'm not sure when I figured that out, maybe as long ago as the first time Cruz came to dinner. But it's important to me to give them to you. It was narrowhearted to think that because Comanches don't own things, owning things isn't a good idea. A Comanche moves his home, along with all his possessions, too often to be able to collect treasures of beauty. So he finds beauty in the land, in the changes of the seasons and the sky.

"But we're going to be staying here a long time, Bay—long enough to have children and for our children to have children. Giving you china and silver is my way of saying there's no reason why we can't surround ourselves with beautiful treasures, no reason why we can't enjoy what's best about the Comanche way of life and life here in Texas, too."

Bay threw her arms around Long Quiet and kissed him hard. She pulled herself from his grasp to say, "I have a gift for you, too." She went to the trunk in the bedroom and took out a package wrapped in brown paper. "This is for you."

Long Quiet took his time opening the present, because it was one of the few wrapped gifts he'd ever received in his life. When he had the package open, his eyes lit with the beauty of Bay's handiwork.

"It's a buckskin shirt and a pair of buckskin trousers," she said. "Sloan provided the deerskin and I tanned it myself, pulling the skin through wooden rings to soften it, the way I learned from Cries at Night."

"They're magnificent." Long Quiet's fingers grazed the fringed trousers; he was awed at the effort it had taken to make the deerskin as soft and supple as it was. He unbuttoned his cotton shirt and ripped it off, replacing it with the buckskin. He crossed his arms to feel how the fringe along the sleeve flowed, then reached up to his breast to fondle the intricate pattern of beads.

"Cries at Night taught me how to do the beadwork. She said it would bring strong medicine to the warrior who wore it."

Long Quiet grinned with pleasure. Because so many Texans also wore buckskins, he could easily wear the shirt and trousers while working on the ranch without anyone ever knowing they were intended for a Comanche brave.

Long Quiet pulled Bay into his arms and held her close for a moment, feeling their unborn babe nestled between them. He breathed the scent of Bay, felt the warmth of her. "I love you, Bay."

"I love you, too, Long Quiet."

He picked her up and carried her back to the huge bed. He laid her down and then joined her. The buckskin fringe of the shirt caressed Bay's face as Long Quiet brushed her hair back from her forehead. And then his lips found hers with a gentle brush, a searching taste, and hungry possession. "I think I'll need strong medicine to make it through the night," he said, smiling.

Then there were no more words, only pleasure. Bay's last thought before she couldn't think at all was that she loved Long Quiet with all her heart and soul, for better or for worse, in sickness and in health, for richer or for poorer. . . .

Bay felt a shiver of foreboding when she saw Sloan riding toward the adobe house. It had only been two days since she'd last seen her sister and the New Year hadn't yet arrived. One look at Sloan's face, and Bay knew her sister hadn't come to chat.

"Rip had a stroke last night, Bay."

"How is he? Is he going to be all right?"

"He's resting. The doctor doesn't know how serious it is. He's lost the use of his right arm and leg, and he can barely talk."

"I want to see him. I want to be with him."

"He doesn't want to see you, Bay. He didn't even want me to tell you what happened. But I thought you should know."

"I'm coming to see him anyway," Bay said, "whether he wants me there or not."

Bay left a note for Long Quiet and rode back to Three Oaks with Sloan. Even though Sloan had warned her, she wasn't prepared for Rip's appearance. One side of his face sagged, and his eyes were dull and lifeless. His skin was pasty white, and perspiration dotted his forehead despite the coolness of the air.

Bay sat in the ladder-back chair beside Rip's bed and took her father's right hand in hers. The once-powerful fist felt like a heavy lump of clay. "I'm here," she whispered.

Suddenly, the fears she'd carried with her on the trip to Three Oaks came spilling out. "This is my fault, isn't it?

Because you don't have the money to cover the loan to Jonas. That's why this happened, isn't it?"

Rip struggled to speak and after much effort managed a garbled, "Want Cricket."

"Sloan sent a message to her. I'm sure she'll be here as soon as she can."

"Want Sloan," he mumbled.

"She had some business to attend to, but she should be back soon. Rest now."

"Go away."

Bay had expected his request for Cricket. After all, she was his favorite daughter. And of course he would want to talk with Sloan, because she could tell him what was happening around Three Oaks now that he was confined to his bed. But she couldn't pretend his order for her to go away was anything less than what it was. Especially when he turned his head away from her and closed his eyes to shut her out.

She sat with him through the rest of the afternoon. Perhaps if she hadn't feared Rip's death, she would never have spoken. But there was the look of death upon him, and so when he woke again, the bitter feelings she'd carried inside for so many years came pouring out.

"Why don't you ever ask for me? It's always Sloan and Cricket, never Bay. You don't want anything to do with me. You never have." She held on to Rip's hand despite the irritated look on his face. "Why can't you love me, too?"

Confusion registered in his eyes. "Love you?"

"Yes, love me. I know I disappointed you, but I tried to be what you wanted me to be. Truly I did. Couldn't you at least have tried to love me in return? Would that have been asking so much?"

His mouth worked, but no sound came out. The tears forming in Rip's eyes frightened Bay because they were another sign of his weakened condition. As far as she knew, Rip Stewart had never cried in his life.

"Shhh. Don't try to talk. It's all right. I shouldn't have said anything."

The more she tried to soothe him, the more upset he got.

"Please, stay quiet. You'll only hurt yourself more," Bay pleaded.

When Rip raised his left hand, Bay grabbed it with hers. "Be still. I won't say anything more."

At that moment Sloan joined them, bringing Long Quiet with her. Sloan saw immediately that something was wrong. "Did he have another attack? What happened?"

"It's my fault," Bay said quickly. "I said some things I shouldn't have."

"No!" Rip's outburst silenced both women. They waited because it was plain he was trying to speak. It took a few moments for him to be able to say, "Not your fault."

"What does he mean?" Sloan demanded. "What's not your fault?"

"The stroke. But he's only saying that to ease my conscience. It *is* my fault."

Long Quiet came up behind Bay and put his hand on her shoulder. "This wasn't your fault, Bay."

"You don't know all the facts. If you did, you'd understand that I caused this tragedy."

"All what facts?" Long Quiet questioned.

"When Three Oaks burned down, my father borrowed the money he needed to rebuild and refurbish the house. He mortgaged Three Oaks to do it. The past two years the cotton crop has failed, and last year the gin had to be replaced as well. Now Rip doesn't have the money to repay the loan, and Jonas has threatened to foreclose."

Long Quiet stopped her with the pressure of his hand on her shoulder. "How come Jonas Harper holds the note on Three Oaks?"

"He bought it from the banker in Houston who made the loan to Rip," Sloan explained.

Bay continued, "When you returned from *Comancheria*

and wanted me to be your wife, I tried to get out of my engagement to Jonas. But he said he wouldn't—couldn't extend the note unless I married him."

"So you agreed to marry Jonas to keep him from foreclosing on Three Oaks?"

Bay met Long Quiet's gaze and said, "I wouldn't have married him for any other reason. If I hadn't gotten involved with Jonas, he might have extended the note for Rip. But once I was . . . I would have gone through with the marriage, but Jonas wanted me to give up my baby—our baby—and I couldn't do it."

Long Quiet pulled her into his embrace, his heart lighter than it had been since he'd come to Texas from *Comancheria*. Here was the confirmation of what he'd come to accept on faith—that Bay loved him and their child above all else.

"So you can see this is all my fault. . . . The strain on my father, the threat of losing Three Oaks—it all must have been too much."

"If what you say is true, then this is as much my fault as it is yours," Long Quiet said.

"It's true, all right," Sloan admitted with a sigh. "If we don't come up with the balance due by the end of the week, Jonas Harper will own Three Oaks."

"How much money do you need?" Long Quiet asked.

"Thousands of dollars," Sloan replied.

"How much, exactly?"

"Six thousand."

"I'll have my banker in Houston write a draft to Jonas for the full amount," Long Quiet said.

Three sets of stunned eyes settled on Long Quiet.

"Where did you get that kind of money?" Bay asked.

"I told you once that my uncle was a banker in New York. What I didn't tell you was that when I returned to Texas, he insisted on setting up an account for me in Houston and depositing my inheritance in it. 'In case I needed it,' he said.

I've never needed it before, but this is certainly a good reason to use some of it."

Sloan whistled long and low. "Some of it?"

"How much do you have?" Bay demanded.

"Enough to buy anything you've ever wanted or needed," Long Quiet said. He saw the look of chagrin cross Rip's face and met it with a wry smile. The man he'd accused of being a poor match for his daughter was going to save Three Oaks.

"Will pay you back," Rip huffed.

"There's no debt to pay," Long Quiet replied. "We're family. What's mine is yours."

Sloan shook her head in disbelief. "This is going to make Jonas furious. He had his greedy fingers all set to grab Three Oaks."

"That's not all he's had his eyes on," Long Quiet said.

Bay shifted uneasily under Long Quiet's steady stare. She didn't have a chance to pursue the matter because at that moment Cricket arrived with Creed. There was so much commotion, Bay easily could have slipped from the room, except Long Quiet took her hand and kept her at his side.

"Guess we should all go and let you get some rest," Cricket said at last.

"Speak to Bay," Rip said. "Alone."

Long Quiet squeezed Bay's hand once before he left her.

When the room was empty except for Bay and her father, he said, "Sit by me."

She sat again in the chair beside the bed but couldn't meet Rip's eyes.

"Look at me," he commanded.

Bay lifted her gaze and met her father's eyes.

"So many plans for you . . . for all of you," he said wistfully. "Nothing like I thought. Wanted the best. Did what I thought right. Don't know how to show you . . . beautiful Bay . . . I love you."

His eyes closed. For a panicky moment Bay feared he'd died. She reached for his wrist to find his pulse. When she felt the faint throbbing beneath her fingertips, she dropped her cheek to Rip's hand. The effort to speak had taken the last of his strength.

Even if Rip died now, he'd given her the reassurance she'd wanted all her life that she was loved by her father. However disappointing she'd been, whatever plans he'd made that she hadn't fulfilled, Rip still loved her.

Bay felt joy crowding out the pain in her heart. She had the love of her husband filling her full, and now the love of her father to set the cup to overflowing.

Bay stayed with Rip for the rest of the evening and wouldn't have gone to bed at all, but Long Quiet came and picked her up once she fell asleep and carried her up the stairs to her bedroom. "Come, wife," he said. "I want to warm my heart with the heat of your flesh next to mine."

"Long Quiet?"

"Go back to sleep, love. You're safe with me."

In the middle of the night, Bay woke again and tiptoed down to Rip's room. Long Quiet found her there in the morning, asleep with her head on Rip's hand.

Bay spent the rest of the week by Rip's side. His condition didn't improve, but neither did it worsen. All those gathered in the house knew they were playing a waiting game with death. In a weak moment, Bay gave way to the tears that had blurred her vision for most of the week but which she hadn't allowed to fall.

"Is he dead?"

Bay jumped at the sound of Luke Summers' voice. She swiped quickly at the tears on her cheeks with the sleeve of her day dress. "No. Just exhausted, I think. What are you doing here?"

"I was on my way back to San Antonio on Ranger business and heard about Rip's stroke. Is he going to live?"

"I . . . I hope so," Bay said earnestly. "But he's partially paralyzed. I don't know how he'll stand it if he has to live as half a man."

"He has a lot of courage. He'll do what he has to do," Luke said. "It runs in the family," he added.

Bay smiled wanly. "I hope you weren't including me in that assessment."

"But of course I was. You've got more courage than both your sisters combined."

"Don't make fun of me," Bay snapped, rising from the chair to face Luke.

"I wouldn't kid about a thing like that. You survived three years of captivity by the fiercest savages on the frontier. You should know it takes more courage to endure than it does to strike out at your enemy so he kills you quickly. If either Cricket or Sloan had been captured by the Comanches, they'd probably have gotten themselves killed during the first three days, trying to escape."

"Did it ever occur to you that I didn't escape because I was too incompetent to do so?"

"You survived. There was nothing incompetent about that."

"Why are you saying all this?"

"Because you need to hear it."

Bay smiled again. "You're right. I do. I just don't know whether to believe you or not."

Luke reached out a hand and smoothed a strand of auburn hair away from Bay's face. "Believe it."

Bay wondered why it seemed so natural for Luke to touch her. She hardly knew him. But there was something about the man . . .

"You look like you could use a break. Why don't you go find Long Quiet."

"You know Walker as Long Quiet? You know he's Comanche?" Bay asked, startled.

"Of course."

"And you don't think less of him . . . or me."

"He's a man like any other."

"I don't understand you, Luke Summers. But I like you."

"Thanks. I needed to hear that."

Bay grinned. "Are you coming?"

"I think I'll sit here with Rip for a while. In case he needs anything," Luke said.

"All right. Call if you need me."

Luke sat by Rip's side through most of the afternoon, trying to make up his mind whether he should reveal the secret he'd kept safe for so many years. He'd been afraid in the prison at Perote that he'd die and Rip would never know the truth. It had never occurred to him that something might happen to Rip.

Now there was a good chance his father wouldn't survive this stroke. Rip would never know that the woman he'd charmed while his wife was pregnant at home with their first child had borne him a son. On the day of her violent death, Luke's mother had been a penniless, diseased whore.

Part of the reason Luke had never told Rip the truth was that he hadn't wanted to hurt Sloan, Bay, or Cricket. He couldn't explain the affinity he felt for his half-sisters, except that they were the only family he had. He'd die himself before he'd let any one of them be harmed. The rest of the reason he hadn't told Rip the truth was that he blamed his father for the circumstances of his mother's death. He wasn't sure he wanted to give Rip whatever pleasure he'd find in the knowledge he had a bastard son.

But he wasn't about to let death cheat him of the opportunity to confront Rip, either.

Rip's eyes blinked and slowly opened. "Why are you here?" he asked.

"I wanted to talk to you."

"So talk."

The words *I'm your son* were on the tip of Luke's tongue, but he couldn't speak them. He couldn't take the chance that the shock of his revelation would cause yet another stroke, one severe enough to kill his father. Instead, he said, "I was wondering if a tough old codger like you is going to let a little thing like a stroke get him down."

Rip tried to grimace, but only half his face responded. The grotesque look would have pleased Rip because it matched his careful, forbidding words, "Nothing is going to keep me down."

Luke laughed. "I could have guessed you'd say something like that."

"Young upstart."

"I'll go find someone to bring you something to eat. You need to get your strength back if you're going to be up on two feet in time for planting the spring cotton."

Luke found everyone eating supper in the dining room, and it gave him a rush of pleasure to realize that by virtue of his blood-tie, he belonged with them. "I promised Rip I'd have someone bring him something to eat."

"I'll take him something," Cricket volunteered.

Luke helped himself to a plate and filled it with food from the sideboard—roast beef, boiled potatoes, green beans, and bread with butter—and sat down at the table in the only available place, Rip's chair at the head of the table.

There was a moment of silent acknowledgment and acceptance of what Luke had done before Creed asked, "How are things in Shelby County, Luke?"

Luke glanced at Bay before he replied, "Rotten to the core."

"So there's corruption in the Shelby County land-title office?" Creed said.

"Sure is," Luke replied. "I not only found charges of theft, but accusations of murders done to hush things up when the theft was found out. The whole county government's corrupt. The citizens are divided into two camps—those who are doing the stealing and those who are being stolen from. Each side has organized an army and the 'moderators' and the 'regulators' have gone to war. It's going to take more than one Ranger to straighten it all out. I'm heading for San Antonio now to talk with Captain Hays. I don't think anything less than martial law is going to solve the problem, and he's going to have to go to President Houston to ask for that."

"What about Jonas?"

There was a moment of silence after Bay spoke before Luke answered, "Jonas Harper is smack in the middle of the worst of it."

Chapter 26

JONAS HARPER HAD DISAPPEARED.

President Sam Houston had declared martial law in Shelby County, and the Texas Rangers had gone to Shelbyville to restore law and order. The evidence they'd found had proved corruption in the land-title office, so they'd proceeded to restore property to its rightful owners—those who were still living. For those who'd been murdered, the Rangers sought justice. Months later, when the hangings began in Shelby County, Jonas Harper remained as elusive as ever.

Bay lived in a state of constant anxiety—afraid Jonas would be caught, and afraid he wouldn't. Because from the moment Long Quiet had agreed to pay the loan on Three Oaks, she'd known Jonas would seek revenge. Knowing Jonas had resorted to murder in the past to achieve his aims had put her on pins and needles wondering when and how he was going to retaliate. The constant waiting for disaster to strike made her short-tempered with Long Quiet over anything and everything. His patience with her only increased her ire.

In the early months of her pregnancy there were times when she'd felt buoyant, awake and alive as she'd never felt before. Now in mid-May, only two weeks away from being full-term, she simply felt fat, ugly, lumpy, and uncomfortable.

"Why do you have to leave so early in the morning?" she complained as Long Quiet rose to go to work.

"It's cooler to work before the heat of the day sets in," he answered her calmly. "If you don't feel like getting up with me this morning, then don't."

"Of course I want to get up with you. What kind of wife do you think I am? No, don't answer that. I hate the way I am right now. I hate myself. I feel awful." She rolled over onto her side and pulled the covers up over her head, groaning into her pillow.

Long Quiet sat back down beside her on the bed and rubbed the lower part of her back on either side of her spine, finding an ache she hadn't even realized was there.

"Mmmmm," she moaned as the tension eased.

He moved his hands to another spot.

"Ahhhhh."

And another.

"Mmmm."

"If you were a cat, I'd say you were purring. Feel better?"

"Mmmm," she replied.

He was grinning, but only because he knew she couldn't see his face. He wouldn't have hurt her feelings for the world, but he found her recent childish petulance so out of character it was funny.

"Do you want to get up, Bay?"

"Mmmmp."

"All right, then get some rest. I'll see you tonight." He reached out a hand and caressed the hard, taut mound that was causing Bay so much trouble. "It won't be much longer until our child makes his way into the world. Be patient, love."

She rolled onto her back again and uncovered her face. He could see the tears in her eyes. "I'm sorry I'm acting like such a ninny. I—"

Long Quiet's mouth came down on Bay's and cut off her apology as he sat down and lifted her up into his lap. He placed his hand on her belly and gently stroked it, then kissed away the tears at the corners of her eyes. "I love you, Bay."

Bay hid her face in his shirt and wailed, "I don't know what's wrong with me today. I feel so strange."

He carried her into the other room and set her down on a chair at the table. "Maybe some breakfast will help."

"Don't you have to leave?"

"This won't take long," he said.

Bay was feeling just awful enough that she not only let Long Quiet wait on her, but she enjoyed it.

He made her laugh with the food he cooked and the way he served it so that by the time the sun was fully up and he had to leave, she was willing to let him go.

"Come home early," she coaxed. "I'll make you something special for supper."

"All right," he agreed, his hands framing her face. "If you promise you'll keep this smile on your face until then."

Bay grinned at the absurdity of smiling through a whole day of being eight and a half months pregnant. "I can only promise I'll be smiling when you get here."

He kissed her hard and left, because he knew that if he didn't he'd end up spending the day with her—and he had work that had to get done.

"I'll ask Juanita to stop by at noon and see how you are."

"That's not necessary. I'm fine. I feel great, in fact, now that I've had some breakfast. Go on, now. Get to work!"

Long Quiet had been gone about an hour when the back pains got worse. Bay pressed as hard as she could with her fists against her back to counter the ache, but it didn't help. She tried lying down, but it felt better to keep moving, so she rearranged the furniture as she'd been meaning to do since the beginning of the year. She'd shoved the table and chairs into the center of the room when she felt the wet warmth flowing down her legs and splashing onto the dirt floor.

"Oh, my." She wasn't so dumb about babies now as she'd been eight and a half months ago. She knew exactly what had happened and what it meant. "Oh, my," she said again. "I'm going to have a baby."

She wished she'd agreed to have Juanita come by at noon, but it was too late for wishing now. "This is supposed to take hours the first time," she said aloud, "so Long Quiet will be home in plenty of time to help."

Only she didn't count on it. More than once Long Quiet had gotten home much later than he'd promised. Tonight might be no exception, and she didn't intend to get caught unprepared. She tried to decide whether she could ride to Three Oaks. She knew there was help there.

She felt fine right now, except for the backache of course, but what if she got halfway to Three Oaks and couldn't get any farther? No, she'd be better off staying right here. At least she had a roof over her head if it rained. Bay looked up at the roof that leaked like a sieve and smiled. At least none of the leaks were near the bed.

Bay made sure there was a clean blanket in the wooden cradle Long Quiet had given her two weeks ago, then straightened the sheets on the bed and put some clean linen down where she could lie to have the baby. She was so involved in preparing everything for the baby that she didn't hear the horse approaching. She wasn't even aware someone was in the house until she turned and found herself facing Jonas Harper at the bedroom threshold.

"Hello, Bayleigh."

"What are you doing here, Jonas? The Rangers are looking for you."

He smiled at her. A sad smile. "I know."

Jonas took a step farther into the room. His glittering eyes were sunken in their sockets, his face was covered with a scraggly beard, and his hair was matted and tangled. His once-fine clothes were wrinkled and soiled, with one sleeve nearly ripped off at the shoulder. He looked like the fugitive he was.

Bay backed up a step but realized she had nowhere to go except up onto the bed, so she held her ground. Despite what she knew Jonas had done, she felt sorry for him. Once, she'd loved this man. Was it the blindness of youth that had kept her from seeing him for what he was? Or had the Texas frontier tested his mettle and found him lacking?

"You shouldn't be here. Long Quiet will be returning soon," she said.

"Worried about me, Bay?"

"Yes."

"I love you," he said.

Bay winced. "No, you don't, Jonas."

"Yes, I do. I want you for my wife."

Bay felt a frisson of fear chase down her spine. "I already have a husband, Jonas. I'm going to have his child." She curved her hands protectively over her belly.

His eyes narrowed with malice as he eyed her protruding stomach. "That can be easily remedied, my dear."

He reached for her and Bay stepped back, now fully alarmed. "I'd like you to leave now, Jonas."

"How could you marry that good-for-nothing half-breed Comanche? How could you let him touch your smooth, white skin? It's really too bad, you know. You'll have to be punished. I could have forgiven almost anything, Bayleigh, but not you lying down under some filthy half-breed. And you can see I'd be doing you a favor if I made sure he wasn't around to defile you any more, can't you, Bay?"

"You're mad!" She backed away from him to the other side of the bed.

He let down the blanket that closed off the bedroom from the rest of the house, then followed her around the bed, backing her into the corner.

"Did you know your Comanche threatened me, Bay? I must say he did a good job of it. I ran all the way to Shelby County and stayed there—until the Rangers started hunting me down. It got to be a choice between shooting a Ranger in Shelby County or coming back here and shooting your half-breed. I figured there'd be less fuss if I finished off the Comanche. So here I am, Bay."

"You're not thinking straight, Jonas. Why don't you go home and—" Bay cried out when Jonas grabbed her by the hair.

"I can't have you warning him, can I, Bay? That wouldn't

do at all. I'm just going to tie you up so you'll be here waiting for me when I get back."

"Jonas, please don't do this. My baby—"

"Don't mention that bastard to me again," he snarled.

Bay held her breath as the whites of Jonas's eyes showed all around. He *was* mad! "All right, Jonas. I'll stay here and wait for you. You go and do what you have to do and I'll be here waiting for you. But don't tie me up, Jonas."

The strip of linen he shoved into her mouth gagged her. Bay fought him then, because she was afraid that if Jonas left her tied up, her baby would be born and die before she could do anything to help it. She clawed his face and heard him yell, "Stop that, you bitch!"

She pounded his chest and face with her fists. She clawed at him again, but this time he slapped her hard across the face. Bay recoiled, covering the red mark on her face with her hand.

Jonas waved his fist at her and said, "I warned you to stop that! The next time it'll be your belly."

Bay swayed with dizziness and almost passed out. She grabbed her belly protectively, but Jonas yanked her hands away and tied them together. Then he shoved her onto the bed and tied her hands to the bedpost.

"That ought to keep you out of trouble."

In the next moment he was gone, as though he'd never been there. Except Bay was gagged and tied to the bedpost.

Long Quiet had captured a *bayo* stallion he thought would be a perfect mate for Golden Lady, but the *bayo* was resisting all his efforts to tame him. He'd finally decided to try an old Comanche trick. He blindfolded the stallion and led him chest deep into the center of a large pond of water. Then he climbed onto the *bayo*'s bare back, grabbed a hunk of the thick blond mane, and slipped off the blindfold.

As expected, the stallion reared and plunged. But the slowing effects of the water on the stallion's movements made it impossible for the horse to unseat its rider. Several *mesteñeros* surrounding the pond kept the horse from coming out of the water, until at last the *bayo* accepted Long Quiet's domination.

Long Quiet rode the stallion out of the water and in a circle around the approving *mesteñeros*.

"He is beautiful, no?" Paco said. "This one, this *hombre*."

"Hombre. I like that tag," Long Quiet said. "That's what I'll call him." He stroked the *bayo*'s neck.

"Do you wish Juanita to visit your wife to be sure she is well?" Paco asked.

"No, I think I'll go see her myself. That'll give me a chance to give Hombre a good ride."

"But first you put a bridle on this horse, no?"

Long Quiet laughed. "If it'll please you, I will. But I don't need it."

Paco snickered because it was true. Long Quiet had a special talent with horses.

Only Long Quiet knew it was the result of having spent a lifetime on horseback as a Comanche.

Since it was nearing noon, Long Quiet sent the *mesteñeros* off to have their meal and to take a siesta. They all promised to meet again late in the afternoon, when the sun was lower.

Long Quiet put his heels to Hombre and let the stallion run. All he needed to do was keep the *bayo* headed in the right direction, and he could do that with the halter he'd compromised on, instead of putting a bridle on the horse. The *bayo* would be tired enough when they got close to the adobe house that he'd be able to stop him with pressure on the halter.

Long Quiet's first reaction when he heard the shot and saw the spot of blood appear on the *bayo*'s neck was fury. As the horse went down, Long Quiet curled himself into a ball and rolled free. He came up running, dodging the bullets that chased him to the safety of a small outcropping of rock.

"I'm going to kill you, you bastard Indian," Jonas shouted. "And then I'm going to get rid of your half-breed brat."

"Come and get me, Jonas."

"I already got Bay," Jonas taunted.

"What are you talking about?"

"I've been to your house. It's not much to look at. How did you talk Bay into living in such a hovel?"

"Where's Bay, Jonas?"

"Oh, she's safe enough," Jonas said. "I left her tied to the bedpost. She kept babbling about having her baby. Maybe it's been born by now. But poor Bay won't be able to do anything about it."

Long Quiet's savage instincts took over. There was only one thing to do with a rabid animal—kill it. "Why don't you come out and fight me, Jonas? Why are you hiding like a scared rabbit?"

"I'm not scared. You come out first, though."

"I'd be a fool to trust you, Jonas."

"I'll throw out my rifle. See?" Jonas threw a rifle out from behind a rise in the terrain, and it clattered down the hill.

"All right, Jonas. I'm coming out. We'll fight this out man to man."

"Sure, breed, you come on out and fight me."

Long Quiet expected to be shot the moment he stepped out from behind the rocks, and Jonas didn't disappoint him. He dodged, but the bullet caught him in the leg. He stood up and waited for the next shot. "Come on out, Jonas. I can't run from you now. And I don't have a gun." Long Quiet held his hands out to show they were empty.

Jonas's head and shoulders appeared above the rise. "I'd be a fool to trust a Comanche," Jonas said, throwing Long Quiet's words back at him. "But I guess you aren't going anywhere with a bullet in your leg."

Jonas trudged down the hill, his Colt revolver in his hand. When he stood directly across from Long Quiet, he said, "I'm going to shoot you dead—and probably get thanked for it by your neighbors when they find out who you were."

"What about Bay?" Long Quiet asked.

"It's too bad about her," Jonas said. "She would have been

a good wife. But you ruined her, breed. She's not good for much of anything now, except laying herself down under a man who needs a fine-looking woman."

One moment Jonas was smirking at Long Quiet, the next he was staring at the knife hilt sticking out of his belly.

Jonas laughed incredulously, blood spilling from the corner of his open mouth onto his white shirt. "That's a pretty good trick. I didn't even see you throw that knife, breed."

Jonas dropped to his knees. ". . . didn't even see . . . that knife . . . coming."

Long Quiet didn't wait to see Jonas die. He headed up over the hill and found Jonas's horse, then rode like he'd never ridden before.

Bay had managed to pull the gag from her mouth, but she hadn't made much progress with the cloth that bound her hands. Her struggles had only pulled the ties tighter and cut off the circulation to her hands. She realized now that the backache she'd had all night long must have been labor, because the pains she was having now felt too strong to be only the beginning of labor.

When the urge to push came, Bay knew she hadn't been wrong. This baby was coming whether she was able to help it into the world or not.

"Bay? Are you all right, Bay?"

"I'm . . . fine . . ." Bay panted. "Baby's . . . coming."

Long Quiet tried to untie Bay's hands, but the cloth was cutting into her flesh. "I'm going to get a knife. I'll be right back."

While he was in the other room, Bay muttered a blistering round of colorful expressions as she began the painful struggle to push a new life into the world.

Long Quiet came back on the run and cut the ties binding her hands. "What was that I heard in here? I didn't know you even knew all those words."

"It hurts . . . you blunderheaded . . . clinch-poop!"

Long Quiet laughed with joy as he chafed her fingers to bring the feeling back into them.

Bay groaned and said, "You'll have to help the baby out . . . and cut . . . the cord that binds us . . . together. I can't do it."

Long Quiet wasn't sure he could do it, either. This was something entirely outside the realm of a Comanche male. "Tell me what to do," he said.

"When you see . . . the head . . . support it until the shoulders come owwwwwwwwwt!" Bay clawed the linens with fingers that felt on fire and pushed with all her strength to expel the child.

Long Quiet was amazed at the sight of a head full of black hair and did what he was told. The shoulders appeared and then the baby slid out into his hands. He scooped out the film inside the baby's mouth, and when he was sure it was breathing, laid the child on Bay's belly.

"Eh-haitsma," Bay said, giving the ritual words a Comanche woman would call from within her tipi if she'd borne a son. "It is your close friend."

"He's a fine son," Long Quiet replied. "I thank you for him." He leaned over to gently kiss Bay's lips.

Between the explusion of the afterbirth and cutting the umbilical cord, it was a while before they had another moment of peace. Bay knew Comanche customs required the umbilical cord to be hung in a hackberry tree. If the cord remained undisturbed before it rotted, the child would have a long and fortunate life. The afterbirth would be thrown in a running stream, to nullify its power. But Long Quiet said nothing about observing Comanche customs—until he picked up his son again.

"I want you to name him," he said.

"I'd like to call him Whipp, if that's all right."

Long Quiet lifted the child up in the air four times, a little higher each time, and said solemnly, "His name will be Whipp Coburn." Then he grinned. "That's only half the naming ceremony, but he's only a quarter Comanche, so I guess it'll have to do."

Bay grinned back at him. "I don't know what brought you home, but you certainly came at the right time. I was worried about you. Jonas was—"

"You don't have to worry about Jonas anymore, Bay."

Bay read Jonas's fate in Long Quiet's eyes. "I'm sorry for him. He was quite mad, you know."

"He was shooting straight enough. Are you up to cutting a bullet out of my leg?"

"What?"

Bay hadn't even noticed his wound.

"I tied my neck scarf around it to stop the bleeding, but it needs some attention."

"Is anyone home?" a voice questioned from the front of the house.

"Is that you, Paco?" Long Quiet called. He limped into the front room.

"Sí." The Mexican stood with his sombrero in his hands. "That Hombre, he came back for his mares without you. The blood she is on his neck. I came looking for you and found the dead señor. I came here as quickly as I could. Do you need Paco's help?"

"What we need is a doctor."

"We?"

Long Quiet grinned proudly. "I have a son."

Paco reached out to shake Long Quiet's hand. "Congratulations, señor. And your wife, she is well?"

"Fine. More than fine. She's great!"

Bay listened to Long Quiet's effusive praise from the other room. Then she looked down at her son. "Your father is very much in love with your mother. Did you know that?"

CHAPTER 27

BY THE FOURTH OF JULY, 1844, BAY WAS READY FOR A picnic. Nursing Whipp every three hours had become a ritual she enjoyed because at long last her breasts were no longer sore. The bleeding had finally stopped, and her stomach was flat again—except for a gentle curve that was a legacy of her pregnancy. The whole family had been invited to their ranch, which Long Quiet had named Golden Valley in honor of the palominos he hoped to foster there. Everyone was supposed to meet at the huge live oak where Bay and Long Quiet had spent so many pleasant afternoons with Cruz and Sloan.

Bay made sure she and Long Quiet arrived early with Whipp so she could greet everyone as they arrived. Sloan, Cricket and Creed came first with Rip, who was well enough to ride in a carriage and could even walk short distances with a cane.

"I want to see this new grandson of mine," Rip blustered as he made his way the short distance to where Bay stood with Whipp in her arms.

"Hmmmph," he said. "Curly black hair and violet eyes." He lifted his gaze and met Long Quiet's with a sardonic smile. "He's a fine-looking boy, all right. Got his daddy's hair and his mama's eyes. Sure enough is going to make the ladies swoon."

"That's what I do best," Luke said, riding up in time to hear the last of Rip's comment.

"What are you doing here, Summers?" Rip asked. "Don't you have any Ranger business to keep you busy?"

"Not anymore, unless I can talk someone into sending some Rangers down to Perote to free the prisoners of Mier." Luke's voice darkened with bitterness. "It's Independence Day, but they're still not free."

"It won't be long now till Texas is a state of the Union," Rip prophesied. "Then Mexico will give up the Mier prisoners in a hurry or face the might of the entire United States."

Bay and Cricket placed Whipp and Jesse on the blankets that had been laid out near one another and sat down to exchange gossip. Already tiring, Rip allowed Sloan to help him sit in a chair that had been brought along and placed at the edge of the blankets so he could survey his assembled family, like a king holding court. Once Rip was settled, Creed and Long Quiet lay down with their heads in their wives' laps, and Sloan and Luke sprawled out nearby.

"I wonder how long this tree has been here," Creed murmured to no one in particular.

"Probably more than a hundred years," Long Quiet suggested.

"I wonder if someone planted it," Bay said, "or whether a seed got carried here by a wild animal or a bird."

"I wonder why it's never been struck by lightning," Sloan said.

Everyone laughed. The trilling notes had barely died on the air when Cruz and Cisco arrived.

Sloan whirled to face Bay. "I told you I wasn't coming if you invited Cruz and Cisco." She scrambled to her feet, but since she'd come in the carriage with Rip, there was no way she could escape.

The instant Cruz set Cisco down off his horse, the boy ran to Sloan. She scooped her son up in her arms and hugged him tight. Very tight. In a moment she became aware that Cruz had walked up beside her. She turned bleak eyes to him. She swallowed hard, but there was nothing she could say when everyone around could hear.

"How about introducing my grandson to me again?" Rip said, breaking the spell between Sloan and Cruz.

Sloan walked over to Rip and set Cisco down in front of Rip. Cruz formally introduced the little boy. "Francisco, this is your Grandfather Stewart. This is Cisco."

Cisco reached out a chubby hand that was met by Rip's huge paw. "It's good to see you again, Cisco. I haven't seen you since you were a tiny baby," Rip said.

"Hello, Grandfather."

"Call me Paw-Paw. Why don't you climb up here and see what I have for you in my pocket." Rip's ears reddened at the astonished murmurs of his family. When Cruz nodded his approval, Cisco didn't hesitate to take Rip up on his offer. When the little boy was seated on Rip's lap, he dipped a hand into Rip's pocket and came out with a short stick of cherry candy. He came off of Rip's lap in a shot and ran as quickly as he could toward Cruz, holding the candy aloft.

"Papa! Look what Paw-Paw gave me! Can I eat it?"

Cruz ignored the start of surprise from Rip when Cisco called him Father and told the child, "A little now, then save the rest for later." He turned and asked Bay, "Will you watch him for a while? I want to talk to Sloan."

"Certainly," Bay said.

Cruz took Sloan by the arm and said, "Will you take a walk with me?"

There was nothing Sloan could do without making a scene in front of Rip. She turned and walked toward the rise that would take them out of sight of the gathering.

That turn of events made Rip frown. "What the hell's going on here that I don't know about?"

Bay and Long Quiet exchanged glances.

"Nothing that I know of," Bay said. "I suppose Cruz wants

to talk to Sloan about Cisco." That would probably come up, anyway, so she hadn't told a lie.

"Hmph!" Rip snorted. "How about somebody fixing me up a plate of food. I'm getting hungry."

Bay gave a smile of relief that he'd let the subject drop and said, "I'll get it."

Sloan walked ahead of Cruz until they were out of sight and then turned to face him. "I told you I didn't want to see you again."

"I want you for my wife."

Determined to discourage him, Sloan demanded, "Why? I could never feel anything for you. Your brother was my lover. He touched me. Every part of me. And every part he touched is frozen now. Why would you want a woman who's dead inside?"

Cruz touched her arm, and Sloan felt an immediate shiver of response. She jerked away, distressed and frightened by her body's wayward reaction to this man. "Don't touch me."

"All right, Cebellina. I will not touch you. But listen to me. I must go to Spain. The patent from the king of Spain granting Rancho Dolorosa to the Guerrero family has disappeared from the county land office."

"How could that happen?"

Cruz grimaced. "I would guess Jonas Harper had something to do with it. We will never know for certain now that he is dead. But I must go to Spain and confirm my right to the land, especially since the annexation of Texas is imminent." He paused and said, "I want you to come with me. I want you to be my wife."

"No."

His jaw tightened. "I will ask you again when I return."

"The answer will be the same."

"We will see."

"No!"

Cruz's gaze was implacable as he said, "We will see."

Sloan knew arguing was futile, so she said nothing. He

would find out soon enough that she would never agree to be his wife. She would not open her heart for any man ever again.

"I will walk with you back to the picnic," Cruz said. "I am sure everyone will be wondering where we are."

Sloan could not stay away without causing speculation. And so, reluctantly, she walked beside Cruz back to the gathering.

Because everyone was having so much fun, the afternoon passed too quickly. As soon as it was fully dark, they lit firecrackers Luke had brought from San Antonio and watched them sparkle and flare against the moonlit sky. Too soon everyone had to say good night and travel home. But they all promised to get together again in the fall, when Cruz would be back from Spain.

Bay had never felt so full of happiness. Nothing could dim her good mood. She chattered the whole way home about nothing. She darted sultry glances at Long Quiet and found them returned by eyes warm with desire. It had been a long time since they'd been able to love one another, and Bay knew that tonight they would be joined again as one.

When they arrived at the adobe house, Bay quickly nursed Whipp, fully intending to put him to bed and end the evening in the way that had been denied her for the past few months.

Only, Whipp wasn't cooperating. As soon as Bay laid him down in his cradle beside the big bed, he began to cry.

"Maybe he's wet," Long Quiet offered.

She picked him up to see if he was wet, but that wasn't the problem.

"Maybe he's still hungry," Long Quiet suggested.

She offered her breast to Whipp again, but after lipping the nipple once or twice, he opened his mouth and let out a wail.

Long Quiet chuckled. "Maybe his belly is full of air."

Bay glared at him but obediently put Whipp over her

shoulder and patted his back. No burp of air was forth-coming.

All of that had taken the better part of a half hour and Whipp was still whining.

"Maybe he's tired," Long Quiet said.

"Of course he is," Bay snapped. "That's half the problem."

The good mood she'd come home with had vanished, and Bay was having to work hard to keep from giving Long Quiet the brunt of her frayed temper. But she still held hope of end-ing the evening in Long Quiet's arms, so she swallowed the scream in her throat and said, "Here, you take him."

Long Quiet reached out his arms for the tiny baby and felt a glow of warmth for his child.

Whipp let out a howl.

"What's the matter with him?" Long Quiet asked, not completely able to conceal the irritation in his voice. "Is he sick?"

"I don't think so . . . unless it's colic."

"Colic? What's colic?"

"It's when a baby cries and nobody knows why."

Long Quiet stared at Bay for a moment and burst out laughing. In a moment she'd joined him, curling up on the bed in giggles. "I have a Comanche nickname for your son," she said between hoots of laughter.

"Oh really? What is it?"

"Give him to me." Bay took the wailing baby from Long Quiet's arms and held Whipp solemnly above her head. "His name shall be . . . Never Quiet."

Long Quiet's face was blank for a moment before a guffaw burst from deep in his chest.

Their laughter dissipated the sexual tension that had built between them on the trip home. Surrounded by the sounds of adult laughter and no longer sensing the nervousness in his mother's body, Whipp abruptly stopped crying.

Bay and Long Quiet looked at each other in amazement and broke out laughing again.

"I guess he doesn't like his Comanche name," Bay said.

"He's lucky we didn't call him Group of Men Standing on a Hill."

Bay howled.

"Or Face Wrinkles Like an Old Man."

She fell back on the bed and settled Whipp facedown on her stomach.

Long Quiet regaled her with funny Comanche names until she laughed so hard she cried. Long Quiet lay down beside her and held himself up on his elbow to enjoy her pleasure. "You're beautiful, Bay."

Bay turned her head to gaze at him. "I love you, Long Quiet. I hoped tonight . . . I wanted . . ."

"Me too," he said.

"But Whipp . . ." Bay looked down to see how Whipp was faring and exclaimed, "He's asleep!"

Long Quiet got up and came around the bed to pick up the sleeping baby and tuck him into his cradle.

"Do you think he'll ever realize how special he is?" Bay asked. "That he's part of two very different peoples?"

"He'll only know what we teach him," Long Quiet said.

"Then I'm glad I married such a wise man," Bay said with a smile. She reached out her arms to Long Quiet and he came into them.

Their kiss was gentle at first, but it had been too long for both of them and their hunger made them bold. Clothes were hurriedly removed until their hot flesh was joined from breast to thigh.

"I've wanted to do this," Long Quiet said as his head dropped to Bay's breast. "I've been jealous of my son." He sucked gently on her breast, and then took as much into his mouth as he could.

Bay felt the tingling sensation that told her milk would soon flow into her breasts. She knew from his groan of pleasure when Long Quiet felt the warm sweet spray inside his mouth. He supped where his son had supped.

Bay had long since lost track of anything except the pleasurable sensations Long Quiet was causing. Her hands were caught in his hair and then strayed to his back, her fingernails scraping his skin as his hands slipped down her belly.

"I love you," he breathed. "I don't want to hurt you, Bay."

"I want you deep inside me," she said.

Long Quiet groaned in pleasure as she reached for him and guided him slowly into her waiting warmth. When he'd lodged himself deep inside her, Bay moaned with pleasure and gripped his buttocks with her legs.

His thrusts began slowly, short and shallow as though he feared hurting her despite her reassurance. But Bay sought his mouth with hers and engaged his tongue in a frenzied duel that provoked a corresponding clash between their bodies. Their climax came quickly, strong and violent. Bay muffled her cry against Long Quiet's chest and he muffled his against her throat. Sated, they both lay panting.

When Long Quiet would have moved away, Bay held him to her. "Don't go," she whispered.

"I'm too heavy."

"No you're not. Stay."

And because it was what he wanted as well, he curled his arms around her and held her close.

"Golden Lady is with foal," he whispered.

"That's wonderful," she whispered back. She paused for a moment and asked, "Why are we whispering?"

"So we won't wake up our son. I don't want to share you with him right away. I have my own plans for how to keep you occupied." He traced the shell of her ear with his tongue and felt her shiver beneath him. "I want to love you again, Bay," he whispered.

"I think I'll call you Man Who Always Wants His Wife," she said, muffling her giggle against his chest.

And in the years that followed, he proved her right.

AUTHOR'S NOTE

——————

I've manipulated the dates of certain events occurring at Castle San Carlos in Perote, Mexico, and taken the liberty of adding another escape to the two that actually occurred during this period.

In July, 1843, Thomas Jefferson Green and fifteen other Texans held prisoner by the Mexicans dug a tunnel under the prison walls and escaped. Despite heavy Mexican guards and manacles, another sixteen men, Mier prisoners, made an amazing escape in March, 1844, by digging a tunnel underneath a wooden floor in the same cell.

On the same July 4, 1844, that the Stewart family was celebrating with a picnic and fireworks, the commandant of Castle San Carlos issued a no-work order and allowed the surviving prisoners of Mier to celebrate the day of American independence by buying mescal, eggs, asses' milk, and a loaf of sugar, which they used to make eggnog. The prisoners borrowed dresses from the soldiers' wives and to the tune of fiddle music proceeded to get drunk, dance, and celebrate. The next day they were back at hard labor.

More than twenty Texans died from the *vómito* epidemic that raged through the prison in October, 1843. By the date of their release, only 110 Texans remained of the 176 originally recaptured after their ill-fated escape attempt in February, 1843.

The Mier prisoners were not released until September 16, 1844, when annexation negotiations between the United States and Texas took a favorable turn. The Texans had been held in Castle San Carlos for a year and absent from their homes in Texas for more than two years. According to one account, when finally released they "sprang like wild beasts from a cage. . . ."

Dear Readers,

I hope you enjoyed Bay and Long Quiet's story. You can find out what "deal" Sloan made with Cruz in *Texas Woman,* available soon wherever books are sold.

The modern-day descendants of the Creeds and Coburns are featured in my Bitter Creek series, *The Cowboy, The Texan,* and *The Loner*. If you like contemporaries in a western setting, you might also enjoy my Hawk's Way series, which focuses on another modern-day ranching family, the Whitelaws. Watch for *Sisters Found* in stores now.

I love hearing from you! You can e-mail me through my web site at www.joanjohnston.com. Be sure to sign up at my web site for my mailing list, so you can receive a postcard when new books are published. If you're using snail mail, a reply might take a bit longer—and I appreciate your patience. Enclose a self-addressed stamped envelope with your letter to P.O. Box 8531, Pembroke Pines, FL 33084.

Happy trails,
Joan Johnston
December 2002

When we left Sloan at the end of
Frontier Woman, she was unwed and
pregnant, and the father of her
child had just been killed . . .

Here's a preview of Sloan's story,
which is told in the third book of the
Sisters of the Lone Star series.

TEXAS WOMAN

It was hard for Sloan to remember the initial joy she had felt at finding out she was pregnant with Tonio's child. Hard to remember the hours when she had pressed her hands against her belly and thought with wonder of their child growing within her. She should have realized something was wrong when Tonio did not immediately offer to marry her when she told him she was pregnant.

"We must wait, *chiquita,*" he had said. "There will be time enough to marry and give the child a name."

Of course he never intended to marry her. It had been devastating to discover he was a traitor, that he had been murdered by one of his own men, Alejandro Sanchez, and that she must somehow bear on her own all the sorrow of his death, the shock of his betrayal, and the shame of being pregnant and unwed.

It had not taken long for her sorrow and shock and shame to become hate and anger and resolution. She had thought it out, weighing every detail, and made the only rational decision possible: She would not keep Tonio's child.

She was bitter and angry for what Tonio had done. She did not think she could love the child of such a man, or even maintain indifference to it. She was afraid she would blame the child for the sins of the father, and she feared the hateful emotions she felt whenever she thought of Tonio and the bastard child she was to bear him. So, to spare the innocent child, she had sought out Tonio's elder brother Cruz, and they had come to an agreement.

Sloan sighed and shook her head. She still could not believe she had acted as she had. She could only blame her actions on the turbulent emotions she had felt at the time. She could vividly recall the disbelieving look on Cruz's face when she told him what she wanted to do.

"You will give away your own child?" he had exclaimed in horror.

"It would bring back too many memories to keep Tonio's baby," she had replied.

"But surely in time the memories will fade," he had said, "and you will want your son or daughter—"

"I will never forget Tonio. Or what he—"

"You loved him, then," Cruz had said, his voice harsh.

"I did," she admitted. "More than my own life," she finished in a whisper. That was what had made his betrayal so painful. It did not occur to her that Cruz would not realize her love for his brother had died with Tonio.

She had watched Cruz's lips flatten to a thin line, watched him frown as he came to his decision.

"Very well. I will take the child. But he must have a name."

"You may call him whatever you wish," she said, in a rush to have it all done and over.

"My brother's son must have his name."

"If you wish to call the child Antonio—"

"You misunderstand me," Cruz interrupted brusquely. "My family possesses a noble Spanish heritage. My brother's child must bear the Guerrero name."

Sloan had not imagined how difficult it was going to be to go through with her plan. She swallowed over the painful lump in her throat and said, "If you wish to adopt the child as your own, I will agree."

"That is not my intention," Cruz said.

She felt the warm touch of Cruz's fingers as he lifted her chin, forcing her to meet his gaze. His blue eyes were dark with some emotion she refused to acknowledge. He could not feel that way about her . . . not when she had been his brother's woman. What she could not accept, she ignored.

His gaze held hers captive as he said, "My brother's child will bear the Guerrero name because you will be my wife."

"That's ridiculous," she blurted, pulling away from him.

"Not at all," he countered, his voice firm. "If you wish me to take the child and raise it as my own, you will marry me."

"That's blackmail. I won't do it."

"Then find another solution to your problem, Señorita Sloan."

The tall Spaniard had already turned on his booted heel before she found her voice. "Wait! There must be some way we can work this out."

He pivoted back to her, determination etched in his features. "I have stated my condition for taking the child."

His arrogance infuriated her, and she clasped her hands to keep herself from attacking him. She held her anger in check, knowing that however satisfying it would be to feel the skin of his cheek under her palm, it would be a useless gesture. She had nowhere else to turn.

"All right," she said. "I'll marry you."

Before his triumphant smile had a chance to form fully, she continued, "But it will be a marriage in name only. I will not live with you."

"That is hardly a proper marriage, señorita."

She snorted. "I don't care a worm's worth about a proper marriage. I'm trying to find a way to compromise with you."

"As my wife, you will live with me," Cruz announced in a commanding voice.

"If I marry you, I'll live at Three Oaks," she snorted.

"Unfortunately, that would make it quite impossible for us to have the children I desire."

Sloan flushed. "I won't live with you."

"Then we can come to no agreement."

Once again, Sloan was forced to halt his departure. "Wait—"

"You agree, then?"

Sloan raked her mind for some way to put off the inevitable and finally came up with an idea. "I'll agree to marry you . . . but I'll live with you as your wife only after Alejandro Sanchez is brought to justice."

Cruz grimaced in frustration. "My brother's murderer may never be caught."

"I know," Sloan replied. "But that is *my* condition." She said it with the same intractability he had used when he laid down his own demands.

"I agree to your suggestion," Cruz said at last. "We will be married now, and I will take the child when it is born and raise it as my own. Ours will be a marriage in name only—until such time as Alejandro Sanchez shall be brought to justice."

It was obvious to Sloan when she shook hands with Cruz to seal their bargain that he expected to find Alejandro within days. But her luck had held. Alejandro had remained elusive, and she had remained at Three Oaks. Over the years, while Cruz had hunted diligently for the bandido, he had kept their bargain and raised her son as his own. Now, at long last, Cruz had found Alejandro. Now, at long last, the arrogant Spaniard would expect her to fullfill her part of their bargain.

And for reasons she could never explain to him, she knew she could not do it.

Sloan jumped away from the adobe wall as Cruz's voice startled her from her reverie.

"I should have killed him when I had the chance."

"The law will avenge Tonio's death," Sloan said.

"Only if Alejandro is still in jail when the time comes to hang him."

A frisson of alarm skittered down Sloan's spine. "You don't seriously believe he can escape, do you? He's tied hand and foot, and he'll be guarded by Texas Rangers."

"He's treacherous and cunning. He must be clever to have stayed free this long. And there are those who would help him escape."

"But—"

Cruz thrust a restless hand through his thick black hair. "But, as you say, I am worrying needlessly. We will surely see him hang tomorrow."

"I won't be staying for the hanging," Sloan admitted. "I dropped everything and left in the middle of the cotton harvest when I got your message that Alejandro had been captured. My responsibilities as overseer can't wait . . . and I have enough nightmares to disturb my sleep without adding one more."

"Do you still see Tonio's face at night, Cebellina?"

Sloan stopped abruptly and whirled on Cruz, keeping her voice low to avoid drawing the attention of those who passed by them. "Don't speak to me of Tonio. And don't speak to me a name intended for a *novia*. I'm not your sweetheart, Cruz, and I never will be."

With a strength and quickness Sloan knew he was capable of, but had never seen for herself, Cruz grabbed her by the waist and carried her the few steps to a nearby alley. He pressed her up against the adobe wall and held her there with the length of his hard, sinewy body.

Sloan saw a ferocity in Cruz's blue eyes, a harshness in his aristocratic features, an intransigence in the jutting chin rent by a shallow cleft, that she hadn't seen since the grim day they had sealed their bargain. There was nothing of the daring Spanish cavalier in the face of the man who held her, only brute strength, iron will, and the knowledge of unrequited love.

"What do you expect of me, Cebellina?" With a hand that trembled under the force of the control he exerted, he caressed a wayward strand of the sable hair that had fostered his nickname for her. His gaze touched her heart-shaped face, her large, intelligent brown eyes topped by delicately arched brows, her short, straight nose, the angled cheekbones leading to her confident chin, and finally her full, inviting pink lips, the lower of which she held clasped between her teeth.

When he spoke again, his rumbling voice held the fervor of someone who has reached the limit of his patience and will not be denied. "I have waited to claim you until Tonio's murderer could be brought to justice. For four long years I have waited! I have kept my part of the bargain we made when you came to me swollen with my brother's child and asked for my help. I accepted Tonio's son from your arms when he was born and took him to Rancho Dolorosa to raise him as my own. And though I was often tempted, I did not ask of you my soul's desire. I did not take from you that for which my body hungered. I waited. And I hunted down my brother's murderer.

"Now you must keep your end of the bargain. I want you for my wife, Cebellina. And I will have you. Whether you see my brother's face in your dreams or not!"

His mouth came down to claim Sloan's, his touch rough with need, his teeth breaking the skin of her lip so she tasted blood. His hands freely roamed her body, commanding a response from her.

Sloan felt the insidious tingling sensation begin deep inside her, felt her lips softening under his, felt her mouth open for his searching tongue that ravaged her, mimicking the movement of his hips against her belly. She felt the rush of passion, felt the desire for him, for the joining of their bodies, begin to well and grow within her, as unwelcome as a weevil in cotton.

She could not allow this! She would *not* let herself be used by any man again. She shoved against Cruz's chest but managed only to break the contact between their mouths.

"Stop it," she hissed. "Let me go."

Her hand rose up between them to cover Cruz's lips. When she felt the wetness on his lips, it caused a shiver of desire within her so fierce that she felt compelled to deny it in words. "I don't want you. I'll never want you. And you can't want me. I was your brother's *puta*. Your brother's *whore!*"

Abruptly, Cruz released her. His blue eyes had become chips of ice. The veins stood out along his neck, and his hands were balled into tightly clenched fists. "Never, *never* call yourself whore. Do you understand me?"

Sloan flinched when he raised his hand, afraid he would strike her. But she stood her ground, waiting. She was Rip Stewart's daughter. It would not be the first time she had been struck in anger. She was no coward; she would not run from him.

His fist unfurled like a tight bud that finally flowers, and his callused fingertips smoothed over her freckled cheekbone in a caress as surprisingly soft as a cactus blossom. "Do you hate me so much, Cebellina?"

"I don't hate you at all."

"Then why do you resist me?"

"I can never love you, Cruz. A true marriage between us would only cause unhappiness for us both."

"I will be the judge of what will make me happy."

"Will you also judge what will please me?"

"Only tell me what I can do to please you, and it shall be done. What do you want, Cebellina?"

"I *don't* want or need a husband."

His mouth tightened, and a flush rose across his cheekbones. "Nevertheless, when Alejandro hangs, you will fulfill our bargain and become my wife."

"I'm going home to Three Oaks, Cruz."

"Go. But know this. When my brother's murder is avenged at last, I will come for you."

Don't miss the thrilling story of the
youngest Creed sister, Cricket, a sharp-shooting
temptress who swears to love no man . . .
until she met the one who stole her heart.

Here's an excerpt of Cricket's story,
which is told in the first book of the Sisters
of the Lone Star series.

FRONTIER WOMAN

SHE BROKE FROM THE TREES AT THE EDGE OF A SMALL OVAL POND almost hidden by the thick brushy undergrowth. She arrived in time to see Rogue, her favorite of the three wolves she'd raised from pups, cracked upon the head by a large branch swung as a club. The wolves hadn't cornered the stag Bay had wounded—they'd caught a man. And he was trying to kill her wolves! In an instant Cricket was off her stallion and standing spread-legged at the edge of the pond.

"You clabberheaded idiot! What the hell do you think you're doing?"

The cacophony ceased, but a heavy tension lay in the air as though a thunderbolt had struck. The man in the pond stared at her, his eyes wide with disbelief. Then the young wolves abandoned him for the new arrival, their excited yowls drowned out by their splashing swim to Cricket's side.

The stranger surged through the water after them with the shouted warning, "Watch out for those wolves!"

"Those wolves are my pets, you beanheaded jackass!"

The man froze in midstride, still wary, but clearly perplexed.

"Those vicious beasts are pets?"

"I raised them myself from pups, and they're not vicious."

"Then perhaps you should have taught them better manners," the stranger snapped, eyeing the bloody gashes the wolves' sharp teeth had torn on his forearms.

"My wolves wouldn't have attacked unless—"

Cricket shut her mouth and squinted her eyes to avoid the barrage of flying water that assailed her from shaking pelts. By the time the wolves were done, a rainbow of crystal dewflecks spattered her golden skin, the soft deerskin shirt that was belted at her slender waist, and the fringed leggings that hugged her lithe figure and disappeared into knee-high moccasins. Cricket leaned down to soothe the hurts of her beasts.

"Poor Ruffian. Oh, Rogue, look at all this blood!" Cricket knelt to check Rogue's wound. "It's not deep, boy. You'll be all right." Cricket smoothed the wolf's wet fur one last time. She swiped the beast's blood from her hand onto her buckskins as she rose to turn her magnificent fury back upon the object of her wrath.

Hip deep in the middle of the shallow pond, lowered club still held in readiness by powerful hands, stood the most proudly handsome man Cricket had ever seen. Water streamed down his face from his wet curls, dripped off his angled cheekbones and jutting chin, and shimmered like a mountain waterfall down his glistening body. His heart-shaped nostrils flared to bring air to the broad, still-heaving chest.

Cricket felt breathless, felt her pulse racing, but told herself it was concern for her wolves that had her so upset. Of course this rugged-looking stranger had nothing at all to do with her pounding heart. She knew better than to let herself think of any man that way. She clenched her trembling fingers into fists and stuck them on her hips.

The man's nakedness had kept her eyes riveted to his body. Her stallion's trumpeting neigh broke the spell and sent her attention to the source of the pinto's interest. Hidden in a brush corral near the pond, five of Rip's mares, which had been stolen a week past, circled in anticipation of the stallion's command.

Cricket's gray eyes narrowed as she brought them back to bear on the stranger. She searched the edges of the pond for the pile of clothing he'd doffed, and finally found it on the far side of the water. A smug smile twitched at the corners of her mouth. Well, well. Her wolves had certainly caught this horse thief with his pants down.

"Who are you and how'd you get here?" she demanded. She flushed as the stranger's topaz eyes boldly assessed her tall, well-curved form.

"I might ask you the same thing," he drawled. "You're a long way from anywhere, little girl."

"I'm plenty big enough to take care of you."

"I'm sure you are. Would you like to join me, or shall I join you?"

The stranger's brazen invitation caught Cricket by surprise, and her belly tightened in pleasure. As though sensing her reaction, the naked man took a step forward.

"You stay right where you are."

The stranger smiled, his eyes revealing his amusement at her response to his blatant virility.

Cricket frowned as she realized the stranger represented a greater—and very different—threat than she'd first thought. She'd long ago made it plain to the gentlemen from the cotton plantations surrounding Three Oaks that Creighton Stewart wasn't about to give them the only thing they wanted from her. This stranger was about to learn the same lesson—the hard way, if necessary.

"I asked you a question, you wet-goose lackwit, and I expect an answer. Who are you and how'd you get here?"

The mysterious man's eyes focused on the bow in her hand and the quiver of arrows slung across her back, as though trying to decide whether she knew how to use them. Cricket smirked. Let him take another step toward her and he'd find out quick enough. Her smoky eyes flashed at him in contemptuous challenge.

Instead of answering her question he asked one of his own. "Who are *you*?"

"That's none of your business." Cricket glanced pointedly at the five horses the stranger had corraled within the bushy barrier. "But I think you'd better tell me where you got those horses."

The man's jerk on her ankles interrupted Cricket's speech, sending her to the ground on her rear amidst a whorl of dust and sagebrush. She was so astonished by his attack she didn't have a chance to move before he rolled over and lunged at her.

Cricket swore a nasty oath when her quiver pressed painfully into her back, as the stranger shoved her down and came to rest on top of her. All thoughts of the stranger's attractiveness faded as she grabbed her hunting knife from its sheath. She got a painful taste of his strength when he knocked it away into the undergrowth.

"No more weapons between us, Brava," he snarled.

A shiver of fear ran down Cricket's spine when she realized the stranger was considerably stronger than she and perhaps even more agile. She lashed out at him with the only weapon she had left, slashing several furrows down his cheek with her fingernails.

"Dammit, that hurt! Settle down."

He captured her punishing fists and fingernails with his powerful hands as she bucked for freedom beneath him. Frantically Cricket tried to bring her knee up to the naked man's considerably exposed manhood, but he was ready for her. He forced his sinewy thighs down hard against her own more slender ones.

"Whoa, Brava. I intend to stay the capable stud I am."

"You bragging ass! You lop-eared mule! Let—me—go!"

"Not a chance."

Cricket shoved with all her strength, but she might as well have been an ant trying to lift a watermelon. Slowly, inexorably the horse thief pushed her wrists into the crushed sage blossoms on either side of her head.

"You won't escape," Cricket hissed.

A broad smile broke out on the stranger's face. It was clear she was in no position to enforce her threat. Cricket turned her face from the horse thief's arrogant grin, her breathing swift and uncontrolled as her thoughts about him.

"You wish to escape," he said.

"Ah, *mi brava,* my fierce, wild one. You answer my question, and I'll answer yours."

Cricket calmly pulled an arrow from her quiver and slotted it in the bowstring. She pulled the bowstring taut, the arrow aimed at the thief's heart, and asked again, "Where'd you get those horses?"

The intense, golden eyes that were his best feature in a face full of perfect features, scorned her use of the weapon, even as his jeering laugh filled the air.

Cricket pulled the bowstring tauter. The man's gaze dropped to her hands, and the laugh caught in his throat.

"Be careful with that thing, Brava," he cautioned. "I'm not ready to be spitted like a beef at Christmas."

"Tell me what I want to know."

The man swore under his breath. But he didn't identify himself.

Cricket held the shaft firm against the gut bowstring. No tremor showed along the muscles of her wrist, even though she'd held the bow thus for almost a minute. She could stand like this long enough to wait out a deer. She could certainly wait out the man standing so irritatingly closemouthed before her.

The horse thief looked from her to the wolves and back again. He stood his ground, club in hand, and stared coldly at her.

Cricket found her patience with the mysterious stranger less great than she'd supposed. "Listen, you hardheaded lug-loaf," she warned, "those mares over there were stolen from Rip Stewart a week ago. Unless you give me some reasonable explanation how you got hold of my father's mares, I don't have much choice except to see you hanged—that is, if I don't kill you first myself."

Cricket felt a swell of satisfaction when the man's whole body tensed warily. At least he'd taken what she said seriously for a change.

"Ah, Brava," he said at last. "I guess you've caught me red-handed."

Stunned by the man's admission, Cricket pondered the situation for a moment. What should she do now? It only took a moment to decide she should take him to Rip. After all, they'd lost the stag, and hadn't Rip admonished her not to come home empty-handed? Cricket grinned as she ordered, "Come out of that water."

The stranger took a step, then paused and looked down. The water now barely kept him decent.

Cricket bit her lower lip when she realized why he'd stopped. He probably thought she was going to be embarrassed at the sight of a naked man . . . or fall in a swoon at his feet. Well, she'd never seen a naked man before, but she knew it wasn't going to have any effect on her. Hadn't Rip made sure she was different from other girls?

"Come out of that water," she repeated.

The stranger snorted derisively once before he obeyed.

Cricket felt the pleasurable tightening again in her belly, as inch by inch the man revealed his powerful stalking form. She'd never imagined a body could threaten so much strength, yet be so pleasing to gaze upon. She felt a fullness in her nipples that was totally foreign, and wondered what it was about this man that caused her body to feel at once both unbearably tense and undeniably languid.

She fought to turn away, but couldn't take her eyes off the stranger's body. Beads of water glistened on the ropes of muscle in his chest and shoulders. Goose bumps erupted on her arms as her gaze followed a long, thin scar that ran diagonally from under his left nipple across the bronzed expanse of muscle-ridged abdomen to the jutting hipbone on the opposite side. She detected another scar that curved along his sinewy flank, leading her eyes to the bold proof of his masculinity. She stared in awe at the sight that greeted her. When he cleared his throat, she raised her eyes to his mocking grin.

"See anything you like?"

Before her shocked anger at his effrontery had a chance to explode, the bloodied stag Bay had wounded crashed across the clearing from its hiding place in the underbrush. Without the necessity for thought, as a reflex almost, Cricket loosed the arrow from her bow, piercing the animal in the heart. The wolves rushed away from Cricket's side to the edge of the clearing to savage the fallen stag.

In that split second Cricket was weaponless and her protective wolves were gone from her side. She watched appalled as the tall, intimidating man dropped his makeshift club and surged through the shallow water toward her.

"Stop! Don't come any closer!"

Cricket could've killed the naked man with bow and arrow before he reached the edge of the pond. Likewise her horse was trained to attack a man on foot at her command, and sh could call her wolves if all else failed. But she didn't wan take the chance of injuring him before she'd satisfied he riosity about who he was, where he'd come from, and v turned her senses upside-down.

Too late, she realized her hesitation had cost her advantage she'd had. She shrieked in pain as th reached her and wrenched the bow from her hand.

"The game's over, Brava."

"Damn you, *horse thief*. Let me go." She grip pivoted, and flipped him over her shoulder stretched out before her on the ground with his

"What the hell?"

The stranger shook his head groggily, tr breath. The bare flesh of his back and buttoc of fragrant columbine. His eyes appeared bleary.

Cricket stood above him with her fi forced her thoughts away from the feel skin where she'd touched him. She ha in a wrestling match, but her lightni instinctively, a result of the hard less

"I warned you, mister. You'd be can. You can't escape. How far chaw-bacon like you can get, nak You'll starve or be killed by some w

The man's jerk on her ankles interrupted Cricket's speech, sending her to the ground on her rear amidst a whorl of dust and sagebrush. She was so astonished by his attack she didn't have a chance to move before he rolled over and lunged at her.

Cricket swore a nasty oath when her quiver pressed painfully into her back, as the stranger shoved her down and came to rest on top of her. All thoughts of the stranger's attractiveness faded as she grabbed her hunting knife from its sheath. She got a painful taste of his strength when he knocked it away into the undergrowth.

"No more weapons between us, Brava," he snarled.

A shiver of fear ran down Cricket's spine when she realized the stranger was considerably stronger than she and perhaps even more agile. She lashed out at him with the only weapon she had left, slashing several furrows down his cheek with her fingernails.

"Dammit, that hurt! Settle down."

He captured her punishing fists and fingernails with his powerful hands as she bucked for freedom beneath him. Frantic, Cricket tried to bring her knee up to the naked man's vulnerably exposed manhood, but he was ready for her. He pressed his sinewy thighs down hard against her own more supple ones.

"Whoa, Brava. I intend to stay the capable stud I am."

"You bragging ass! You lop-eared mule! Let—me—go!"

"Not a chance."

Cricket shoved with all her strength, but she might as well have been an ant trying to lift a watermelon. Slowly, inexorably, the horse thief pushed her wrists into the crushed columbine blossoms on either side of her head.

"You won't escape," Cricket hissed.

A broad smile broke out on the stranger's face. It was clear she was in no position to enforce her threat. Cricket turned her head away from the horse thief's arrogant grin, her breathing as harsh and uncontrolled as her thoughts about him.

"I have no wish to escape," he said.

loosed the arrow from her bow, piercing the animal in the heart. The wolves rushed away from Cricket's side to the edge of the clearing to savage the fallen stag.

In that split second Cricket was weaponless and her protective wolves were gone from her side. She watched appalled as the tall, intimidating man dropped his makeshift club and surged through the shallow water toward her.

"Stop! Don't come any closer!"

Cricket could've killed the naked man with bow and arrow before he reached the edge of the pond. Likewise her horse was trained to attack a man on foot at her command, and she could call her wolves if all else failed. But she didn't want to take the chance of injuring him before she'd satisfied her curiosity about who he was, where he'd come from, and why he turned her senses upside-down.

Too late, she realized her hesitation had cost her whatever advantage she'd had. She shrieked in pain as the stranger reached her and wrenched the bow from her hand.

"The game's over, Brava."

"Damn you, *horse thief*. Let me go." She gripped his wrist, pivoted, and flipped him over her shoulder so that he lay stretched out before her on the ground with his head at her feet.

"What the hell?"

The stranger shook his head groggily, trying to catch his breath. The bare flesh of his back and buttocks nestled in a bed of fragrant columbine. His eyes appeared confused and a little bleary.

Cricket stood above him with her fists on her hips. She forced her thoughts away from the feel of his hair-roughened skin where she'd touched him. She hadn't intended to engage in a wrestling match, but her lightning-quick reactions came instinctively, a result of the hard lessons Rip had taught.

"I warned you, mister. You'd better give up while you still can. You can't escape. How far do you think a flapdoodle chaw-bacon like you can get, naked and unarmed in this land? You'll starve or be killed by some wild—"

"Ah, *mi brava,* my fierce, wild one. You answer my question, and I'll answer yours."

Cricket calmly pulled an arrow from her quiver and slotted it in the bowstring. She pulled the bowstring taut, the arrow aimed at the thief's heart, and asked again, "Where'd you get those horses?"

The intense, golden eyes that were his best feature in a face full of perfect features, scorned her use of the weapon, even as his jeering laugh filled the air.

Cricket pulled the bowstring tauter. The man's gaze dropped to her hands, and the laugh caught in his throat.

"Be careful with that thing, Brava," he cautioned. "I'm not ready to be spitted like a beef at Christmas."

"Tell me what I want to know."

The man swore under his breath. But he didn't identify himself.

Cricket held the shaft firm against the gut bowstring. No tremor showed along the muscles of her wrist, even though she'd held the bow thus for almost a minute. She could stand like this long enough to wait out a deer. She could certainly wait out the man standing so irritatingly closemouthed before her.

The horse thief looked from her to the wolves and back again. He stood his ground, club in hand, and stared coldly at her.

Cricket found her patience with the mysterious stranger less great than she'd supposed. "Listen, you hardheaded lug-loaf," she warned, "those mares over there were stolen from Rip Stewart a week ago. Unless you give me some reasonable explanation how you got hold of my father's mares, I don't have much choice except to see you hanged—that is, if I don't kill you first myself."

Cricket felt a swell of satisfaction when the man's whole body tensed warily. At least he'd taken what she said seriously for a change.

"Ah, Brava," he said at last. "I guess you've caught me red-handed."

Stunned by the man's admission, Cricket pondered the situation for a moment. What should she do now? It only took a moment to decide she should take him to Rip. After all, they'd lost the stag, and hadn't Rip admonished her not to come home empty-handed? Cricket grinned as she ordered, "Come out of that water."

The stranger took a step, then paused and looked down. The water now barely kept him decent.

Cricket bit her lower lip when she realized why he'd stopped. He probably thought she was going to be embarrassed at the sight of a naked man . . . or fall in a swoon at his feet. Well, she'd never seen a naked man before, but she knew it wasn't going to have any effect on her. Hadn't Rip made sure she was different from other girls?

"Come out of that water," she repeated.

The stranger snorted derisively once before he obeyed.

Cricket felt the pleasurable tightening again in her belly, as inch by inch the man revealed his powerful stalking form. She'd never imagined a body could threaten so much strength, yet be so pleasing to gaze upon. She felt a fullness in her nipples that was totally foreign, and wondered what it was about this man that caused her body to feel at once both unbearably tense and undeniably languid.

She fought to turn away, but couldn't take her eyes off the stranger's body. Beads of water glistened on the ropes of muscle in his chest and shoulders. Goose bumps erupted on her arms as her gaze followed a long, thin scar that ran diagonally from under his left nipple across the bronzed expanse of muscle-ridged abdomen to the jutting hipbone on the opposite side. She detected another scar that curved along his sinewy flank, leading her eyes to the bold proof of his masculinity. She stared in awe at the sight that greeted her. When he cleared his throat, she raised her eyes to his mocking grin.

"See anything you like?"

Before her shocked anger at his effrontery had a chance to explode, the bloodied stag Bay had wounded crashed across the clearing from its hiding place in the underbrush. Without the necessity for thought, as a reflex almost, Cricket